The WAY of MUSIC

AURAL TRAINING FOR THE INTERNET GENERATION

ROBIN MACONIE

D1522633

The Scarecrow Press, Inc.
Lanham, Maryland • Toronto • Plymouth, UK
2007

SCARECROW PRESS, INC.

Published in the United States of America
by Scarecrow Press, Inc.
A wholly owned subsidiary of
The Rowman & Littlefield Publishing Group, Inc.
4501 Forbes Boulevard, Suite 200, Lanham, Maryland 20706
www.scarecrowpress.com

Estover Road
Plymouth PL6 7PY
United Kingdom

British Library Cataloguing in Publication Information Available

Library of Congress Cataloging-in-Publication Data

Maconie, Robin.
  The way of music : aural training for the Internet generation / Robin Maconie.
    p. cm.
  Includes index.
  ISBN-13: 978-0-8108-5879-4 (pbk. : alk. paper)
  ISBN-10: 0-8108-5879-7 (pbk. : alk. paper)
  1. Music appreciation. I. Title.

MT6.M136 2007
781.1'7—dc22   2006028974

CONTENTS

*In affectionate memory
of Frederick Page*

The WAY *of* MUSIC

PREFACE

Welcome to a new series of courses in classical and world music and its human messages, for students of all cultures and abilities. In easy, conversational style, and drawing on the author's *The Second Sense: Language, Music, and Hearing* (2002: The Scarecrow Press; 0-8108-42424), the one-volume series has beneficial applications in attention recovery, aural comprehension, and higher reasoning, while at the same time awakening self-confidence and appreciation of traditional musical cultures, through a repertoire of programmed exercises in critical thinking and listening. Conceived to satisfy a longterm hunger for aural awareness materials for use in general education, the series is attractive and easy to read, providing a plain, flexible, jargon-free and reader-friendly introduction to the place of music in world history and culture. Written in the language of the nonmusician, the series is also suitable for upper level nonmusic courses in aesthetics, cultural history, literature, language, and psychology. Each course programme is designed to function equally as self-teaching or classroom study and discussion material, and to be led by nonspecialists as well as teaching staff with formal qualifications in music theory. For Book 5, access to good quality audio reproduction is recommended, and full references are provided for cd titles recommended in the text.

Conceived as a "paper website," this unique series combines the convenience and cheapness of print media with the complete freedom of access of a software package. The books can be studied individually or sequentially, and the reader will encounter plentiful cross-references and revisions of critical points from book to book. When studied in sequence, the series builds from a foundation in attention training and aural skills grounded in real-world experience, to focus with greater specificity on the meanings represented in patterns and symbolic processes of classical and world music traditions. Books 1 and 2 inquire into the hearing process, while books 3 and 4 consider the layers of significance—intellectual, social, acoustical, and emotional —revealed in specifically musical actions.

Book 5 provides a core survey of over 100 samples of recorded classical and world music, incorporating birdsong, speech, famous works by 60 named composers and authentic examples of 26 national and ethnic traditions, exploring the history of music from earliest times to the present day. Book 6 brings together a collection of 101 adult reactions, representing a variety of ethnicities and skill levels, to two versions on record of the same slow movement of a Beethoven piano concerto. This study offers a fascinating insight into gender, culture, and nationality issues that influence listener perception. The Beethoven movement is a representation in music of conflict and conflict resolution with class and gender implications. The solo piano represents the artist, the orchestra the masses. Individual interpretations reveal the richness and subtlety of different shades of meaning that can be read into relationships described in musical terms.

❧

BOOK ONE

101 Ways of Hearing a Dog Bark

1

What you hear is the truth.
The rest is up to you.

2

A dog barks:
Woof! Woof!

3

An unseen dog that barks
is still a dog.

4

If you can hear it,
then you can hear.

5
In a bark,
a dog exists.

6
A dog exists,
you exist.

7
In the bark of a dog,
the world exists.

8
A bark, a dog, a person listening,
a world in relation.

9
A dog barks
in order to hear.

10
The sound of its voice
is the sound of its world.

11
The sound of its voice
is the sound of your world.

12
A dog, a chicken:
what's the difference?

13
A dog may howl at the moon
but a chicken commands the sun to rise.

14
A dog barking is a
sign of life.

15
At the time of barking
a dog hears only itself.

16
To anyone listening, the sound of a dog barking
is like pebbles rattling in a wooden box.

17
To a dog, its bark
is the sound of the universe shaking.

18
Woof! Woof!
Once for surprise, twice for emphasis.

19
A dog is in control of its body
but the sound it makes is out of its control.

20
A barking dog
is breathing out.

21
Before and after,
relative silence.

22
The sound of a dog barking
is only the air in between dealing with the pressure.

23
A dog barking is converting stored
energy into radiant energy.

24
The sound of a dog barking
can only spread outwards.

25
The energy in a dog's bark
is as much as its lungs can hold.

26
A bark is powered
by compressed air.

27
The farther a bark travels in every direction
the less you hear in any one place.

28
A dog that barks
is a dog provoked.

29
When the barking stops,
its cause may remain.

30
A bird in flight, a barking dog:
air resistance.

31
A dog that barks
is showing its teeth.

32
A dog barking
has clear airways.

33
A dog barking
declares itself.

34
A dog barking
is standing upright.

35
A dog that barks
has energy to spare.

36
A dog barking
discovers its place.

37
If a barking dog is not here but there,
then there is not here.

38
By the time you hear a bark
it has already happened.

39
By the time you are sure it is a dog that is barking,
the sound has already passed into memory.

40
Before it barks
there is no dog.

41
When the barking stops
the dog stops.

42
A dog that barks
is using remote control.

43
A dog that barks
is switching channels.

44
The note of a dog barking
changes its world.

45
Where a barking dog can be heard
defines its territory.

46
The louder the sound,
the greater the silence.

47
A breeze is blowing:
the sound travels.

48
In the sound of a dog barking
you can hear that snow has fallen.

49
In the sound of a dog barking
you can hear that the air is dry or damp.

50
In the ambience of a dog barking
is an entire neighborhood.

51
In the pitch of a dog's voice
is the size of the dog.

52
In the fullness of a dog's voice
is its presence.

53

In the intensity of a dog's voice
is its excitement.

54

In the certainty of a dog's voice
is its maturity.

55

In the steadfastness of a dog's voice
is its purpose.

56

In the definition of a dog's bark
you can hear that it is in or out of doors.

57

A bark is rhythm,
a howl is melody.

58

Rhythm signifies action,
melody a state of being.

59
The direction from which a dog is barking
is in the ears of a listener.

60
A dog that barks
is telling the truth.

61
A dog barking
is not in pain.

62
A dog howling
is filling the void.

63
A good keeper
knows a dog's voice.

64
The expression of a dog's voice
is never the same.

65

The character of a dog's voice
is in its face.

66

The dog that barks once
may bark again.

67

In the expectation of a second bark,
we experience time.

68

The first of two woofs
is always louder.

69

Unexpected is real:
the rest, imagination.

70

In recognition we understand
persistence of being.

71
A barking dog
is fully awake.

72
A barking dog
is a wake-up call.

73
Whoever hears a dog bark
intrudes in its space.

74
The dog that barks
is upbeat.

75
The dog that barks
is in good shape.

76
The power of a dog barking
is its physique.

77
The sharpness of a dog barking
is its reaction time.

78
The dog that barks first
may not have to fight later.

79
A barking dog
is imitating human speech.

80
A dog does not bark
and eat at the same time.

81
A bark is for warning
and also for confidence.

82
One breath, two woofs:
flash, bang.

83
Between the first woof and the
second, a moment of absence.

84
The second woof
prolongs the first.

85
The first woof initiates the action;
the second completes it.

86
The repetition of a bark
embodies time, form, and directedness.

87
The second woof is more predictable
than the first.

88
A dog barks
to clear its throat.

89
A dog barking
resembles the action of a musical instrument.

90
The sound of a musical instrument
combines force and resistance.

91
The greater the resistance,
the more structured the vibration.

92
In resistance is constancy,
in flexibility is change.

93
Whatever is flexible
is also uncertain.

94
The message of a bark
is not in the tone quality but in the intonation.

95
To bark one time
is the work of a moment.

96
To do it again
is a matter of practice.

97
Practice
is memory.

98
Air goes in, food goes in,
bark comes out.

99
A dog breathes
by opening its throat.

100
A dog barks
by closing its throat.

101
The sound of resistance
is a musical note.

BOOK TWO

Walking the Dog

1
What you hear is the truth.
The rest is up to you.

In order to come to a decision at all about what a sound is, or what it appears to be, you first have to believe that what you are hearing is a real event, and that your ears are not playing tricks.

Every sound you hear is a test of your hearing. Hearing is a two-stage process. The first stage is capturing the sound, the second stage is interpreting it. Capturing sound is done by a person's ears, which are sensing devices. Your ears do not think for themselves, but they do process sound in ways that enable a person's brain to interpret it. But in order to interpret any sound that you hear, you make a decision to trust the evidence of your ears. This is what is meant by "hearsay evidence." Among visual cultures, hearsay evidence is thought to be less credible in matters of law, than evidence given in writing that can be read and disputed. What that means in everyday life, is that when we hear a sound, we are only able to come to a conditional judgement about what it is. That decision is also influenced by personal issues and circumstances, the world we know, and how we organize our life.

2
A dog barks:
Woof! Woof!

"I am my master's dog; Bow-wow!" as the saying goes. We say "Bow-wow!" but in reality, in English, a bark sounds more like "Buff-wuff," like the words *rough* and *tough*. When a dog barks, there are usually two parts, a Bow and a Wow. A repeated action such as this is a basic indicator that the source of the sound is a living creature and not a random natural event. Here is a proverb: "A tree falls only once." Some natural sounds repeat, like a bouncing table-tennis ball or a dripping faucet. In that event we hear the sound not as a random event, but as an organized process.

3
An unseen dog that barks
is still a dog.

A sound is not the sign of an event, but the event itself. The name we give it, "dog," is the sign. A recording of a dog barking is also a sign, not the sound of a real dog. You do not say of a real dog barking that it sounds realistic.

4
If you can hear it,
then you can hear.

The world of sounds is a picture in constant renewal. Sounds come and go: if that were not the case, the environment would quickly become intolerable. Our eyes tell us that the environment stays in place and is always complete; but for those who cannot see, who are forced to rely on the alternative senses of hearing, touch, smell, and taste, the real world is a constantly changing mosaic of momentary impressions. The more dependent we are on the sense of hearing, the more appreciative we become of what we are able to hear, and the limits of hearing.

5
In a bark,
a dog exists.

In identifying a disturbance as a dog barking, the listener in effect "calls the dog into existence." That notion of a revealed reality is the underlying meaning of the bible creation myth, which says that the world and its inhabitants were created, not by waving a magic wand, but by the declarations of a divine voice. Each individual human being constructs a personal world from the evidence of the senses, but without absolute certainty: first, because the evidence available to any one person is patchy, and second, because the extent of individual potential knowledge is limited in space and time. In order to account for the world as a collective and transcendent reality superseding the perception of any one individual, it is necessary to invoke a superior being with absolute powers.

6
A dog exists,
you exist.

From being aware of the dog barking, one is aware of still being alive and of hearing as a function of being alive. The world of our perceptions is a combination of several different worlds: what we see, what we smell, what we hear, and what we touch and taste. These several worlds are quite distinct in their formation and very different in nature and scope. To advance from a perception of multiple coexistent worlds to the perception of a coherent and unified world requires intelligence and also some degree of compromise with the sensory evidence.

7
In the bark of a dog,
the world exists.

On the basis that a barking dog exists, and that the person listening also exists, the notional existence of a larger world that includes them both is a reasonable and a convenient extrapolation.

8
A bark, a dog, a person listening,
a world in relation.

The dog exists to me by virtue of its bark being heard by me, likewise I exist to me by virtue of existing in relation to the dog, and the world exists by virtue of the relationship manifested between me and the dog, since I do not identify myself with the dog but the dog, through its bark, as something else.

9
A dog barks
in order to hear.

Though all of us were told at school that you cannot talk and listen at the same time, in the real world we do it all the same. It is only reasonable to suppose that a being with the ability to make noises of various kinds also has the mechanisms to monitor the sounds it makes. The interesting question in the case of a dog barking is whether the sounds a dog makes are as well adapted to its own hearing as to the hearing of its human carers. If barking is a dog's imitation of human speech, then as an adaptation for the hearing of another species, it may arguably be less suited to the hearing of other dogs, among whom howling is the preferred mode of conversation. If the action of barking were physically ill-adapted to the species, we might expect to find evidence of stress or damage to the vocal parts of dogs who bark a great deal.

To say that a dog barks *in order* to hear is to say that a dog or a human being uses its voice in part as a sounding device, not just to communicate with others but to create an audible feedback from the environment in general (as, for example, when a person shouts into a well, or sings in a cathedral). Paradoxically, however, most of the sound a dog or a singer makes is detected within the vocalist's own head, and therefore masks the same sound as it would be heard in the environment. (That is one reason why people shy away from the recorded sound of their own voice as something alien or distasteful.) If all of the sound a person vocalizes were heard inside the person's head, then barking or singing would serve no useful purpose in arousing a sense of the surrounding space.

That dogs continue to bark, and people sing, is a fair indication that not only after, but during the act of speaking a listener is able to detect a residue of the vocalized sound from which an impression of the acoustic environment can be sensed. Logically that residue would have to be (a) delayed in transit, because milliseconds of time elapse while sound travels out into the environment and is reflected back to the sender; and (b) at the higher end of the frequency range, since high frequencies are not transmitted within the body because the tissues covering the inside of the mouth are soft and absorb them. For both active (voice) and passive (hearing) mechanisms located in and about the same compact structure (the skull) simultaneously to emit powerful acoustic signals and monitor considerably weaker reflections from the environment, suggests a processing regime particularly sensitive to fringe effects in the higher frequency range. Laser interferometry works by matching a very precise signal against its reflection from a distant body, and it tells us only one thing, which is how far away the body is. Animal and human hearing employs very much more complex acoustic signals across a wide range of frequencies, and is thus able to build up a more detailed image of a surrounding space. The broken texture of human speech, with its random alterations of pitch, mixture of tone and noise elements (vowels and consonants) and frequent micro-pauses, makes it a richly suitable and highly sophisticated signaling material.

10
The sound of its voice
is the sound of its world.

It follows that the image of the acoustic environment available to a dog *while it is still barking* is derived from the minute differences between the sound it is generating and the reflected sound it is receiving. We know that bats navigate in the dark with the aid of ultrasound signals. That dogs, human beings, and other creatures are unable to produce or detect ultrasound does not mean that they do not use the sounds available to them in a similar way, though the level of definition of an environmental image is bound to be much less satisfactory at lower than higher frequencies. Since the sound of a bark or a voice, unlike a laser, is not a single frequency at constant amplitude, but is randomly changing in both frequency and amplitude, it is reasonable to suppose that sudden shifts in frequency and amplitude, such as at the beginning or the ending of a word, are particularly useful in highlighting delays in acoustic response.

11
The sound of its voice
is the sound of your world.

Paying attention to the sounds of others is a lot less hazardous than making your own noise and running the risk of drawing attention to yourself. For the listener on the sideline, being able to monitor the environment through attending in silence to the sound of some other source, such as a dog barking or a person singing, is both easier to do and more energy-efficient: but it means you have to rely on the quality of the signal you are given, which is not always entirely satisfactory.

12
A dog, a chicken:
what's the difference?

A dog, a chicken, a human being, a sheep: "all creatures great and small" that contribute to the world of sound, are connected to one another through the process of sound propagation, which is the same for all who inhabit the air. The atmosphere is common to all; it is at the same pressure for all; and it responds in exactly the same way to sudden localized changes of pressure, no matter how large or tiny the creature involved. The laws of sound propagation and the speed of sound are the same for everybody, even though the mechanisms for initiating and detecting pressure changes in the atmosphere vary considerably from one creature to another. A sense of absolute consistency in the transmission of sound is fundamental for survival. It is how we can be sure that the voice of a chicken is indeed that of a chicken and not a dog's voice at a higher speed, as might be the case if you were listening to a tape recording.

13
A dog may howl at the moon
but a chicken commands the sun to rise.

Different creatures create different sounds, and that is how we can tell one from another. For larger creatures the medium of air is relatively thin and easy to penetrate; larger creatures also have more power at their disposal. For smaller and lighter beings such as birds and insects, the air is thicker and offers greater resistance, on the one hand making it easier to fly, but on the other hand making it more difficult to communicate over long distances. Compared to the soft tissue structures of dogs, sheep, and human beings, for example, birds and insects such as cicadas have evolved very different mechanisms for the production of high-frequency, high-intensity sounds that can be heard a long way away. These compact, hard-tissue structures produce bursts of clicks or rasping sounds. Different animal sounds reveal different mechanisms; these in turn relate to the plasticity of the air relative to the size of the animal and its disposable energy. That there are ritualistic implications in the signaling activity of animal life in relation to the sun and moon, is recognized in the mythology of many cultures.

14
A dog barking
is a sign of life.

A sign of life is a very welcome impression if you happen to be in the middle of a desert, stranded at the side of a country road, or in any other isolated situation. A garden without birds, or a park with no wildlife, is an unnatural and somewhat disturbing place. Any sound that breaks the silence is an encouraging reminder that wherever you happen to be is capable of sustaining animal life. (A silent environment can also be momentarily confused with a sudden loss of hearing.) Telling one animal's sound from another involves a sense of time as well as pitch. At the moment a sound is first detected we cannot know whether it is produced by something living or dead, or even whether it may be an illusion produced by a glitch in our own hearing. Among the features that distinguish a vital sign from a chance event like a falling object are qualities recognizable as shape and pattern. For a sound to have shape it needs to have continuity and be heard to evolve; to have pattern it needs to have repetition. Both shape and pattern are temporal processes, even though they may appear instantaneous.

15
At the time of barking
a dog hears only itself.

Barking, like human speech, can be used as a means of self-defense. By filling one's own space with sound, a person defends that space from unwelcome invasion by the voices of others. When two people are in conversation and one interrupts the other, the gesture acts to repel the other and occupy and control the space they have in common.

16
To anyone listening, the sound of a dog barking
is like pebbles rattling in a wooden box.

A gravelly voice describes a kind of rattle in which the pebbles are the vocal folds, the action setting them in motion is the forced emission of pressurized air from the lungs, and the box itself is the resonant cavity of the mouth. The barking gesture is compared to the motion of shaking the box.

17
To a dog, its bark
is the sound of the universe shaking.

The louder a person or animal vocalizes, the louder it appears to itself. In an extreme situation, a primal scream can be understood as an attempt to obliterate the environment altogether. We say of a solo singer or musician that they perform "as if possessed," or as if lost to the outside world.

18
Woof! Woof!
Once for surprise, twice for emphasis.

What is interesting about a double action of this kind is the exact correspondence between the way the sound is processed in purely mechanical terms, and the intention that the gesture is presumed to convey. The moment of onset is the moment of greatest change in the environment, which is also the time of greatest uncertainty and sensitivity. We do not know, at the moment of onset, what a sound actually represents. The natural human response is bound to be the same to any sudden event, since every sudden event contains the same possibility of danger So whether or not a sound is intended to arouse alarm, any sudden transition from silence to sound is enough in itself to generate the same alarm response.

At a very basic level, a repeated gesture can also be interpreted as the animal reassuring not only any listener that it is real and ready for action, but also as designed to reassure *itself* that the sound it has just heard was in fact its own voice under its own control. At various other levels repetition is able to convey emphasis, confirmation of intent, and also completion.

19
A dog is in control of its body
but the sound it makes is out of its control.

The word "expression" means "projecting outwards." The whole point of a dog barking, or of any animal emitting a sound, is of letting go, of acting in a way that has influence beyond the body reach of the animal itself. Once a sound is emitted, it cannot be recalled, though sooner or later the sound will die away. Retaining control as an alternative to simply letting go, involves modifying the sound during the process of generation, and for that to happen continuity of action is essential, for example a howl in which the tone is heard to rise and descend in pitch. In music, as in the rattle of a rattlesnake, the desired effect of a sound perceived as in progress but incomplete is the same. Both are designed to fixate and hold the attention of the person listening, the intended victim. A sound that is able to be prolonged indefinitely can have the effect of putting the listener in a trance of unfulfilled expectation. The abrupt tones of a dog barking are sharp warning signals of short duration that have no powers of fixating or hypnotizing a listener's attention.

20
A barking dog
is breathing out.

This is a fact. Just try talking and inhaling at the same time. The valve mechanism in the throat opens to allow air to enter the lungs, and closes to allow food and drink to enter the digestive tract. These actions are involuntary. Vocalization arises as a reflex action associated with breathing that an infant learns to control by manipulating the muscles that act on the tissues of the larynx to influence the expulsion of air. Effective vocalization draws on energy stored in the tissues and lungs. The same combination of resources is used to power wind instruments in music. A fundamental limitation of sound production for the voice and wind instruments in general is "the length of a breath." Bagpipes employ a windbag as auxiliary lungs, and are thus able to continue playing indefinitely without audible pausing for breath. The ability to prolong sounds indefinitely is highly prized in some cultures, as well as being a feature of instruments such as the pipe organ and harmonium, that are associated in western cultures with religious ritual. Rare examples of wind instruments in which sound is produced by both sucking and blowing, include the mouth harp and concertina.

21
Before and after,
relative silence.

The world of sound is perceived as a collective mosaic of intermittent signals, both accidental and intentional, and their reflections. The sounds we make of our own accord contribute to that mosaic of signals in our immediate environment, and in that degree to the constant renewal of that world image. All sounds die away sooner or later, so the world of hearing is never complete at any one moment. Like a television image, it is built up by an ongoing scanning process. To creatures like us who actively contribute to the acoustic environment, advantages arise: first, from the control that is more or less consciously exercised over the signals we produce and thus over the reflected image we receive, and second, from the fact that the sounds we produce are tuned specifically to human hearing and are therefore a more efficient means of inquiry into the world around us. The silence into which all sounds inevitably decline is a blessing in that it offers a listener relief and time to reflect on what has been heard, and also in the opportunity it allows for improving the signal through repetition, and for social interaction.

22
The sound of a dog barking
is only the air in between dealing with the pressure.

"There is nothing between us . . . just air," as the actor observed. By definition, if a sound is not tangibly connected with the actions of our own body, it is the effect of an action elsewhere. The sounds we make are correlated with the actions we take to produce them, but sounds that reach us from elsewhere do so as independent disturbances of air pressure detectable only by our ears. While it may be convenient to think of a dog barking as the sound of a dog, and though from observation and imitation we learn to recognize what kind of action is associated with the sound, in everyday reality what we are responding to is atmospheric disturbance and no more. All that we actually hear is a process of redistribution of excess pressure introduced into the atmosphere by accident or design.

23
A dog barking
is converting stored energy into radiant energy.

Life itself is a complex of energy transactions sustained by the storage and release of energy within the tissues. Surplus energy acquired in expansion of the lungs in the service of taking in oxygen can be used to power the emission of patterns of pressurized air. Normal breathtaking and heavy breathing involve the same mechanisms as vocalizing, but are simply different ways of shifting air from place to place. For sound to be detected by human ears the associated fluctuations in atmospheric pressure occur with extreme rapidity, in a range between 20 and 16,000 or more alterations or cycles per second. At such high rates of change the air behaves more like a solid than a gas, so the sound of a dog barking is not like the wind, but more like *the air ringing*.

24
The sound of a dog barking
can only spread outwards.

Let go a tied inflated balloon and it falls to the floor, because the air inside it is compressed, making the total air and balloon together heavier than the surrounding air. The compressed air in a balloon is stored energy that can be released in a number of ways. Burst it with a pin, and all the energy is released at once, with a bang. Let the balloon go without tying the neck, and the air rushes out of the tube with a whoosh, making the balloon fly round the room out of control. Pinch the neck flat between fingers and thumbs, so that the air escapes only a little at a time, and it makes a sound like a baby crying. By pulling on the rubber the release of energy is slowed down to produce a continuous wail that can be manipulated in pitch and rhythm to imitate an animal or person. Of all the possibilities of using the energy stored in a balloon, a slow release technique is clearly apt for communication.

In every case, when the energy locked in an inflated balloon is allowed to escape, it rushes outward and a sound is created. The whoosh of a balloon that is let go, is only turbulence or rushing wind. When a balloon is burst, the change of pressure is virtually instantaneous, and a shock wave radiates out from the invisible boundary between high and normal air pressure. When the air in a balloon is released slowly by pinching the neck, a stream of pulses of energy is released as the compressed air inside forces its way between the stretched rubber surfaces, which open and close hundreds of times in a second.

Sound travels outward from the source, for the reason that a shock wave can only expand away from a zone of higher pressure into a surrounding region of lower pressure. That is how and why sound propagates from the source to a listener at a distance. Sound travels faster than the wind, because the pressure patterns in sound as we hear it are transmitted directly through the substance of the air and not by the movement of air.

25
The energy in a dog's bark
is as much as its lungs can hold.

The bigger the dog, the bigger a noise it can make, but there is always a limit to the amount of energy an animal of any size can dispose of at any one time. The size of a dog affects not only the amount of air it can hold in its lungs, but also its vocal folds, the pitch of its voice, and the length of time it can continue to bark or howl continuously.

26
A bark is powered
by compressed air.

Compression in this case applies not so much to the natural condition of air in the lungs, as to pressure applied to the lungs via the ribcage by related muscles. Controlling different sets of muscles to influence both the emission of air and the tension of the vocal folds makes the human voice a very versatile instrument. When a person whispers, the vocal folds are relaxed, and the sound of the voice is essentially the sound of puffs of air, which you can feel by holding the palm of your hand in front of your mouth. A whisper is perfectly intelligible to a listener close by, but is not very useful for public speaking. A whisper is unable to convey intensity of expression. In order to express changes and degrees of emotion, access to tone of voice is required, and tone is produced by controlling the stiffness and shape of the vocal fold tissues in the larynx.

27
The farther a bark travels in every direction
the less you hear in any one place.

Vocal energy comes in packages, and the size of the package is limited by the size or energy capacity of the animal. Energy radiates outward in concentric shock waves or pressure differences. The energy of each wave is the energy released at a particular instant, which is a fixed amount; and because the energy surface expands like a balloon, it gets progressively weaker, eventually merging with the random motion of molecules of the atmosphere that is thermal energy. If you are trying to read by the light of a candle, the farther you move away, the less light is available to fall on the page, because even a candle sends its light in every direction.

For a dog, of course, the fact that a bark travels in every direction is a matter either of indifference, or pride, or expediency, or all of these things. For human beings, however, the idea of being able to channel energy in a particular direction, or toward a specific individual, and excluding others, has many attractions. It may seem paradoxical that the human body is designed to exercise so much control over voice production and yet have so little control over where the sound goes once it leaves the lips. Among many ancient cultures the issue of otherwise wasted energy is addressed and harnessed in the form of simple tube resonators such as a didgeridu, horn, or speaking trumpet. Being able to focus the energy of a sound in a certain direction confers advantages in distance signaling and can also be construed as a demonstration of supernatural power. The design and evolution of wind instruments reflect the development and increasing sophistication of human understanding of fluid dynamics, as expressed in irrigation, water-powered devices, and aerodynamics, and in the design of airways such as chimneys and jet engines.

28
A dog that barks
is a dog provoked.

A barking dog can be a public nuisance, but the reason for having a dog in the first place goes back to a desire for the protection of life and property. A domesticated dog shares and defends the space of its master, and barks when that space is invaded. Because barking is an inherently wasteful expenditure of energy, it is not normally a frivolous activity. When a sudden alarm of any kind is sounded, whether by a dog, a flock of geese, a church bell, or a parked car, the inference to be drawn is of a change that threatens the peace and stability of the local environment. By definition, the threat itself is silent. An alarm signal is designed to draw attention to the locality of a perceived threat, but in the absence of speech is usually insufficient to identify it.

29
When the barking stops,
its cause may remain.

When an alarm signal dies away, peace is restored. After the doorbell rings, and the door is opened, and the visitor is admitted, both the reason for the disturbance and the disturbance itself have been dealt with. But in many cases, after the sound dies away, doubts continue to linger. That a dog stops barking does not necessarily indicate that the situation has returned to what it was before, only that the threat is under control—at least for the time being. Any sudden disturbance is a reminder that a breach of the peace is always possible, and that vigilance is an ongoing process.

30
A bird in flight, a barking dog:
air resistance.

Birds fly by trading muscular energy against the resistance of air, and learn to take advantage of changes in the pattern of airflow to conserve energy in flight. A dog barking trades muscular energy against air resistance at a molecular level, using the reflected energy from nearby surfaces to amplify its voice.

31
A dog that barks
is showing its teeth.

A dog opens its mouth in order to bark, and in doing so exposes its teeth. If the air temperature is cold, it may even feel the cold in its teeth. It does no harm, and may improve the effectiveness of the gesture, to make baring the teeth part of the display. Alternatively, barking may be interpreted as a secondary effect of baring the teeth in the first place. After all, many dogs snarl before they begin to bark. Since the same mechanisms are involved in eating as in speaking, it is perhaps not surprising that for many cultures the act of reading aloud, which is taking in knowledge, is akin to chewing and swallowing, which is taking in food. To *ruminate* is to think as well as to digest. To "eat your own words" is to swallow your pride.

32
A dog barking
has clear airways.

To speak with your mouth full, on the other hand, is (a) hazardous, since you may choke; (b) bad manners, since eating interferes with the action of speaking and disturbs the clarity of what you are saying; and

(c) impracticable, because you are trying to use the same apparatus to do two different things at the same time. For effective signaling, care and preparation are required. Even trumpet players have to take time out from playing to clear the condensation from their instrument.

33
A dog barking
declares itself.

A dog is not a ventriloquist. In barking it draws attention to itself. To draw attention to oneself in so public a fashion in the wild is not always a good idea. A dog will bark because it is accustomed to feeling secure, and for the sake of maintaining that sense of security. A concert violinist feels much the same way. In the protected environment of a concert hall, the solo artist can feel confident about being the focus of attention.

34
A dog barking
is standing upright.

Snoring is for lying down, singing is for standing up. Sitting down is good enough for conversation, but not for addressing a large gathering without a microphone. Standing up also looks better, and affords the speaker a better view. For a dog, a parliamentarian, or anyone in between, assuming an upright posture shows that the speaker is a person ready for action. A string quartet is a musical conversation as though seated around an invisible table. An orchestra is a seated assembly led by a standing conductor, and it is the person standing up who takes the lion's share of the credit. Among the exceptions in musical performance are the solo pianist and the solo cellist, both of whom perform sitting down, with the inherent disadvantage of loss of mobility. The image of exercising power while remaining seated is more readily associated with royalty, bank managers, and driving fast cars. Even the cello started life as a solo instrument to be performed standing up, the instrument resting on a cushioned stool.

35
A dog that barks
has energy to spare.

If you are going to impose your presence on the world at large, it is best to be fit, and a useful strategy to have enough energy in reserve to meet any challenge that might arise.

36
A dog barking
discovers its place.

Routine is a feature of animal as much as human behavior. Actions of an habitual kind form into patterns, and eventually become more or less automatic. The advantages of settling into a routine are that over time the sequence of tasks is managed more efficiently, which also translates into a saving of energy. When a child learns to walk it also learns to run: in acquiring the coordination for walking, it also saves enough energy to allow the action to be speeded up. Routine exploration of the environment is a normal function of everyday life because people or animals cannot be everywhere at once, even on the internet. Routine behaviors of all living creatures are linked to the ongoing maintenance of a personal world image. Work routines are patterns also incorporated in music, so that in performing a song or movement one is reinforcing or teaching the rhythms of work or dance. Even a dog barking is part of an ongoing process which is sometimes defined as the rhythm or cycle of life. The less attention one has to devote to the routine itself, the more alert one can be to any unforeseen changes that may happen along the way.

37
If a barking dog is not here but there,
then there is not here.

In some parts of the world it is customary to answer a telephone call
with the question "Are you there?" implying that on the evidence of
the voice alone, one can never be sure. The same kind of uncertainty
that used to be attributed to spirits in limbo, is felt nowadays about
information in *cyberspace*, another antique term for a place that is
neither here nor there. When the barking of a dog invades a listener's
personal space, one is aware of it as the *sound* having arrived, but the
physical *dog* (for want of other evidence) being somewhere else. If the
dog itself is not here then there has to be somewhere else for it to be,
by definition a place out of reach of the listener. Like the ghost of
Banquo in Shakespeare's *Macbeth*, the dog's voice enters our space as
an immaterial presence, one that may however exercise the option of
invading in person at an imminent later stage. So it is in the listener's
immediate interests to pinpoint the real location of the dog and be
ready to take appropriate defensive or evasive action. To do that you
have to believe that the real dog is somewhere else, and that its space is
separate and distinct from your own.

38
By the time you hear a bark
it has already happened.

Somebody remarked of René Descartes, the philosopher who observed
"I think, therefore I am," that by the time he got to his conclusion he
was already relying on memory and may therefore have been mistaken.
If Descartes had been writing his thoughts down at the time, which is
very possible, he would not have needed to rely on memory because
the evidence of what he had started out to say would be there in front
of him, continuously in view. For other listeners, however, the issue of
memory is very real, firstly because sounds take a finite time to arrive,

secondly because they die away rapidly, and thirdly because human hearing itself is a temporal process with built-in delays and buffers that protect the ears from the damaging effects of sudden loud noises in nature. (The same mechanisms however *do not protect* the hearing of young listeners from long periods of exposure to amplified rock music at extremely high intensities.)

Sound at sea level travels at about 340 meters per second, so by the time the sound of the dog barking from your neighbor's front garden over the road reaches your ears from 34 meters away, it has been delayed by 0.1 second, which is the sort of delay that we hear on television interfering with the conversations between prime time newscasters and reporters on location. After the sound reaches the ears of the listener, the response time of human hearing is subject to further delays: because human tissue is flexible, because the sound has to be analyzed, and because the resulting messages have to be sent along nerves to the brain, all of which takes time. If a person is not already on the alert, there may be a further delay in processing a sound in thinking about it. So there are both physical and psychological factors that enter between the time the dog actually barks and the time it triggers a response in the listener's mind. Fortunately, sound travels so much faster than any living creature that even after the sum total of delays is taken into account, there is still usually time to get out of the way. Much of the history of warfare, as a matter of interest, has been geared to the development of missiles that travel silently, or faster than sound, to ensure that by the time the shot is heard, the bullet has already reached its target.

39
By the time you are sure it is a dog that is barking, the sound has already passed into memory.

A listener's immediate reaction to a dog barking involves a number of processes that jointly come under the definition of short-term memory. However, in order to identify the disturbance as *a dog barking*, you have to know what *a dog* is, which means you have to have heard a dog before, preferably more than one dog and at different times. That knowledge is stored in long-term memory, and recognition of the sound as a dog barking is usually described as a matching process, though that is most likely an oversimplification. If music rather than a visual imaging process is taken as the template for auditory memory, the various attributes of a dog barking: pitch, rhythm, accent, timbre, etc., are stored as separate impressions in a network of different locations recognizable not as a single item but as a configuration.

40
Before it barks
there is no dog.

A dog may exist in potential when a listener can neither see nor hear it, and for its owner a belief in the continuing existence of a family pet is not only understandable but necessary if one is intent on stocking up with pet food at the supermarket. For those without a dog the continuing existence of a neighbor's dog is neither here nor there as long as the animal is not creating a disturbance. We coexist with the rest of the world, including the neighbor's dog, on a strict "need to know" basis, which means that we only need to take a dog's existence into account when it barks, and not in between. A person's individual world is made up of the impressions and sensations that matter, and a barking dog, if one is not a dog owner, is only rarely part of that network of resources.

41
When the barking stops
the dog stops.

Unless, of course, it is biting your leg. The "down time" of a serious and unexpected disturbance can take longer to get over than a bark of greeting encountered in passing, and will continue to cause concern as long as the perceived danger remains, or until it is otherwise resolved, such as by the listener going somewhere else. The natural outcome of a recovery process, however, is elimination of the disturbance from the normal routine of daily life. To all intents and purposes, when calm is restored the dog ceases to exist, only a trace remaining in memory.

42
A dog that barks
is using remote control.

Television did not invent the remote control. Any living air-breathing creature with a powerful voice uses it to control the environment. Baby animals do it by instinct, and adults by choice. The great advantages of controlling the environment through sound signals are that it is proven effective, avoids the embarrassment of confrontation, and does away with the need for direct physical intervention.

43
A dog that barks
is switching channels.

Using the voice for remote control is analogous to a person switching channels, action prompted by a sense of disquiet with the world as it is presented, and a desire for change to an alternative life situation toward which the observer feels more comfortable and in control.

44
The note of a dog barking
changes its world.

Babies also cry as a form of remote control, though the life situations with which they are wrestling tend to be driven by internal appetites and sensations. That babies, blackbirds and bull terriers alike are able through sound to manipulate the world of other living creatures to their own advantage lends interest to the study of musical and vocal behaviors as command and control strategies in their own right. Music builds on these survival skills, and music also plays a prominent role in human rituals, which evolve as social protocols to deal with unseen threats in the local environment.

45
Where a barking dog can be heard
defines its territory.

A church bell rings out over the village and into the fields where the villagers are working. The judge bangs his gavel to bring the court-room assembly into order. In an airplane, electronic chimes sound over the public address system to remind passengers to fasten their seat belts. The siren of an approaching police car tells everyone in its path to get out of the way. In outdoor situations where a signal has to travel great distances, and also in crowd situations where there is already a lot of noise going on, words are not much help: you need strong, audi-ble shapes that are easy to identify. Call signs and alarm cries are abundant in nature, and children are taught from a very early age that the sheep goes baa, the cow goes moo, and the duck goes quack–quack–quack—that is, to recognize different animal sounds and under-stand that each is associated with a very specific creature and degree of danger.

In the act of vocalizing and hearing the sound of its own voice, a dog finds itself in the center of the action. When you are in the center, it is difficult to tell where any external boundaries may be. That a barking dog is defining its territory is not necessarily what the animal thinks, but is certainly what the listener thinks, a reasonable conclusion in the circumstances, considering the way lesser animals respond to the calls of larger predators.

46
The louder the sound,
the greater the silence.

Loudness in itself is only part of the story. One thunderclap among many is just another thunderclap. The impact and effectiveness of a signal like a dog barking depends not so much on how loud it is in a scientific sense—though naturally it has to be loud enough to reach a listener in the first place—but in its degree of contrast with the background sound in the environment. For small- and medium-sized vocal creatures like birds, dogs, and human beings, distant calls differ from local calls in the way they use energy. A relaxed human speaking voice covers a broad spectrum of frequencies, from low chest tones to the hiss and click of consonants, which are high-frequency noises. These different frequency layers are not all equally adapted to traveling long distances through the atmosphere, one reason why the referee at a football match uses a high-pitched whistle to call the teams to order, rather than his voice. To signal over a distance as effectively as a whistle, one has to change the way the voice produces sound, so that most of its energy is focused in the higher frequency range. The tradeoff of long-distance signaling is that much of the ability to form words is sacrificed, but since words would not be discernible at a distance anyway, that is not much of a loss.

The most effective contrast to a bark or a speech is silence. However, silence is not always easy to find. In a noisy environment other forms of contrast are necessary. Noise by definition is all around, and lacks overall pattern or shape. For a meaningful signal to overcome a haze of noise, it may only be necessary for it to show greater consistency: in pitch, by reducing the amount of fluctuation to a small number of notes; in rhythm, by adopting a regular pattern; and in location, by the individual standing still rather than moving about. Standing with your back to the wall can also help, since the sound energy that would otherwise be lost behind your back is reflected forward, making the voice appear twice as loud. Many musical instruments are well adapted to be heard in the marketplace.

47
A breeze is blowing:
the sound travels.

If the air through which a sound is traveling is itself in motion, as in a breeze or wind, the sound is carried along in the direction of the air current. If the wind is coming toward a listener, it will carry sound from farther away; if blowing in the other direction it may prevent it from reaching the listener. When a wind is blowing, the speed of sound remains unchanged, but the mass of air through which it is traveling is also moving. A different situation arises for the sound of an airplane flying overhead. In that case the object producing the sound is moving, not the air, and the plane is moving at a very much higher speed, with the result that the sound waves radiating from the airplane are compressed in the direction of forward motion, and stretched apart behind it. The change in tone a listener hears as an airplane passes overhead is the audible effect of its speed of travel.

48
In the sound of a dog barking
you can hear that snow has fallen.

Sound is a perception of pressure waves traveling through the air as though it were a solid body. For human beings snow is a soft covering, but for sound propagating at 340 meters per second, it is a hard and unyielding reflecting surface. We speak of sound *dying away* as it loses energy, and for most people losing energy is the same as running out of energy and getting tired, so the impression created is of a sound that gets tired. We also talk about sound in a room being *absorbed* by thick curtains and soft furnishings, suggesting that its energy is soaked up like water in a sponge. Both impressions are somewhat misleading. Energy is transferred but not lost. A small amount of the energy in sound is converted into heat, through forcing air molecules into motion back and forth as the pressure waves pass through. Some energy is lost to structures like spider webs or windowpanes that convert the airborne energy into structural vibration. Most of the energy in a shock wave however is dissipated by contact with complex surfaces that at high magnification add up to an area much greater than the volumes they occupy, like the surface area of a sponge or deep pile carpet. Out of doors vegetation such as hedges, the leaves on trees, and grass on the lawn present surfaces that at a microscopic level are just as hard as window glass to incident sound waves; but because they are not large and flat barriers but complex structures presenting multiple angled surfaces, their effect is to scatter the incoming pressure wave into a mass of incoherent fragments that ricochet from blade to blade and leaf to leaf, unable to escape. But if snow has fallen and covers the trees, the hedges, and the grass with a thick and relatively smooth coating, the energy in a sound wave is no longer broken up and trapped, but reflected back into the open air. That is why sound carries farther in winter and sleigh bells can be heard from far away.

49
In the sound of a dog barking
you can hear that the air is dry or damp.

After snow has fallen, the air is usually dry. In times of mist or high humidity, the air is moist, with tiny droplets of water floating freely in the atmosphere, ready to condense as dew on the leaves of plants or as steam on windowpanes. Mist and fog not only make it hard for people to see, but to a lesser degree they also affect the sounds we hear. The droplets of moisture form a cloudy barrier that extracts energy from sound in the higher frequency region that normally makes sounds appear crisp and well-defined. The higher frequencies in a sound are the more rapid fluctuations in pressure: at this order of magnitude the suspended droplets are as big as punchballs, set in motion by the shorter wavelengths while the larger and more powerful undulations pass through undisturbed. The world of sound is muted in foggy weather, which is why foghorns emit low, penetrating tones. In music and acoustics, the deadening effect of suppressing the higher frequencies of a sound, for example by laying a cloth on the surface of a drum, is also called "damping" the sound.

50
In the ambience of a dog barking
is an entire neighborhood.

There are two spatial components of any sound you hear, like a dog barking. The "direct" sound comes in a direct line from the source to the listener, in this case from the dog's throat to your ears. If a dog is barking or a small child calling from a long way away in the grassy center of a public park, all you are likely to hear is the direct sound and no reflections, given that there are no objects near the source to reflect and reinforce the sound, and that the grassy surface traps sound, in the manner already described, rather than reflecting it. The reason a shepherd whistles instructions to his dogs in the field is because his sheep are covered in wool and do not reflect sound any better than a grassy pasture. They are forced to rely on the direct sound. In the absence of reflections a distant sound is thin and small, but in a normal suburban environment a whistle or bark bounces off houses, paved roads, parked cars and other hard surfaces in the neighborhood. Some of that "indirect" component of reflected sound is returned to the caller, the dog or small child, and some is diverted toward the distant listener. A typical suburban neighborhood consists of hard paving, walls, cars, telephone poles, trees, gardens, and hedges. Since reflected sound reached the listener by an indirect route, it takes longer to arrive and arrives out of focus, but because the indirect signal diverts energy from a much larger surface area than the original source, it is often more powerful than the direct sound.

After becoming aware that sound is reflected by solid bodies one learns by investigation and experiment that flat surfaces such as still water are good reflectors, whereas negatively curved or concave surfaces such as cliff faces can influence the spread of sound and even bring it to a focus. Anthopologists now believe that prehistoric cave paintings are often markers of acoustically special locations where the voice is noticeably amplified or prolonged.

51
In the pitch of a dog's voice
is the size of the dog.

The size of an animal affects its muscle power and lung capacity, which in turn influence the loudness of its voice and how long it can sustain a cry. An animal with a larger head also has larger vocal cords, giving it a deeper voice. When a child grows into an adult, the voice "breaks" as the vocal cords experience a growth spurt, an effect common to both sexes but usually more noticeable in males than females. There are two ways of evaluating the pitch of a voice: the actual note of a particular bark or call, and the relative pitch, which corresponds to its natural range of variation. Professional singers are trained to sing with control over a much wider pitch range than normal, giving the voice a supernatural quality. The throat singers of Tibet and Central Asia cultivate techniques of throat muscle control that enable singers to produce voice sounds of extremely low pitch and enhanced resonance.

52
In the fullness of a dog's voice
is its presence.

Presence is how close a person is heard to be, or a dog, judged by the sound of the voice. It is a perception of amplitude or fullness, terms sometimes mistaken for loudness. A nearby voice appears louder and clearer because more direct energy reaches our ears, but whereas loudness refers to the peak energy level, or the loudness of the loudest part of a sound, amplitude or fullness refers to the totality of range or spectrum of the sound that a listener is able to discern, from deep chest tones to sharp clicks and hissed sibilants, many of which are only audible at close range. These more subtle sounds in the more sensitive areas of hearing give a voice a quality of intimacy or presence. Whispering, which is vocalizing without any voice tone, is an intimate manner of speaking that relies on the more subtle nuances of voice, such as breath noises and chest cavity resonances, rather than the powerful midrange of throat sounds.

53
In the intensity of a dog's voice
is its excitement.

Intensity is another word that implies loudness but does not mean quite the same thing. A loud voice can be loud and effortless at the same time, while intensity of voice has more to do with raising the level of activity associated with the sound and any change in the quality of sound that may result. A whimpering dog is not louder than a barking dog, but its sound is more intense. Intensity highlights or distorts certain features of a normal sound to an abnormal degree, for expressive or emotional effect.

54
In the certainty of a dog's voice
is its maturity.

Good judgement lies in knowing when to start, and when to stop talking. Uncontrolled barking wastes energy, time, and patience, and may even provoke the aggression it may have been intended initially to deter. A good watchdog is a professional: quick to respond, authoritative in tone, confident in manner, and economical in performance. Clarity and economy of gesture are the hallmarks of maturity in vocal behavior as in any other action.

55
In the steadfastness of a dog's voice
is its purpose.

Firmness or steadfastness of character are qualities of evenness of tone and consistency of gesture in a voice. To produce a consistently even tone a musician has to demonstrate exceptional physical and mental control that remains unaffected by momentary distraction. A performance displaying such control is more than a show of exceptional skill. It is also the mark of dedication to a chosen goal, and indifference to any danger or distraction that may be encountered along the way. Such dedication to the task is a highly valued element of leadership.

56
In the definition of a dog's bark
you can hear that it is in or out of doors.

As one might expect, to a listener in the street the sound of a dog barking inside a house sounds muted compared to one barking outside. Instead of radiating outward in every direction, the shock wave is contained and circulates within the room structure before emerging from an open or closed window or door. If the window is closed, what a listener outside hears is the glass vibrating with a sound that is also colored to some degree by the interior cladding. The sound of a barking dog in an empty room retains a lot more of its initial energy than for a room fitted out with carpet, curtains, and soft furnishings. The flatness of a vibrating windowpane also means that the pressure waves radiated from it are more flat than spherical, which means that a sound heard from behind a closed window is more limited in directionality than the same sound produced in the open air. In music there are many instruments that make use of shaped containers for added and directed resonance, notably the piano, harp, acoustic guitar, and violin family. The curvaceous "box" of an acoustic guitar reinforces the string tone in similar ways to the reinforcement of a dog barking in an empty room, or the sound of an empty drink bottle when you blow across the open end. The "air tone" is the product of the shape and volume of air within the box, and the overall pattern of back and forth motion of sound waves in the interior cavity of flat and curved reflecting surfaces. The "wood tone" is an additional coloration of tone arising from the flexibility and grain of the wood used in its construction, its degrees of motion, and the surface coating applied to it.

57
A bark is rhythm,
a howl is melody.

Rhythm and melody are two major elements of music, and they arise from perceptions of movement and direction in human and animal speech. By rhythm we understand pattern and repetition of gestures or phrases, as in a chicken clucking, a duck quacking, and a dog barking. Rhythm in nature is associated with actions that break down into a succession of smaller repeated actions, as when a bird digs for a worm or a builder hammers in a nail. Above all, rhythm is associated with movement in space, whether walking, hopping, running, or flying. The breakdown of larger movements into smaller repeated actions comes about because animals have to move in order to survive, and because they have to manage movement in ways that suit their bodies, whether they have two, four, six, or a hundred legs, or wings. The ultimate goal of movement may be to obtain energy in the form of food, but the repeated actions needed to achieve that goal also cost energy, and the best way of conserving energy is by moving in a rhythm, finding the most efficient action for taking one step, and then repeating it over and over. So a rhythm encountered in nature implies both goal-directed action, and the movement required to achieve the goal. These associations are also very strong in music.

By movement animals and people explore and keep watch on their territory, and for people as well as animals movement is also required to maintain physical contact with family and friends. Rhythmic actions imply awareness of time, both in the small-scale sense of the management of movement from step to step, and in the larger sense of actions directed toward an ultimate goal.

Howling is very different behavior from barking. Dogs howl in groups for much the same reasons as gospel choirs sing in chapel or team supporters chant at a football match: to socialize, express collective identity, demonstrate group security, and also to savor a transcendent emotion that may or may not be fuelled by food and drink. The characteristic features of a howl are continuity of action, indefinite duration, absence of interruption, and beauty of tone; in a collective howl a listener can also discern a desire for corporate unity and endurance beyond the limits of a single breath. These tendencies are also features of ritual singing in many ancient cultures.

A dog cannot howl while on the run. In howling an individual voice scans the spectrum of audible frequencies like a radio ham sweeping across the wave bands, in search of a familiar reflection. The purity of tone and scanning action of a howl up and down in pitch make it a very apt acoustical process for sounding out the environment, most notably the focused intensity of the signal, which like a radio beam is constant in amplitude and concentrates all of the animal's energy into a narrow bandwidth. Signals of precise pitch, gliding tones in particular, are ideal for sending and monitoring at the same time, since the narrow frequency band they occupy at any one time leaves the ears free to pick up any sound in higher or lower regions of frequency space. The values music and musicians attribute to purity, intensity, and continuity of tone reflect the same deep associations of scanning with self-reflection, friendship or loss, and sense of place.

58
Rhythm signifies action,
melody a state of being.

Rhythm is dynamic gesture that sends a message of the physical qualities and potential of the sender. Melody is static, in the sense of conveying a moment of self-reflection as well as in the functional sense of a signal designed to enhance a sense of place. In western music, an emphasis on rhythm tends to provoke a physical response in the listener and is associated with a faster tempo, whereas melody normally evokes a more emotional response and is generally associated with a slower tempo. Since the western social and cultural revolutions of the eighteenth and nineteenth centuries, rhythm in music has acquired more positive, and melody rather more negative associations, related directly to social attitudes toward action and change, and involving a mistaken perception that the values melody stands for are emblematic of human weakness, when in fact they arise from a heightened sense of personal reality.

59

**The direction from which a dog is barking
is in the ears of a listener.**

A listener can estimate how far away a dog is, from the loudness and fullness of the signal, but the direction from which the bark is coming is not a property of the sound itself, but of the hearing of the listener. Ears come in sets of two. People and animals have dual hearing for a useful and also paradoxical reason. The useful aspect of dual hearing is that a listener hears everything twice, through left and right ears, and the brain performs a form of triangulation on the two signals to work out the location of the dog barking. The movement of a shock wave through the air is fast enough to give the impression of the same event reaching both ears at once, but not so fast as to prevent differences between the two signals being detected when the brain matches one with the other. These differences can be summarized as variations in arrival time, since the ear nearer to the source of sound will hear it first, and phase differences, which relate to the perceived misalignment of positive and negative pressures in the two signals because of the time of arrival difference between the left and the right ear. These critical differences are extremely subtle in themselves, but cumulative in effect: the longer the dog keeps barking in one place, the more certain a listener can be of its true location.

The location of a barking dog or other noise is mapped onto a mental image of the environment, but of necessity a sense of location itself is first and foremost the expression of a personal relationship, an understanding of where the dog is in relation to you rather than where it is as a position on a satellite navigation system.

The paradoxical consequence of dual hearing, as with dual vision, arises from the fact that like vision the left and right images are not identical: what is heard is neither one, nor the other, but the difference. An object's location in space is encoded in the differences between the two signals, and it takes a brain to work them out. Both seeing and hearing are active brain processes applied to passive sensing mechanisms, and because what individuals see and hear is influenced by what they are familiar with, or what they want to see and hear, people do not always agree on how to interpret the evidence presented to them: either what they are hearing, or where it is. We all have a different point of view, but the reality is somewhere in between.

60
A dog that barks
is telling the truth.

The first rule of listening is trusting the evidence of your ears. If you hear a dog barking, then that is only what you think it is, but what you think you hear is a response to something you actually heard, and that is real. Even if you make a mistake, and it turns out that what you thought you heard was a trick of hearing or imagination, that does not make the event any the less real or truthful, since the reality is that you thought you heard something, and that is the truth. A popping in the ears may not be the sound of a dog barking, but it still tells you the truth about the state of your hearing, just as those moving points of light in your field of vision, "seeing stars," are the real effect of a sudden bump on the head. The truth of the experience is a separate issue from the accuracy of the description given to it.

That is the subjective truth of the experience of hearing a dog bark. The objective truth implied by saying the dog is telling the truth is also a complex judgement. It has to do with whether the dog actually barked, whether it intended to bark, and whether the bark was intended to mislead. These are issues of the kind that arise in a debating situation or in legal argument in court. In the real world the simple point is that if the dog did in fact bark, then that is the truth, it happened, and that truth, the fact that it happened and that the observer was aware of it, is not changed by any other consideration of purpose or intention on the part of the dog. What the dog does afterwards may help to explain the barking, but cannot change its truth value as a timely gesture.

61
A dog barking
is not in pain.

A dog may yelp in pain or growl in anger, but if it barks, it barks in self-defense, or simply to be sociable. The rhythm of a bark implies a readiness for action, which would be inappropriate for an animal in distress. It is reasonable to infer from a healthy bark that the animal is "in good voice" with all that implies: good condition, and good spirits.

62
A dog howling
is filling the void.

Is it reasonable to infer that a howling dog is therefore in pain? What emotional states, if any, does a dog experience? The experience of pain in human beings is a contentious enough issue in itself without invoking the sufferings of animals. Since any form of vocalization wastes energy, energy that a suffering person or animal would rather conserve, in reality most physical pain is endured in silence. Communities join in weeping and wailing as expressions of collective pain, or emotional solidarity with the sufferings of others, and they are able to do so freely because they are not themselves suffering physical pain.

Perhaps it would be more helpful to characterize pain as a state of being in which physical sensations are greatly intensified and thus harder to deal with. Certainly the characteristics of being in pain are reflected in those features of a howl or melody that have already been noted: a heightened sense of continuity, an acutely intense and highly localized tone, and a refusal to budge. The cyclical form of Purcell's famous aria "Dido's Lament" brings all of these qualities to bear on the lyrical expression of personal tragedy.

63
A good keeper
knows a dog's voice.

To know a dog, or a person, or any animal, by its voice is to have a distinct impression in memory of the tone qualities and resonances that are special to the individual, the same as a musician recognizes in a favorite musical instrument. Mimics who specialize in Elvis impressions have to do more than just copy the singer's lyrics and style of singing; their goal is to capture the identity of the voice itself, and that identity is conditioned by the the vocal cavity, the shape of the mouth interior, the tension of the muscles of the throat, and the way the facial structure moves. During the act of vocalization the soft tissues inside the mouth cavity—lips, tongue, and throat muscles—are constantly changing shape, affecting the pitch of the voice as well as the volume of air space within the vocal cavity, and thus its momentary resonance. But at the same time, certain features of the voice remain constant in all situations, and these are the features that give a voice its personal identity. The roof of the mouth, the teeth, jaw, and nasal cavity are among the rigid or invariant features of the facial structure that color the voice. The collective term for the identifying qualities of a voice or a musical instrument is its timbre or tone color. The timbre of a musical instrument, which is a largely rigid container or conduit, is much easier to identify and relates to the materials of which it is made and its interior shapes, whether it is a cylinder, conical, lens-shaped or spoon-shaped, and so on. The shapes of musical instruments are crucial influences on the sounds they make and how the sound is directed,

64
The expression of a dog's voice
is never the same.

It is only in a recording, or the movies that both the circumstances and the detail of a person's words or actions are exactly repeated. For centuries the idea of absolute identity in human affairs was thought to be an idea beyond human experience. Identical twins were a gift of the gods. The ancient Greek philosophers concluded that everything in human experience is change, and nothing on earth is ever the same. At the same time, human life is ruled by cycles: the sun rises and sets, the phases of the moon regularly wax and wane, and the seasons and tides also ebb and flow. Individual life is unavoidably committed to continuous growth and change, and even the structures and routines of social life, like language and crop cultivation, though established on concepts of identity of purpose and meaning, are in practice subject to constant modification even as they modify the environment. That the words and actions of living creatures are never identical in shape or context suggests that they can never be exactly the same in meaning, implying not only that dogs may bark for different reasons, but that people can never agree. That being the case, society can only function by appointing leaders whose interpretations of reality they are willing to abide by.

Both science and music arise from the counter-claim that identity, or exact repetition, can be found in the properties of things, if not in the things themselves. It does not matter what the caller says for a listener to recognize who the person is on the other end of the line, and it is not necessary to know every customer personally in order to design a bicycle.

65
The character of a dog's voice
is in its face.

The facial structure is a constant, and the bark a variable, but behavior is also a constant. Character, personality, temperament, and status arise from consistencies in the relationship of the vocal gesture and circumstances of provocation to the permanent qualities of the voice as an instrument and the clarity of the signal. Character is "star quality" without the script.

66
The dog that barks once
may bark again.

Dogs are normally taciturn creatures. They do not cluck to themselves like chickens, nor do they break spontaneously into song like birds in the wild. When a dog barks, it is generally for a reason. That in turn is a major incentive to employ dogs as pets, to give the alarm in an emergency. Sometimes the sound of a dog barking is enough to deal with the situation, bring help or scare away an intruder. But unless and until you observe the confrontation for yourself, you cannot be sure what it is about, and even if you arrive on the scene in time to see the next-door cat scampering away, it does not mean that the cat was responsible. The very fact that a bark works by remote control and avoiding direct physical contact also means that the source of provocation has not been touched and may well return.

The significance of barking, as for human speech, lies not in its ability to deal finally and completely with a disputed situation, but as a means of controlling it in the short term to the satisfaction of the parties involved. When a dog barks for the first time, the question that lingers in a listener's mind is whether the gesture has been effective in dealing with the emergency. If the problem does not go away, the barking is likely to recur, and further action may need to be taken.

67
In the expectation of a second bark,
we experience time.

There is a movieland saying, "Waiting for the other shoe to drop."
There are certain gestures in vocalization that imply incompleteness
and await a response. The upward inflection of a question asks for an
answering downward inflection. The bark of a dog may also convey a
threat: go away, or I will bite. The abruptness of a bark can be construed as a message that the animal is not one for small talk, that
barking is only a preparation signal for tougher action, and that the dog
is not going to waste time or energy arguing with an intruder. Anyone
alarmed by a dog barking will experience a down time wondering what
the dog will do next. Alarmed or unconcerned, the listener now knows
that the dog is there and that any plans for immediate action will have
to take the dog into account.

Any situation of heightened awareness is a time experience. Composers are skilled at making incomplete opening statements that grip
the attention. Schoenberg makes the distinction between a "theme" that
is necessarily incomplete, like the *dit-dit-dit-dah* of Beethoven's Fifth
Symphony, and a melody that comes fully equipped with a beginning,
a middle, and an end, like the anthem "God Save the Queen."

It is equally the case, of course, that a barking action is a form of
negotiation. A barking dog is one that is not biting. In barking rather
than opting for physical combat the dog is literally saying "This is my
position: what are you going to do about it?" A dog barking is a good
role model for dealing with difficult situations.

68
The first of two woofs
is always louder.

Impact is relative. The first woof breaks the silence, so the contrast is
more marked. The second woof echoes the first, so can be compared

with it. When two similar events are heard one after the other the second can be evaluated in terms of the first, for differences in emphasis that might indicate emotional direction, or indeed movement in space. If there is no difference, the gesture is emphatic; if the second is stronger, the emotion is increasing; if weaker, the animal is losing interest. The same with position: two barks from the same place shows the dog is holding his ground, but if the second woof comes from a different place, depending on the quality of the bark it might indicate the dog is in active pursuit, or in retreat.

Repeated sounds are associated in nature with echo, the delayed reflection from a flat surface of an original sound; echo is also associated with call and answer communication in the animal world, in which the response from a distant fellow creature is a repetition of the original call. Echo effects are often encountered in music, either as dialogue between a solo leader and the chorus, for instance in gospel music, or to give an illusion of space, as in baroque instrumental music in which loud phrases alternate with softer, more "distant" repetitions. Repetition in dialogue is also a way of registering the full significance of a message received, or of a promise being made. Marriage is all the more impressive in involving an exchange of vows that are spoken by the celebrant and repeated by the couple. In civic rituals of confirmation of public office, of taking the oath, or becoming a citizen of a new country, repetition symbolizes commitment. In the most solemn moments of human life, oral traditions still tend to prevail.

69
Unexpected is real:
the rest, imagination.

The proverb says, "To the blind all things are sudden." The blind would disagree. Blind people out of necessity have a more acute sense of hearing than sighted people. Visually-oriented cultures imagine that vision confers foresight, the ability to see what is coming, and that blind people lack foresight, being deprived of vision. What sighted people tend to forget (until they watch a mystery or horror movie) is that they can only clearly see in one direction, which is the direction they are already going. People cannot see what is behind them, and to see they also need light. A blind person can navigate just as effectively in the dark as in daylight, and has the significant advantage of being able to hear voices and movements to the side and behind just as clearly as those to the front. The sighted person says, but I too have hearing, I can do that too. But to have as well-developed a sense of hearing as a blind person takes a lot of effort and practice. An unsighted person moves with a great deal more care and precision than a sighted person, often with the head tilted slightly upward, to hear forward more clearly.

That normal people avoid sudden or unexpected events as often as possible is certainly true. The image of a world in which "all things are sudden" is one of unconditional helplessness against attack from those who have the advantage of speed or sight. Pattern and orderly routine in daily life are adaptations of behavior that not only improve the quality and efficiency with which life is maintained, but also reduce the incidence of unexpected events to a manageable level. Not to avoid the unexpected completely, since a life of total routine (such as the stereotyped office environment) can easily descend into an inhuman and robotic existence. The ideal is a situation of balance in which the organized person is prepared to deal with the unexpected and not always trying to avoid it. The unexpected is also a proof of the reality of the world in which we live out our routines. Since such an experience could not possibly be a figment of the imagination, it must be an effect of a real world outside the imagination.

70
In recognition we understand
persistence of being.

Hearing is a constant in a world of intermittent, short-term sounds. If every sound were perceived as completely new and different from anything anyone had heard before, aural life would be a total confusion. Since both in logic and in reality every sound we hear is likely to be unique in some way, the question has to be why we do not live in total confusion anyway, and arising from that, how it is ever possible to recognize sounds as being the same. The answer in logic is that if everything is different then our knowledge of the world can only be conditional, so we choose to live in a buffer zone of possibility rather than a world of absolute certainty. In a practical sense, it means that everything we hear and do is part of a cumulative process of gathering and sifting the evidence.

In an inconstant world, maintaining a sense of continuity of personal being assumes a high level of importance, and provides a real motivation for detecting similarities and consistencies in the encounters of everyday life, such as eating and drinking—and also walking, since walking is repetitive action, and dogs and human beings are not like slugs and snails, in constant contact with the ground while they move about.

71
A barking dog
is fully awake.

Nobody ever heard a sleeping dog bark, or even a dog that was only half awake. In order to perform, a player has to be on full alert. The bark is both a statement of alertness and a demonstration of it.

72
A barking dog
is a wake-up call.

There is a nobility in barking to alert a potential enemy, rather than using stealth to surprise and defeat the intruder. In a practical sense the dog is unsure who the intruder is—or even if there is any intruder at all—so that part of the reason for barking and thus declaring oneself amounts to a challenge to the unknown opponent to come out into the open and make its intentions plain. That perceived opponent could also be you, the listener. You are already awake, but your thoughts may be elsewhere. The thought that one may have been targeted by a hostile dog is good reason to come to your senses and review the situation in which you find yourself. That the dog barks first before taking any further action can be regarded in this light as a charitable gesture.

73
Whoever hears a dog bark
intrudes in its space.

Whether the dog knows you are there, or is unaware of your presence, does not matter. Whether the supposed intruder responds to the bark by revealing itself does not matter either. The efficacy of a barking action is the same whether the intruder fronts up or runs away. If it rises to the challenge, then the bark has done its job and the situation is clear. If it runs away, the bark has succeeded in chasing away the intruder and protecting the property from occupation. On the other hand, if no intruder is revealed the bark has also been efficacious in disposing of the threat, which is shown to be either not there at all, or to have been intimidated into silence.

From a listener's point of view, the only prudent response to a dog barking, however briefly, is to review the situation as though oneself were the object of attention.

74
The dog that barks
is upbeat.

Upbeat is a term from music. It implies a positive attitude, readiness for action and taking control. It says, let's deal with this.

75
The dog that barks
is in good shape.

Readiness for action suggests not only physical fitness and acute sensitivity to changes in the environment, but also a willingness to be provoked, often a sign of youth and inexperience.

76
The power of a dog barking
is its physique.

There are ways of estimating the general health and strength of a dog, but at a particular moment in time the proof of its real condition has to be in demonstration rather than mere appearance. The power of a bark is a significant indicator of lung capacity and muscular strength, especially in and around the mouth, which is a dog's major offensive weapon.

77
The sharpness of a dog barking
is its reaction time.

In order to judge its reaction time, an observer should ideally be aware in advance of what the dog is barking at, and the simplest and most effective gauge of a dog's speed and intensity of reaction is to provoke it oneself. There are levels of provocation, from teasing and cruelty to conversational and affectionate dialogue with a pet who is also a friend and companion. Whether the occasion is an angry encounter, a casual chat, or a learned debate, all dialogue involves provocation, assertion of territoriality, and a testing of physical and moral strength. In nature, speed of response can be a life and death issue; in political debate it can mean the difference between triumph and humiliation.

78
The dog that barks first
may not have to fight later.

Barking, as we have said, is wasteful of energy, so a sensible dog will ration the use of its voice, to save energy, to maintain the element of surprise, and in order not to shout itself hoarse. The tradeoff of barking first is that once its cover is blown the intruder will see no point in proceeding, so the dog will avoid further expenditure of energy and associated risk of injury.

79
A barking dog
is imitating human speech.

The broken texture of barking is not a feature of dog vocalizing in the wild, for which reason it is sometimes suggested that the behavior is in imitation of human speech, the dog's carer being effectively the "top dog." A dog is trained to obey simple one-word instructions, which are not very different in kind from barking gestures—a commanding officer "barks" orders to his troops in the same manner and to much the same purpose. Loudness, brevity, and economy in giving orders aid coordination in the ranks, or one may say more cynically that the same combination is more likely to provoke an instant collective response that will be more or less coordinated by default.

That barking in dogs is imitation of human speech begs the question of whether from the dog's point of view barking is any more useful than howling, its natural mode of communication in the wild. The domesticated dog does not roam in packs but lives, usually alone, or in twos or threes, with human beings in a house and garden of limited area. Barking may be considered an adaptation not just of humanized dogs to their human companions, but of their habit of voice to a more suitable style of vocalization for territorial defense, and for signaling, in a built environment.

80
A dog does not bark and eat
at the same time.

The mouth is a versatile piece of anatomy with which a person or animal takes in oxygen, expresses affection, communicates, defends itself, and eats and drinks. It is close to the brain for speed of reaction, and works in close partnership with the eyes, nose, and ears for maximum coordination of sensory information.

Eating engages the lips, teeth, tongue, and throat muscles, which is why it is neither polite nor prudent to speak with your mouth full. In addition, one's sense of smell is distracted during eating, and the vocal folds are otherwise engaged in their primary function of closing the airways, ensuring that masticated food does not take a wrong turning and enter the lungs by mistake. Eating, breathing, and barking all require the mouth to be open and empty to begin with.

81
A bark is for warning
and also for confidence.

Barking is both a gesture of recognition, "Hello there," and also a warning signal provoked by the unknown: a footfall, a voice, a scent. The action of sounding the alarm and at the same time flexing one's auditory muscles acts as a self-test as well as intimidation, like a driver of a sports car revving the engine to listen to its comforting growl.

82
One breath, two woofs:
flash, bang.

A double bark, "Woof! Woof!" is achieved in a single breath and thus a single action expressed in two gestures, of which the first contains the element of surprise, and the second acts as confirmation. Human beings do the same when they knock at a door. One knock could be an accident or a trick of hearing, but two knocks one after another give the action definition as well as emphasis. It is interesting to note that for the "Knock! Knock!" action to be effective, the time gap between the two knocks has to be quite short, about as short, in fact, as between the first and second woof when a dog barks. The speed of repetition is governed by the recovery time of the muscles, also taking into account the recovery time of the hearing of the person listening. Too long a gap between the two, and the sense of connection diminishes, eventually to a point where the knocks become two separate actions and not a single action in two parts. In music the critical distance between successive stimuli is called the pulse or beat.

83
Between the first woof and the second,
a moment of absence.

If a bark were a solitary event, just a single woof, it would define a single instant in time. Before it, silence; after it, silence, and the bark in between. But a single woof almost never happens. If it did, we might not recognize it as a bark.

A double bark, Woof! Woof! is something else. A double bark conveys intention. It has a structure. A double bark is two barks with a break in between: a bark before, and a bark afterwards, separated by a silence. The silence has duration: it is a measure of time and an experience of time.

A perception of time is not in the position of the second hand on a clock, or the number displayed by the seconds digits on a digital watch, but in the movement of the second hand to a new position, and in the change of shape of the seconds digits on the watch to a new number. The experience of time is an experience of change, and for change to be perceived requires awareness of an initial state and a subsequent state.

84
The second woof
prolongs the first.

A double bark begins with a woof and ends with a woof. The silence in between, to pursue the clock analogy, is a time of transition, of time passing. Since the woof action is the same both times, the gesture does not develop. The opening statement is the same as the concluding statement. "I bark, therefore I bark." If the first bark is regarded as a spontaneous gesture in response to an external stimulus, since it comes out of nowhere, the second bark may be regarded as a deliberate act, since it arises in the context of the previous bark.

85
The first woof initiates the action;
the second completes it.

Life is continuous. Everything a living creature does is the precursor of what it does next. Actions tend to be segmented, while the "passions" (senses of vision, hearing, taste, touch, smell, and the emotions associated with them) imply continuity. Continuity of experience is always difficult to quantify. A dog howling is giving expression to the paradoxical uncertainty of a world in perpetual motion, an existence without definition. The sacred songs of Hildegard von Bingen express exactly the same melancholy perception.

   It would be easy to say that a dog barks in two short actions simply because it cannot bark in one continuous action. The mechanism does not allow it, just as the only way for a person playing a plucked string instrument like a guitar (or koto, or harp, or mandolin) is to repeat the action to sustain the level of an opening sound. But that is not true, since dogs can also howl, just as a string instrument can be played with a bow as an alternative to being plucked. The action of barking thus represents a choice in favor of segmentation in preference to the continuous movement of a howl or bow. If there is a choice involved, one can ask what the advantages are. There could be a social advantage for a dog in the imitation of human speech. In adapting to human speech patterns, which are highly segmented, a dog would learn to appreciate the perceptual advantages of the broken texture of human speech, with its mixture of tones and noises, as an instrument of environmental assertion and control. Rapid and seemingly random changes of signal from fixed tone to gliding tone, and from tone to noise, provide useful information across the range of hearing while remaining relatively transparent to the speaker and listener (there are holes in the sound that one can listen through).

86
The repetition of a bark
embodies time, form, and directedness.

Despite its simplicity, the double action of a dog barking has all of the essential features of a formal statement. It attracts and holds a listener's attention; it has a beginning, middle, and end; it defines a relationship; it defends a position; it embodies a personality; it articulates a temporal process; and it conveys a positive message.

87
The second woof is more predictable
than the first.

The first woof of a double always contains an element of surprise for the dog, since the first of two also has the role of testing the system, and the system includes not only the dog's vocal mechanism but its hearing mechanism as well: in effect asking "Is this real? Did I do that?," and the follow-up bark answering "Yes, I did, what a voice" and "the way it sounded was this." There are two views on speech acts. The traditional linguistic view is that speech is a process directed toward the satisfactory articulation of words; the alternative view of motor phonetics is that words are the audible byproduct of physical gesture. If linguists were to take account of animal communication, they would find it more difficult, one suspects, to defend the primacy of language as a social construct and the individual speech act as a personal and therefore trivial instance of word selection and interpretation. For human beings in normal conversation, talking is a social activity as well as a sharing of information, meaning that the activity of talking is as important for many people as what they might be talking about.

88
A dog barks
to clear its throat.

But, you may say, it wouldn't be barking if its throat wasn't already clear. How can an action be preparation for itself? The simple answer is that dogs are not logical animals, but running through this entire discussion of what a dog is actually doing when it barks is the message that simple things have many reasons, and as a design issue it makes perfect sense for an action such as barking to fulfill the task of clearing the airways as part of its function of testing that the airways are clear in the first place. Suppose that you had heard a cough and a splutter rather than a bark. You would rightly conclude that the dog had something in its mouth. If the action dislodged a particle of food stuck to the back of the throat, then the bark would have fulfilled a back-up role of clearing the throat. The listener's problem lies in having separate terms for a cough and a bark, and in not realizing that the two may be connected.

89
A dog barking
resembles the action of a musical instrument.

The voice is the original musical instrument. Alternatively, a musical instrument is a tool devised by human beings to make specific kinds of noises, some of which are voicelike, others not. The action of playing a musical instrument converts muscular energy into sound energy. Physical movement is generally silent: take away the clogs from a clog dancer and you will not hear very much. For airbreathing animals in the natural world, whether a snake, a lion, or an eagle, it is a matter of survival to avoid making unnecessary noise. When wild animals vocalize or behave noisily, it is usually either out of the abandonment of the chase, or from a position of desperation.

Musical instruments transform gestures into sound that would otherwise remain silent. The meaning of the sound is interpreted as the meaning of the gesture, as when the doctor tells a patient to say "Ahh!" the word has no meaning other than to show that the mouth is wide open. In the movies, and in computer games of combat there is a longstanding convention of using sound to add impact to a punch to the body. In real life there is little or no sound to a violent blow, the throw of a spear, or running barefoot across the plain.

The main reason for reproducing silent actions as gestures in sound is for telling a story, which is a means of storing and reproducing the experience. In order to convert a silent gesture into sound, a physical gesture is needed along with a resonating structure that vibrates in response to the physical gesture. The resulting sound gesture becomes both a description of the physical action, and a demonstration of the vibrating and resonating apparatus. In music it is the same. When a violin is played, the gesture is the bowing action, the vibrating agent the string, and the resonator the box. For a dog barking the gesture is the muscular spasm, the vibrating agent the vocal folds, and the resonator the lungs, mouth, and nasal cavities.

In considering the effectiveness of a musical instrument as a converter of gesture to sound we need to ask how well the sound conforms to the action, and although at a fundamental level the sound is bound to correspond with the action taken to produce it, there is a higher perception of a dog barking as a symbolic gesture, because it is a form of display, and because barking cannot be an entirely accurate expression of behavior that is normally silent.

90
The sound of a musical instrument
combines force and resistance.

Barking could also be described as conflicted breathing. People gasp with emotion and splutter with rage, so it is not an entirely unfamiliar process. The distinction of barking, as of vocalizing in general, lies in the way the apparatus of breathing—the lungs, the airways, the chest muscles, the soft tissues of the mouth, throat, and larynx—are reconfigured so that instead of operating smoothly in cooperation, they work in structured opposition. If newborn animals did not cry spontaneously, it would be impossible to teach them. Voice production is centered on the vocal folds, which form a valve structure at the entrance to the airways to the lungs. In breathing, eating, and drinking the valve opens and closes spontanously, but if food "goes down the wrong way" as we say, or the airways become congested, the animal or person is forced to take action to free the blockage. That ability to tense or relax the valve tissues in the larynx is the key to vocalization in which the same tissues are stiffened intentionally to close off the normal flow of air. In that way air pressure builds and eventually forces its way between the closed vocal folds to be emitted as a series of pulses, a process analogous to the sound emitted from an inflated balloon when the neck is drawn apart between fingers and thumbs. The element of self-imposed internal conflict, of natural body processes deliberately set in opposition, is a paradoxical feature of speech that brings to mind the inner conflicts and pressures that are supposed to motivate human actions.

91
The greater the resistance,
the more structured the vibration.

When a dog is persuaded to sing, the sound it produces is a howl rather than a bark. This is interesting for a number of reasons, in the first place because the dog understands singing as howling, secondly because the howl, though more musical than a bark, is conventionally speaking a more primitive form of vocal behavior, thirdly because howling (i.e., music) is a social activity for dogs as well as human beings. The purer, more focused and sustained tone of a howl is produced by a combination of breath control and deliberate tensioning of the vocal folds. A howl is thus more motivated than a bark, with aesthetic as well as functional implications.

In a practical sense, the greater the stiffness of a vibrating body, the greater the force that is needed to make it change shape, and the more regular the resulting vibration, tending toward a tone of constant pitch. When a structure is forced out of shape, if it has resistance it will seek to go back to its original shape, and if steady pressure is applied, a steady vibration is produced. The tone of a guitar is directly related to the motion of the string that has been plucked and transferred to a resonating chamber, but the sound of a voice is more like the ripple effect created as a consequence of interfering with the airflow.

92
In resistance is constancy,
in flexibility is change.

To tune a guitar, a musician winds up the tension of each string to a point where it sounds the right note. The tension in the string is the force holding it tight, and the materials and thicknesses are different for strings of higher and lower pitch. Compared to a rubber band, a guitar string is stiffer material, strong enough to be wound up to a very high tension without giving way. A rubber band changes its note in response to how vigorously it is plucked. The same is undesirable in music. We require a string at high tension consistently to sound at the same pitch, no matter how soft or hard it is played, and it is this inner strength and consistency of tuning that gives the musician control and freedom of expression. In singing, however, the tension applied to the vocal folds is constantly changing, since a voice in effect is a one-string instrument. This puts the voice of a professional speaker, actor, singer, or evangelist at serious risk of wear and tear from the strain of constant exercise of vulnerable throat tissues.

93
Whatever is flexible
is also uncertain.

The advantages of a musical instrument over the voice are first, greater rigidity of structure and thus greater reliability and consistency of tone; second, that the instrument is a renewable structure independent of the performer, so any wear and tear does not directly impact on the physical well-being of the performer; third, that being independent of the body of the performer it extends the signaling capabilities available to the musician beyond the normal limitations of voice production to include higher, lower, clearer, more rapidly inflected sounds, and even chords. The great virtue of the voice, a flexible instrument, is its versatility; the complementary advantages of musical instruments are consistency and reliability. Musical instruments are among the first scientific instruments in human history.

94
The message of a bark is not in the tone quality
but in the intonation.

A listener is alert to stable features of a vocal or instrumental signal, and also to elements of change. Static features allow the signal to be identified: what or who is calling, the condition of the sender, and where it is at. If the signal has a message to deliver, that message is expressed in terms of changes within the signal, in pitch, timbre, loudness, rhythm, and so on. Spoken language is a system of formalized changes or configurations; expression is the addition of otherwise unpredictable dynamic or directional indicators.

95
To bark one time
is the work of a moment.

Any new action taken in isolation, or any historic event, is linked to the particular person, time, and place it occurred, and a value attaches to it. In western cultures uniqueness in art and achievement is highly prized, on the basis that progress is socially desirable, that it involves change and risk, and that it is often achieved through the actions of a gifted individual. What is valued in artists and poets may also be frowned upon in ritual celebrations where exact adherence to tradition is strictly required.

The same respect for individual action is shown toward a solo musician in relation to a group, acknowledging the individual qualities a gifted person may bring to the form of an original work through the display of individual skills, through improvisation, and for classical music especially, in the personal interpretation of a precomposed work.

96
To do it again
is a matter of practice.

In any repeated action the first attempt provides a template for the second and subsequent attempts. Among oral cultures, repetition is the key to learning: the teacher speaks, the class repeats. In music and drama the role of leading actor or soloist is of a person having special powers of innovation in thought and action; in science and magic, the gifted individual may be considered to have powers even over nature itself. To be original, or even "an original," is to act and think in ways that are unprecedented. Solo action is fascinating but also unverifiable. We do not know its truth for sure. When only one person is speaking or playing, there is always the possibility that the person is making it up.

That perception is transformed by repetition of an action by the same person, or by a group, for example a chorus. Wherever there is repetition, there is a script. If a group of people say the same words, or perform the same actions simultaneously, it is by definition not spontaneous but premeditated and scripted behavior. Scripted behavior is a matter of practice. It involves the sublimation of personal identity and individual freedom in the interests of a corporate goal. A collective statement or action signifies collective agreement with an earlier statement or action, the group behaving literally as one body. Corporate endorsement by a chorus has the same effect as resonance in acoustics. A chorus creates a halo of assent around the solo performer analogous to the reverberation of a sacred cave or cathedral in response to a solo singer. It is an interesting example of live behavior imitating inanimate nature, and demonstrates that at a fundamental level human hearing does not discriminate between living and nonliving sounds in the environment. Or rather, that everything in the environment is suffused by an animating spirit.

97
Practice
is memory.

If there is a script, the repeated information is written down, in a book, a play, a musical score. In the absence of a script, the learner relies on memory. Exact repetition does not confer total understanding, but in most cultures learning by rote is regarded, if not as a guarantee, at least as an essential precondition to understanding. Among ancient and modern oral traditions learning by repetition and memorization are essential for the preservation of community identity and history. In the absence of print documentation, the formal structures and rhythms of traditional poetry and myth provide a system of classification of experiences stored in oral memory, as well as organizing them in patterns that assist the memorization process. Brevity, economy, the use of stereotypes and symbols, and the development of a rich text base with multiple meanings, are features of oral traditions. Among modern print cultures many of the older poetic conventions of assonance, rhyme, rhythm, and form are discarded or suppressed in favor of text and word formations perceived as authentic, individual, and new, designed for silent contemplation rather than performing aloud.

The development of printed notations for music freed the art of music from the formalities of oral memory and allowed music to develop structures of a complexity inconceivable without visual aids. The relationship of classical to popular and world music today is essentially that of a print-based, visual culture to the oral traditions of ancient times.

98
Air goes in, food goes in,
bark comes out.

There are intriguing symmetries in the various roles of the mouth, of which the symmetry of direction, in and out, is only the most obvious. Breathing and barking (or speech) are different ways of processing air; breathing an *involuntary* process of extracting life-sustaining oxygen from *incoming* air and thus altering its chemical composition, whereas barking (or speech in a human being) is a *voluntary* process through which air is processed and *expelled* in the form of pressure waves, altering its physical composition. Breathing and barking or talking are relatively *intangible* processes interacting with the *gaseous* envelope that interpenetrates everything; eating by inversion is both a direct *contact* process involving teeth, touch, and taste, and also the physical consumption and assimilation of solid and fluid *materials* previously leading a more or less independent existence in the external environment. Breathing prolongs the state of life, but eating is necessary for dynamic growth.

Ancient cultures, the Greeks included, recognized the existence of two worlds: an internal world of sensations that are tied to the individual, and an external world of other things and other people that live independently. Their difficulty lay in how to account for the real existence of an external world when the only evidence of it we have is the "hearsay" of internal neural activity. That eating, breathing, and speech employ the same orifice could almost be seen as a divine ruse to persuade the human species of the reality of an external world other predatory animals have little occasion to doubt.

99
A dog breathes
by opening its throat.

To be open to breathing is to be open for anything. That is the fundamental risk.

100
A dog barks
by closing its throat.

To close the aperture at the vocal folds and noisily expel air from within the lungs, is more than just holding one's breath to keep evil influences at bay. In going on the attack to counter a threat of invasion by unseen forces, gaseous or spiritual, the speaker faces the opposite danger, of loss of consciousness of the external world.

101
The sound of resistance
is a musical note.

A musical note is very rare in nature. The howl of a dog is one example. In human beings the same process is called singing, and the word "singing" is also applied to the sound of a kettle letting off steam, to power lines suspended between pylons vibrating in the wind, to the wind blowing through a narrow passageway, to the sound of a circular saw cutting through wood, and other sounds in the environment that stand out for their unusual precision and persistence of tone.

The key attraction of musical sounds of steady pitch is that they are so much easier to hear. Since the human voice is made of soft materials, it is not as easy to produce sounds of constant pitch as it is to hear them. Some of the earliest musical instruments: bone flute, bamboo flute, gourd flute, ocarina, antelope horn, trumpet fashioned from a conch shell, didgeridu, are adaptations of natural materials that are hard rather than soft. Being made of hard material, they can produce a constant tone when blown correctly. Not only are they better adapted to producing a steady tone that is easy to hear, the tone also remains constant from one performance to the next, which means these instruments can be recognized for their distinctive qualities of tone. In turn this makes such instruments apt for sending messages across distances greater than the human voice would carry. The combination of superhuman range and unnatural stability of tone leads to these artificial sounds acquiring a supernatural status, which is why such instruments are often associated with religious ceremonies.

Since these instruments are unable to pronounce words, however, the role of articulating sacred words with constant tone and supernatural precision falls to a special class of human beings who are trained to control their normally unstable voices and produce steady tones while at the same time forming those tones into speech. The combination of exceptional physical and emotional self-control associated with religious chanting is highly regarded as a prescription for achieving a correspondingly higher state of being. At a deeper level, however, musical sounds are the consequences of normally mute structures, often under tension, responding to potentially catastrophic forces. That perception of ideal beauty and order *necessarily* arising from a situation of extreme tension, tribe against tribe, or between male and female, underlies most of the great tales of myth and legend in all human cultures.

❦

INTRODUCING
BOOK THREE

Wherever there are people there are usually dogs, and where there are dogs there will be barking. If you are traveling anywhere in the world and hear a dog barking, it makes exactly the same kind of sense wherever you are. Listening is an excellent way of locating yourself in the environment. There are no rules, only natural abilities that can be applied as one chooses to any situation.

Sounds are amazingly complicated. The fizz of soda being poured into a glass; the buzz of conversation in a coffee-house; the chorus of cicadas around the pool in high summer—even the sound of busy traffic in the city as you are waiting to cross the road is a mysterious torrent that like a river is always moving and yet always in the same place. Other favorite sounds of mine are the light saber fights in the *Star Wars* movies; a hamburger sizzling; native birds in the wild; footsteps in gravel; a distant passing freight train heard late at night; an acoustic guitar; a solo cello playing in a church.

A dog barking is one person, but in real life groups of animals as well as people talk and listen to one another as a community, each managing to select from all the talking going on the particular sounds that are important and needing attention: a distress cry, a hungry child, a signal that means food.

The amount of information a person is able to hear in the sound of a dog barking just one time, is an indication of the amount of thought the person can bring to events in real life. It is our choice how much and what we hear, and therefore what we learn: but it is a choice that can only be exercised once the basic skill is acquired. Given the potential of a dog barking, imagine the quality and complexity of information to be discovered in extended items of music created with instruments designed to weave intricate and beautiful patterns of sound.

BOOK THREE

Strings, Surfaces, and Empty Spaces

———————

1
All music
is intentional.

2
All your responses
are true.

3
Boredom
is not a response.

4
Do not misjudge
your emotions.

5
Do not
apologise.

6
You are the advocate,
nobody else.

7
Seeing is believing;
hearing is comprehending.

8
If you can hear it,
you are hearing who is doing it.

9
As long as you are listening, you
may as well pay attention.

10
The name of a sound
is not the nature of a sound.

11
An instrument can do more than speak,
and also less.

12
Music is greater than language, because only in music
is there a possibility of complete agreement.

13
Both music and language
define ways of hearing.

14
Without words,
anything is possible.

15
A musical score is not what you hear,
it is what you do.

16
A change of instrument
is a change in hearing.

17
Music is not the accompaniment:
it is the ritual itself.

18
Rule one:
defend your space.

19
To control your space,
you need an instrument.

20
The world of music
is the perception of a musical instrument.

21
The only certainty
is error.

22
Without notation
there is no error.

23
Freedom from error
is not freedom.

24
The story of music
is the story of civilization.

25
Music is about
information management.

26
Music is about
people management.

27
There are two types of musical instrument:
the voice and the rest.

28
A musical instrument
is a storage device.

29

A musical instrument
is a measuring device.

30

A musical instrument
is a sensing device.

31

A musical instrument
is a switching device.

32

A musical instrument
is a signaling device.

33

The voice offers control,
the instrument, reliability.

34

A voice is one person,
an instrument is every person.

35
Singing is inside your head,
playing an instrument is outside your head.

36
The notation of music
is external memory.

37
Naming the notes A to G
arranges pitches in a line.

38
Naming the notes A to H
allows for changes of key.

39
Sharps and flats
are morally suspect.

40
A seven-note scale conforms to a seven-day week
and a seven-planet universe.

41

Naming notes

shows an ability to make distinctions.

42

The oldest string instrument

is a bow.

43

The oldest wind instrument

is a bone.

44

The oldest keyboard instrument

is a set of panpipes.

45

The oldest percussion instrument

is a shield.

46

A mask, a high collar

magnify the person.

47
Accents, diacriticals, and punctuation marks
are music notations.

48
Music arises
from noise.

49
Music is easier
to hear.

50
A four- or five-note scale is for outdoors,
a seven-note scale for indoors.

51
In the forest, birds sing in tune;
in the open plains, they sing in rhythm.

52
The echo of a man's voice is a child;
the echo of a child's voice is a child.

53
A gothic cathedral
is a forest in stone.

54
Air is invisible, sound is invisible,
music is invisible.

55
A voice and an instrument
are a coupled system.

56
A group of similar instruments
is a choir.

57
A group of different instruments
is a band.

58
A choir is for harmony of tone;
a band is for harmony of action.

59
A choir signifies many;
a band, diversity.

60
A person can sing and play the guitar at the same time, but
a person cannot sing and play the flute at the same time.

61
The harp is to the longbow
as the trumpet to the musket.

62
A band, an industry;
an orchestra, an army.

63
The note A
is the length of a stride.

64
The note F is 6 feet,
and B flat 9 feet.

65

Middle C and its octaves
are powers of 2.

66

A scale model
is a model of a scale.

. ~ **67**

A church or temple is bigger inside
than it is outside.

68

The greatest harmony of all
is the unison.

69

An orchestra
creates its own space.

70

Written music
has its advantages.

71
A concerto
is about leadership.

72
A suite of dances
is about the nature of time.

73
In music for keyboard, there
is neither continuity nor intonation.

74
A movement of music
is about movement.

75
A modern orchestra
cannot hear itself playing.

76
Following an opera is like reading a novel;
following a symphony, like navigating in traffic.

77
Start together,
finish together.

78
A standing soloist is a team leader;
a seated soloist is a team manager.

79
A cadenza is about
making it up.

80
Notation simplifies
for the sake of complexity.

81
Plainchant notation
recognizes sequence, not time.

82
Standard notation
converts time into space.

83
The evolution of western music
is a history of dealing with the unpredictable.

84
Baroque music is dedicated
to mechanical time.

85
Classical music is about
dealing with the inevitable.

86
The eighteenth century elite discovered stress,
the nineteenth century bourgeoisie celebrated it.

87
One length,
many lengths.

88
One length,
many strings.

89
One tension,
many lengths.

90
Stand, process, walk,
dance, skate, tumble.

91
The end is silence:
so what?

92
The universe
in the sound of a bell.

93
First, second, third harmonic:
Parent, child, ghost.

94
In a choir,
nobody wins.

95
A choir, an orchestra,
an acoustic.

96
A flute,
an irrigation system.

97
A violin, a piano,
a suspension bridge.

98
A lute, a biwa,
a satellite dish.

99
A valve trumpet,
a water closet.

100
A pipe organ:
air conditioning.

101
Alpha to Omega,
the length of a string is infinite.

INTRODUCING
BOOK FOUR

Where there are words, there is the possibility of disagreement. That is normal. But language is not the only way of making a statement: for people living in affluent countries, who you are and the values you recognize can be expressed very clearly in the choices you make, the clothes you wear, or the car you drive. Because it is like a language but does not need words, music can help in the process of finding out how in fact agreement is possible, and why language succeeds as well as it does. The advantage of studying music over language or literature is that choosing music eliminates huge areas of potential disagreement over what words actually mean, while allowing everyone to focus on those aspects on which agreement is inevitable.

The transition from environmental noises and their meaning to music and its potential for carrying information may appear to involve a quantum leap of the imagination, especially for listeners who have little or no acquaintance with western classical music or world music of different cultures. After all, it involves a shift in focus from simple to complex, from individual actions to collective actions, from animal to human consciousness (which is what language implies), from short-term statements to extended narratives, and from oral to written cultural traditions.

However, unlike reading and writing, which are highly specialized techniques of information processing with distinct cultural conventions attached to them, listening to music involves human mechanisms of ear and brain function that work in exactly the same way for music as for navigating through the sounds of everyday life. Because it builds on shared human perceptions, music is truly a universal medium of information exchange, from listening to which it is possible to determine the patterns and preferences of different cultures with unexpected clarity.

BOOK FOUR

Reflections

1
All music is intentional.

Music sounds like that because somebody wanted it to sound like that.

2
All your responses are true.

When you listen to music for the first time, your responses are telling you something that is true of the music, of the listening situation, and of yourself.

3
Boredom
is not a response.

Boredom is not being able to focus. Listening is a life skill. When you are bored you are not asleep but rather in defensive mode. Self-defense is a strong response and a valid reaction. A negative reaction is just as true as a positive reaction, and usually more interesting.

4
Do not misjudge your emotions.

A new experience can take an observer by surprise. If you dislike a new experience, ask yourself whether the negative reaction is because of being caught unawares, rather than because you don't like the experience. An experience that makes a person feel uncomfortable is often one that touches the person deeply.

5
Do not apologise.

A listener's responses are true, and they are all you have, so they are worth taking seriously. You may want to ask *why* they are true, to convince yourself and others.

6
You are the advocate,
nobody else.

Whether or not a piece of music or a work of art is to a person's taste is not the issue. The point is how you deal with it as critic or advocate. In order to convince anybody else, you have to convince yourself. And that involves acknowledging what, in fact, it is.

7
Seeing is believing;
hearing is comprehending.

In music, what you don't see is what you get. What you see at a concert of music is a group of people, mostly seated, making movements with objects of various kinds in their hands or held to their lips, forming more or less coordinated gestures on cue from a person who is standing with his back to the camera like a surgeon in an operating theatre. What you see is a mystery. What you hear is coherence, harmony, and change: a dynamic of structured and constant renewal that is made necessary, in the absence of any spoken narration, by the simple fact that sounds do not last forever. The message of the visible world and of the visual arts, is of things that remain the same; the message of music is of the evanescence and recurrence of all things. Through music an audience becomes reconciled to the experience of a provisional reality, and to the passage of time.

8
If you can hear it,
you are hearing who is doing it.

Through sound one becomes aware of the person performing, the quality of the instrument being played, the materials of which the instrument is made, how it is played, and the quality and experience of the person playing it.

9
As long as you are listening,
you may as well pay attention.

Some people go to a concert in order to sleep. Others go in order to admire the skills of the musicians. It is not about any of that. Music raises the ability of the listener to process complex simultaneous events in real time. Classical music of different periods not only demonstrates acoustical complexity, but also how to manage complexity in the way you listen. The different historical and cultural styles of music also reflect differences in the management of information.

10
The name of a sound
is not the nature of a sound.

A sound has many names in music: a flute sound, a violin sound, a harp sound; a plucked sound, a blown sound, a struck sound; a high sound, a low sound, a gliding tone. Instrument names are convenient labels to attach to entire repertoires of sounds. Pitches are abstract terms. All such names are merely guiding threads in a labyrinth of audible possibilities. For the sake of connecting sounds that vary in unpredictable ways, listeners resort to naming actions or instruments that in reality represent coincidence or consistency—a tone of voice, a smooth delivery—rather than describing the sound itself. What the ears actually hear is much more to the point: sounds of touch, of friction, of pressure, of tension, of weight or lightness. To describe the totality of a musical experience in terms of what an audience actually hears would be complicated beyond words, not because the experience is beyond human comprehension, but because mere language is inadequate to the task.

11
An instrument can do more than speak,
and also less.

A musical instrument cannot speak, which may make it less than a human voice. An instrument may guide the intonation of a reciting or speaking voice and thus ensure a more accurate reproduction of the intended meaning of a poem. Or it may accompany a voice and in so doing convey a tone that the individual voice may not be able to reproduce, either because not all voices and personalities are the same, or because production of the tone of expression intended by the poet or composer is impeded by the actual process of forming and speaking words, and by the need for words to be spoken in a certain order if they are to make sense. A "song without words," or an aria for a solo instrument, in that sense liberates the meaning of a poem from the mechanics of delivering a text, but at the cost of leaving the text unsaid.

The ancient Greeks understood that a musical instrument could serve as an aid to accurate reproduction of an epic poem, and also as a medium of inquiry into nature. They also realized that in its other guise as "the food of love" music could also affect the mind and encourage the release of inhibitions. During the era of church patronage of music in Europe, the use of musical instruments was sanctioned for the accompaniment of a text, as a means of clarifying an authorized intonation and in that way ensuring that the correct meaning of a socially significant message was preserved from generation to generation. By 1600 the evolution of a universal system of notation, a software that any voice or instrument could act upon, had stimulated a new instruments-only aesthetic that deliberately sought to exceed the limitations of the human voice. Much to the concern of the ecclesiastical authorities, the practitioners of this new musical science also liberated music from the duty to serve the expression of a sacred text. In non-western theocracies disapproval or prohibition against purely instrumental music is still encountered. In the west itself, the shock of liberation continues to resonate in the popular fiction that music is essentially meaningless.

12
Music is greater than language,
because only in music
is there a possibility of complete agreement.

Mendelssohn declared music to be superior to language, for the reason that it is pure feeling uncontaminated by thought. To Socrates and the school of Pythagoras, for whom musical instruments such as the monochord were devices for calculating mathematical ratios, music transcended all other forms of experience because only in music was it possible to demonstrate identity. No two sticks, no two stones, no two fish, plants, or people are identical, so the issue was whether it was possible to talk about nature in universal or general terms applicable to

collections of the same thing. Music not only demonstrated that two
voices or two strings could sound at the same pitch, but also that the
vibration of a single string contained a multiplicity of pitches, each
representing an exact fraction of the length. The invisible world of
sound and music was thus canonized as the realm of essential forms.

13
Both music and language
define ways of hearing.

At first encounter, a foreign language sounds like an incoherent babble
of sounds. Over time, a listener becomes aware that the apparent chaos
has certain regulating features, among them pattern (rhythm, emphasis), tempo, texture (incidence of consonants), and tone (incidence and
location of vowels). These external features of language express the
preferences of the culture of the language user, and in the long run
influence and even limit the ability of the language to convey ideas or
feelings. These cultural differences affecting language are if anything
more clearly expressed in music. Compared to western classical music,
which is largely confined to a very limited range of pitches, cultures
such as classical Indian music and classical Japanese music are considerably more refined in tone.

14
Without words,
anything is possible.

As long as music is regulated by a text, sacred or secular, the art of
music could be said to consist in serving the needs of a text. These are:
definition of the syllable, accentuation, articulating the beginning and
end of a phrase and a sentence, emphasizing the most important parts
of a sentence (for example, by lengthening or decorating the syllable),
and maintaining the integrity of the thought. Stave notation arose out
of the same historical necessity as punctuation, for the purposes of

standardizing pitch and timing. Instruments were brought in to substitute for voices or to strengthen the intonation of the choir. As they became more familiar with reading notation, musicians realized that their instruments could play beyond the limits of the voice, and as notation became more versatile, the idea of a purely instrumental music took hold. Italian composers of the late 16th century were among the first in Europe to identify the potential of purely instrumental music to express nonliterary, distinctly secular and progressive conceptions of time, space, conflict, harmony, and competition.

15
A musical score
is not what you hear,
it is what you do.

When the cylinder phonograph arrived on the scene in the early twentieth century, many promising young composers were inspired to make field trips to record and transcribe folk songs and melodies that it was feared might otherwise be lost to posterity. What these composers discovered, if they did not already know it, was that the apparently easy and simple music of oral cultures is virtually impossible to write down. The system of music notation that had been supposed to raise classical music to a higher level than folk music, proved unable to handle the subtle intonations and timing of music of oral traditions. The conclusion to be drawn is that music notation is a compromise in every way, and not a true description of an aural event. What it also implies is that when classical notation was developed, choices were made, among them an executive decision that personal tone and subtleties of expression were qualities not merely unsuited to notation, but also inappropriate for the uses for which notation was designed. (A parallel debate continues to be argued concerning the competing social and personal values of the written as against the spoken word.)

That notation has limits implies that a performer has to "interpret" the notes on the page to realise their expressive implications. The alternative view, drawing on the music of Bach and Mozart through to

Stravinsky and John Cage, says that the performer's role is not to
"interpret" but simply to reproduce a written text. That in turn implies
a European classical aesthetic geared to the limitations of notation and
employing a mode of expression that, like diplomatic code, reveals its
true meaning through a careful reading of the choice of terms and
protocols rather than in the passionate rhetoric of oratory. By late
medieval times, music notation, along with Latin, became recognized
as a truly international language, and the successors of the touring
troubadours of medieval Europe, as accredited exponents of a medium
of expression with a written language that was universally recognized.
That composers were able to gain employment and for their music to
be performed in countries across Europe without regard to the local
spoken language, tells us a great deal about the values attached to
information sharing and reproduction across regional boundaries a
thousand years ago. That the tone of classical music conforms to a
diplomatic neutrality of expression makes perfect sense in such a context. This time-honored appreciation of the value of neutrality in
information sharing was lost on the newly-enfranchised majorities of
the nineteenth century, middle classes brought to power under the
banner of nationalism, for whom the passions were more natural, and
therefore of greater value.

16
A change of instrument
is a change in hearing.

If Romeo and Juliet in Shakespeare's play were to exchange their lines,
it would either be a comical mistake or a deliberate study in gender
typing. That the words of a play, or the notes of a musical score, are
available to be interpreted by any voice or instrument, is part of the
larger proposition that language makes it possible for different people
to say the same thing, and thus to mean the same thing, and by doing
so, to be able to reach an agreement on what has actually been said.
What gives significance to the signing of an international treaty, as
much as the content, is the ceremonious affirmation that agreement is

possible at all.

In transferring a notation from one voice to another, or from one instrument to another of a different family, it is easy to identify the transaction as a form of information sharing in which the information content is the printed score. In practice, however, when different instruments perform from the same musical score, what is most obvious from the way they *sound* is their differences. Romeo does not make a convincing Juliet. Her words do not fit a male character. The text on the page remains the same, but the totality of meaning implied by the delivery of the text by a particular person or instrument will always reflect the special circumstances of the individual case. This has serious cultural implications when the printed text or music to be interpreted is from a much earlier period, or is supposed to preserve traditional values. It is even today a matter of spirited debate whether an authentic performance of early music is at all possible, since (the argument goes) there are so many unknowns, and musicians today cannot imagine themselves back to earlier times. That musicians should therefore abandon the search for authenticity and adapt older notations to the more advanced technical possibilities of modern instruments, as has often been argued, is in effect declaring that the printed score is the only information that it is possible to discuss, and certainly the only information of which an interpreter can be certain. The performance then becomes a layer of actuality superimposed on the text, and whether it is faithful to the text becomes something we can never know. It is a short step from that position to concluding that the musical text has no reliable meaning, and therefore nothing to tell us. It only serves as a vehicle for a performance that may be more or less exciting to the listener, an experience defined as a momentary rush of adrenaline, which is not the whole story by any means.

The traditional view that the meaning of a piece of music, or poem, or work of art, is somehow distinct from the individual performance or experience or opinion, leads to a style of performance in which the personality is more or less suppressed. We understand a suppression of personality (and thus, of personal accountability) in the role of the messenger in Greek tragedy, in the white-faced expressionless character of Pierrot, in the mime, in the masked characters of

Indian and Japanese drama, in the blank innocence of Buster Keaton and Charlie Chaplin from the silent movie era, and (for music especially) in the studied impersonality of ballet. In considering the traditional role of the performer in the history of music, from plainchant to Mozart, Satie, Stravinsky, and Webern, and also in cultures outside the western tradition, values of impersonality and precision tend to outweigh any alternative values that might be attached to subjective motivation or emotion. Lack of expression on the part of a performer does not mean absence of expression, nor is it absence of meaning. It is simply a way of indicating that the expression and the meaning are locked in the text, and by implication, that both are independent of the performer.

17
Music is not the accompaniment:
it is the ritual itself.

To set words to music, compose music to a movie, or be entertained by a marching band during the intermission of a football match, is to cast music in the role of a cosmetic addition to an event or activity that could get along quite adequately without it. Take away the music, however, and the experience is incomplete. To watch a movie with the sound track removed is to understand how important a role music plays in maintaining the attention of the viewer, defining the emotional content of a scene, and even enabling the viewer to anticipate developments in the story of which the actors are supposedly unaware. Without such guidance the viewer (alas) would have to rely on the acting and the script.

A state funeral without music, an opera or ballet without music, a country and western classic ballad without music, a wedding without music, a marching band without music—all are certainly possible, but all are more difficult to manage, to follow, and to enjoy. In order to sing along, and thus fully participate, an audience needs the music as well as the words. Take away the music and a marching band will find it more difficult to march and turn in step. In order to stay focused and to know when to stand up and when to sit down, visiting foreign dignitaries at a state funeral or other solemn occasion rely on the music, and since the music is the same for all visitors, whatever their culture or nationality, their actions are not only coordinated in fact, but expressing actual as well as symbolic agreement. Even the piped music in a supermarket or shopping mall has the important function of enhancing a visitor's purchasing experience. Take away the music, and the environment becomes just another shed, fairground, or stage set.

In understanding the extent to which music defines, controls, coordinates, and satisfies the emotional conditions of a public or private function, to that extent one is in effect conceding that the event itself is musical in conception.

18
Rule one:
defend your space.

The personal space of any individual is that zone, more or less defined by one's extended reach, within which a person feels secure. The marketing of a car is essentially the selling of a notional personal space, and a car remains a personal space even when the owner is not at the wheel. For one's personal space to be invaded, whether in a crowded environment or by an unwelcome approach—for example, by a traffic warden—is often interpreted as an invasion, or even as an assault. For a musician about to perform, whether in the street or onstage, the first rule of music is to assert possession of one's personal space, and from there to control the movements and attention of those otherwise out of reach. If the audience members have paid to occupy their places, they may already for that reason be motivated to listen. Some may be more interested in the buzz that comes from being exposed to amplified sound at dangerously high intensities, than in the message or charisma of the lead singer. By convention an audience at a rock concert is noisier, because of the amplification, than an audience at a classical concert, where the musical message is considerably richer in information content and subtler in expression. But whether designed for the market square or a private mansion, most music of any kind involves controlling an audience. Totally improvised music relies on the personality and skill of the performer, and even a music bereft of content, such as John Cage's *4' 33"* for a silent pianist, relies on the power of social convention to maintain public order.

The loud chords at the start of a rock concert fulfill the same function as the tuning up of a solo violinist or acoustic guitarist at a classical concert. They define the musical space—pitch, loudness, tempo, tone quality—within which both the players and the audience will function. The prelude of a classical suite of dance movements for harpsichord is not itself a dance. It too is a composition that defines the terms of the concert: what the instrument is and sounds like, and how it relates to the acoustic or room space in which the concert is to be given, which is a matter of setting the levels (the music of a prelude is composed in a way that allows the performer to adjust the tone or speed while performing). The opening statement of any concert for symphony orchestra is also of particular interest, both for the way it acknowledges the presence and provokes the attention of an audience, and in the way it suggests the direction the music is to take.

19
To control your space,
you need an instrument.

Some people are valued for who they are, others for what they say or do. Along with the rewards of becoming a beauty queen goes the duty of making public appearances. By definition an appearance is a message in itself, whatever the messenger might have to say by way of product endorsement. Music, on the other hand, involves more than just appearing onstage: a musician is expected to make a statement. Something to say means time to fill, so the making of a statement is also about filling time in an acceptable way.

Musicians specialize in particular instruments because the latter are available to be chosen, but in choosing an instrument one is also choosing to go with the set of possibilities and limitations associated with it. That range of expression is contained, up to a point, by the instrument itself, and more explicitly in the catalogue of music composed for the instrument or available to a performer. In theory any musical instrument can appear in a solo performance; by convention however the role of soloist is limited to instruments of exceptional range, such as the piano or violin, or those of great antiquity and cultural significance, such as the flute.

Compared to the piano, tuba, pipe organ, or even the singing voice, an instrument such as the flute is relatively small in *volume* (a word incidentally implying space as well as loudness). All instruments have the advantage, over the voice, of purity and penetration of tone, and those of smaller size are generally lighter and quicker in response than their larger counterparts, qualities that more than compensate for any shortfall in power.

20
The world of music
is the perception of a musical instrument.

Any world or totality of experience is one of three things: the totality of a person's experience; or the totality of everybody's experience, past and present; or the totality of everybody's experience, past, present, and future. In real terms we can only know our own experience, which is neither very much nor very certain. The experiences of others, past and present, are of interest to us because we have to deal with them, in part as a means of escape from the closed circle of personal experience. Consideration of the possibility of new experiences is also of therapeutic value, whether these already exist in the experience of others or have yet to be discovered.

A musical experience may consist in the activity of a single instrument but more usually involves a number of instruments. The world of music at any one time consists in the possibilities available to the instrument, determined by the composer, and reconciled to the skills of the musician involved. In this three-way interplay the instrument stands for a species (or ancestry) of instrument, and (according to its chronological age), to the relative permanence of a particular form and repertoire of musical possibilities. The performer in turn represents a level of individual skill measured against what the instrument is designed to do, what it may have achieved in the past (for instance, in recorded form), and may still be capable of doing in the future (the ever-present possibility of doing something completely new). Finally, the composition itself (assuming the performance is from a score and not an improvisation) amounts to a résumé of possibilities in the imagination and to the practical knowledge of the composer at a particular time.

21
The only certainty
is error.

Remember the saying: A solo performer might be making it up, but a choir always has a script. A solo performer is at liberty to make changes in the text, either deliberately to change the meaning, or accidentally to obscure the meaning, and since there is only one person in charge of delivering the message it is (supposedly) impossible to tell if the message is true to the original. A diplomatic courier in medieval times would deliver the message orally but carry a written scroll for backup. The role of an "interpreter" in present-day international affairs is similar to a solo performer: to render the text of a state visitor in the local language, but in a plain style stripped of any added expression, since a listener is also exposed to the body language and tone of voice of the visiting speaker. Immunity has been granted to the messenger from early times because it was recognized that responsibility for the message content lay elsewhere.

That an interpreter has the power to change the meaning of a musical message is recognized in the status that is accorded to the role of the virtuoso since the era of the traveling composer-performer in the nineteenth century. That change of status reflects a change in audience perception of the role. In earlier times a musical message such as a symphony was intended for an audience sensitive to the diplomatic, intellectual, or social implications of any display of data processing and people skills. After Beethoven, the message changes from data processing and people management to mass entertainment, and the role of the soloist from diplomatic messenger to revolutionary leader. A choir by definition is working to a script, but the effect of multiple voices reading from the same cue-sheet is that the message of the text loses immediacy and becomes stereotyped, in the manner of a classroom of first-graders greeting their teacher: "Good mor–ning Miss Spen–cer." A formalized or rote statement is diminished in implication, not to mention sincerity, and certainly lacking in clarity and nuance. What it projects is an uncomprehending solidarity, which has its own uses.

22
Without notation
there is no error.

The notion of truthfulness to a composer's or playwright's intentions originates in a need among earlier oral cultures to store and retrieve the information on which social life relied and in order that social identity could be maintained from generation to generation: through stories embodying local customs, rituals, genealogies, great battles, natural disasters, and heroic deeds. In the absence of computers, cameras, and print technology, oral cultures evolved methods of storing important information in encrypted form, as myth, art, drama, poetry, and music. The role of music in all of this was a mixture of stage management, audience control, and interpretation: helping to maintain an authentic tone of voice, and appropriate emphasis, in the delivery of an historic narrative.

With the arrival of notated music came a perception of musical performance as fidelity to the written or printed text. Until a music is written down, the idea of wrong notes has no meaning.

The written or printed score is no more than a guide to a performance that requires an interpreter to bring it to life and deliver at least a potential for meaning. A recording stores and allows for the reproduction of a performance, in which not only the notes but the authentic tone and delivery of the lead soloist are available in perpetuity. For the musician, the documented recording can easily be accepted as a standard against which a live performance is judged. In this way, by a curious reversal, the author of a text becomes the slave of an interpretation that, by the time a live performance arrives in town, has already passed into the cultural memory of an audience. In measuring the performance of a song from a live concert recording by the Rolling Stones, for example, against the "original" studio recording, the keen listener may discover uneven balance, audience noise, and deliberate distortion of lyrics and melody: errors in the reproduction of a text already sacred to the audience, deliberately done to reinforce a perception of the event as real, live, local, and not simply miming.

23
Freedom from error
is not freedom.

Since a written music score is necessarily incomplete, and in any case ambiguous, a "perfect score" as synthesized by a computer can only be a literal reproduction of what is written, and that, for most listeners, is not what a real musical experience is about. Stravinsky remarked that he felt most free when he was composing to rules, adding that the composer was free to invent his own rules. "Free music" as the Australian composer Percy Grainger imagined it, is a paradoxical concept, since it cannot exist out of a context of music that is not free, as a cadenza is only free in relation to a formal musical structure. Improvisation in jazz and other music traditions is also based on templates or models: in jazz, on familiar songs, and among more ancient traditions, on the choice of a scale or mode, and of a rhythm. The artistic merit assigned to improvisation in these instances reflects the same leadership values as those associated with inspired decision-making in a critical situation, even though in music the art may seldom rise above inspired rhetoric.

24
The story of music
is the story of civilization.

Oral culture is the basis of human civilization. Like other creatures we are born able to hear, but not to speak, see properly, read, or write. Our understanding of the world is based on learning to navigate in a sensory maze in which the senses of smell, initially fuzzy vision, and hearing offer clues to the reality of an extended environment out of immediate reach. Urban humanity today is relatively insensitive to smell. The visual world is seen as a deceptive environment of camouflaged predators and alternating light and darkness. Vision itself is an ongoing task of focusing and refocusing, limited to a small target area in front of the face.

Sound and hearing provide the most reliable continuous evidence of the world around us. We can hear sounds through a full 360 degrees, not just in front, and the sounds are always perfectly in focus. Sounds do not deceive, nor do they threaten. They are there to help. And since the sources of sound are largely invisible and constantly available, night and day, they can be personified and honored as manifestations of benevolent spirits who watch over humanity. In a cathedral there are many hiding places, but the sound of a single singing voice is able not just to fill the void, but reach into the most inaccessible space and find out whoever is hidden or lost.

The social power of music to coordinate actions and harmonize relationships is self-evident. Among other roles, music and musical instruments were developed for distance communication and for aiding in the storage and retrieval of information on which the life and identity of an oral community depended. The history of musical instrument making is a chronicle of developing understanding of materials, shapes, ducts and containers, of resonance, of the mysteries of the unison and harmonics of strings and tubes, and the relation of pitch to length and tension. Astronomers from the era of the pyramids to the age of Isaac Newton observed the motion of the planets and the stars, the sun and the moon, and wondered how it was possible for the universe to hold together as a vibrating system comprising multiple cycles, all predictable but seemingly out of synchronization. And to explain the universe as a stable but dynamic system they resorted to musical models such as a vibrating string or a bell.

In the late twentieth century leading figures in theoretical physics continue to speculate about the secrets of the universe, employing much the same repertoire of acoustic images as the soothsayer of ancient Babylonia: unseen dimensions, particles that pop in and out of existence, vibrating strings, and reflecting surfaces.

25
Music is about
information management.

Music notation is a graph. It evolved throughout the middle ages and attained its standard form in the late renaissance. The earliest attempts at notation were intended to record the dynamics of formal or intoned speech, to preserve in written form how a voice inflects to express the precise meaning of a text. Early attempts included writing the actual words higher or lower on the page to indicate movement up or down in pitch. A transitional form of notation survives in current use as punctuation marks and diacriticals (circumflex, acute accent, tilde, etc.). Signs such as the comma, colon, and question mark were devised to indicate a change of pitch level, others a movement in pitch within the syllable. These alterations of pitch were designed to emulate the natural inflections of formal speech. Notation became abstracted over time, partly through the steadying influence of the choir, partly through the use of musical instruments, including the organ, to regulate pitch. The more abstract the system became, the more it evolved away from its original role as speech transcription toward a medium of inquiry into tonal relations.

By the sixteenth century stave music notation had largely reached its present-day form. Other notations called tablatures existed (and still exist today), but these were limited to instruments of one class and indicated only where the fingers should be placed on the strings rather than the pitches to be played. Tablatures were eclipsed by the new system, which employed a *great stave* or grid of horizontal lines on which compound signs expressing pitch, time, and duration were positioned, to be read and intoned by any voice or instrument of appropriate range. Because the new notation was truly universal, it became possible for music to be composed for large ensembles, of a diversity of voices and instruments from different families and traditions. As the orchestra and its repertoire became more specialized, the structures and patterns of music became more intricate. Stave notation allowed composers to create and manipulate musical figures on paper, and, starting with J. S. Bach, to visualize interlocking structures more complicated than it was possible to hear in one's head, or follow in real time.

Such process planning skills eventually provided models not only for mass production in the industrial era, but also for battle strategies, competitive team sports, and even the organization of a modern democracy.

The achievement of a truly universal music notation involved a number of steps, of which the first was the conceptualization of pitch and time as dimensions of a virtual space, and the second the establishment of chronometric time as a means of quantifying and ordering durations in graphic form. Because they were not tied to particular musical instruments, the discoveries of music notation were also available to be applied to encoding dynamic processes in general as a connected series of positional indications in virtual space-time. The astronomer Kepler used stave notation to record particulars of the orbital motion of the planets. Mechanical engineers transferred positional information from stave notation to pegs fitted onto giant rotating cylinders that interacted with keyboard mechanisms to play tunes on peals of steeple bells for the townsfolk to enjoy. Miniature pin cylinders were fitted into musical boxes and later into the first chiming watches. As more durable paper became available in Europe, imported from the Far East after 1750, information originally encoded as pegs on drums was reinvented as punched cards for playing the keyboards of mechanical organs by compressed air. In the Napoleonic era, the same method was adapted by Joseph Jacquard to program and control mechanical looms. Musical box cylinder technology was also adapted to program mechanical dolls to dance, write their name, and draw in pen and ink. A direct line can thus be traced from international agreement on a universal musical notation in 1600 to the punched paper tape of the early computer era, and thereafter to the technology, as well as the musical content, of the digital disc.

26
Music is about
people management.

People react to music in different ways. Some dance, some sing, a few do both at once. We take it for granted because everyone knows that singing and dancing are what music is for. Plato, who was a bit of a killjoy, realized that for music to affect people spontaneously in such a way it must be working at a subliminal level, and since singing and dancing were intimately associated with partying and other delinquent behavior, that access to music should perhaps be restricted.

The objection that music provokes disorderly behavior is still encountered in newspaper reports of drunken fans singing rather too loudly during or after a football match. It is an interesting moral objection because the whole point, then as now, is not that music triggers *disorderly* behavior, but that in reality it is capable of stimulating *coordinated* behavior of an uninhibited and sometimes antisocial nature. It is, I suspect, the cocktail of instinctive discipline and irrational motivation that rings alarm bells among the socially responsible majority. All the same, these are not disordered situations. A truly chaotic situation will self-destruct for lack of direction. The problem where music is concerned is not that it creates chaos but rather that it creates spontaneous order, a unity of purpose that in the absence of moral leadership can easily turn nasty.

That music organizes people spontaneously tells us a great deal about it and us. There is a scene in Antonioni's movie *Blow-Up* where David Hemmings in the character of a fashion photographer coaches girlfriend Lynn Redgrave in how to move in front of the camera. He puts a record of Latin American club music on the turntable, and she moves awkwardly; he then tells her to move *against* the beat, which involves a conscious effort on her part and produces an immediate and dramatic change in the poise and elegance of her movements. The moral is that when music is playing it is easier and more instinctive for an audience to move to the beat without thinking, than to move and act independently. On another level, music notation introduced new possibilities of complexity in the organization of groups of musicians. These musicians had to be able to read music, in real time, from the printed page, and at the same time stay coordinated as an ensemble. The three levels of complexity of notated music can be compared to the three levels of organized action at a football match: the cheerleaders, the marching band, and the game itself. The cheerleaders are a line of people moving in unison, their role being to excite team supporters to a sense of unity of purpose. That is organization at the level of unison plainchant. The marching band combines music and formation marching, which is complex pattern-making in which each member of the band has a different part to play and trajectory to follow. That is organization at the level of a Haydn symphony. The game itself is a test of the abilities of each team to respond in a disciplined and coordinated way to an unpredictable situation. The closest musical equivalent to a situation such as this is perhaps dixieland jazz.

27
There are two types of musical instrument: the voice and the rest.

The voice sounds internally, other instruments sound externally. The voice is made of soft stuff, other instruments are made of hard stuff. Because the voice is produced within the head cavity, the act of vocalizing interferes directly with the act of listening. We hear internally as well as externally, but the internal voice is dampened by the presence of soft tissue and in more subtle ways a vocalist's attention is distracted by bone-conducted vibration and the physical gestures involved in forming and generating sound. Medieval scholars distinguished the internal world of individual perceptions (the mind, the world inside your head) from the real external world in which we all live. Though we believe in a real external world our knowledge of it is limited to the way sensory data is processed inside the brain. We are in effect trapped in the world of our imagination.

In vocalizing, however, human beings (as well as other creatures) are "expressing themselves,"—literally sending signals from within out into the wider world, signals designed to engage with whatever it is out there, as confirmation that there is indeed another world beyond the limited data available to the imagination. Inherent in all vocal behavior is this fundamental sense of sending a message to, and making a connection with, the outside world. Proof of the existence of an external world is also confirmed by unexpected events that occur beyond our control.

Every other instrument, by contrast, is already "out there" to touch, hold, strum, pluck, beat, or blow. When sounds are made using another instrument than the voice, there is no longer any confusion, as in vocalizing, between what we hear internally and externally. When you play a drum, or a violin, you do it *silently*. You go through the motions. The instrument makes the sound. It is quite a different monitoring process. On the one hand, it is much easier to hear the effect on the environment of a sound made by an instrument. The ears have a clear signal. On the other hand, what you are listening to is the aural effect of actions controlled from within the body and directed by the mind, so there is also an interest in matching the sound with the action taken to achieve it, and discovering the most efficient moves for producing the best sound. If "best" sounds like an aesthetic judgement, it is. The basis of a good sound is its effectiveness as a signal for monitoring the environment, which is also a way of saying that the aesthetics of music is no different in kind from the aesthetics of car horns.

The vocal mechanism is made of soft stuff, subject to continuous muscular adjustment, and that makes it an extremely flexible and subtle signaling device. Musical instruments are made of hard stuff for precisely the contrary reason: so that the sounds they produce will be the same every time. Consistency is a feature human beings demand of the external world, because a sense of security in the continued existence of a real external world depends on evidence of consistency rather than the appearance of continuous change. In this sense musical instruments are also scientific instruments, since they embody perceptions of the real world and behave in the same way for different performers.

28
A musical instrument
is a storage device.

Devices for the storage and retrieval of information are not peculiar to the digital age. The function of storage devices is to store information externally rather than in individual human memory. It is culturally important for societies to remember things, and it is always an advantage if the information to be remembered is available in permanent form and not just in the fallible memories of individual persons. The other advantage of storing information separately is that the same information is available to different people at different times, and while the information content may vary in the way it is interpreted from generation to generation, the data record itself remains the same, and thus its intended significance is always potentially retrievable. The imaginative task of interpretation consists in part of intuiting the original conditions that made the information worthy of storing in the first place, a task aided by consulting the instrument originally designed to reproduce it.

A telephone directory contains information most people would not see the need to remember in full; by comparison a musical score is a storage device containing instructions for the reproduction of a piece of music. A *manuscript* musical score is richer in information by virtue of the composer's handwriting and corrections containing clues about how the music was assembled, the historical period in which it was composed, and the physical and mental state of the composer.

It is easy to suppose that before visual music notation was invented, the only means of storing a piece of music was in human memory, to be passed from teacher to pupil. To the extent that a piece of music is identified with a given composer and fixed arrangement of instruments and voices this may well be true, even though the identification of a composition by name and as the work of an individual composer is comparatively rare in Europe until late medieval times. In the absence of a written score, instruments themselves were regarded as repositories of information about music and its organization. Twentieth-century research into musical and pitch memory has established that melodies are recalled as rhythms and shapes, and not as exact sequences of precise pitches. It follows that the way music is written is not an image of the way it is stored in memory. So notated music as it is read is not a template of how the information is *stored*, rather of how it is *reproduced*.

If psychology is correct and melodies are stored in memory as gestural information, then the process of information retrieval involves fitting the remembered gesture to the correct scale or mode. Exact recall is not difficult to achieve, however, if the appropriate scale or mode is already stored in the lengths of tube of a set of pitch pipes, or the strings of a harp. A dedicated instrument embodies the further advantage of a tone quality as well as preserving an authorized range of notes within which the voice is required to move. Different instrumental timbres may also be employed to specify or enhance the interpretation of a poem or lyric: a flute by nature expressing the idea of breathing and continuity of life, in contrast to the plucked strings of a harp that convey a sharper sense of moment to moment experience that rapidly dies away.

29
A musical instrument
is a measuring device.

We start with the proposition that tone is measure. An audio engineer or producer entering an unfamiliar concert hall takes soundings of the acoustic, to judge its quality as a recording venue. This ritual involves moving to different locations in the hall and clapping the hands, loudly, one clap at a time. A clap is a noise or dense bandwidth of sound that ricochets back and forth throughout an enclosed space. If by any chance a zing or a twang is detected—a wiry, metallic resonance at a particular pitch—it means that an audence's enjoyment of music may be spoilt by the same obtrusive sound, which is an unwanted peak in the hall resonance produced by acoustical feedback.

Any hall or corridor with parallel walls is sure to produce peak resonances, which arise from its constant width and the fact that different notes in the scale are associated with specific wavelengths. A wavelength is the distance between successive crests of a sound wave. For example, the wavelength of middle C is about 4 feet 4 inches, or 1.3 meters. For every pair of facing parallel walls there is a series of pitches whose wavelengths exactly fit, reflecting back and forth between the walls exactly like male and female lines in classical dance approaching and receding in wavelike motion (indeed it is tempting to suppose that the two may be related). The consequence of introducing a burst of sound between parallel walls is to set up an oscillating process at an audible frequency corresponding to the distance between them. Every container of sound, from the cavity of a microphone to the interior of a concert hall, has the potential to generate peak resonances, and since western music moves constantly from key to key and note to note, exposing a range of different wavelengths, it is inevitable that a musical performance taking place in a concert chamber with parallel facing walls will interact at some point with the wall-to-wall dimensions of the auditorium to enhance notes in a certain spectrum of wavelengths. The natural tonality of an architectural space may in fact be designed to assist musical performance, as suggested by the deliberately musical proportions of Palladian interiors; but the objective of assisted resonance can only be attained in this way at a cost of limiting performances in such places to music of a single key.

The architect Palladio was not only aware of the musical consequences of parallel walls, he actually designed mansions to proportions corresponding to musical intervals. It is possible that he was motivated merely by aesthetic and philosophical conventions of beauty, but the possibility cannot be ruled out that in doing so the architect was deliberately constructing spaces intended to provide assisted resonance for music. That would be fine if all the music one wanted to play was in the key of C, or F, or G: the simple ratios of 3 : 2 that govern the tuning

of members of the violin family. Then, if players tuned to the wavelengths of the room, their sound would be mysteriously reinforced by
the acoustic at the tonic and closely related keys. Unfortunately for
Palladio, at the time he was constructing his musically-proportioned
mansions, composers and instrument makers were already moving
toward a new kind of music modulating freely from key to key. For
this new and restless music a different kind of architecture was needed,
one that did not favor one set of wavelengths over the rest. That task
was successfully addressed by baroque architects.

In this connection attention is inevitably drawn to those musical
instruments that are continuously adjustable in pitch, including the
slide trombone, its toy variant the swanee whistle, and the antique
tromba marina, which despite its name is a one-string bass fiddle
designed to produce strong harmonics. These instruments stand out as
suitable for monitoring room acoustics for structural resonances, since
in the presence of a tone of sufficient power gliding gradually up the
octave a point is reached where the pitch coincides with the wavelengths between the walls and is suddenly louder and more prolonged.
From measuring the length of the pipe or string at this moment, it
becomes a simple matter to work out the relationship between the
sounding pitch and the distance from wall to wall.

30
A musical instrument
is a sensing device.

An aeolian harp is a simple wooden frame with strings tuned to
different pitches stretched across it. It hangs in a tree and makes a
singing musical sound that rises and falls in pitch in response to the
action of the breeze. When you hear it sound, you know there is a
breeze blowing, and from the sound changing in pitch, a listener
becomes aware of changes in the force of the breeze. A variant is a set
of chimes, in tubular metal or bamboo, that hangs in the back porch
and clinks or clacks quietly, again blown by the breeze. With wind

chimes, as the breeze increases in force, it is the density of the musical clatter that changes from isolated tones to clusters, and then to clusters in rhythm. A bead curtain at the entrance to a Turkish restaurant, or the sleigh bells attached to the swing door of a corner store, make pleasant rustling or chiming noises as a person enters, to alert the proprietor that a customer awaits attention. In many parts of the world ritual and formal dancers wear garlands of shells or tiny jingles around their necks, arms, and ankles, in order that their movements may be clearly heard as well as seen. Translating inaudible movement into audible gesture offers a number of advantages in monitoring a situation and regulating movement. When the process to be monitored is a natural event like the wind, there is also a latent scientific component to observing the natural action and its consequences.

Musical instruments are also sensing devices, in that the sounds they produce are the audible by-product of the gestures required to play them. For most of the time a listener is only interested in a player's actions in so far as they deliver a smoothly modulated tone. But solo musicians perform in a manner intended to draw attention to their own exceptional skills, often by playing music faster than anybody else, or reaching higher notes than would be thought humanly possible. A great deal of music is composed with technical display in mind. The nineteenth-century piano studies of Moszkowski require a superhuman speed and delicacy of touch comparable to a mechanical player piano, and the eighteenth-century trumpet concerti of Michael Haydn are showcases for players able to reach extremes of register equal to the highest top notes of a Dizzy Gillespie. Audiences are understandably enchanted by such displays, but to turn every concert item into a speed or endurance trial is probably a mistake.

31
A musical instrument
is a switching device.

Some instruments—for example piano, harp, panpipes, xylophone, or tubular bells—incorporate an entire range of notes, and the music played on these instruments involves the player in moving back and forth across the keys from one note to the next. Each note has its own separate mechanism, exactly as every letter of the alphabet has its own key on a computer keyboard. Writing by hand involves forming a sequence of letters (your signature, for instance) as a continuous line, in order that the action may be distinctive enough for a signature to be recognized as genuine and not a "forgery"—a quaint, antique term for a simulation intended to deceive. In the real world a high value is placed on the signature as a badge of authenticity. That a signature is often illegible as a sequence of letters is not the point: what matters is the quality of the gesture.

Keyboard instruments, whether for word processing or for making music, offer the alternative advantages of legibility and precision. Since every key is programmed to a specific pitch, a performance consists in selecting a preordained sequence of keys. It is no longer necessary to find the correct pitch, only the correct key. The instrument itself is designed for consistency of touch from key to key, reducing the task of performance to a task of selecting keys in the right order and with the right degree of emphasis (though the earliest keyboard instruments such as the pipe organ, harpsichord, and musical box were also designed, like the later typewriter, to eliminate differences of emphasis).

A keyboard is a digital device, both literally in that it is controlled from the fingertips, and also in the dictionary sense of reducing continuous images to a mosaic or sequence of data points that can be readily stored. Keyboards are instruments intended by design for the reproduction of a musical text in a way that eliminates human expressive variables such as intonation, dynamics, and touch.

32
A musical instrument
is a signaling device.

That, of course, is obvious. A simple rule of thumb is that the louder the instrument, the more effective it is for sending messages over long

distances. Bells in steeples, trumpets on the battlefield, horns on the
hunt, long horns heard in the Swiss Alps and in the valleys of the
Himalayas, are all designed to send simple strong signals to scattered
local populations or groups. When these instruments are brought into
an enclosed space they are naturally treated with respect, since at close
quarters the sounds they produce can do serious damage to human
hearing.

For instruments to communicate effectively out of doors, without
amplification, there is normally a tradeoff between power and range of
notes. With increasing distance the perceived loudness of a signal
diminishes and the timbre also simplifies leaving only the strongest
elements audible. And because audibility has to do with the sensitivity
of human ears as well as the strength of an acoustic signal, it should
come as no surprise that the most penetrating elements of a musical
signal are also in the frequency zone of human speech discrimination,
the region where vowels can still be distinguished. Both Joan of Arc
and Dick Whittington discerned voices in the swinging partial tones of
distant bells, and made decisions on where their lives were to go from
what they thought those voices were saying.

Instruments of music designed for enclosed spaces are more muted
in tone, but their variety of tone and expression is considerably enhanced. The complexities of organization for which European classical
music is celebrated express a number of key motivations, of which the
first is a desire to unify the written language, the second to create
harmony out of diversity, and the third to achieve all of this within a
controlled acoustic environment free of external distraction.

33
The voice offers control,
the instrument, reliability.

Having said that, the controls available to the human voice are subject
to available limitations of pitch and tone. Speakers and singers alike
are able to exercise the most varied and subtle controls in the more
comfortable midrange; as the the voice rises or falls from the median

zone of pitch or loudness, other factors such as vowel discrimination and consonant articulation become harder to manage. An instrument such as the oboe or clarinet employs much the same power mechanisms as the voice, but substituting a single or double reed and tubular resonator for the tissues and cavities of the throat and mouth. Playing a woodwind instrument means that more energy and attention can be focused on tone control over a greater frequency range than is possible with the singing voice, and that greater overall consistency of tone quality is reliably maintained at greater extremes of register. An indication of the stresses to which the human larynx is subjected can be gauged from the fact that the reeds of these wind instruments, which are made of flexible cane, actually wear out after a relatively short period of use, and have to be replaced. By comparison the vocal cords of a trained singer are expected to perform to the same high standard for a professional lifetime.

34
A voice is one person, an instrument is every person.

The trivial interpretation is that your voice is your own, but an instrument can be played by anybody. There is only one Elvis, but any number of tenor saxophones. What we identify as the individual voice arises from a combination of lifestyle, training, and mainly the configuration of the face. Unlike human beings, tenor saxophones are built to a uniform specification, though a fine instrument of any kind in the right hands will always stand out.

Just as interesting, however, is the uniqueness of a performing style, whatever the instrument. That a listener is able to identify a particular musician through recognizing the way an instrument is played is another remarkable aspect of the art of music, especially given that the music being performed, as is usually the case in western classical music, has been composed by somebody else.

That audiences value individuality so highly, especially in solo performers of exceptional talent (and to a limited degree among the orchestra rank and file, where opportunities for solo performance are rather more scarce) says something about attitudes to progress and competitive skills in a democracy. It says quite a bit, too, about the middle-class values that have dominated classical music since the early nineteenth century, a post-classical society that finds physical prowess, speed, and technical dexterity easier to cope with, and a good deal more explicit, than any message the composer may wish to say. It is also unfortunately the case that many gifted performers on the classical concert circuit prefer the comfort of familiar repertoire to the challenge of newer music.

35
Singing is inside your head,
playing an instrument is outside your head.

One of the interesting consequences of singing being an internal process, like thinking, is that by analogy it accounts for the power of music at a concert to influence an audience collectively. If a concert— whether popular or classical—is characterized as a form of surrogate singing, a perception implied by the convention of singing along with the music, then the sound of the music "out there" is available to be construed as simply the external reverberation of an internal mental process. One of the desirable, though dangerous, side effects of ampli- fication at a rock concert, is that at very high intensities the reproduced sound is able to obliterate awareness of the real-world acoustic. This cannot happen at a symphony orchestra concert, even though the loud- ness (decibel) levels attained by a 100-piece orchestra playing *Bolero* by Ravel are capable of generating an equivalent thrill among those in the front seats. The reason why the sound of an amplified rock band of five to seven players can be more dangerous to listen to than a symphony orchestra of 100 players lies in the high intensity and high coherence of the amplified audio signal projected like a laser beam out of powerful speaker towers directly into the ears of the young audience. It is very different from the sound a symphony orchestra makes, which is a mixed frequency signal, produced by a much larger number of players, and a signal that is both incoherent in itself (because of the number of players and instruments) and in the experience (because the direct sound emanates from a large platform area and is mixed with ceiling and sidewall reflections that tend to neutralize dangerous peak frequencies).

36
The notation of music
is external memory.

To say in self-defense that one was simply following orders is no longer enough. There is a moral component. Nobody is likely to suffer permanent damage from exposure to music, other than loss of hearing if your taste is for heavy metal. The moral component consists in knowing that orders are necessarily incomplete. A musical score can say only so much. A musical score is not brought to life simply from the fact of being performed by musicians who are not yet dead. Nor is it a corpse to be resuscitated, Frankenstein fashion, by a charge of electricity from beyond the grave. The moral component of a musical interpretation consists in taking responsibility not only for what the composer has written, but also for what the composer has intended, and that is a matter of intelligence.

Inspiration means taking breath (as in taking a deep, deep breath). Taking breath is not the same as mouth-to-mouth resuscitation. An "inspired" performance is fully conscious, alert, and self-aware to the highest degree. For an interpretation to be truly inspired, a musician has to understand two things: first, that the notated score is incomplete, and second, that notation is imperfect, in the sense of being misleading if taken literally. To appreciate how notation can mislead requires an understanding of where it is inadequate. Pianists today do not have to think about exact intonation, because it is a matter beyond their control. Piano tuners worry about intonation, because that is their job. It is a worry because tuning a piano so that every triad is perfectly in harmony is an impossible task: it cannot be done. When J. S. Bach composed his sets of preludes and fugues to defend the compromise tuning of the well tempered keyboard, composers and performers routinely tuned their own instruments, so were very much aware of the effect of a particular temperament (system of tuning) on a musical performance. Scholars analysing the preludes and fugues of Bach, or indeed the piano music of Chopin, discovering that certain keys and combinations of notes have been avoided, enable performers to interpret this music with a sensitivity to the implicit compromises of tuning, and how potential false relations between intervals are disguised in the score, for example, by ornamentation.

In areas of doubtful interpretation, such as grace notes, small notes that approach an accented note from above or below, a keyboardist has no option than to play the notes the keyboard allows. But if the same music were to be played by a Japanese koto, for example, or an Indian sitar, the same notations might be interpreted as a bending intonation, which is a form of expression available to these instruments. European composers, even as long ago as the sixteenth century, were aware of and occasionally influenced by non-European musical traditions. It is entirely possible that some of the grace notes of Scarlatti, Mozart, and Haydn may have been intended to express the bending of a note, or the rising or falling inflection of a single pitch, and not two pitches one after another. After all, a flute or violin, or even an oboe is able to bend the pitch of a note. In swing bands, the simple two-by-two patterns written in the sheet music are rhythmicized into threes, while singers and lead guitarists of the rock and roll era continue to bend the notes of a melody for expressive effect as a matter of course.

In discovering where the limits of classical notation lie, and then measuring them against the natural tendencies of expression in the music of oral cultures (including rock and roll), it becomes possible to see beyond the literal reading of a printed text to possibilities of natural expression, such as bending notes, that lie beyond.

The vocabulary of classical music notation is a rich and varied mixture of note symbols, which came first, and expression marks, which came later. It is a system containing many redundancies, in which there is often a tension or ambiguity in relationship of the more "objective" components, such as pitch and duration, to the more "subjective" elements of tempo, alterations of tempo and dynamic, accents, form, and ostensible idiom. Indications of a composer's deeper expressive intentions may sometimes lurk unnoticed in the ambiguous middle ground between what the printed notes say and peripheral marks suggest.

37
Naming the notes A to G
arranges pitches in a line.

The white notes on a piano keyboard are named A to G, and form a continuous scale from low to high. They were named A to G because the next note after the seventh note G moves into a higher octave, and the cycle A to G repeats. The formation of white notes in a line from A to G arose from the invention of keyboard devices over a thousand years ago embodying the radical new concept of pitch as a spacelike continuum from low to high. Such a conception can be traced back to the panpipes of ancient times—bundles of tubes organized from long to short—and to the harp of ancient Egypt, a frame with a sounding board on which strings of graduated length were mounted in order. (Interestingly, the bundled pipes making up the traditional Japanese *shô* are not graduated in length, suggesting a more hierarchical attitude to pitch where every pipe has its place.) The main advantage of tubular pipes over strings as sources of pitch is that they stay in tune; in turn, the advantage of the stringed harp over the panpipes is that more than one note can be played at a time, so harmonic relationships can be demonstrated and compared. Given that the strings of a harp are maintained at the same tension, it is possible to translate musical ratios into relationships of length and proportion. For thousands of years, European designers and builders of palaces, temples, and great cathedrals were guided in their work by simple ratios based directly on harmonic intervals and their transpositions. In the absence of efficient and universal systems of measuring and calculating, dimensional ratios expressed as musical intervals provided a reliable method of computing the proportions of structures to achieve consistent and harmonious results. The grand cathedral organ of medieval Europe can thus be interpreted as a massive musical keyboard calculator bringing together the pitch stability of tube resonators with the superior programmability of the harp.

The importance attached to scale relations in music is indicated in religious art, in which angels playing a variety of instruments signify a higher value to music than celestial entertainment, and also the status accorded to music in the *quadrivium* of medieval learning, alongside arithmetic, geometry, and astronomy, subjects ranking higher than grammar, rhetoric, or logic, yet further proof of the deep involvement of music in the sciences of mathematics, measurement, and the study of natural dynamics.

38
Naming the notes A to H
allows for changes of key.

In Germany the diatonic (white-note) keyboard is named A, B, C, D, E, F, G, H—the name B (which in other countries means the white note B natural) being given to the black note otherwise known as B flat. On a trivial level it allows for the musical spelling of the name B–A–C–H as B flat, A, C, B natural, which of course is after the fact and not an explanation. A scale only of white notes offers only a limited number of changes of key without "false relations" or out-of-tune intervals: C major, A minor, D minor, a reasonable key of G, and an F major with a nasty tritone. By adding just one note and assigning the name B to B flat, the F major dissonance is removed, the new scale permitting a choice of three key centers: C, G a fifth higher (in the ratio 3 : 2), and F a fifth lower (in the ratio 2 : 3). The tuning of violins in fifths, and viols, guitars, lutes and other portable string instruments in fourths, is not only a reminder of the importance of these simple ratios, but also an indication of how numeric ratios embodied in intervals and chords were calculated. When a violin tunes up, for example, the open strings A–E, D–A, and G–D are all perfect fifths, expressing the ratio 2 : 3, but put together in ascending order, the ratios of successive open fifths correspond to raising that initial ratio by powers of ⅔, which is not the simplest of mental arithmetic. The evidence of the added note H suggests that its German inventors were well advanced in their calculation of harmonic ratios.

39
Sharps and flats
are morally suspect.

Theoretically the white-note scale is perfect. It divides the spectrum of pitch into seven notes, as the week is divided in seven days and the night sky is transected by seven planetary bodies moving at different speeds. Isaac Newton, continuing the practice, divided the visible spectrum into seven colors, adding indigo, the color of a dye discovered in the Americas and immortalized as the blue of blue jeans, the color of labor, to make up the number seven.

The white-note scale is perfect if the music you wish to play or sing is in the key of C major. But human voices are not all tuned to the same register: some prefer to sing in higher keys, some lower. It was to allow music to be played in a different key (or *transposed*, moved to a different position on the keyboard) that the black notes were introduced to the octave, occupying positions literally over the cracks between the white keys. These additional notes disturbed the sevenfold symmetry of music, the week, and the planets. While seven notes still made a perfect scale, it was not possible to create seven perfect scales from the same seven notes on the keyboard. Once the principle of changing key was accepted, the serious intellectual challenge arose of finding a system of tuning that would allow a musician to sing or play in any key.

The task was complicated by the fact that subtle differences in tuning emerged with every alteration of key, and it became a topic of learned debate whether more black keys and split keys should be added to the keyboard, or whether a compromise tuning using fewer added notes would be acceptable. Eventually a solution was reached adding five black keys to the seven white keys to make the twelve-note chromatic scale of pitches as we know it today. The number twelve was found acceptable because the seven days are divided into two sets of twelve hours, alternating light and dark, so the change from seven to twelve can be defended as reflecting a change from a larger single perspective to the possibility of multiple view-points based on the idea of subdivision of the scale into dark and light tonalities. It is nevertheless interesting that even today musicians choose to speak of an *octave* (eight notes) and avoid speaking of a *seven*-note scale, and contrarily speak of a *twelve*-note chromatic scale in preference to a *thirteen*-note chromatic octave. Seven and thirteen are odd numbers having magical significance, while eight and twelve are even numbers and mathematically related, 8 being 2 raised to the power of 3, and 8 : 12 expressing the ratio 2 : 3.

40
A seven-note scale conforms to a seven-day week and a seven-planet universe.

Cosmologists have always dreamed of finding a simple formula to connect matter, time, and the laws governing the behavior of the smallest conceivable particles of matter through to the distribution of galaxies throughout the entire universe. That similar dreams were entertained by medieval European disciples of Babylonian science is of interest as much for the persistence of a Grand Unified Theory mindset among the scientific community, as for the *prima facie* evidence of a willful harmonization of music, time, and astronomy at the time of the medieval *quadrivium*. (The seven "planets," incidentally, are the sun, moon, Mercury, Venus, Mars, Jupiter, and Saturn.)

41
Naming notes shows an ability to make distinctions.

When a violinist plays up the scale, there are no keys to aim for, as for a pianist, nor are there frets across the fingerboard as for a lute or guitar, to ensure that the string is *stopped* or shortened to exactly the same length. What this means is that, like a singer, the player of a violin or viol has to find the right note by touch or guesswork, and for that reason can never claim to be playing exactly the same pitch every time. That is a disadvantage for those who think of music as a form of mathematics, playing with exact quantities. On the other hand, if music is about harmony (ratio, geometry) rather than quantity (counting, arithmetic) then the advantage of being able to adjust the pitch of the voice or violin by minute amounts, is that perfect harmony can still be attained for every chord in every key, which is not the case for instruments of fixed tuning.

The violin, with its flexible tuning, was developed in Italy during and after the Galileian era of trial and controversy over the fixed tuning of keyboard instruments, so the fact that the violin family are of adjustable tuning, and not of fixed tuning, is of historical significance. The violin was also valued for its expressive potential; like the voice, it could imitate different tunings and bend a note at will for emotional effect. That the modern orchestra is based on the violin family, and not on recorders or lute consorts, tells us something of the new mathematics of the renaissance era, an age of perspective (changing scale) in painting, and musically an age of modulation, which is movement within the pitch space characterized by constant adjustment of the base value represented by the key.

<h1 style="text-align:center">42
The oldest string instrument
is a bow.</h1>

All stretched-string instruments are related to the bow and arrow, or at least the bow. The connection is clearly visible in surviving examples, from the African continent, Mongolia, and elsewhere, of one-string fiddles in the shape of a longbow, with a bowl or gourd resonator attached to one end.

A longbow is not designed for music, but for hunting. The musical connection lies in the use of a stretched string as a source of power.

The mark of a well-made and powerful bow is in the tension of the string, a property relying both on the manufacture of the string (from the dried sinews of an animal), and the strength and resistance of the wooden bow itself.

In the absence of devices for calculating tension and quality of manufacture, and lacking even the concepts of tension and measurement, the hunter relied on the sound of the string in tension, both in its undrawn state and when an arrow was inserted. If the sound was a musical note of distinct pitch, and its vibration strong and lasting, it showed that the string was of good quality. If the hunter had difficulty hearing the sound of the bowstring, it could be amplified by resting one end of the bow in a bowl or against the dried skull of a deer, acting as a resonator, and the other end against the listener's temple. In that way the hunter was able to monitor the tension of a bowstring as a function of its timbre and relative pitch.

When an arrow is inserted in a bow, the optimum location is the exact midpoint of the string. This midpoint coincides in mysterious fashion with the node or deadpoint of the first harmonic, so a hunter would have learned from experience to find the midpoint by plucking the string and searching out by touch the point at which the pitch suddenly rings at an octave higher. As the arrow is drawn back, the string is stretched to a degree of maximum thrust, and its tension and associated pitch gradually rise. Here too the point to which the bow is drawn back can be judged by the change in pitch of the string, an especially useful division of labor since the hunter's gaze is necessarily fixed on his quarry. From mastering the art of making and using a longbow a hunter acquires a limited vocabulary of musical signs: a bass note representing the string in tension, but at rest, the first harmonic representing the optimum location for inserting the arrow, and a scale of still higher pitches representing degrees of increasing tension as the arrow is drawn back before being released.

The longbow has remained a principal hunting and fighting weapon among the world's cultures for thousands of years, and it is only natural that its acoustical characteristics should have attracted the attention of the best minds of the community in endeavors to understand the principles of arrow propulsion and thus design better, more powerful, and more efficient weaponry. These studies would be focused in particular on the relationship between the speed of the arrow and the tension of the string. In such a knowledge context, which has major survival implications, the development of instruments such as the harp by which a numerical value (equivalent length) can be assigned to degrees of change in bowstring tension and associated pitch, makes a great deal of sense. Having been constructed for scientific purposes (in this case, ballistics), such instruments then become available for musical entertainment.

43
The oldest wind instrument
is a bone.

When the marrow is sucked out of a bone, a hollow tube is left that may either be open at both ends or open at one end and closed at the other. Blowing across the open end of a hollowed-out bone produces an audible resonance of constant pitch. The same effect can be heard by blowing across the mouth of a drink bottle. To produce a steady musical note takes a bit of practice, and the cut aperture needs to be clean, with a good edge. In blowing a steady stream of air across the cut end, one is effectively trying to put more air into the tube than it will hold.

Since bone is a rigid material, air pressure within the tube builds up before escaping, and as long as the airflow directed by the player remains constant, a cycle of alternating higher and lower pressure is produced in reaction to the piston-like up and down movement of air within the tube. That cycle of pressure change is audible as a tone of constant pitch. By experimenting with different bones one discovers that some make a better sound than others, and that bones of different length or width sound different notes. From such experimentation comes an understanding of pitch as a property of the sounding length of the tube. The next step, adding finger holes to vary the sounding length, is an application of that understanding as a means of varying the pitch.

44
The oldest keyboard instrument
is a set of panpipes.

Hollow tubes of bamboo or cane are more readily available and easier to manage than bones, which may take a long time to accumulate through hunting, and may not exhibit as good a consistency of diameter and tonal quality. A set of panpipes does not look like a keyboard, but it embodies all of the most important design features of a keyboard instrument such as a pipe organ. Consistency in the manufacture of cane tube resonators points to an interest in making an instrument of consistent tone. Each note in the scale is assigned to a separate tube, which is then shaped and tested until the pitch is right, at which point the tube becomes a permanent record of the note, and the collection of pipes, of a scale of pitches. The object of making such an instrument is self-evidently to have a collection of pitches permanently available, so that the performer does not have to tune the instrument every time, or have to figure out the location of the note on a fingerboard, as one has to do with a violin or guitar. Implicit in the creation of a uniform set of pipes is the intention to secure uniformity of tone quality or waveform throughout the scale.

Since expression in music arises from nuances of accentuation and intonation, an instrument that eliminates uncertainties of intonation can also be interpreted as an instrument intended to eliminate the variables of artistic expression. The value of being able to manipulate the pitch and accentuation of a note, is a value invested in freedom of choice and also in a moral obligation to seek harmony. These values can only be articulated if pitches can be finely adjusted in performance. Panpipes are not designed with flexibility of intonation in mind, in fact the opposite. By implication, such an instrument is intended to be played by people lacking in knowledge or concern for the art of intonation, and thus unaware of the higher implications of perfect harmony.

The legend of Apollo and Marsyas tells of a challenge to Apollo, the god of stringed instruments (and also of the longbow) brought by Marsyas, represented as a Pan-like satyr with goat's horns and lower body. Marsyas rashly claimed superiority for his pipes over the strings

of Apollo. The contest was adjudicated by King Midas, famous for his
golden touch. Midas decided in favor of Marsyas, and Apollo, greatly
roused, inflicted the ears of an ass on the king to show his disapproval
("cloth-eared"); he then flayed the unfortunate Marsyas alive (expressing an opinion that the satyr was thick-skinned and therefore totally
lacking in sensitivity).

Depicting the performer of panpipes as a satyr is a condescending
way of implying that the maker of such an instrument is a rustic sim-
pleton who has no appreciation of the higher values of art. It is the
attitude of a cultivated humanism that cannot see the value of an
instrument designed for consistency and accuracy of response, eliminating the variables and uncertainties of human performance. In fact,
these are the values of science. The panpipes can therefore be understood as a scientific rather than a musical device. In the more than a
thousand years of evolution culminating in the baroque organ, European engineers enlarged the pipes, developed an independent power
source (the wind chest) to guarantee evenness of air pressure, and
installed a servomechanism (the keyboard) to ensure complete uniformity of intonation and attack. This huge effort in science and engineering was undertaken under the patronage of the church, and it is
something of an irony that just at the time the organ was finally
perfected, in the era of the Inquisition, the church authorities were
beginning to lose interest in the scientific applications for which the
instrument had been conceived.

45
The oldest percussion instrument
is a shield.

As seen on television, police reservists advance on a group of protesting citizens, rhythmically clattering their batons against clear plastic
shields.

46
A mask, a high collar
magnify the person.

In acting or ritual the mask or helmet is a disguise that both neutralizes the individual personality and allows an actor to assume the character of a hero or messenger of the gods. Dark glasses are today's mask of preference, but as well as hiding the eyes (even now considered as gateways to the soul) the traditional mask provides a rigid resonating surface to amplify and direct the voice. A singing or declaiming voice, as delivered by a masked actor in front of a large audience, will also gain a hardness of tone or, in the case of a Darth Vader or knight in armor, an alien and perhaps intimidating metallic quality.

The bishop's mitre, a stiff two-sided hat in the shape of an arch projecting high above the head, may also have originated as a device for amplifying the voice, in addition to adding stature and thus magnifying the authority of a religious leader. The magnificent starched and ruffled lace collars that surround the face in portraits of Queen Elizabeth I are also intimidating in their way, and may have had a secondary purpose of reflecting and magnifying her speaking voice in court. A judge's wig, unfortunately, has no such effect.

47
Accents, diacriticals, and punctuation marks
are music notations.

Sharps and flats change the inflection of a note. F sharp is still F, but tuned upwards, "sharpened," gained tension, and given an edge. If F sharp had been considered a different note from the outset, it would have been given a different name. On the white keyboard F comes after E, and on rare occasions is notated E sharp; but F sharp, which is higher than F by the same amount as F from E, is still called F and not I, J, or K. The F sharp key on the black keyboard also does duty for G flat, but as G flat it is supposed to sound different, a G that has been lowered in tension and therefore sounds duller or more muted. The difference between a "flat key" such as D flat major, and the corresponding (*enharmonic*) "sharp key" of C sharp major, would seem to be more psychological than real, since exactly the same keys are employed. In practice, a performer will tend to play music in a sharp key with a more edgy tone, and in a flat key with a softer touch.

Such subtleties remain in written language, in French, for example, to distinguish the upward inflection of é, as in *épée* (foil), from the downward inflection of è, as in *règle* (rule), and the combined up-and-down inflection of ê, as in *fenêtre* (window). When reading aloud, quotation marks have the effect of raising the pitch level of the text enclosed within, to show that it is another person's voice, as it were, and not the voice (or opinion) of the actual reader.

48
Music arises
from noise.

John Cage thought that any kind of sound could be musical in effect, and devised concert scenarios in which the unexpected was likely to happen. He had the advantage of living in an age of concert halls, which are protected environments, and of sound recording, which is able to amplify, isolate, and preserve incidental noises for posterity. When a transitory sound or noise is caught on tape or disc it becomes transitory no longer, and thus material for artistic or scientific inquiry.

That music exists at all reflects a human preference for sounds of a musical nature, for reasons of perception (that musical sounds are easier to hear and process), and also for aesthetic reasons (that they convey an awareness of the supernatural and the beautiful). Musical sounds are steadier, longer-lasting, and more efficient for audition and communication, and the fact that they are rarely encountered in nature and mostly discovered as a consequence of human ingenuity, gives them special status in human and tribal relations, as well as in human-animal relations (tending sheep or cattle, issuing commands to hunting dogs and falcons). When a musical signal is heard, a listener knows instantly that this is the sign of another human being. In the heat and clamor of battle, the call of the trumpet can still clearly be heard, advising combatants to fall back or advance.

Awareness of the superior audibility of music over speech and other noise returned to public attention in the early years of sound on film, when makers of animated movies suddenly realised that adding dialogue in English (or any other language) would have the effect of drastically reducing international sales of their entertainments. In addition, the quality of sound reproduction in movie houses was often so bad that recorded dialogue, even in the appropriate language, was difficult for an audience to follow. At that time music established itself as the preferred accompaniment to cinematic action, not only because it was easier to listen to than spoken dialogue, but also because, as a universal language, its message could be understood around the world.

49
Music is easier to hear.

Noise has its uses, as a means of shielding the listener from distractions, and as a specific against silence, since an absence of sound can be just as disconcerting as too much. For a holidaymaker lying on the beach on summer vacation, the natural sounds of surf, seagulls and cicadas create a paradoxical impression of undisturbed tranquility. Across the world, in public squares and private courtyards, architects and engineers erected fountains: to cool the air, to aerate the water and prevent it from stagnating, and in order for the sound of falling water to create a zone of peace and quiet, and also privacy, for people to sit and hold a conversation without being overheard. In libraries, where people are asked to avoid making unnecessary noise, a screen of low level background noise is provided by air conditioning. Background music is out of place in a library for the same reason that many consider it an intrusion in supermarkets and elevators, as an unnecessary distraction from the task in hand. Part of the increasing appeal of third world music to first world audiences must lie in the fact that it occupies a middle zone between the distracting presence of familiar music, and the unsettling absence of no music at all.

50
A four- or five-note scale is for outdoors,
a seven-note scale for indoors.

Folk music is recognisable around the world for its typical melodies based on five notes. The five-note or pentatonic scale is a five-point division of the octave, from the tone of an open (unstopped) string, on a guitar for example, to the tone produced when the string is stopped an octave higher, at the halfway point. After the unison, which is when two strings or pipes are tuned to the same pitch, the octave is the next significant consonance, because an octave defines a space between two notes, one lower, the other higher, a space that also sounds as a unity and is thus closed and not open. (The higher pitch of an octave in fact vibrates at twice the frequency of the lower.)

Between the lower and the higher notes of the octave lie other notes that are not identical with, but sound more or less harmonious with them. In order to create melodies to imitate the natural rise and fall of the voice with notes that are also reasonably harmonious, some way of fixing these intermediate pitches has to be found. That folk melodies tend to favor a division of the octave into five, whereas classical diatonic music is based on a seven-note scale, can be partly explained by the fact that folk music originates out of doors, whereas classical music by and large is music to be made indoors. A melody sung out of doors has to make larger distinctions in pitch if it is to be heard over a reasonable distance without amplification. The workers in the cotton fields whose songs created the blues, were not singing to relax but as a team to keep their spirits up and maintain a rhythm. That they sang to a five-note scale also has to do with the structured way in which the speaking voice deals with distance communication.

The shorter the distance a voice has to travel, the better the signal; and the better the signal, the easier it is to make distinctions. The scientist Fritz Winckel observed that classical seven-note music belonged to the concert hall, and atonal or twelve-tone music to the recording studio, where microphones bring the listener even closer to the musicians.

51
In the forest, birds sing in tune;
in the open plains, they sing in rhythm.

A forest habitat, the "dark woods" of fairytale, is a resonant environment in which the trunks and limbs of trees assist the propagation of sound, rather than hindering it. That songbirds of the forest tend to sing with purer tones, while related species living in the plains "rely more on temporal coding" in signaling, can be attributed to the advantages of assisted reverberation. The multiple tall tree-trunks of the forest behave like a walled space or room, reflecting and prolonging an acoustic signal.

When a sound interacts with multiple reflections of itself, the more structured it is in the first place (the more musical in tone), the more these multiple reflections interact positively to make it last longer and travel farther, which is a saving of energy for the animal or bird. You and I experience the same benefit when we sing in the shower and imagine ourselves to be much better singers than we thought. The small reflective enclosures of a shower or bath act to steady the singing voice and reinforce the stronger and more musical frequencies in the vocal signal.

52
The echo of a man's voice is a child;
the echo of a child's voice is a child.

The interiors of cathedrals, museums, mausoleums, art galleries, and historic railway stations, as well as the entrance lobbies of leading financial institutions, are often stoneclad and larger than life public spaces that tend to intimidate visitors just a little. Glass and polished stone are chosen not just because they are durable materials and easy to clean, but because they reflect and amplify the casual sounds of ordinary life, like footsteps and conversation.

When a person comes into a reverberant environment, the enhanced impression of space combined with a heightened sense that one is disturbing the tranquility of the space simply by being there, make one feel as if under a magnifying glass, exposed to the scrutiny of the building's unseen occupants. The effect is entirely acoustical in nature. Responding to the heightened acoustic, adult visitors instinctively lower their voice, try to keep the children quiet, and go about their business as discreetly as possible. Reverberant spaces are very effective in instilling a sense of awe.

In contemplating the vastness of a canyon or a cave, making a noise is sometimes permitted, and through doing so visitors are able to discover what kind of call is most effective and how long it will continue to sound. In order to hear a reverberation or echo, some of the original sound has to be reflected back to the source. We distinguish a reverberation, which is like a shimmering aura that dies away gradually, from an echo, which is a sequence of disconnected coherent reflections of an original sound gesture, seemingly returned in answer. The fascination of an echo is that it can repeat whole words and phrases and thus appear to be speaking. In order to travel the distance required to produce an echo, the energy of a chanting or calling voice has to be concentrated in the middle range of frequencies, which is why people employ a higher-pitched voice in the open than is normal for indoors. Rituals exploiting echo or echo-like dialogue between a lead singer (or *cantor*) and a congregation are universal in cultural history. They lead to the puzzling discovery that when an adult male voice is singing (and the voice of a celebrant is traditionally male) the returning echo is heard at a higher octave, which to some listeners might indicate that the echo is the voice of a spirit, or at least some other being.

Among many religious traditions, ancient and modern, including Greek and Russian orthodox ritual, Tibetan chant, and throat singing traditions of Mongolia, Albania, and the island communities of the outer Hebrides, techniques of vocal resonance are cultivated for outdoor singing across remote valleys, and for religious ceremonies in reverberant temples, as though to emphasize the difference between the real earth-bound voices of the celebrants and the disembodied and elevated resonances heard in response, that float high in the air like the angels of religious art.

53
A gothic cathedral
is a forest in stone.

By its very nature a forest not only enhances sound, it also tends to exclude the light, so any creature that makes the forest its home will tend to rely more on hearing to survive. The great cathedrals and temples of Europe and the Middle East were constructed, in some cases over many centuries, as monuments to religious faith. In structure they are very different from temples in many other parts of the world, specifically in size, volume, and acoustic qualities, with rows of high, branching interior columns that interlace at roof height to create complex vaulted reflecting surfaces resembling the lofty trunks and interlocking crowns of an ancient forest.

Compared to the much smaller chapels built to serve the religious needs of local communities, the vast spaces of these cathedrals might appear superfluous, ostentatious, or merely made for effect. As acoustic structures, their size makes a certain amount of sense, however, especially when considered in relation to the music created within them. "Magnification" is a recurrent term of traditional ritual, for example the Magnificat, and the size of a great cathedral is appropriate and necessary to accommodate instruments of the power and frequency range of the pipe organs installed in them. In addition to their religious function (indeed, because of it) cathedrals are also monuments to an oral tradition of knowledge, acoustic laboratories in which an intellectual elite sought to understand the dynamics of the universe through acoustic modeling. Today that role has been largely taken over by astronomy, and temple domes to the visual science can be found scattered on high remote vantage points throughout the world. Astronomy is also concerned with magnification, and with understanding the universe.

We have no difficulty with the idea that the larger the reflecting mirror, the farther into space it is possible to see, and the more therefore it is possible to know. Acoustic magnification had a similar scientific purpose, achieved by transposing pure tones and tonal relationships from higher to lower octaves. In building pipe organs containing families of similar pipes extending from the very small to the extremely large in size, reaching from the highest to the lowest extremes of audibility, organ builders were enabling research into the profound mysteries of the unison, harmonic intervals and difference tones, and the fact that two separate vibrating signals actually reinforce and stabilize one another at a distance, without the instruments touching. Using the extended range and consistency of tone of the pipe organ, effects of consonance and dissonance observable in the voice range could be transposed and recreated in much lower octaves where their slower vibrations could be more readily measured and counted. Working with low frequency signals meant having to construct tuned pipes of enormous size, and develop reliable power sources to operate them, requiring not only metallurgical science but also engineering skills of a high order. Low-frequency sounds are extremely power-hungry, large-scale vibrations. By way of example, the wavelength, or distance between pressure peaks, of bottom C on the piano, vibrating at 32 cycles per second, is about 35 feet. To conduct research on pure tones of this order of magnitude, immensely powerful bellows and correspondingly large resonating chambers are necessary.

54
Air is invisible,
sound is invisible,
music is invisible.

Ancient ritual also makes the distinction between action and intention, the tangible and the merely (or not so merely) imaginary. Dividing the world into "things visible and invisible" might appear to be drawing a contrast between the real world of substantial things and the world of the spirit. It is no less likely to be striking a balance between the equally real worlds of vision and hearing. In the movie world, all the same, music is the unseen spirit that motivates the action, triggers lust and remorse, and guides the expectations of the audience who, finding themselves literally in the dark, are invisible to the personalities onscreen.

55
A voice and an instrument
are a coupled system.

For a flute or oboe player, the instrument is an extension of the voice. Musicians *sing* through their instrument: not literally, perhaps, but emotionally. The instrument behaves like a voice, but a voice having exceptional powers of extended range, greater tone control, the ability to play rapid complicated passages, and so on. To hear musical instruments as extended voices is to appreciate the range and precision advantages they have over the human voice, advantages arising in part from their freedom from a text. After the emancipation of the voice in the age of Monteverdi, when the first operas launched a new and deliberately naturalistic vocal style, the next level, as it were, was to extend the human voice to emulate an instrument, and we hear the result very clearly in the heroic solos of Vivaldi ("Lauda Jerusalem"), Handel ("The trumpet shall sound" from *The Messiah*), Mozart (the Queen of the Night aria from *The Magic Flute*), and elsewhere. Strength, range, absolute control, and purity of tone are highly prized qualities of dramatic singing in the western classical tradition, and they are expressed in an idiom that invites comparison with a musical instrument. The much-feared and maligned male *castrato* voice was revered as having the power of an adult male, but the high pitch, intensity, and purity of tone of a trumpet. The last genuine castrato died in 1921, but the fashion for male solo voice singing in the soprano range returned in popular music of the late twentieth century, in the vocal style of soloists like Freddie Mercury of the band Queen, for example, a voice of a timbre and intensity to complement the sound of an electric guitar at the upper extreme of range.

The idea of a coupled system in which the voice and the instrument each fulfill and complete the other, is perfectly embodied in the traditional singer-songwriter who accompanies himself or herself on acoustic guitar. This lyric tradition can be retraced through the lute songs of the sixteenth century, via the traveling minstrels of the Middle Ages, back to the eras of Greek lyric and epic poetry, even to the time of King David and his lyre. When the singer is also accompanist, the complementarity of voice and instrument is most clearly apparent. The instrument offers precision of intonation, against which the voice may be heard deliberately to waver and break for expressive effect. The instrument is able to add emphasis and intensify underlying emotion, including taking the voice to a higher level, the voice however has the further dimension of language, the added value of key words and figures of speech having the power to trigger a cascade of associations in the minds of a listening audience.

56
A group of similar instruments is a choir.

A choir is for church, a chorus for opera and musicals, and for pop music the same are called backup singers. The musical definition of a choir is of a group of instruments of the same family, not just the human family, but also a brass choir (trumpets, trombones), a consort of recorders (end-blown flutes of different sizes), or viols, lutes, a string quartet, even a group of saxophones. The criteria are uniformity of tone and intonation allowing for a perfectly blended harmony, coupled with extension of range, from bass to high treble. A choir or consort is a multi-part ensemble that can also be construed as a living keyboard, performing like a pipe organ, but in a secular environment, so outside the jurisdiction of the church.

A choir brings human flexibility of intonation to the previously mechanical task of exploration into harmonic relationships, especially involving modulation from key to key. When limited to a keyboard instrument such as an organ or harpsichord, a composer (in the role of researcher) is obliged to make the best of a fixed scale of pitches that being programmed in advance cannot be adjusted during a performance. Since all keyboard tunings are compromises with perfect (universal) harmony, a keyboard composer is forced to negotiate carefully from key to key, and navigate around difficult keys, those in multiple sharps or flats that sound disconcertingly out of tune. A choir, on the other hand, is able to move from key to key with ease, adjusting the harmonies from chord to chord as the music progresses (the word *progression* in music evoking the image of a pioneer navigator, like Vasco da Gama or Francis Drake, sailing into uncharted waters). The madrigals of Gesualdo reveal the inherent strangeness of harmonic logic to great intellectual and emotional effect. The ideal of complete tonal and harmonic integration combined with total flexibility of tuning survives today in the slightly tongue-in-cheek idiom of the barbershop quartet or choir.

57
A group of different instruments is a band.

When different instruments are combined in the same group, the same integration of tone as a choir is clearly impossible. In a band, also called by the old name of *broken consort*, unity of tone and expression is not an option, so a band stands for unity of action, and unity of purpose. The different instruments in a band have distinct sounds and personalities related to what they do best. The image that comes to mind is the old fable of the organs of the body ganging up against the stomach because its belching offended their sense of corporate dignity. The moral of that tale, as we know, is that each organ of the body has a special role to play, and when they work together everybody benefits.

A modern rock and roll band is a broken consort in this classic sense. Each member has a distinct role: the drums, to provide a steady beat and cue entries; the bass guitar to provide a harmonic foundation; the rhythm guitar, to fill in the harmonies; the lead guitar, to partner the voice, and the lead vocalist, to fill in the words and give the band an emotional identity.

58
A choir is for harmony of tone;
a band is for harmony of action.

Considered as a social group, the image of a partnership of specialists united in the service of a common goal has perhaps more to offer an audience than the choir model of corporate integration and conformity. A symphony orchestra is a broken consort on a larger scale, while a military wind or brass band is more of a choir, an association under-lined, if that were necessary, by the uniform dress and strictly uniform marching associated with a military band.

59
A choir signifies many;
a band, diversity.

Competing images of corporate might (the choir) versus cooperation among experts (the band) also have something to tell us about the way society organizes itself and the premium it sets on individual skill and expertise. A choir expresses the values of citizenship, in comparison with which a band celebrates the contribution of teamwork and individual skill. The same drama of competing social orders, pitting uniformity of collective action against unity of purpose that recognizes individuality, is played out every time music for large numbers is composed and performed.

60
A person can sing and play the guitar at the same time,
but a person cannot sing and play the flute at the same time.

The issue here is complementarity once again. If an instrument sub-stitutes for the voice, it imitates and extends the voice, so it may be perceived as voice-like, but having superhuman extra capabilities. In the case of a wind instrument, like the flute, the similarities extend to dynamic intonation and phrasing, which are controlled by the same breath action as the voice and are subject to the same limitation of the length of a breath.

The violin was also designed to imitate the more powerful tone and dynamic inflection of a solo voice, in contrast to the corporate plain tone quality of the viol, an instrument more suited to ensemble work. A violin has greater control over expressive shading than a flute or wind instrument, and can even play two notes at once, which the voice cannot do. Woodwind instruments, while controlled by the breath, remain essentially instruments of fixed tuning, since the player cannot reposition the holes at will.

It follows that where a voice is accompanied by a guitar—or piano, harp, or lute—it is natural for the voice to emphasize the more flexible qualities of which it is capable, and the accompanying instrument complementary values of stability and precision of tone. By the same token, a wind instrument is implicitly a voice with added instrumental qualities.

61
The harp
is to the longbow
as the trumpet to the musket.

Apollo, the Greek god of music, was also the god of war, his weapon the longbow. The two roles are connected. A bow uses the power of a string in tension to propel an arrow swiftly to a distant target with enough residual force to penetrate and kill it. Apollo's instrument of choice is a lyre, sometimes represented as a violin, but in any case a frame on which a number of strings, perhaps seven, are strung to provide the notes of an ascending scale or mode. The mastery embodied in both archery and playing the lyre is a knowledge of the power implications of a string at different degrees of tension. When a bow is drawn prior to releasing an arrow, the tension of the string increases to an optimum level, and this change in tension is audible as a change in pitch. Since the bowstring remains the same in length, the difference in pitch cannot be related to a change in length, as is the case with a guitar or violin. It is due to the addition of a mysterious property of added force of which the change in pitch is the outward sign.

One way of measuring the increase in tension (and thus, latent force) in a bowstring is by matching the pitch of the bowstring with a harp, noting which string is in unison with the bowstring at rest, and which other strings coincide with the pitch of the bowstring as it is drawn back to the release position of maximum tension. In this way the different degrees of tension in strings of the same length (the bow, or lyre) can be equated to different degrees of length at the same tension

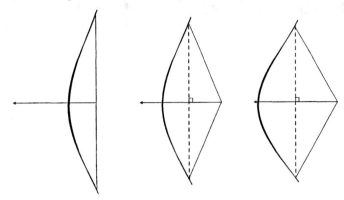

(the harp), and vice versa. Degrees of tension in a bowstring can also be visualized geometrically as a series of right triangles of which the bowstring at rest forms the vertical, the distance the arrow is drawn back the horizontal, and the drawn bowstring the hypotenuse. The changes in pitch of the bowstring as the arrow is drawn back can then be correlated with angular displacements in relation to the line of the bowstring at rest, and beyond that to the ratios of length of the sides of the right triangles formed as the arrow is drawn back.

From the ancient Greeks to the time of Galileo, Marin Mersenne, and Isaac Newton, scholars struggled to explain the relationship between stopping a string (shortening its length) to raise the pitch to a chosen note of the scale, and increasing the tension of the unstopped string to attain the same note. Arguing from the analogy of a spinning weight on a string, they hoped to explain how much the relative orbital motion of a planet was an effect of distance (the length of the string), and how much of mass (the weight on the end). The relationship of length to tension can be expressed as a form of inverse square law. Thus, raising the pitch of a string by an octave is equivalent to shortening the length of a string by half (½) or increasing the tension by 4, the square of the reciprocal: $(\frac{2}{1})^2$. Pythagoras tells us that the square on the hypotenuse of a right triangle is equal to the sum of the squares on the other two sides. By a curious coincidence, the increase of force acting on the arrow (using the diagram as a guide) is also equal to the square on the hypotenuse of the right triangle formed by the drawn bowstring.

There may seem little to connect the straight trumpet and the blunderbuss, an early firearm, other than the shape of the barrel. But the acoustic connection is similar in principle to that of the longbow in relation to the harp or lyre. In both cases the critical issue is of harnessing power and directing a projectile to a distant target. The longbow draws on knowledge embodied in stretched string instruments, while the new firearms destined to supersede the longbow in turn draw inspiration from the design of a musical instrument whose function is to project a focused beam of sound energy in one direction. A trumpet is a straight tube, like the barrel of a gun, but with a flared end. The sound of a trumpet is produced by the explosive emission of compressed air through the mouthpiece into the tube, while the flared end is designed to aid the passage of sound waves into the open air, making it easier for the player to continue playing, and to hold a steady note. It may well be that the first muskets were crafted with trumpet-ended barrels in the belief that, as for the musical instrument, the flared end would improve directional accuracy and avoid blowback.

62
A band, an industry;
an orchestra,
an army.

The industrial revolution in western manufacturing came about after successive social revolutions during the late eighteenth century led to a change in the way society perceived and organized itself. In mass production of cheap goods for a mass market, society acknowledged the new status of the tradesman and citizen—and the rise to power of the middle class—along with the introduction of new methods of manufacture to streamline production of consumer items in quantity. The new production line approach emerged from the example of the western orchestra and its development from the time of Bach and Vivaldi in the early eighteenth century to the time of Haydn and Beethoven a century later. The early baroque orchestra was a small band of variegated instruments controlled from a keyboard, a model of integrated teamwork in which different but equal team members cooperated under strong, literally "hands-on" leadership. Nearly everybody had a different role to play in the team; the baroque concerto grosso emphasized coordination in the performance of interrelated tasks to attain images of a precision and complexity beyond the capacity of a uniform choir or consort. The 104 symphonies of Joseph Haydn trace the development of the orchestra from the tight ensemble of the concerto grosso era to the greatly expanded collective of skilled players of the late eighteenth century, a body considerably more flexible in organization and no longer dependent on direct control from the keyboard. A late Haydn symphony is a model musical production line in which the rank and file "workers" are highly skilled artisans, all capable of assuming leadership roles at different times.

Through the Mannheim era to the final decades of the eighteenth century the skill levels in an orchestra increased to a point where the interpretation of a symphony came to express a collective responsibility shared between the conductor and a number of soloists. By 1800 the orchestra had developed into a workforce able to function equally well as a totality or as a collective of specialized task groups, and this versatility in turn is reflected in the symphonic music of the period.

The new style of team management relied on universal literacy among orchestra players, on a uniform language of command (standard notation), and finally on a network of leadership (interpretation) skills allowing responsibility for the course of the operation to be delegated among specialized individuals from time to time.

The symphonic model was destined to revolutionize warfare as well as the peacetime production of consumable goods. That Haydn's and Mozart's new prototype of guerrilla warfare was resisted by the military for over a century, from the nationalist campaigns of the eighteenth century through to the disastrous wars of the nineteenth and

early twentieth centuries, can be interpreted as a refusal by an aristocratic elite to abandon the classical model of mass troops led from the
top. We see the same attitude still reproduced today in the action and
music displays of the military where troops march as a group, en bloc,
in step, to music of a uniform beat. If the music of the modern army
were truly to reflect the complexity and professionalism of today's
fighting forces, it would have to sound more like Mahler, Schoenberg,
Stravinsky, or Stockhausen, than Sousa or Elgar.

63
The note A
is the length of a stride.

Since the white notes of the keyboard are named A to G, the note A has
to mean something: *alpha*, the beginning of the sequence, the starting-
point, the first letter of the musical alphabet. A above middle C is the
tuning pitch for an orchestra, and for a string quartet. It brings the
group into harmony. The note A is a standard for the violin family and
larger ensembles including the violin family.

Today we think of a note as a location on a keyboard, or as a
sound of a certain frequency. Over the centuries the frequency associated with the tuning note A has risen from around 415 cycles per
second in the time of Mozart to about 435 in the time of Schubert and
upward to 440 in the early twentieth century. Nowadays a concert A of
442 cycles per second is not uncommon. The relationship between a
note and a number of cycles per second does not mean very much to
the casual listener. Furthermore, it relies on an exact measurement of
the length of a second, which is an achievement of relatively recent
times.

In the age of Leonardo da Vinci time could not be measured with
the kind of accuracy needed to make the modern concept of frequency
in cycles per second meaningful, or even conceivable. Prior to the
Napoleonic era, the length of a foot or an inch could vary from state to
state. The ancients did not calculate in cycles per second, but what they

did understand were the twin concepts of unison and wavelength, the distance between successive pressure peaks that varies with pitch and can be related to the ringing sound of distinct pitch that resonates between parallel walls.

What this means is that in earlier times, before time and length were exactly computable, rituals of tuning, of coming to the unison,

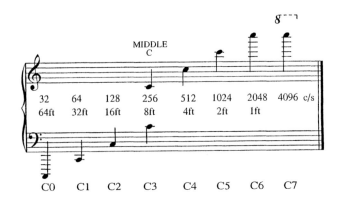

C pipes in the organ as powers of 2

and singing or playing in simple harmonies, were charged with considerably greater mystery and significance to contemporary audiences than they are today. As the purest and most accurate indications of measurement and proportion available, musical relationships stood for the hidden laws of proportion that ensured the world and the universe remained stable and in balance. The Vitruvian figure of renaissance art showing a standing male with arms and legs apart, most famously represented in the image by Leonardo da Vinci, is of interest not simply as a standard figure showing the ideal proportions of the human body, but as a statement of harmonious dimensions and ratios to be applied in design and architecture. Today we give the name "ergonomics" to the science of designing buildings, tools, and items of furniture to a human scale. For architects in the Rome of Vitruvius the standard units of measurement were the height of a man and the length of a pace. People were not so tall in Roman or renaissance Europe. Assuming a speed of sound of 1100 feet per second, wavelengths of 5 feet for height and 2 feet 6 inches for a pace correspond to frequencies of 200 and 400 cycles per second; for a height of 5 feet 6 inches and a step length of 2 feet 9 inches, the corresponding frequencies are 220 and 440 cycles per second. An orchestra tuning to A is thus tuning to the standard dimensions of a Vitruvian figure. The range of pitches between 400 and 440 cycles is equivalent to the range of tuning frequencies for A in use through to the end of the eighteenth century, after which they were reassessed scientifically.

64
The note F is 6 feet,
and B flat 9 feet.

For the violin family, the tuning note is A. It is hard to imagine how the name A could have been assigned if it were not the first note to be named and the note of first importance, as the wavelength of a measure equivalent to the height and step length of an ideal human being. The height of a human being is a hypothetical ideal. That woodwind and brass bands tune to B flat rather than A might seem to suggest a conflict of standards. The more likely reason, however, is that wind instruments are tubes and pipes, and that the standard length of a pipe is a tradesman's measure and not a philosophical or aesthetic talisman.

65
Middle C and its octaves
are powers of 2.

The C major scale is the major scale containing all seven white notes, and for that reason may have been regarded as somewhat special. Middle C lies approximately at the midpoint of a modern keyboard, and so occupies a privileged position at the mid-point between the treble and bass clefs of keyboard notation. Why it should enjoy special status is the interesting question. If it were really so important, why is the note called C and not A?

The answer may lie in the tradition of organ building that classifies pipe sizes in octave groups counted from C to C rather than from A to A, and referring to these registers in terms of the length of a C pipe, which happen to be multiples of 2 feet, from 2 feet in the treble, through 4, 8, 16 in the bass even to 32 or 64 feet in the sub-bass register on some larger instruments. In wind instruments like the trumpet, oboe, or clarinet, the physical length of the tube does not conform to the wavelength of its fundamental pitch. These differences arise because the sounding length of the instrument is affected by variations in the inner shape of the tube and the shape of the bell. For organ pipes in C, however, tradition recognizes a concordance between the length and the frequency of a pipe, both powers of 2.

Middle C in that sense is literally the key connecting music as a study with astronomy, geometry, and architecture. Its significance is numerical. An octave in music is a mystery equivalent to doubling the square in architecture. The development of equal temperament, coinciding with the invention of logarithms, connects musical scales and progressions with recursive calculations of compound interest and cyclic phenomena such as the orbital motions of the planets. The slide rule, for centuries employed for rapid calculation until the arrival of the pocket calculator in the late twentieth century, is marked in a manner resembling the fingerboard of a guitar or monochord, and calculations made with the aid of a slide rule are similar in nature and effect to the chord changes and modulations of music.

66

A scale model

is a model of a scale.

Perspective in painting, scale projection in mapmaking, and key modulation in music are variant applications of the same art of scale modeling originally developed for music. Like the different pipes of an organ, families of musical instruments such as recorders, viols, oboes, and lutes were designed to provide uniformity of timbre from bass to treble. The violin family of cello, viola, and violin are scaled in proportion to the first, second, and third harmonics of a harmonic series. By contrast, variant sizes of trumpets, horns, and clarinets in B flat, C, D, E flat, and F are simply designed to cope with the intonation problems arising from classical modulation. Music that modulates from key to related key is a music of changing scale, and for that reason the latter instrumental families are genuine scale models.

67
A church or temple is bigger inside
than it is outside.

Fractal geometry teaches that length or surface area is relative to the unit of measurement. In acoustics, the size of an interior space, as expressed in the time it takes for a sound to die away, is related to the surface area reflecting the sound and not to the gross dimensions of length, breadth, and height the structure may occupy.

The principle of maximizing the internal surface area is the same for a cathedral as for the lungs of a human being, to present the greatest possible surface in contact with the air. External size and volume on their own are of little significance acoustically, which is why retail warehouses, aircraft hangars, exhibition centers, and some modern places of worship such as Coventry Cathedral in England, are dull and uninviting spaces. Ignorance of the role of surface shape and area in the propagation of sound may partly account for the increased use by architects of amplification systems in modern churches and temples, as well as for the externally bizarre shapes of some postmodern concert halls.

By contrast, the music of traditional ritual corresponds to a knowledge of acoustics acquired through centuries of trial in historic places of worship, environments where natural speech is normally unintelligible but the sound of plainchant, assisted by the reverberation of a stoneclad interior, can be heard and understood by large numbers of worshipers.

The multifaceted interior surface of a gothic cathedral not only enlarges the area reflecting sound, but also selectively enhances different parts of the frequency spectrum according to the relationship of the wavelength to the detail of the structure. The wavelength from pressure peak to peak of a 64-foot low C, for example, measures about 35 feet, and of an 8-foot middle C, about 4 feet 4 inches. Longer wavelengths are relatively immune to obstacles and surface irregularities, while medium wavelengths around middle C are broken up and reflected by sculptures and furnishings on a human scale, and the smallest audible frequencies, such as voice consonants and high harmonics, are scattered by cornices and decorative additions measuring in inches. As the sample wavelength decreases, the interior surface area interacting with it increases, in exactly the same way as in fractal mathematics the length of a coastline increases as the chosen unit of measurement diminishes in size. When music is performed in a cathedral, however, larger and smaller frequency scales are perceived simultaneously, so at one and the same time a listener is aware of a very low-resolution image of the space at the lowest frequencies, along with progressively higher degrees of resolution at the higher octaves.

68

**The greatest harmony of all
is the unison.**

The unison is remarkable. Without any knowledge of music, a child can sing in tune with its mother from an early age. The actual skill involved may amount just to singing a pitch that excites the inner ear at precisely the same location that is already being stimulated by an external voice or instrumental tone. Acoustically the unison is the most perfect experience of tonal agreement, involving two or more sounds of the same wavelength coming together and reinforcing one another in a common external air space. The experience of a sung tone being reinforced from outside, as it were, is not in itself very unusual. Long before mastering the intricacies of spoken language, a young child with normal hearing learns that a sustained tone produced spontaneously sounds louder in an enclosed space than out of doors. Since young children enjoy emitting high tones of constant pitch, it is only a matter of time before they learn to associate a strong reinforcement of the voice with particular environments like the bathroom, the playground drainpipe, the school corridor, and the cave.

What makes a unison of two or more voices or instruments appear so magical is the awareness of a concord that is consciously produced, draws strength from different sources, and creates a positive feedback that every participant can recognize and appreciate. Acoustically the unison not only returns each individual voice with interest, it also takes on a life of its own and on occasion can even appear to move stereophonically in the space between singers. Philosophically, the unison amounts to a proof of the reality of a world of other people beyond the reach of the individual. Symbolically, the unison amounts to a total merging or sublimation of an individual voice (and thus, of the persona) in another voice or group of voices (representing the beloved or the cause to which one is dedicated).

Musically the unison is the only harmony able to unite instruments of contrasting timbre. When two voices move out of unison, the audible interference effect is of a tremor of increasing rapidity. Subtle effects of such a kind, more usually associated today with electronic tone generators, were once cultivated by small groups of chamber singers as expressive effects signifying absolute (that is, divinely ordained) harmony and not merely subjective emotion.

69

**An orchestra
creates its own space.**

The symphony orchestra as we know it is a multi-person and multiple timbre instrument of great range and variety, with powers of expression extending from simple lines to acoustic patternmaking of a complexity at the limits of human comprehension. During the seventeenth century, under the influence of a new humanism, instrumental music of a secular nature emerged, dedicated to action and representing new values of individual skill and competitiveness in defiance of the older values of music for the church, which for centuries had cultivated a music of the intellect focused on the conservation and clarification of a sacred text, and the revelation in music of privileged and otherwise hidden laws of harmony and proportion in the universe.

The musical priorities of the earlier sacred era were embodied in the organ and the acoustics of great churches. The most complicated product of human ingenuity of the age, the pipe organ amounted to a laboratory for research into the tempered scale—and, by extension, into the harmonization of all vibrating systems. The resonating chambers for these sounding devices amplified and sustained interval and tone ratios so they could be more clearly evaluated.

As patronage moved out of the church and into the homes of wealthy aristocrats interested in the pursuit of science and technology, music's philosophical agenda changed from preserving the past to discovering the future. Part of that future lay in organizing people to do complex tasks; another part was involved in modeling the dynamics of temporal structures and processes becoming increasingly visible in the heavens through telescopes, and computable with newly accurate mechanical timepieces.

The new musical environments provided by the aristocracy were less reverberant and more lively acoustic spaces allowing much greater freedom in key movement and flexibility in pace. As the baroque orchestra evolved, it assumed the character of a living pipe organ in which the pipes are replaced by human performers of various instruments standing closely around the conductor at the keyboard. In the absence of the cathedral's rolling ambience, the function of reverberation chamber was gradually assumed by the string section of the orchestra, which acting in chorus generated a pleasingly diffuse quality of tone, but with the significant advantage of being able to change tonal orientation at a moment's notice.

Since over a number of centuries architects and musicians had come to agree on a correlation between the measurements of an acoustic structure and tonalities of the same wavelength, the ability to change key at will could be construed as an ability to change the virtual dimensions of an acoustic space. Baroque architecture assisted in the exploration of tonal and spatial relationships by creating concert chambers of deliberate complexity and asymmetrical design, replacing the static, parallel walls of traditional domestic architecture in favor of dynamic combinations of voids and warped surfaces resembling the shape of the violin itself.

70
Written music
has its advantages.

Most ensemble music around the world, and certainly most popular music, is performed without sheet music. It is composed, learned, and played, as they say, "by ear," meaning from memory. In the absence of a written score, such music relies on the talents and sympathies of the players. It is never exactly the same from one performance to the next.

Classical music is written down. Performing music from a printed score is like reciting a poem or reading a play. The performers have to discover a meaning in the text and then a character and dramatic purpose in the roles assigned to them. In doing so they also have to learn to be comfortable with social codes and relationships that may well be alien to them. For an audience the test of a performance is whether it has conviction. The message or moral argument is a separate issue.

Among oral cultures, pop music in particular, the question of "conviction"—whether an artist means what he or she is singing (given that he or she has composed the lyric and music, and probably put together and rehearsed the backing group and vocalists as well) makes little sense. The artwork is the person, take it or leave it. However slight its emotional and musical impact may be, the authorship of such a work, and the authority or authenticity of the collective performance, is hardly in doubt.

Since truth to oneself has become a major moral issue in consumer culture, the objection to classical—that is, scripted—music and drama as artificial, simulated, and untrue to life, and therefore unworthy of attention, has to be taken seriously. We can begin to deal with that objection by asking what classical music can do that is different from popular music, and what advantages arise from those differences that music of oral cultures cannot achieve.

For a music (or verse) to exist in written form means 1. that other people also have thoughts and experiences; 2. that these can be shared; and 3. that in sharing them we may discover what we have in common with other people. The first level of interpretation is reading; the second, interpretation; the third, assimilation. The earliest musical scores were written by hand, in large format, for choir singing in church. There was only one score to read from, like singing lessons from a blackboard at school: the lead singer stood close to the music and guided the choir by pointing with a finger or stick. When you are singing and reading at the same time, there is not much scope for expressing personality, but in church or classroom individual personality is not a priority. What is interesting is the experience of what might be called *singing outside yourself*: of coming to grips with the reality of an acoustic and social world that has a separate agenda.

Writing music down is not simply what you do when the melody has already come into your head. Notation creates the possibility of designing music on paper, of creating patterns of harmony and line that would be impossible to invent or discover spontaneously. Some of the earliest music for viols survives only in separate parts. There is no full score. The experience of four musicians reading a musical score around a table from four separate parts thus becomes an exercise in detective fiction in which four individual lifelines are superimposed and make sense in ways that cannot be foreseen but only experienced in the act of playing. That people's lives share certain themes, but not always at the same time; that people pursue independent paths that in a strange way also influence one another; and ultimately, that independent action is also compatible with social harmony, are the kinds of moral lessons to be drawn from performing written music as distinct from playing rock and roll.

A vital consideration in written music is the ability to organize events in time, and in different timescales, like an architect who visualizes an entire structure in advance and can alter, adjust, take in the larger view, and then zero in on the detail to create a richly satisfying habitation experience that can be enjoyed over and over again in different ways and from different directions. Based on the experience of composing part music to be read from opposite sides of the same table, some composers were inspired to experiment with themes turned upside down or back to front, or even combined in simultaneously time-compressed and expanded forms. As notation developed in precision, music itself became more daring and abstract in ways beyond the reach of popular song, and increasingly detached from the emotional interpretation of a private experience in verse.

71
A concerto
is about leadership.

Whenever a solo performer appears with an orchestra, to all intents and purposes the soloist is in charge. Music is old-fashioned in that way. As the orchestra evolved, in the time of Vivaldi and Corelli, a leadership structure gradually emerged that is not very different from the organization of a session orchestra for a studio recording today. The concerto can be regarded as an extension of baroque orchestra practice. In the early days the conductor directed the orchestra from the keyboard, and the principal violinist (or another soloist) led the melody. In a modern concert hall, which is somewhat larger than a private salon, the quiet tones of a harpsichord are difficult for an audience to hear, but for eighteenth-century players standing around the open casework the sharp wiry tones of the harpsichord were audible enough to keep them in tune, which was probably the main idea. (The wiry sound of the harpsichord, by a curious coincidence, also resembles the twanging peak resonance between parallel walls.)

In addition to keeping everybody in tune, the conductor would signal the entrances and exits of the various players. To the conductor's right, in good view of the orchestra and the audience, stood the leader of the orchestra, usually the principal violinist, sometimes a flutist. The leader or concertmaster's role was to act as the public face of the ensemble, and indeed to lead, that is, to inspire and coordinate, those playing the melody line. The baroque orchestra in many respects resembles a high school orchestra of today that has a few talented and experienced players along with a "rank and file" of apprentice players (the conventional use of military terminology is interesting here). Since a concerto is also music without words, its meaning is not immediately obvious to an audience. The concertmaster's role is to shape and direct the flow of a principal melody, using a combination of body gesture and improvised flourishes to keep the orchestra in line and in step, and convey some essence of the expressive purpose of the composition.

By the end of the eighteenth century the orchestra had become well enough established and trained to function as an ensemble without direct assistance from the keyboard. The role of soloist in a concerto changed from keeping order in the ranks to putting on a show. Like a magician, the soloist became a larger than life personality, a commanding presence, consummate psychologist and master of techniques and special effects designed to dazzle the audience. Like the concertmaster of earlier times, the soloist also worked to a script, but with leeway to embroider, improvise, and "create the character" of the solo part.

72
A suite of dances
is about the nature of time.

With no words to set to music, the question of motive arises. If a music is not for singing, then what is it for? Early classical composers found themselves in a secular context in which they were free to experiment without the church authorities breathing down their necks. Science and technology were rapidly advancing. Notation itself had created the possibility of defining and exploring musical space. The new spaces set aside for musical performance were neither huge nor highly reverberant, so composers no longer had to contend with reverberation times of 3, 4, or 5 seconds slowing the music down and muddying the texture. Instead, they could make music move at any speed, and thanks to the new transparent acoustic of wood and plaster rooms, were able to embrace complexity without fear.

Society in the late seventeenth and early eighteenth centuries became very focused on time management, a trend literally encapsulated in the navigational chronometer and pocket watch. During that period, music for orchestra was the only public activity clearly modeled on a conception of clock time as a measure completely separate from the time of human experience, or even the logic of causality. While a song could always be construed as a sequence of lines of poetry forming a sentence, and a dance as a sequence of moves forming a pattern, and both song and dance expressly as definitions of time on the human scale of the actions required to articulate them, instrumental music by contrast was largely mechanical in interest: it had no reason to be concerned with human affections or rhythms, as long as the separate parts were playable and perfectly synchronized. A Bach Brandenburg concerto is an experience as abstract as observing the movement inside a pocket watch, and every bit as fascinating.

The many suites of dances dating from the early classical era, composed for solo keyboard and for orchestra, are not necessarily to be taken as evidence that the aristocracy were obsessed with dancing. Though modeled on dance forms an audience would be expected to know, a dance suite is music for listening, not physical participation. The composer's interest in dance forms, in turn, is as descriptions of human experiences of time in relation to the chronometric time of music notation. A dance suite asks: Why does this music feel fast or slow, light or heavy? What is the nature of human time experience? Such questions make no sense in a cathedral environment, not because they are irreligious, but because the acoustic does not allow for them.

73
In music for keyboard,
there is neither continuity nor intonation.

The Italian word *legato* is used of a melody or phrase that flows from note to note. It shares the same root as *ligature*, a term in surgery for stitching a wound: that is, joining together or reconnecting what has been divided. It is a useful analogy, since frequency in nature is a seamless continuum from low to high, but in musical notation and for many musical instruments the pitch dimension is segmented artificially into modes or scales of distinct tones. So the term *legato* is literally an instruction to make whole and bring back to life that which has been reduced to a sequence of steady states or notes, just as images in the movies are "joined together" in conformity with the timescale of human vision, so that a sequence of stills may be restored to an appearance of living action.

Literally to join the notes of a melody to make a continuous line, as for the letters in joined-up writing, is certainly possible with certain instruments. String players employ *portamento*, sliding the fingers up and down the fingerboard, for discreet voicelike transitions in melody phrasing. Louder and more dramatic effects are possible for slide trombones, which can change the pitch of certain notes by as much as half an octave, a special effect called *glissando*. In American country and western music both voice and guitar employ a typically wavering intonation to convey an impression of raw country realism, tearful emotion, and perhaps the contributing effects of alcohol as well. Similar devices of bending the tone are also encountered in classical music for expressive effect, and to indicate a change of key.

Too much unsteadiness, however, makes music difficult to listen to, and in this respect the reality of human emotion has to be weighed against the necessary artificiality of delivering a coherent message: you cannot weep and recite poetry at the same time, and expect an audience to take on board both the grief and the poem. In the long run it is the poem that counts. We are drawn back to the basic consideration that while the real world, including human feeling, is constantly in motion, the only way of seeing order and pattern in the world is by segmenting time into moments, taking measurements for every moment, and only afterward connecting the dots. The keyboard typifies that analytical approach to reality. On a piano you can play any number of dots but you still cannot create a line or bend a note: all a pianist can do is create the illusion of line and intonation by arm gesture and body movement. Around 1900 the industry sought to improve piano-roll technology to reproduce not just the notes of the printed score but also the expression marks of a living performer. Sensing mechanisms attached to the piano keyboard registered the pressure applied to each individual key. It was found that the entire personality of a great pianist and interpreter was encoded in the simple timing and pressure modulations of a performance.

74
A movement of music
is about movement.

Time and motion study addresses the efficiency with which people perform routine actions. An interest in the nature and experience of time is to be expected among European composers of the seventeenth century who have only just acquired a standard, internationally recognized notation suitable for the task, along with desktop keyboard devices (harpsichord, spinet, virginals) for their reproduction as music. The baroque dance suite belongs to a period of intellectual inquiry into the motion of human bodies corresponding to the interest of contemporary astronomers in the motion of celestial bodies. A dance suite for harpsichord by Domenico Scarlatti can be read as a document of the characteristic tempi, rhythms, and melody inflections of a range of court and folk dance types. It is both a test of the precision of western notation, and an analysis of the features of music modeled on human movement that are associated with very specific intensities of feeling, including sensations of time. Human time as a sensation is very different from clock time, which is an artificial measure. French composers such as Lully and Couperin were particularly attracted to the problem of quantifying human movement, and along with developing the metronome (a device for measuring tempo), the art of ballet considered as an art of precise movement developed in France out of that interest. Ballet allows an audience to observe human movement objectively.

The same interest in reconciling absolute (clock) time and human experience continued in a more abstract sense in the era of the classical symphony. The sections that comprise a symphony or string quartet are called movements and only rarely by the names of dances, as in the convention of labeling the third movement a minuet and trio. Although no longer modeled directly after dance forms, the first movement, slow movement and fast final movements of classical music are no less interested in discussing the nature of time, and the paradoxical nature of human perception. In familiar works such as the Mozart *Eine kleine Nachtmusik* and the symphonies of Beethoven and Schubert we can discover the same chronometric pulsation recurring in moderate, slow, and fast movements alike.

In the twentieth century, composers struggled to create a music to accompany the fractured continuity, and abrupt changes of pace, of action movies. Because they had to work fast to meet production deadlines, many composers adopted the device of composing a score timed in seconds, to a metronome beat of 60 per minute. You might imagine that music composed to a uniform 60 beats per minute—a totally neutral timescale—would be incapable of conveying any quality of action or emotion. In practice, however, movie composers from Erich Korngold to John Williams have shown that it is indeed possible to compose music that an audience perceives as fast, slow, tense, relaxed, dramatic or dreamlike, all to the same 60 per minute pulsation of a stopwatch. In the last resort, as they discovered, an audience's sense of pace in music comes down not to how fast or slow a music is counted, but to the degrees of change: melodic, rhythmic, and dynamic, of the musical action.

75
A modern orchestra
cannot hear itself playing.

A conductor today is a lonely figure standing on a podium with his back to the audience and waving a stick. His role is silently to coordinate, by physical gesture and facial expression, an orchestra grown to a hundred or more players spread across a platform nowadays so vast in extent that it would take a sound nearly one-tenth of a second to travel from the left side to the right.

The size of a modern orchestra is partly due to an increase in instrumental resources, including a vastly extended range of exotic percussion accumulated during the nineteenth century, an era dedicated to collecting ethnic and natural artifacts from all parts of the world. But the modern orchestra is a response to an increase in size of concert halls to cater for larger public audiences, creating a need for greater numbers of players.

Bigger concert arenas and more players do not mean better performances. They lead to a loss of clarity and definition, and compensating tendencies toward brighter contrasts and more theatrical performance styles. In addition to the audience experiencing a loss of acoustic definition through excessive numbers, the members of a modern symphony orchestra find themselves less able to hear themselves play, compared to a chamber group of half a dozen players who know one another well, sit facing one another, and maintain good eye and ear contact to create a music of exact precision of tone and timing. Whether recording in the studio or performing in the concert-hall, a modern symphony orchestra is so large an ensemble that the players cannot afford to rely on their hearing alone for entrance cues or coordination. From his position in the center the conductor provides visual cues that, traveling at the speed of light, are instantly recognizable to everybody.

76
Following an opera
is like reading a novel;
following a symphony,
like navigating in traffic.

Opera is drama set to music. Drama has a story. Audiences like a story being enacted onstage because it makes the music tolerable and easy to follow. Many think that the function of music is to help define characters and plot situations. After all, that is its role in musicals and movies. The test of music composed to support drama, or comedy, or animated film, is whether it stands on its own as a collection of songs or as a symphonic suite, without visual images in support. Music for dance makes perfect sense in a concert setting, as does music for ballet, which is dancing with a storyline. The underlying role of dance music is to tell the dancers what to do, so the entire programme of movements and characters is reflected in the forms, energy levels, and emotional states of the musical score. In a movie or a play, however, the music's role is usually reserved for episodes of special importance. Unlike a classical play or ballet, the action of a movie tends to be fragmented and discontinuous, with frequent changes of spatial and temporal perspective. The music does not control the action, but enhances it in certain locations.

Movie music also has to share the sound track with dialogue and sound effects, and is subject to the final decision of the producer, to be faded in, up, down, or out as the movie takes shape. The conditions of movie making do not allow the composer to have full control over the action, the timing, or even the dynamic levels of a performance. With music in control of the drama, events tend to move at a different pace. In opera, with some exceptions, the action tends to be slower than normal, to allow the full significance of the drama to take effect musically.

In ballet or Broadway musical, action is expressed symbolically in dance, with and without song. The physical action of dancing gives the drama a sense of continuity and a pace that relates to realistic behavior and timing. Compared to stage drama or ballet, a movie is neither continuous nor realistic in action. Rather it offers a rapid succession of situations and momentary events, geared to the attention span of the viewer, and not to the exacting pace of real life. With the exception of music for animated film (which by definition is unrealistic), whenever movie music has tried to keep pace with movie action, it has not been successful.

That classical music follows its own rules of plot and character development in a nonvisual arena is difficult for many nonmusicians to understand, because the movies have conditioned audiences to a music that plays a decorative and not a controlling role. In addition, the visual action accompanying a concert has little to tell an audience about what the music is saying.

77
Start together,
finish together.

To ask what the storyline of a symphony is, is to expect that a symphony has a narrative to deliver, like a novel or movie. An opera or a ballet clearly has a plot of some kind, though there is more talk than genuine action in an opera, and only action of a stylized kind in ballet. The idea of an entertainment without a plot may seem pointless. Already values begin to kick in. But how do you "know" there is a plot in a novel or a movie? You can only answer that if you have already read the book or seen the movie. The point of having a plot is as a reason for reading the book or watching the movie in the first place. In the ideal situation, the first encounter, a reader has no idea what the plot is. The reason for sticking with it is to discover what the story actually is. If you already know the story, through having seen the movie or read the book, then watching or reading it again is for another reason, perhaps to do with observing the skills and techniques of writing, acting, or plot development. The more familar a story line becomes, the more a reader can be expected to perceive it as a formula designed to hold the attention, and less as an authentic experience. Diaries and documentary films are recordings of reality, and we know from these sources that the message of real life is not a continuous narrative at all, rather an experience of moments of crisis separated by long periods of tedium.

If there is a message in fictional narrative, it is surely one of having a goal and finally achieving it. In other spheres of activity that goal is called winning, a curious feature of sports activities in which the participants start in line in an orderly fashion at a precise moment in time, only to finish in rank disorder a moment later.

The essential features of an abstract musical narrative are of interest because music is by definition a process in motion. In a novel or movie, and even in real life, one is always looking for an incentive to do something, set a goal, make a decision, turn a page. Music on the other hand is already a temporal process: it is already about managing change. As the advertising man said, the object is not to catch your reader's attention, but to hold onto the attention you already have. In music likewise, the composer's and performer's task is not to generate movement, but to articulate and direct (or indeed, "conduct") a flow inherent in the dynamic of sound generation and renewal.

78
A standing soloist is a team leader;
a seated soloist is a team manager.

Up to the time of Weber and Beethoven in the early nineteenth century, an orchestra used to play standing up. Either they had not learned how to perform sitting down, or it was considered impolite for musicians as servants to sit down in the presence of their patrons and superiors. There were exceptions: the cellist, the organist, the keyboard player. Standing up has its advantages, allowing greater freedom of upper body movement, better breath control for wind players, and improved visibility.

A solo singer invariably stands to sing, as does a massed choir. For any vocalist, standing up is essential if you want to make a good noise. Even at a football game the team supporters will stand up to sing or chant in celebration of a goal well scored. Nowadays standing up to play in a symphony orchestra concert is a duty reserved for those who need to be visible, like the conductor or the soloist, or those who could not otherwise manage their instrument, like players of the xylophone, hand cymbals, or tubular bells.

That the hand actions of a conductor may sometimes resemble those of a Barcelona traffic officer on point duty during the rush hour, tells us something about the inherent dynamism of traffic and music, and the responsibility of those in control of the flow to keep things moving freely, not because the movement in itself is beautiful or meaningful, but because a good circulation is essential for a healthy body. Music is not a race: though having said that, it would be interesting to imagine what a race in music would sound like, and how it might be organized.

There are two kinds of soloist in a concerto: those who stand up (for example, the violin, flute, or trumpet) and those who sit down (cello, piano, or organ). Both are figures of leadership, but a leadership of different kinds. Those standing up are like team captains, high-ranking players and visible role models who are part of the team and direct the action from positions in the field. Like the baroque concert-master, the standing soloist in a concerto inspires the members of an orchestra to a sense of unity of purpose, to raise their game to a higher level, and to perform at their best in the heat of the moment. A seated soloist, by contrast, relates to the style of leadership of the baroque conductor at the keyboard, whose role, supported by cello and bass to either side, is essentially strategic. The player of a melody instrument is focused on the melody, which is about carrying the movement forward and keeping the players together in moment to moment synchronization. The player of a keyboard instrument or a bass line, on the other hand, is much more focused on the formal process from a management perspective, in the longer term.

79
A cadenza
is about making it up.

The eighteenth-century cadenza originated as the ultimate test, in a concerto, of a solo player's nerve, skill, and ingenuity: a real moment of truth. A cadenza (the Italian term implying closure and also a personally distinctive manner or style of delivery) often occurs toward the end of a first movement. The orchestra comes to a halt at a point where the musical argument seems undecided where to go or what to do. The conductor puts down his baton and looks at the soloist as if to say, it is up to you, action superhero, to bridge the gap between the point we are now at, and a successful conclusion. Ideally, to improvise. This is a staged crisis in the familiar tradition of the medieval knight errant, the lone cowboy, or the costumed crusader, a device to reinforce the message of the solo artist as a figure of extraordinary mental and physical powers who can be relied upon to defend the community against anarchy and natural calamity. The soloist in a cadenza acts entirely alone. It is a strangely critical image of leadership, when the troops have come to the realization that they can go no further. A leadership, furthermore, very much in the image of the visionary— grand duke, scientist, artist, philosopher, or political leader—whose role is to demonstrate, by a combination of will, physical prowess, and devotion to the public good, how threats to civic order are to be dealt with. For the aristocratic audience of Haydn's day there was a reassuring subtext to the conventional image of a leadership representing an elite, and a general public (the orchestra) that without intelligent direction is bound to descend into inaction and silence. It is also truly weird to reflect that the cadenza, in which those leadership qualities are supposedly demonstrated, is itself a show of anarchy in all but name.

There are compensations. The music up to the moment of the cadenza has all been scripted. By implication, the performance is a replay of a work of musical fiction that already exists in printed form: it is therefore old news. For a cadenza suddenly to break into the routine of a scripted event, is like breaking news interrupting a television drama at a crucial stage. In its original definition, the cadenza is made up on the spot. It is not part of history, rather a glimpse of actuality defined by a particular location and individual performance: a unique token of the special chemistry that exists at that moment alone between a soloist, a composer, and an orchestra—and, to be fair, with an audience as well. Among oral cultures, that sense of immediacy and creative excitement is everything that music is about; for western middle-class audiences, however, the conventional image of inspired (improvised) leadership is a matter for excitement mixed with unease. Today, sadly, the cadenza is part of the script along with the rest of the concerto, and all we are left with is the appearance of brilliant improvisation, of making it up as you go. Audiences of the twenty-first century are more cynical about superheroes. There are, nevertheless, stunning examples of scripted cadenzas, for example in the violin concertos of Schoenberg and Berg.

After the 1939–1945 war, a conflict that in many ways brought awesome closure to a century and a half of nationalistic militarism, a younger generation of avant-garde composers renounced the traditional paradigm of leadership in favour of a music of utopian anarchy in which every member of the orchestra would be expected to contribute creatively to the shape and direction of every piece. In many ways their ideal musical form was a cadenza in which everybody took part. That idea shook the classical music profession (conductors, concertmasters, educators, music teachers) to its very foundations. While such a radical approach is only gradually beginning to win acceptance in the concert arena of western music, it has served in the meantime to awaken public interest in the music of nonwestern traditions where improvising plays a major role. In modern theater, film, and dance, improvisation has become an essential part of training and preparation for a solo artist. At the present time, computer games are the most highly developed participatory arts in the form envisaged by composers of the 1950s, and it is a matter of some significance that so many games of this kind are predicated on themes of combat and destruction.

80
Notation simplifies
for the sake of complexity.

Formality has its uses. In musicals there are special moments when the leading actors stop talking and begin to sing. When that happens, the illusion of realism is set to one side and idealism and art take over. The song captures the emotion of the drama and expresses it in an elevated mode that is both easier to grasp than casual conversation, and also connects the emotion, through its standard terms of reference (song structure, key, instrumentation, etc.) with an entire class of such songs already stored in a listener's memory to be called upon to reinforce a private interpretation of the situation presented onstage.

The formalized intonation of a song is not altogether unnatural. In casual conversation the voice is an extremely volatile instrument, and the uncertainties of pitch and timing work in normal situations where the participants are closely related, in spatial as well as emotional terms. As soon as one begins consciously to deal with a larger, more anonymous, and more distant audience, a more formal style of speaking has to be adopted; that change to a more vibrant, more consciously articulated and pitched style of speaking sends out a signal that the message is something that everybody should hear. There is a musical cadence to declarations of a public nature, when a voice is heard to say "Hey, you! Yeah, you!" or "Dearly beloved, we are gathered here . . ." or "The curfew tolls the knell of parting day . . ." or "Come on down!" or "Hip, hip, hooray!"—more like a singing voice than a talking voice. In fact, a listener can recognize the melody and rhythm of such phrases even if the words are unclear, which makes a stylized delivery useful, indeed essential, for communicating in a crowded and noisy environment. A song simply takes the natural formality of public speech and sets it to music, which allows the message to be reinforced by a supporting group of musicians playing in the same key and with the same tempo and rhythm.

The notation of written music builds on that natural tendency not just to simplify the pitch levels and transitions of heightened speech, but also to steady the pace and rhythm of a vocal message. Once specific pitch and time values have been allocated to a song, other players can be brought in to accompany the singer with a reasonable certainty that the more complex result will still make musical sense.

81
Plainchant notation recognizes
sequence, not time.

Timing is the most obvious and profound distinction between religious ritual and secular music. A regular pulsation is characteristic of routine and repetitive actions, such as walking, digging, hammering a nail, and riding a bicycle. Cyclic actions represent the most efficient use of energy in the completion of larger tasks, and breaking down a larger task into smaller, repetitive tasks is an element of good design. Cyclic processes underlie much of what we know of the universe and of human life: the months, the tides, the seasons, birth and death. In creating musical models of steady rhythm and a constant, repetitive beat we are acknowledging not only the significance of regularity in human affairs, but a connection between the cycles of human life and the mysterious cycles of nature and the universe. The ritual waltzes of Vienna are images of the orbital motions of the stars and planets as well as representing the endless movement of the river Danube. Paradoxically, cyclical procedures tend by their very nature to turn into habitual actions or routines to be performed without thinking. It follows that if there is a message to be delivered that requires the highest degree of listener attention, a formulaic approach can often be counterproductive. Strong rhythms and occasional rhymes are found in Shakespearean drama and also in hip-hop. Rhythm and rhyme are cyclical devices that attract and hold the listener's attention, but rhythm and rhyme also carry the risk of distracting attention from what words are actually saying, or what they may be intended to mean. The deliberate avoidance of a beat in religious chant, recitative, and in many modern plays and poems, is done with the intention of concentrating the mind of the listener on the full meaning of what is being said *as it actually unfolds*. It says, in effect, listen, do not guess, do not anticipate, do not prejudge.

Just like a cadenza, or an unmeasured prelude by Louis Couperin through which a performer accommodates the sound of a harpsichord to an alien acoustic, a music with no rhythm builds on the assumption that the only true reality is experienced in the unexpected or the unpredictable. Aleatoric and chance music in the late twentieth century also tap into that tradition.

82
Standard notation
converts time into space.

In the notation of plainchant, all the notes look much the same. They are square or diamond-shaped notes with thin vertical stems, produced by simple strokes of a square-cut quill pen, and all notes of whatever shape are of essentially the same value, as locations on a graph. There is not much difference between reading plainchant and reading a money market report. The movement of stocks and shares is depicted as a line on a graph in which a reader may discern a trend. The vocal line of a plainchant is depicted as data points, sometimes grouped into formulae, that the act of singing converts into a line of melody with its own inherent fluctuations of emphasis.

As long as the notes of plainchant are sung in the correct sequence and to the correct syllables of a text, the notation has done its work. The actual timing of a chant from syllable to syllable is determined by the number of notes assigned to each, which can vary with the significance of the syllable or word, and the choice of a speed of delivery appropriate to the prevailing acoustic and the requirement of clarity.

With the introduction of time controls into music notation, responsibility for the timing of a musical message is shifted from weighing the syllable to choosing and counting the beat. A new style of reading is required, one that because of the new hierarchical organization of time—into beats, measures, phrases, sentences, sections, up to complete movements—is capable of being interpreted on a number of different levels at once, in the same way as the movement of a share price can be evaluated simultaneously in the shorter and longer term. As a temporal event, an interpretation of a classical movement replaces the simple moment to moment progression of plainchant with the sense of a continuously updated temporal perspective in which a balance has to be struck between present and future trends.

83
The evolution of western music
is a history of dealing with the unpredictable.

All of us are locked into a present existence as well as a present locality and identity. At the same time, we are surrounded by change: cyclical change, as night follows day; growth, which is directed; and natural catastrophe. How we live can be read in the strategies individuals and societies develop to maintain self-control and at the same time manage change. A survival strategy defends the status quo and is resistant to change; a progressivist strategy cultivates change; a supremacist strategy imposes change. Some change is inevitable and we learn to live with it: for instance the tides, which are predictable, and the weather, which is not so predictable. Some change is positive, and we are able to profit from it. Other change is unwelcome, and we have to deal with it. A key element in managing change is the recollection of previous events, the risks they pose, how they evolve, and the best way of responding to them. Collective memory, expressed and handed down in the form of myth and ritual, is a powerful therapy as well as a teaching aid for the new generation. As an element of ritual, music has the remarkable property of leading the listener through time as if through a maze, in one continuous flow, a palpable thread connecting the immediate past through to the immediate future, at the very same time as the ritual itself is looking back to a more distant past and preparing ahead for an uncertain future.

Since music is manifest change, it is possible to read a strategy for managing change into the way it is organized. Ritual actions, drama, and epic and lyric poetry employ stylized forms, rhythms, and modes of utterance to aid the preservation of experience in oral memory and ensure the accurate recovery of ancient wisdom. Music assists in the preservation of forms and also in the recovery of meaning, in the first instance through instruments that pass from generation to generation as tangible records of cultural attitudes and preferences: to vocal movement in pitch, to the use of sustained or unsustained tone, for location indoors or out of doors, size of audience, and style of performance. The same richness of cultural association a collector values in a Stradivarius violin or a classic guitar, is also discoverable in the sound and substance of an ancient gong or whistle. The invention of a reliable visual notation introduced the radical possibility of creating a music that was no longer tied to preserving the past, but open to speculation about how past, present, and future might be connected.

84
Baroque music
is dedicated to mechanical time.

Notation freed instrumental music from its traditional obligations of enhancing and preserving a vocal line, and after 1600 western classical composers entered an era in which traditional vocal forms were deconstructed and reconfigured in denser and more abstract orders in which time is treated as a spatial dimension. The keyboard Preludes and Fugues of J. S. Bach are examples of open and closed expository forms that articulate time but do not always convey a human dimension of temporal experience or quality of movement. For Bach, the inflexible beat, representing the tick of the clock, is all the motivation he needs. The excitement of a mechanical movement is that, once started, it continues on its own momentum at the same pace, without deviating, until it can go no more. Seen on a larger human scale, the tragedy of a work such as the *St. Matthew Passion* is embodied in the music's sense of total and absolute inevitability, an unstoppable flow colored at times by searing dissonances on the downbeat. Whether the movement is outwardly fast or slow, the drama consists in the fatalism or conscious resignation of a living subject to the inevitable march of time.

In the operas of Wagner that sense of tragic inevitability is associated with a narrative development depicting the ebb and flow of human experience seemingly in real time. To audiences of the early twentieth century, Debussy and Stravinsky introduced the fractured continuity of the movies, exploiting tensions between chronometric time, progressing in exact increments; montage, which rearranges the normal flow of events in an arbitrary order representing time as space; and the action content of individual scenes, which maintain the fiction of real-life and real-time causality.

85

**Classical music
is about dealing with the inevitable.**

Dance is of interest to baroque composers as a temporal art of both ritual and emotional implications. Since dance is a human activity, it is adapted to human limitations and traditions, so its value as insight into chronometric time, time in the abstract, is necessarily limited. As the chronometer isolates time from human experience, so the experimental procedure set in place for the sciences by King Charles's Royal Society sought to eliminate human variables from the observation and description of natural change in chemical, biological, and other reactions. In this context, classical first-movement form, the three-part procedure of exposition, development, and recapitulation typical of the symphony, sonata, concerto, string quartet, etc., can be construed as an expression of scientific experimental procedure in musical terms, whereby first and second subjects are exposed, tested, and combined in various ways in the hope of obtaining a reaction that may lead to a better understanding of the nature of each. The classical mind neither denied nor sought to avoid change in nature, but through knowledge to control it.

86
The eighteenth century elite discovered stress, the nineteenth century bourgeoisie celebrated it.

Stress is implicit in the rise and fall of a voice, especially when the voice is accompanied by an instrument in which the strings are graded by tension. An increase in stress is associated with improved musicality of tone. A normal speaking voice is relatively relaxed, but a voice making a statement before an assembly, or insisting on a particular line of argument, is steadier and more focused in pitch; to this extent music can be regarded as an art of managed stress. The lyre is an instrument of multiple strings of the same length that in order to sound a scale of pitches are tuned to increasing degrees of tension. So to play up and down the scale on such an instrument is to go up and down a scale of degrees of stress. The greater the tension applied to a string, the sharper and cleaner the sound, employing the word "sharp" in the sense of a sharp note in a scale. When a string is relaxed to change the mode, it will sound "flat," with a duller, less edgy tone, as well as being lower in pitch.

The voice of a person driven to an emotional extreme becomes more tense and more shrill in tone. The art of controlling the emotions when under extreme pressure is identified in music with a performer's control of intonation at extremes of range. Stress is not just about "raising the voice" in a literal sense, but about exaggeration in every "raising the voice" in a literal sense, but about exaggeration in every dimension: pitch, loudness, speed, and rhythm. That Apollo, the god of war, was also the god of music, tells us that for the Greeks power and authority were invested in the tension of the bowstring as in the voice.

European composers in the late eighteenth-century era of "storm and stress" found themselves having to reconcile the dispassionate classical ideals of an aristocratic elite with the growing unrest of an increasingly well-organized and professional proletariat. The later symphonies of Haydn and Mozart display unmistakable signs of tension within the ranks, a particular irony since the musicians of a private orchestra were themselves leading representatives of a newly politicized professional class. So much so, that the intricate and powerful music they were paid to perform could be interpreted not only as a demonstration of an orchestra's skill in executing complex tasks, but also as timely warning of the collective wrath to come.

The romantic celebration of heroic leadership is in part a legacy of the overthrow of classicism, and a tribute to the stereotype hero as a charismatic individual driven by passion rather than reason, very much in the mold of an opera star or concerto soloist (of the concertmaster variety). From the nineteenth into the twentieth-century world of comic strip and movie fiction, the romantic image of the hero as stress master continued to prevail, despite a revival of classical values of education and calm intelligence in the studiously uncharismatic heroes of detective fiction from Dupin via Holmes to Poirot and beyond. That romanticism coincided with a period of intense scientific interest in human drives and motivations is to be expected. The same interest was to lead to the invention of the X-ray and sound recording, and the discoveries of Freud.

87
One length,
many lengths.

Replacing a set of panpipes by one pipe with many holes makes a lot of sense. One pipe is easier to manage, its tone quality is consistent, there is better continuity between notes taken with the same breath, and most of all you can let your fingers do the moving rather than having to move your face from pipe to pipe. When the fingers are in charge, speed and pattern-making take on a new dimension; and when the mouth and lips are focused on one place, more effort can be directed to tone control. The external metalwork of a modern flute, oboe, or clarinet, consisting of finger extensions, levers, and caps, was introduced to cover finger holes relocated out of normal reach by manufacturers for the sake of more reliable pitch and consistent tone. The caps on a modern wind instrument add a distinctive soft click to the tone quality.

88
One length,
many strings.

There is no fingerboard on a lyre or harp. To change the note, you change the string. If there are only a few strings to choose from, a musician's freedoms of expression are limited. If all the instrument is intended to do is cue a singing voice, a limited range of notes may not be a problem. Since a singing voice is sustained by vowels, when a voice sings in unison with an instrument of uniform timbre, it is not only amplified, but differences in vowel quality also become apparent as variations in timbre: *ee, ah, ow, oh, oo, er*, etc. The musical potential of vowel resonances is celebrated in folk traditions of jaw harp and mouth music, and preclassical poetry that is rich in alliteration and assonance.

In some instruments strings are doubled for added loudness, for example, the lute, mandolin, and twelve-string guitar. The fewer the strings, however, the less there is to go wrong, and greater control over uniformity of tone. Tone control is one reason why the strings of a guitar or violin are organized in a narrow band down the center of the instrument, rather than set wider apart.

Between the harp principle of many notes and one sounding length for each, and the flute principle of a single mechanism containing length by moving the fingers up and down a fingerboard makes an excellent compromise, since it is still possible with such an arrangement to play chords as well as single notes.

89
One tension,
many lengths.

As we have seen, the design advantages of a harp over a lyre are structural as well as procedural. An instrument of many strings of the same tension but varying in length is not subject to uneven distribution of stress across the frame, allowing the frame to be of lighter construction. On the other hand, relative equality of tension across the range means that a change of pitch is unaccompanied by a change of tone, so music for harp (harpsichord, cymbalom) is relatively impervious to stress (and thus more suitable for heavenly angels).

It was to allow for the expression of modulated emotion after the manner of the violin that the Italian Cristofori introduced the touch-sensitive, hammer-action keyboard in the early eighteenth century. The new *fortepiano* (meaning "loud/soft") introduced a new aesthetic of dynamic gesture replacing the old impersonality of tone. Through the classical era to the age of Beethoven and Schubert, the fortepiano combined the tonal uniformity of same-gauge strings, a legacy of the harpsichord, with the dynamic expression of a keyboard action responsive to finger pressure.

During the nineteenth century, partly in response to the increased size and capacity of concert halls, and partly in response to audience taste, piano manufacturers introduced the altogether heavier and more resonant *pianoforte*, an instrument designed for consistency of power across the pitch range, rather than consistency of timbre. The effect of this change of focus from tone to dynamics can clearly be heard in performances on modern instruments of items from the classical and early romantic repertoire, including many well-known pieces by Mozart, Chopin, and Beethoven ("Für Elise" for example, or the third movement of the "Moonlight" sonata).

90
Stand, process, walk,
dance, skate, tumble.

The history of aviation from kites and balloons in the time of Mozart to stealth aircraft in the Stockhausen age is a little like human progress in learning to walk. The first stage is getting up and staying up; the second is learning how to move from place to place without falling. In the third stage, speed, and in the fourth, endurance become priorities. For the specialist in movement, the stage after that is becoming an athlete, an army recruit, or a fashion model. For others, the next stage is getting drunk. Part of the attraction of intoxication has to be in the sense of loss of mobility, of revisiting the experience of learning how to stand and how to walk without falling over or losing consciousness. That controlled instability can actually improve mobility was the surprising message of the design of the new joint European multi-task combat jet aircraft.

In poetry and music alike, an artist has choices in the way movement is controlled. Interpreting poetry in motion is called *scansion*, and the unit is a *foot*, so in effect a poet's choice of rhythm is intended to convey a definite impression of placing one foot after another, or staggering, or galloping—or even of standing still. Since human beings move about on two feet, there is a sense of greater stability in rhythms of two and four, and of greater dynamism in a triple rhythm. To Shakespeare's audiences the unequal five-step rhythm of iambic pentameter represented a radical new dynamic of unstable movement that also proved to be an ideal vehicle for naturalistic speech. In the later prose and poetry of Milton, the dynamics of rhythm combine with those of logic and grammar to generate sustained and directed thoughts of exceptional duration. An analogous experience of directed instability can be found in the dynamic equations of rhythm, theme, and key transition in the music of J. S. Bach. (Handel's "Hallelujah Chorus" from *The Messiah*, by contrast, emphasizes stability: the setting of a text reduced to a statement that does not go anywhere, expressed in harmony and rhythm that emphasize the dynamics of standing still, presenting arms, or knocking in fence posts.)

91
The end is silence:
so what?

A lot of classical music ends with a bang of some kind, as if to say, wake up, we've arrived. Like the beginning of a work, the ending marks a point of transition from sound to silence, or at least, from the experience of sound structures of unusual complexity and definition, to a mundane world of noise. Whatever message the content may appear to deliver, the musical experience itself is of an order in the phenomenal world arising out of a supernatural clarity of perception. Silence has rather bleak connotations of absence of people, loss of motivation, and interruption of communication. In romantic opera, silence is often a metaphor for death, implying in turn that life consists in singing at the top of one's voice, which is really rather silly. In reality, sounds do not last indefinitely. Noises, speech, and music come and go. The end of a symphony is simply the point at which the activity stops. Stopping is good. It allows the listener (who has been listening all this time in silence, but is very much alive) time to reflect.

Silence can also happen by accident. A power surge: the lights go out, the hi-fi goes dead. Either the event ends of its own accord, or is brought to an abrupt halt by circumstance or choice. The argument for letting the music take its course is that only after considering all of the information presented is it possible to decide precisely what message it intends to deliver. But in either case, the fact of a work of music ending in silence does not mean that it is finished, since even an interrupted experience continues to resonate in the memory. The music is over. It will return. Let the conversation begin.

92
The universe
in the sound of a bell.

In many old cities of greater Europe the community identifies itself with the sound of a bell. Even the name of the old city may sound like a bell, combining a clash with a resonant hum: *London, Lyons, Ulm, Wien, Rome.* A good town bell is large, expensive to make, built to last, and has a powerful voice. Musically speaking, a bell is a fascinating instrument of complex tone containing many partials. A deep-dish solid bronze resonator of circular section and conical shape, a bell is set in vibration by a heavy clapper impacting at a single point. The resulting pressure wave travels in both directions around the perimeter, at the same time as the bell swings back and forth on an axis perpendicular to the rim. Carefully-engineered variations in the thickness of the metal create a ringing complex of inharmonic partials—one tone containing many resonances that are not precisely in tune with each other. The metallurgical reason for making a bell ring at harmonically unrelated frequencies might well be to avoid undue stresses building up and cracking the instrument like a wineglass; however, the practical consequences of out-of-tune partials are that they bring greatly improved sustain and a voice-like quality to the timbre, both enhanced by the effects of swing movement. In Mozart's and Beethoven's time, the multiple strings of a fortepiano note were tuned to exactly the same pitch, producing a tone quality of strong attack but rapid decay. Today, by contrast, the strings of a pianoforte are deliberately tuned slightly out of unison, to give a more bell-like tone that lasts longer and contains attractive shifting inner resonances.

Philosophically speaking, the complex timbre of a great bell can be understood as an acoustic model of the known universe—in effect, the "music of the spheres." Its sound allows a listener to reflect on the viability of a dynamic structure in motion, of which the constituent partials are not in simple ratios or in phase.

93
First, second, third harmonic:
parent, child, ghost.

Western religion and many other varieties of spirituality insist on the reality of the invisible, the operation of unseen forces in human life, and the continuing existence of the spirit after death. Among visual cultures such precepts are difficult to grasp. That they are rooted in oral culture suggests that in common with mythology and legend, certain kinds of religious symbolism may conceal a knowledge of acoustics that may be incomprehensible either because it deals with the natural behavior of vibrating systems that are normally invisible, or because it draws on analogies with the behavior of vibrating systems to account for the relationship of humanity with the rest of the natural world.

Music is full of such mysteries. That the first harmonic of an open string, at the midpoint of the string, is a tone higher in pitch but in perfect accord with a lower fundamental that is the tone of the entire string, is a fact of acoustic life requiring an ingenious explanation. When you have two "voices" of which the generator is the lower voice and the greater length, and the dependent voice higher in pitch and shorter in length, then the image of father and son is an appropriate metaphor. To go beyond that point and explain the third harmonic, however, is something else, since the third harmonic is not the same note, but an octave and fifth higher. To explain the third, fifth, and higher harmonics one has to resort to the difficult concept of a moving spirit independent of the generating pitch.

94
In a choir, nobody wins.

A choir or a chorus is a group. The group stands for society at large. The role of the chorus in Greek drama is to comment on the actions of the leading characters, who briefly enjoy or endure the consequences of rising to positions of influence. The chorus in Bach's *St. Matthew Passion* represents the mixed reactions of the townspeople witnessing the events of the drama, while the chorales sung by the congregation during the oratorio are a genial addition providing moments of contact with the past, and meditation on the events of the drama, for communities in the present. In the role of society, a chorus provides a sounding board for the actions of charismatic, powerful, or otherwise independent individuals, like the figure of Coriolanus depicted in Beethoven's "Coriolan" overture, a character only loosely based on

Shakespeare's play. Coriolanus was a general who saved his community from defeat but was unable to get along with other people, even his own family. A solitary figure himself, Beethoven unpicks the contemporary fiction of the romantic hero to reveal a rancorous and driven obsessive whose will to win has nothing to do with destiny, and everything to do with planning, patience, meticulous attention to detail, and complete dedication—along with the psychological insight that these very same qualities can make a human being impossible to live with.

The soloist can make it up, and the chorus has a script. The hero, by the same token, has free will, offset by the chorus, representing consensus, public opinion, and also tradition. The drama of individual initiative encountering and eventually prevailing over collective opposition is universal. The message of the chorus is that nobody wins, but everybody is changed.

95
A choir, an orchestra,
an acoustic.

That a choir or an orchestra is a group of people in the literal sense, acting as a team in a practical sense, and apt to assume the role of human society in a dramatic sense, does not by any means exhaust the possibilities of meaning inherent in the opposition of solo and multiple unison voices or players. There is an acoustic dimension. A solo voice, *because* it is only one voice, brings clarity, virtuosity, and individuality to the interpretation of a dramatic or musical text; a chorus, on the other hand, signifies diffusion, unanimity (collective agreement), and stability. A solo voice represents the possible, but the chorus (or so the analogy reads) represents the truth—or in science, the endorsement of one's peers. The image of a chorus is of society as a resonator, a sounding board, a closed unit, like the hollow box that amplifies the thin, pure sound of a guitar or violin string.

Acoustically speaking, a reverberation defines a space as a crowd reaction defines a society. A reverberation amplifies a signal but does not initiate a signal; it indicates the extent of immediate influence of a message, but at the same times returns that message in a blurred and confused state. That mixed metaphor of power, endorsement, and also relative incoherence carries its own message about society and its response to individual initiative.

96
A flute,
an irrigation system.

Innovations in flute design are associated historically with discoveries in fluid dynamics. The hydraulic pump invented by the Roman Ctesibius, in all likelihood with air conditioning applications in mind, became the inspiration for the pipe organ; a mechanical flute invented by the Arabic engineer Abu Al-Jazari in the tenth century was created to address an analogous problem of loss of water pressure over distance in irrigation systems; while development of the "beak" end-piece of the recorder in Elizabethan times, to divide the flow of air into the pipe for the sake of a steadier tone, directly influenced the design of fireplace chimneys of improved updraft, and indirectly, much later, the intake design of the jet engine.

97
A violin, a piano,
a suspension bridge.

Managing stress is not just a musical metaphor. In order to convey and control the stress levels of human emotion in song, it was necessary to find ways of illustrating and managing stress in a musical instrument. As we know, the Greek lyre consists of a set of strings of equal length across a frame connected to a sound box. The earliest lyres may have been improvised from the dried-out horns and skull of a deer or antelope, the horns providing a frame and the hollow skull a resonator. A natural framework of this kind is solid and strong enough to handle the unequal strains of strings of varying tensions, and the result is an instrument of considerable iconic significance, but of disproportionate size and weight for the sound it produces.

The ideal string instrument is light, strong, and of full tone. To design an instrument of the power and warmth of (say) a Spanish acoustic guitar is not a trivial task. Since the strings of a guitar are relatively straight and the bridge a relatively low projection, the front plate of the instrument takes most of the strain of the six strings pulling against it, and trying to bend it into an arch. Even though the wood grain follows the line of the strings, a flat guitar front plate will inevitably succumb to the constant tension of the strings. The violin-makers of Cremona were not only great artists but very resourceful engineers in wood. Among their many innovations in the management of string tension, the design of the bridge and sound box are of particular interest. A violin bridge is a curiously shaped and perforated wedge of hardwood, much higher than a guitar bridge, over which the strings are stretched. The effect of a higher bridge is to bend the strings in an arch. The violin-maker's second innovation lay in developing a lens-shaped sound box, convex both front and back. By analogy with the optical lenses of the new telescope and microscope, the violin body was designed to modulate and magnify the tone in ways unavailable to the plainer and flatter box design of the earlier viol. Violin sound is designed to be more vibrant, more radiant—indeed, more unstable, —and most of all to be a more suitable medium of individual expression. But the instrument is also extremely strong for its weight and power. Though a violin bridge may succumb to stress with time, many instruments of great age remain in active use, having survived over centuries with their tone intact, and even enhanced.

During the nineteenth century the tuning of orchestral instruments was lifted by up to three semitones (a 20 percent increase in pitch, or 400 percent increase in tension) to add penetration and brilliance of tone. That huge added stress brought structural problems. It led to the fingerboard of the violin being tilted back in relation to the front plate, instead of lying parallel to it, as in Haydn's day. The lessons learned from the management of string tension and disposal of excess vibratory energy, not only in the violin family but also in pianoforte design, contributed to the knowledge base from which the great suspension bridges of the late nineteenth and twentieth centuries were constructed.

98
A lute, a biwa,
a satellite dish.

A lute, a mandolin, an Arab lute or *oud*, or a Japanese biwa are plucked string instruments sharing an outward resemblance to a spoon or ladle. A spoon or ladle is more than just an implement to carry liquid from the plate to the mouth; for a chef or professional taster of tea, the bowl should not only contain a fluid but also reflect its color to the eye and concentrate its flavor to the nose. The acoustical purpose of a spoon-shaped sound box is similar in kind: to bring the sound of the strings to a focus and radiate it upward through the circular aperture in the flat upper surface. Unlike the lens-shaped violin family, the concave interior of a lute is designed with a single listener in mind. It is not wholly irrelevant to recall that the convex lens telescope of Galileo's era was developed with magnification in mind at the same time as the lens-shaped violin, eventually to be superseded by a reflecting instrument in which the priority shifts to the collection of light, and bringing it to a focus for a single observer, by means of a concave reflector.

99
A valve trumpet,
a water closet.

However improbable it may appear, the brass band of the industrial age came into existence as a byproduct of advances in public sanitation. The valve technology introduced to instruments of the bugle, trumpet, and horn families in the nineteenth century brought a new versatility of tone control to historic instruments of traditionally fixed tuning. It did so by enabling the flow of air to be instantly and easily diverted to auxiliary coils that in effect lengthen the tube and thus alter the

The valve technology introduced to instruments of the bugle, trumpet, and horn families in the nineteenth century brought a new versatility of tone control to historic instruments of traditionally fixed tuning. It did so by enabling the flow of air to be instantly and easily diverted to auxiliary coils that in effect lengthen the tube and thus alter the instrument's fundamental pitch. Such innovations in airflow control coincided with advances in civil engineering undertaken to ensure the efficient distribution of fresh water in urban communities, and separate disposal of waste water, to ensure the elimination of disease and maintenance of public health.

The same valve technology led to the manufacture of a new and populous class of brass wind instruments of the bugle family, only some of which were destined to find a home in the modern orchestra. The German Richard Wagner and the French composer Hector Berlioz were among a small number of composers to lend their authority to the incorporation of new brass sonorities in the symphony orchestra. The traditional brass band, a family of keyed bugles designed for uniformity of tone and ease of performance, after the somewhat archaic model of the recorder consort, was adopted by the military and industry, and has since gone on to fulfill a public role as an outdoor ensemble.

100
A pipe organ:
air conditioning.

Why the pipe organ was invented is a mystery, even to organists. But then, why any musical instrument was invented is an issue all too often outside the scope, and interest, of musical experts. After two centuries of archaeological science and a century of forensic science, it is surely time to consider the design and philosophical implications of the instruments people make, collect, play, and compose for. Musicians, especially in the west, often present themselves as a rather closed community, dedicated to mastery of an instrument or to the finer points of an esoteric art disconnected from the skills, interests, and histories of other arts, sciences, and professions.

That no musician today appears to know why the pipe organ was invented in the first place, given the complexity of the task, its scientific and technological implications, and the fact that the effort occupied some of the best intellects in Europe and Byzantium for over a thousand years, is a rather sad reflection on the priorities and limitations of musicological practice over the past two hundred years.

What is missing is not evidence, but insight. We can begin by questioning the all too superficial assumption that the organ was developed as a musical instrument from the outset, and could not have been developed with some other end in view. The Roman Ctesibius was a hydraulics engineer. Wealthy Roman communities were interested in keeping their mansions warm in winter, and the water pump developed by Ctesibius makes use of the pressure from a water tank, a standard feature of a Roman mansion, to force the flow of warm air through pipes to the various rooms. Needless to say, a hydraulic pump is not a musical instrument, but as a pump it offers practical advantages of power and constancy of air pressure. How might the inventor demonstrate to a skeptical investor that his hydraulic pump will deliver hot air at the same pressure to every outlet? He makes a small model of a sealed tank with a number of outlets in the top. Into each of these outlets he places a whistle. Each whistle sounds at a different pitch to enable listeners to judge the equality of pressure at each outlet by comparing their relative loudness.

The demonstration attracts wide attention from the general public and building professions. Hey, says a bystander, you could play a tune with that contraption. Another, more philosophical observer realizes that the combination of controlled air pressure and simple waveforms could be applied to the study of tone ratios and interference effects.

101
Alpha to Omega,
the length of a string is infinite.

There is an old saying, how long is a piece of string. With his *Three Standard Stoppages* of 1913–1914 artist Marcel Duchamp contrived to answer the riddle by allowing three straight horizontal threads to fall from a height of one meter onto a horizontal plane "to create new shapes of the measure of length." Alas, he missed the point. The riddle is musical, and the string in question is one string of a musical instrument, perhaps the monochord of ancient times.

Assume the string in question is a guitar or cello string. "Alpha and Omega" are the first and last letters of the Greek alphabet, and the biblical phrase is also a figure of speech for the first and final cause of everything. This is interesting as a definition of the whole of creation as an alphabet, some thousand years in advance of the genetic code and binary code. It is also interesting as a musical figure of speech, given that letters of the alphabet are assigned to notes of the scale. Both the cello and the guitar have an A string; the letter names B, C, D, and so on are points in line up the string. Since the A of an A string is associated with the nut at the upper end of the string, the opposite end of the string, where it is stopped at the bridge, must be the Z, the omega, the ultimate barrier.

So then, what is the length of the string from A to Z? What determines the length of this piece of string? If the length is measured in feet and inches, as Duchamp supposed, there would be no mystery and no point. On the other hand, if length is a question of how many letters (notes) are contained between point A and point Z, the answer is an infinite number, and the string is therefore of infinite length.

BOOK FIVE

Sound Bites

INTRODUCTION

A sound bite is a sample of music, a section of a movement or a complete short movement that has a single statement to put across within the attention span of an average listener. An attention span is the length of time during which a listener can stay focused. The examples in this study are under five minutes in length, or they make their point in five minutes or less, so they are also suitable for study in a class or lecture period of fifty minutes. That young children and adolescents have a short attention span is a myth fostered by an older generation, said of the very young, because their minds have not developed, and of teenagers, because their minds are on other things. Language and mobility are great assets, but also great distractions. Prior to acquiring speech and mobility, infant children are already displaying enormous powers of concentration. Those powers need not be lost. Education for that reason is also attention training, to enable students to remain focused on a topic of observation or discussion for longer periods, and thus to develop analytical skills. Because it has a higher information content and is less strongly identified with the personal attachments of young listeners, music, and especially classical music, is perfectly adapted for attention training and the development of listening skills.

A good listener is a better student and a nicer person. Music is not a foreign language with a history and rules that have to be learned. Rather, it is a universal mode of communication that speaks directly to listeners of every culture in terms of the most self-apparent and natural human perceptions: being, space, time, action, stress—and of course, emotion. Though the repertoire of classical and world music is unbelievably vast, the basic terms of musical expression are relatively few and not at all difficult to grasp. Learning to listen to music is not dependent on knowing dates, names, or the finer points of performance. The present programme deliberately avoids aesthetic and historical doctrines in order to concentrate on the messages that emerge from the music itself. And as we know from Shakespeare's example, you do not have to be able to spell in order to listen and write well.

The content of a musical statement is *the way in which it is heard.* Music without words communicates in two ways: firstly and trivially, in what it declares; and secondly and more significantly by actually setting limits to what may be communicated. The conventional view that only words can convey information, is only a way of saying that words are the only information worth talking about, which we all know is not the case. A listener is much more deeply involved with the possibilities of a medium of expression than the expression itself. The limitations of any mode of discourse are associated with a certain kind of experience: for example, wailing is associated with grief or pain, and speed with excitement.

To acquire listening skills you have to be able to listen in the first place, and in this sense suitable acoustic, technical, lighting, and seating conditions are absolutely vital. A portable "boom-box" cd player sitting on a table is about as useful for reproducing the finer details of classical music, in home or classroom, as a cell phone for a movie. Because it is recorded to the highest standards, classical music deserves to be experienced in depth, not just for the music but for the recorded ambience as well. Good audio equipment is no longer an expensive item. Good quality headphones are a less expensive and portable option. Once a suitable listening environment is provided, all the other benefits of creative listening, including a greatly improved attention span, will follow naturally.

Music that can make a listener curious is music that touches, bonds with, and influences the way that person hears and processes sound. In influencing the way a person listens, music has the power, at least temporarily, also to change the way a person thinks: a powerful reason why music since ancient times has been regarded with suspicion, by intellectuals and guardians of public morals, as a form of mind control. It has always been tempting for those who are convinced that music has no meaning to interpret music with which they are not comfortable as the rebellious by-product of temporarily charismatic or renegade individuals. Blaming the artist or composer leads to the comforting fiction that such people are "not like us," which is actually rather sad. On the other hand, the creeping fiction that classical music is somehow élitist is simply an echo of a culture of fear and ignorance that has continued to reverberate among the middle classes since the time of the French Revolution.

For a listener, the fundamental issue is always: why am I listening to this? And the answer is essentially practical: it lies in something about the music that is able to attract and hold a listener's attention. For young people this attraction may be summed up in the personality of a star performer; for others it might be a curious sound, an enviable technique, or an intensity of expression. It might be complexity. In making the inquiry, however, every listener is actually embarking on a personal discovery, to find out what the mind is actually doing when a person listens deliberately and critically. From determining what a listener is actually capable of hearing, it is possible to infer the wealth of implication that flows from hearing itself.

This selection of pieces is eclectic, personal, and of course limited to items of a certain duration that are acoustic in nature (i.e., normally performed without amplification), and interesting for young people to listen to. Each item has been chosen because it is intriguing or special in some way, and to demonstrate a particular mode of musical communication. How much a listener actually hears in the music will determine how much the listener is able to report about it: the only failure lies in having nothing to say. The development of listening skills and writing skills go together. The method is simple: listen, make notes, then discuss. There are *no right answers*, only longer or shorter

stories that may be more or less consistent with what the music appears
to be saying. That measure of consistency emerges in discussion. It
expresses consensus. Consensus allows for differences in interpretation that reflect personal or cultural differences. These in turn are
interesting on another level. By avoiding aesthetic dogma one is able to
distinguish self-evident processes and techniques within the music on
which all can agree, from individual preferences and perceptions that
not all will recognize but that deserve to be acknowledged with tact.

For myself, listening to these music samples and discussing them
with students of architecture, art, jewelry, computer animation, con-
tinuation art (comics), furniture design, and interior design was an
enormously interesting and instructive experience. Young people of
artistic gifts who have not been exposed to classical music discover it
to be a world of acoustical design to which they can readily relate, and
from which they have something valuable to learn. In turn, their fresh
responses draw attention to aspects of classical music that classically-
trained musicians take for granted, or may never even have noticed. It
came as a total surprise to me, for example, to discover that students in
their early twenties, attending their first symphony orchestra concert,
could be so impressed at the sight of two dozen violin bows moving in
synchronization: a reminder not only that most other artists work in
isolation, but also of the special contribution of classical music to the
development of the very team organization skills that—whatever moral
value we may choose to attach to them—have played so important a
role in the rise of industrial economies. Other students were genuinely
captivated by the idea of a work of art recreated anew at every performance. "It's not like a painting," said one, speaking of Stravinsky's
Rite of Spring. "You can't recreate a painting brush-stroke by brush-
stroke. A painter cannot create that reaction. The masters of art don't
compare to the masters of sound. The person who forms sound creates
an environment that affects emotions and thoughts. *It is very complex
and strange.*" To a musician, such observations are pure gold, not to
say profoundly insightful.

What an individual listener discovers in a piece of music is a
personal matter. There is no argument with that. Listening can only be
encouraged. The implications of those aspects of a piece of music on

which all are agreed, are something else. On its own, being able to listen is a life skill. The benefits of better listening will be seen in higher grades across the board. A community with improved listening skills will create better and bigger audiences for classical and world music, take an interest in more challenging and dynamic concert programmes, and sponsor more interesting creative work in music and sound. Most important of all for the future of classical music in contemporary society is the encouragement, through listening, of present and future audiences. As one young writer shrewdly observed, "The only way that one could misinterpret music is by not interpreting it at all."

Defining music

Music does not exist in a vacuum. When a dog barks, the event is an indicator of time, space, and identity. Whether or not the animal in question is aware of time, space, and identity are philosophical issues that need not concern us. What matters is how the act of barking is interpreted, and we know very well that the perceptions of a human audience are programmed to interpret barking, or any other acoustic signal, in these terms and the terms of what they imply: alarm, danger, good health, and so on. It is the same for a musical event.

Any action that occupies time and space is also an experience of time and space, just as any expression of temperament or emotion in sound and gesture can be read as a real or simulated experience. We tend to regard dramatic art, including music, as simulated rather than real, because it is done for an audience, involves the use of props, and so on. Even scripted art, however, allows for the insertion of an authentic emotional response, and in many cultures the only authentic art is that which is executed in the heat of inspiration. This also affects our understanding of music.

Music and speech are display activities with information sharing implications. We can reach a basic understanding of what music is by considering the acoustic activities of animals and birds in the wild, and acoustic signaling, including traffic related protocols, in the human environment. Birds and animals emit cries for a number of reasons: to assert themselves, to navigate in the dark, to signal distress or authority, and to influence the behavior of anyone listening. We make a distinction between speech acts or signals that are private in nature or for personal reassurance, and those that, being directed to the attention of others in the group, or to other species such as predators, might therefore be said to have a useful social or communicative function. The value of studying signaling behavior among wildlife arises from a reasonable perception of the purity and effectiveness of animal and bird cries, both for personal identification and for influencing the actions of others. Survival in the urban jungle has led to a corresponding vocabulary of communication signals being devised with human needs in mind: a repertoire of car horns, truck horns, police, ambulance and fire appliance sirens, bicycle bells, bells at railway crossings, air raid and emergency evacuation sirens, etc.—functional non-verbal acoustic signals that at the same time communicate very specific messages. Because they are geared specifically to human hearing, traffic signals are a simple and effective additional starting point for an inquiry into musical meaning.

In making a distinction between display and content of an acoustic signal, one is drawing a line between personality and aesthetics at one extreme—display features that are unique to the individual—and its social or communicative function—features that are common to the species or group. The expressive dimension of a signaling gesture is a listener's perception of where it stands on an imaginary line between the two. Other factors implicated in distinguishing private and public-orientated gesture include perceptions of acoustic action as:

> subjective or objective;
> spontaneous or goal-directed;
> isolated or group-related;
> a response to silence or noise;
> a response to social indifference or acclaim;
> delivered indoors or outdoors;

—and so on. None of these is particularly mysterious. An instinct for self-preservation affects the behavior of all; we are constantly exposed to the assertive or compliant behavior of others, we understand the rules of social intercourse even though we may not choose always to adhere to them, and for that reason we are all perfectly well equipped to identify with the tensions and motivations of others, at least those within our culture or society.

I

PARTS OF SPEECH

Saying it right is about having something to say, and how you say it. Speaking without ideas, simply to arouse attention, is sometimes called *patter.* The content of patter is not in the meaning of the words, but in the attention of the listener, and attention is aroused by the expectation of meaning that comes with speech activity. Patter can be useful in regular speech as a way of *spacing ideas* so the listener has time to digest what you are saying before you move on to your next point. There are many ways of doing this. One is telling jokes, because your brain keeps on working on the serious stuff while your audience is waiting for the punchline. Another way is to repeat what you have said, but in different words. That can be helpful if the listener was not paying attention the first time, or didn't fully get the message. A third is by asking questions as you go, to make sure your audience is listening. A fourth is slowing the flow of ideas by saying "Um" and "Ah," as if you were improvising. Any one of these can also work against you if it gives an audience the impression you are not really sure what you are talking about. There is always a limit however to how much patter a listener can take. If the person you are talking to decides there is no content in what you are saying, it becomes noise and the person loses interest.

Music follows similar rules.

There are three parts of speech: the *idea*, the *form of words*, and the *delivery*. The idea is the *point* you wish to make; form is the *composition* or how you put it in words; and delivery is the *performance*:

the way you say it. All three should work together to reinforce your intended meaning.

The way you speak influences what you mean. Diction and tone of voice identify the speaker as a person and demonstrate attitude; energy and enthusiasm express self-belief and confidence and influence the bonding process with an audience; finally composition and performance skills ensure that what you are saying is strong and memorable. Effective speaking is also influenced by situational and environmental factors. Talking to a close friend over lunch, asking a question in conference, reporting an emergency by phone, and acting in a play, are four very different situations in terms of audience relations, the distance over which the voice has to carry, the loudness and tempo of the voice, the amount of background noise involved, and so on. In music the same adaptive processes are clearly audible.

1
A Drum all alone

Mohammad Esmai'li, *zarb* solo. 4:55 minutes. In *Iran: Persian Classical Music*. Elektra Nonesuch 9 72060-2 (track 4).

What can you say about a piece of music with no melody, no words, and no harmony? Is it music at all? This music track is from Iran. The *zarb* is an open-ended, bottle-shaped earthenware drum with a skin stretched over the wider end. When you first start listening, all you hear is a drum. The more you listen, however, the more you hear. The art of drum music is like the art of drawing with a pencil: you only have one basic color. The art consists in finding a whole palette of different sound qualities and textures using only your hands on the drumskin. Fast patterns use the individual fingers, as on the piano; sharper accents use the tips of the fingers all together, with the full weight of the hand; deeper pulses are made with the heel of the palm pressing into the skin to change the tone or produce a deep ringing tone; an iron ring on one finger strikes the edge of the skin from time to time. Patterns of pulses come and go with amazing speed, holding the listener fascinated. Some of these patterns are ancient and full of meaning. Within the drum tone there are subtle alterations in pitch, depending on which part of the skin is struck. The deep ringing tone is the resonant air tone of the drum, the sound you hear if you blow across the open end of an empty drink bottle. The power of the performance lies in a careful blend of tradition, which gives consistency, and artistic license, where the performer invents or is inspired to decorate the pattern in an individual manner, which adds the spice of novelty.

Do not ask if it is music. If you would feel like clapping at the end of a performance, it is music. Do not ask if it is art. If the skills involved are more than you could do yourself, it is art. The person who is able to perform to such a level of skill not only has a great memory and a mission to preserve important cultural information; he (she) is also in great physical shape, with two good hands, excellent coordination, acute responses, stamina, charisma, rhetorical skills, and other highly valued personal qualities.

This is music to be played in concert indoors, seated on a rug to isolate the subtle details of finger action acoustically, or out of doors, seated against a wall for a stronger sound. The intricate rhythmic patterns are well suited to communication in the open air, bringing structure and grace to a backdrop of ambient noise.

2
A Shinto chant

O-hitaki matsuri: Ceremonial chant from the Fire-burning festival of Kobe, Japan. 3:00 minutes. In *Kagura: Japanese Shinto Ritual Music.* Hungaroton HCD 18193 (track 7).

This track also challenges conventional definitions of music. It is a live recording of chanting on one note by a small number of unison voices led by a priest. Because there is only one note being sung, there is no melody, and because the prayer is being chanted to a constant pulsation, there is no rhythm either. The only accompanying effects are an occasional *whoosh* of a burning torch swinging close by the recording microphone. So: no melody, no rhythm, no harmony, no variation in loudness. The image is *constancy in all things.*

A good precept to keep in mind when listening to any music is: "Could I sing to this music? Could I dance to it?" If you can imagine yourself singing to it, then that is a sign of melodic interest—even in the absence of a tune. Melody is not just about movement in pitch; it is also about *line* and *continuity*. Of the two, continuity has special significance in the chanting rituals of many musical traditions where to take a breath, and thus break the flow of the chant, carries the risk of breaking the spell or letting in the devil. The Shinto chant is very easy to sing along with, since there is only one note: but you need to know the words, and that is the point. Though not for dancing, monotone chant is also very appropriate for following a moving target in an outdoor procession in a relatively noisy environment, since the persistent repetition of a single pitch is easier to locate and track than music of changing pitch and accent.

The imagery of constancy and lack of expression conveys a literal meaning of devotion and self-denial. The performance moves in space and time, but the music itself remains motionless. The only changing element is the syllabic coloration of the tone with every vowel change: a feature that connects this chant with other traditions of mouth music that also focus attention on the inner harmony of voice resonances. Because it is constant in pitch, tempo, timbre and loudness, from a modern communications viewpoint monotone chant is the complete antithesis of chaos or noise, which is characterized by constant change in every dimension. It is significant that this chant is celebrated in an outdoor location against a backdrop of crackling fires and crowd noises.

3
Birdsong in the forest

Pukaha: Songs of the Forest: The Awakening. Birdsong recorded at the Mt. Bruce native bird reserve. New Zealand National Wildlife Centre Trust XB1003 (track 1, 8:00). www.mtbruce.doc.govt.nz

The forest and the cave are naturally reverberant places. If you get lost in such a place, you cry out, and the sound of your voice sends ripples of pressure into the surrounding air, where they are caught and reflected by the irregular hard surfaces of boughs and trunks of trees, or the clefts and protrusions of cave walls. Some of that reflected sound is returned to the person crying out, as though the spirit of the forest or cave were calling back in reply. Reverberation is the halo effect of multiple reflections from surfaces at different distances. Near reflections are stronger and virtually instantaneous; those from a greater distance are weaker and delayed in time. Most sounds consist of a mixture of longer and shorter wavelengths. A wavelength is the distance between successive peaks of pressure. For signaling and navigating in a cave or forest, higher frequencies are more useful because their shorter wavelengths are better suited to detect smaller objects in the environment, like a moth to a bat. In music, for example, the violin A string sounds a note of a fundamental wavelength of 30 inches, and soprano high C has a wavelength of about 11 inches, but there are much shorter wavelengths (partial tones) mixed in with these to give the instrument its special tone quality. The effect of a signal combining with multiple reflections from the environment (as for a person singing in the shower) is that the longer wavelengths tend to be reinforced, while the shorter wavelengths cancel one another out. Birds are more efficient signalers than human voices in the forest. Human song is continuously fluctuating in frequency and amplitude, but birdsong consists of bursts of high-speed pulses too fast for human ears, and is thus able to detect objects at a much higher resolution.

All creatures communicate more tunefully in a reverberant enclosure, because clear and stable pitches are more precise, reinforced by local reflections, and carry the signal a greater distance. And for those who are lost in a cave and trying to call directions to a rescue party some distance away, there is a further advantage in calling in a singing voice, in a monotone, like the Shinto priest, because the cave wall reflections turn the fluctuations of a normal speaking voice into an incoherent noise, but amplify a voice singing on one note.

4
The Voice of Florence Nightingale

Florence Nightingale recorded in 1890. The Wellcome Trust: http://library.wellcome. ac.uk/doc_WTX023017.html. Also the Royal College of Nurses website: http://users. rcn.com/borneo/nightingale/nutting.htm.

There is still something a little spooky about hearing the recorded voice of an historic figure long dead. Florence Nightingale's message is all the more effective in this sense because she is quite deliberately addressing future generations, including listeners of the present day, to remind them of the duty they owe to the disabled veterans of past wars. Though her deliberate tone of voice and steady delivery are partly in response to the primitive technology of the earliest cylinder recording, they are also normal features of a public speaking voice in front of a large audience. The arrival of portable cylinder sound recording technology in the last decade of the nineteenth century ushered in an era of busy research into folk music and oral language traditions. The pioneer philologist Paul Kretschmer made a field trip to Lesbos in 1901 to record examples of Greek dialect on the new equipment. In his report he observed in some puzzlement that the spoken voice did not record satisfactorily, however singers "were less timid of the apparatus." The real reason for what he interpreted as timidity, is that everyday speech tends to fluctuate in loudness, leading to frequent "dropouts" or loss of signal, whereas singing is more focused and consistent in tone and loudness, and produces a better signal for transmitting and recording. So by a twist of fate, research into the distinctive sounds of language became redirected toward the music and accents of folksong.

In casual, intimate conversation the vocal mechanism is fairly relaxed, but when one is delivering an important message before a large, even if imaginary, audience, musical factors come naturally into play. Florence Nightingale's speech is carefully modulated in pitch and rhythm, and at one point there is a hint of a tremor of emotion (which is also a musical effect). It is not quite singing, but very close. The voice has a personal quality or timbre that identifies her as a distinct individual. Her words are delivered in melodic cadences that allow a more distant listener—distant in time as well as space—to make sense of every syllable, and understand the weight of every word in its sentence and context. Intonation is a key ingredient of the sound bite, whether the voice is Florence Nightingale, Churchill's "We will fight them on the beaches" speech, or Martin Luther King Jr. proclaiming "I have a dream."

These voices and their speeches are memorable, not just as images of great and charismatic individuals, but as compositions of tone and rhythm that continue to resonate with listeners in the present. They are memorable in part because they are musical; they also demonstrate the effectiveness of musical qualities in delivering a message, and in anchoring the message in the minds of present and future generations.

"Singing is just like talking but uses a lot more air."

5
Herb Morrison reports the "Hindenburg" disaster

Herbert Morrison reporting the arrival of the German airship "Hindenburg" for station WLS from Lakehurst, New Jersey, on May 6th, 1937. Numerous online and cd sources including: *20th Century Time Capsule,* Buddha Records 744659633 2 (track 8), and *The Century in Sound,* The British Library National Sound Archive NSA CD8 [ISBN 0-7123-0511-4] (track 19).

"Oh, the humanity!" What makes this recording so memorable for it to appear in nearly every compilation of recorded events of the twentieth century? To be sure, the explosion of the "Hindenburg" airship was a disaster, a human tragedy, a setback for the future of air passenger transport, and a death knell for the airship. It was a newsworthy event. What makes this particular radio newscast so powerful is the audible transformation of one person's voice in the face of an unexpected and terrifying event where the speaker's own life is suddenly in danger. When a professional newscaster loses his cool, it impacts every listener. The example tells us a great deal about *delivery*: how we instinctively react to the musical qualities of a speaking voice. You do not have to understand the language in order to appreciate that something terrible has happened. That information is embedded in the changes of rhythm, melody, tempo, and accentuation of the words: a transformation so effective that even when the speaker is not making sense, or lapses into silence, the drama and emotion of the event is still tangible.

In Greek tragedy, bloody events by convention took place offstage and were relayed to the audience by a messenger. When Oedipus puts out his eyes in Sophocles' tragedy, you do not see it, rather you hear about it. By following the event through a witness the audience is forced to experience it at the pace and intensity of real life, along with the actual complex of emotions that accompany moments of great stress. In the same way, through the broadcast recording a listener experiences the "Hindenburg" disaster in *real time*, as it actually happened. That experience is not so much in the words, as in the involuntary music of the vocal performance.

A newscaster is supposed to stay on top of events. A newsworthy event such as the arrival of an intercontinental airship is prepared for in advance. The news media are invited and provided information about the aircraft and its distinguished passengers. Morrison has a script to deliver, not totally without emotion, but in a controlled manner that allows for a hint of excitement. Outdoor news microphones in 1937 were robust and designed to catch the speaker's voice and not much else. In those days, cigarette smoking added an attractive edge and texture to a broadcaster's tone. As Morrison begins his broadcast, his voice is steady in pitch and even in pace, with only slight changes of pitch to avoid monotony and draw attention to aspects of interest such as the prevailing weather conditions.

You do not hear the actual explosion, or hardly at all. What you hear is the reaction. A steady, urbane, controlled description to a prearranged script is suddenly transformed into the voice of tragedy. When emotion strikes, the reporter struggles to maintain composure and continue speaking, since it is his professional duty to report, and only through what he says is his unseeing radio audience able to follow what is going on.

We hear the emotion in a number of ways that distort the regular flow of information as delivered up to the moment of tragedy. He is initially lost for words, and has to improvise, since the events are not going according to the script. His formal radio persona and polished vocabulary abruptly give way to the urgent tones and rough grammar of the working man: "It's crashing terrible!" Instead of moving at a steady pace, the reporter's voice alternately tumbles over his own words and leaves involuntary gaps to take in the horror of the situation. Instead of holding the microphone close to his face to maintain a steady signal, you can hear his voice zoom and fade in amplitude as he gestures, microphone in hand, at the spectators surging around him. As the horror sinks in, his voice cracks, and veers wildly up and down in pitch.

Thanks to recording, we can relive momentous events through the images and voices of those who actually observed them. Before the era of recording there were other tragedies, battles, and natural disasters that impacted on society and that communities wanted to preserve in memory for future generations, and they did so through the words of poets and dramatists, and the performances of great singers and actors, known as *interpreters* because they were able to recapture, through the music of the voice, with or without the aid of an instrument, the emotion and the experience of the recorded event. They did so by modulating the voice between the two extremes of absolute and impartial objectivity and overwhelming emotional involvement.

In 1986 the world witnessed a similar disaster when the space shuttle "Challenger" exploded soon after launching. This time, however, the whole world was watching the event on television. The voiceover from mission control did not have to convey the emotion of the event—or rather, did so by eloquent understatement: "[silence]. . . . Clearly a major malfunction."

6
Traffic horns

This material should be familiar to most readers. Recorded sources are freely available on sound effects discs and movie soundtracks.

The first car "horn" was a red flag, chosen because the authorities thought that a visual warning would be more effective than an acoustic signal. Today the use of a flag is restricted to presidential motorcades. The horn is altogether a more effective way of alerting other people and other vehicles. In the eighteenth and nineteenth centuries the more or less musical note of a post horn, a straight trumpet—played from the rear of the vehicle to avoid frightening the horses—signaled the imminent arrival of a stagecoach to those waiting ahead. With the coming of steam power, whistles replaced bells on trains and boats, but it was not until the fast-moving 1920s that the bell was eventually superseded by the siren on fire engines and ambulances.

In today's motorized world there are many signals. Some are visual. If you are driving a car and want to change direction, those who may be affected can already see you, so a visual signal is sufficient. A visual signal affects only those who are watching, but an acoustic signal affects everybody indiscriminately. That is the power of sound: you can hear it even when you are not looking. Acoustic signals in a stable environment can be extremely complex and long-winded: that is what music is about. In the dynamic environment of the urban freeway, on the other hand, the acoustic message has to be immediate and to the point, because for every message there is an appropriate response, and any delay in comprehension could be dangerous.

In the world of car horns as in the world of music there are universal conventions. Size is one. A small vehicle such as a bicycle makes a small sound; a large vehicle such as a freight train makes a big sound. The power of the signal is related to the size of the vehicle and the range within which it has to be heard for others to take suitable evasive action. For a bicycle or golf cart, that range is relatively small —as also for the beep-beep-beep of a larger vehicle such as a bus or delivery van backing up, since in this situation the vehicle is travelling very slowly and is more concerned to alert pedestrians than other moving traffic.

Alarm signals fall into two temporal classes: the momentary beep and the continuous blare. A short beep tells the listener "I am here" which is usually reminder enough. A continuous alarm, on the other hand, whether it is the alarm clock ringing to wake you up, or an ambulance approaching from a distance, is a signal *that will not go away unless the listener does something* like getting up or moving aside to let it pass. Emergency signals such as the fire services or ambulances also have an emotional component, expressed in the relentless oscillating wail that has strong associations with distress. A continuous sweeping signal, like a dog howling, is a sign of instability, and instability is invariably emotional, whereas an abrupt signal, like a dog barking, is simply an assertion: I am here, and this is my place. Of course that message can change. Holding down the horn button can express anger, tooting in rhythm to show delight that your football team has won the series, while (in a rare example of the inappropriate use of music) a car horn that plays "La Cucuracha" is calculated to annoy an entire neighborhood and may even be breaking the law. These changes in implication are all consistent with the fundamental associations of loudness, duration, and rhythm on a listener's perception of what a signal is intended to mean.

The largest rail and road vehicles often have multiple horns that sound more or less in harmony. Sometimes the harmony incorporates a tritone, a dissonant interval with symbolic overtones of fear and doom. Some horns are more friendly: for example, the added 6th chord C–E–G–A is popular with freight locomotives in the USA, while others prefer a warning tritone F–B. Unlike the wavering signal of a police car or ambulance, the stable harmony of a train or interstate truck horn is designed to convey size and power but without provoking unnecessary distress. An alarm signal that lasts for an indefinite period has the added advantage of signaling speed and direction of movement; if you are in its path, it gets louder, but if you are already out of the way you can clearly hear it pass by or fade away.

Alarm signals and their associations are a part of music too. If your audience is making a noise, as is often the case at the beginning of a concert, the first few chords of an overture or symphony are sometimes loud and assertive, designed to bring listeners to order and take control of the space. In his "Surprise" and "Drumroll" symphonies, the composer Joseph Haydn takes delight in lulling his listeners to sleep, only to wake them with a sudden loud bang.

"When I was in grammar school, whenever we heard an ambulance siren we had to say a prayer."

"The horn lets those in range realize the person wants others to know not only that they are in that location, but also that something is up."

7
Tuva chant to a cliff
"Kyzyl Taiga" (Red Forest). Long song performed by Kaigal-ool Khovalyg. 2:19 minutes. In *Tuva, Among the Spirits*. Smithsonian Folkways SFW 40452 (track 16).

For communicating at a distance singing is better than regular speech, indoors or outdoors. That is a given. If you were asked where music came from, and why it evolved in the first place, this would be a good place to start. Singing is common to all cultures. It is related in principle to the signaling behaviors of other animal species. It is true that among human tribes, singing is a vehicle for words, and for that reason may be considered superior to the singing of species that do not have speech. But in reality communication in words is only possible over relatively short distances—and for best results, in a controlled environment or enclosure. If you are stuck on a mountain or down a pothole, or even trying to shout a message of encouragement to the umpire at a sporting event, words are not much help. The message is in the delivery, not the content.

The singing in this example is recognizable as an invocation to the spirit of a place. Though we think of spirits as invisible entities of tradition and myth, their existence as guardians of specific locations can be inferred from small rituals of this kind, where the act of singing generates a strong audible response that lingers after the human voice has ceased. Here the singer is directing his voice across a river to the cliffs on the far side. The distance involved is quite considerable. What makes this example so fascinating and mysterious is that the reflected sound, the reverberation, returns *at a higher pitch* than the singing voice: an octave higher to be precise.

There are simple reasons for this. A singing voice contains a number of partial tones of different wavelengths that collectively sound as a single pitch because they are all vibrating in step. Some partials however are more powerful than others, and it is these midrange frequencies that stay the course over longer distances while the longer wavelengths dissipate into thin air. A singer would not notice the difference in the shower, or in a concert hall, because the distances are small and the reflected sound reinforces the voice in a positive way. It is only when the voice travels the relatively long distances associated with outdoor life that one begins to notice that the reflected sound—of male voices in particular—is higher in pitch. If the reflected voice is not the same as the singer's voice, it must be the voice of some other spirit. And since that other voice is only heard in a certain location, it has to be the voice associated with the spirit of that place. Since the difference is only audible when an adult male is singing, and not for female or children's voices which are naturally higher in pitch, the inference to be drawn is that only adult males have the special power to summon up the spirit voices of sacred places.

8
Tuareg medicinal chant

Incantation and dance of the Tuareg people (Mali) to drive away fever, for female and male voices and hand drums. 6:57 minutes. Elektra Nonesuch 9 72073-2 (track 5).

In the plains where there is less natural reverberation than in forest habitats, birdsong is more rhythmic than tonal in emphasis. The same is true of human music. Tonal music involves listening to the environment, "sounding it out" as it were, and taking advantage of the positive reinforcement of an acoustic signal to develop a music of complex patterns of stable and distinct pitches. In locations where the acoustic is relatively unresponsive, where the notes of a song or cry are lost in the grass instead of resonating off tree trunks and cliff faces, there is less benefit to be gained from precise intonation. This example of music from western Sahara embodies a number of features typical of a plains environment: a drone, drums, complexity of multiple voices and rhythms, and a leading voice that glides or scans in pitch rather than moving between fixed pitches.

The medicinal purpose of the song is to evoke a trance-like state, and within that state of suspended awareness, to stimulate the fever patient into extreme activity that will sweat out and drive the fever away. The lead singer is a female specialist who encourages the patient by example. Her wailing intonation is a characteristic expression of emotion and suffering, and her improvised patter, an allusive montage of phrases in various languages, draws on an intuition of meaning beyond rational consciousness. This wailing is offset by the steady drone of the other singers, which is both mesmerizing in effect and provides a firm tonal reference. A drone can be understood as an out-of-doors substitute for the sound of a reverberant interior. It conditions a listener's hearing so that notes of the song that are in tune with the drone are emphasized, and in that way enables the improvised melody to be understood as a pattern oscillating between dissonance (pain) and tonal resolution (relief of pain).

9
Fandangos
María Soléa (voice) and Paco del Gastor (guitar). Improvised song in the gipsy flamenco tradition of Andalucia. 4:34 minutes. Recorded live. Nimbus NI5168 (track 6).

Among all cultures, music is a natural medium for the relief of anxiety and stress. Sometimes the emotional pain runs deep. A great artist can give expression to feelings that the rest of us do not know how to deal with. When such a song is created on the spur of the moment, the effect on a responsive audience can be especially powerful and immediate. Improvised song has the special potency of the here and now: in this case a moment of creation, late at night, in which surreal, dreamlike images drawn from the cultural memory of a community are distilled in words and music through the inspiration of a gifted visionary, the singer María Soléa, aided by guitarist Paco del Gastor and encouraged by a small but appreciative audience.

As the music begins, the guitar strumming fiercely to inspire a sense of urgency and energy, one can hear the singer warming up, testing her notes, and murmuring to her accompanist or to herself. Suddenly the words come: verses that speak of universal emotions, fear of the unknown, relief after forgiveness, and bitterness at the hardness of a man whose beauty is as a diamond.

Catching the emotion of the moment, and connecting with the emotions of others, are universally valued qualities of art and performance. Inspiration cannot be planned for, or read from a script. In classical music, which is largely performed from a score, a bravura performance is one that takes liberties with the text, and feeds off the emotion of listeners.

10
Gregorian chant
Recommended: Extracts from the Proprium missae in Epiphania Domini. Choir school of Benedictine monks of Münsterschwarzach Abbey, directed by Fr. Gödehard Joppich. In *Music of the Middle Ages*. DG Klassikon 89. 439 424-2.

Gregorian chant is among the earliest written music in the western classical tradition. It is sung here alternately by unaccompanied lead singer and chorus, singing in unison. This is music for an enclosed and reverberant space. The great cathedrals of late medieval Europe are impressively large stone structures combining the acoustics of the underground cavern and the forest—indeed, the interior columns rising to interlaced ribs at roof level are often carved to resemble a petrified grove of enormous trees.

A walled enclosure excludes the distracting sounds of the outside world, and the intricately sculpted interior of fluted columns, voids, tombs, side chapels, and carved screens exposes a lot of shapes and surfaces to ambient music, from the very large to the relatively small. It is this large and complex surface area that sustains the lingering reverberation and gives Gregorian chant its soothing and tranquil character. This music does not have a regular beat imposed on it; it is music for words, the words are sacred ritual, and they are sung at a rate determined by the need for clarity of diction and meaningful continuity.

A lingering acoustic helps to create the same sense of a sacred and spiritual space as the reverberation of the cliff across the river to the singing of the herdman of Tuva. But because the reflecting surfaces in a cathedral are close at hand as well as far away, the acoustic influences the style of singing in the same way as the forest environment influences the singing of birds. Near reflections reinforce and stabilize the tone, encouraging a controlled music of clearly-defined and stable pitches. The style is a little slower than the newscaster of the radio era, and a little more formal; the movement of the vocal line also resembles Florence Nightingale's intonation, rising and falling by degrees carefully judged for clarity of diction, phrasing, and subtle emphasis, rather than to express personal emotion. A slower pace than normal speech confers weight and dignity, and allows for greater variety of pitch without compromising intelligibility.

Note that chant is sung at constant amplitude, again for reasons of clarity. If the voices were to vary in loudness, quieter passages would be drowned out by louder. For similar reasons, the singing also maintains an optimum steady pace, because a reverberant acoustic does not tolerate unduly fast or slow singing. The singing is unison, so the congregation can hear, not only that the singers are in perfect agreement with one another, but also that they are also "at one"—in total agreement—with the answering reverberation.

Plainchant is an austere religious music designed to express ideal qualities of steady resolve, calmness and clarity of purpose, continuity with tradition, and freedom from stress. There is, however, room for a certain kind of emotion and expression to emphasize parts of the sung text that are especially significant. If the medieval singer wants to celebrate a holy name, for example, the syllables of the name may be stretched out and decorated like an oversized capital letter in an

illuminated manuscript. Here the art of singing is an art of vocal illu-
mination of a sacred text. Because he sings the verses solo (and is a
more accomplished singer than the others) the leader has a freedom of
expression unavailable to the chorus. The lead singer sings more
clearly and with more artistry, but the combined voices of the unison
chorus have more weight and substance. The solo voice conveys the
promise of inspiration, whereas the fuzzier delivery of the chorus
delivers the security of consensus.

11
Broken consort

Martin Codax: "Mandad' ei comigo" (My love is coming home). Early 14th century. 2:39
minutes. Maria Kiek and Sinfonye. In *Bella Domna*, Hyperion CDA66283.

This is a very public love song, sung by a woman to celebrate the safe
return of her partner from a trip away, a separation that in the four-
teenth century might have been long and fraught with danger. The song
was discovered written on a parchment concealed in the original bind-
ing of an old book. The melody is composed on just six notes and
flows up and down in a wavelike motion.

The strength of the melody expresses the strength of devotion the
woman feels for her man on his safe return. This music belongs to the
same era as plainchant, but it sounds very different. Plainchant is for
unison voices, that is, multiples of the same kind of sound: a *harmony
of sameness*. The listener to plainchant receives an impression of *total
conformity*. This music for mixed instruments is a contrasting example
of a "broken consort": a mixture of tone qualities creating an impression of *unified diversity*. We call this a *harmony of difference.*

The song in this interpretation is a lively pattern of triplets, easy to
follow and easy to remember: a three-line verse form, a sequence of 11
three-beat measures phrased in three-note groups centered on pitches E
and C, which are also a third apart.

When multiples of the same instrument or voice create harmony,
as in plainchant, there is a high degree of mutual reinforcement of the
tone, and a strong message of corporate unity. When different instruments and voices play together as a group, the same fusion of tone is
not possible: instead, the message is cooperation rather than unity. In a

broken consort the individual members can be clearly distinguished. Their cooperation is a *voluntary* matter, unlike the blending of voices (or strings, or brass instruments) which is *intrinsic* to the species. So the music of a broken consort—even a rock band—also sends a clear message of goodwill.

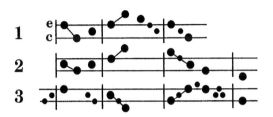

Mandad' ei Comigo: verse

The instruments in this arrangement are: drums, Celtic harps, a hurdy-gurdy, and the female voice. Because they are all different, instead of striving to all sound the same, the various instruments of a broken consort are chosen to enhance specific aspects of the song for which they are best suited: beat and rhythm (drums); keeping the voice in tune (harps); and maintaining an underlying harmony (hurdy-gurdy). (The hurdy-gurdy is a laptop string instrument of buzzing tone, driven by a crank handle, that produces a constant drone and has a rudimentary keyboard for playing melodies of limited range.)

So a broken consort is a small community of specialists playing different patterns but in a common cause. This is music in celebration of human rather than spiritual emotions, to be sung out of doors rather than in a church setting—hence, in the absence of strong reverberation, a music that relies on the coordinating power of a strong beat. Here too the subtext of the difference in timing is that church music is *timeless* and expresses a connection with tradition, whereas secular music celebrates a *temporal* human experience that connects emotionally with other human beings at a given moment. The message of voices singing plainchant is that the timing is in the text; but for a broken consort, timing is an externally applied means of managing complex actions. The need for a regular beat as an objective measure is more likely to arise from activities where people are doing different things than when they are all doing the same thing. Plainchant is self-evidently music about words. Even if you don't know Latin, it is perfectly obvious to a listener that the activity of solo and corporate chant is dedicated to the preservation, enhancement, and delivery of a text of some significance. It is not like gospel singing, where the preacher and the choir get carried away with enthusiasm and the watchword is joy and freedom from oppression. The tone and manner of plainchant is more precise, as for a doctor, scientist, or judge, and reinforces a message of the duties and values by which a community lives. The celebrants of plainchant are male, the public servants of the day, whose duty it is to uphold the law. When they sing, they don't get emotionally involved.

12
Devout emotion
Hildegard von Bingen, "O vis aeternitatis." 12th century, 7:56 minutes. Sequentia. In *Canticles of Ecstasy*. DHM 054742 77320 2 (track 1).

Something very different is happening in this song by Hildegard von Bingen, a female member of a religious order, a scholar and intellectual from the plainchant era whose music was definitely not to the liking of the ecclesiastical authorities and was suppressed and unappreciated for seven centuries after her death. Commentators (invariably male) complain at her imperfect grasp of Latin, but what really offended the critics was Hildegard's celebration in music of powerful emotions of love and personal commitment, feelings that the religious administration felt should be kept under wraps. And so it remained until the emancipation of women movement of the 1970s rediscovered her music and brought it back into the public domain.

The emotion of this song is very poignant, but also very determined. One has the feeling that, unlike conventional plainchant where the music is a vehicle for a text, here the lyrics—the words of which are hard to discern, even for those who understand Latin—are less important for the meaning they contain, than for the emotion they convey. Like Gregorian chant, this is unison melody for alternating solo and chorus, supported by a discreet drone played by medieval fiddle.

Whereas plainchant is a deliberately articulate style of singing, with careful stepwise changes of note for more or less every syllable of a public ritual, the song "O vis aeternitatis" conforms to a highly ritualized and intense expression of pain, despair, passion, or ecstasy. The female voice ranges over a much greater interval than orthodox masculine plainchant, rising and falling on a tide of emotion, but not giving up or letting go. The female quality of being a medium comes through just as clearly in this austere sweep of melody as in the cascading wail of the Tuareg medicine song. In both cases the meaning of the words is less important than the ebb and flow of an intensely focused experience. Gliding tones and melodies are disliked by the male of the species because they convey uncertainty and loss of control, and interfere with the safe delivery of a text. The more nurturing message of Hildegard and her female followers, however, is that emotions are part of the human condition, and that a music that embraces emotion is better able to deal with it.

13
Freezing time

Perotin, "Viderunt omnes." 13th century, 11:36 minutes. The Hilliard Ensemble. ECM New Series 1385. 837 751-2 (track 1).

How is a composer to express the idea of infinity? The great cathedrals of Europe are superhuman in scale, beyond the accommodation needs of communities of the day. It is natural to associate size with power, so only natural to construct buildings on a superhuman scale as virtual habitations of divine spirits of supernatural power. But how to express infinity or eternity in a musical sense? Logically, in a music that seems —even if only momentarily—that it could last forever.

In two celebrated settings dating from around 1200, "Viderunt omnes" and "Sederunt principes," the composer Perotin juxtaposes a musical setting of long, drawn-out syllables, with voices moving in a jaunty, dance-like rhythm. This early form of multi-voice polyphony is known as *organum* and until recently was disparagingly mentioned in history books as a primitive stage in the development of classical harmony. The harmony is certainly austere, mostly in intervals of a fourth or fifth, and an occasional third. This apparent poverty of harmonic invention can be excused on the acoustic ground that fourths and fifths produce strong audible combination tones that blend and interact with an accompanying drone, whereas smaller intervals do not.

What is so clever and fascinating about "Viderunt omnes" is the appearance of being able to switch timescales from a perception of *no change* (the drone), to *slow motion* (the changing syllables "Vi–de–runt" etc., to *fast motion* (the dance-like ornamentations). The coexistence of multiple timescales is a conception we normally think of as very modern, as for instance in the music of Olivier Messiaen or Karlheinz Stockhausen, and it may in part be inspired by an imagery of the relative motion of the sun, moon, and stars, as much as by the idea of human life and timing coexisting with eternity.

What makes the juxtaposition all the more satisfying is that the various timescales are in effect "color-coded" with the appropriate mood. The message of the sacred text is solemn, detached, conveying an impression of permanence and harmony as vast and enveloping as the cathedral of Nôtre-Dame in Paris where the music was composed. It is offset by the jaunty triple rhythms of the faster harmonies which, like the gargoyles and gremlins hidden in the crevices of a great cathedral, reveal a lively human presence, clearly secular and humorous in tone, capable of lurching into momentary dissonance, and thus prey to the sins, errors, and conflicts of human affairs.

In addition to showing an interest in modeling a music of multiple timescales, "Viderunt omnes" is the sort of music one would expect to be written by a composer, and for an audience, who have an interest in studying the inner harmonies of speech. As the music makes the transition from vowel to vowel, from [i] to [e] and then [u], a listener hears the change of vowel very clearly as a change of coloration of the syllable, almost as though the resonant space itself is changing shape: now higher, now wider. Such an interest in the inner partial structure of vowel sounds is a key aspect of a broader interest in the association of tone-color and meaning, also reflected in throat music and jaw harp traditions, that would eventually lead to the development of the renaissance organ, the first instrument of programmable timbres.

14
Vowels and consonants

Thomas Tallis, "O salutaris hostia" for choir. 16th century, 3:34 minutes. Winchester Cathedral Choir, David Hill. In *Tallis's 40-part Motet and other cathedral music.* Hyperion CDA 66640.

Polyphonic or multi-part music is a development in western music of a new and complex form of musical discourse made possible by the development of a notation to visualize and manipulate melodic shapes, and to calculate harmonies in dynamic progression. No matter how calculated a music may be, if it is to be performed in a cathedral environment with a lot of reverberation, it still has to accommodate to the same acoustic conditions as plainchant, if the message is to be clearly audible.

In chant or song of any language, it is the *vowels* that carry the melody line, and the *consonants* that separate one vowel from another. Another way of looking at it is to say that the vowel sounds express the emotion of the song, while the consonants deliver the meaning. Since consonants are in effect bandwidths of noise, and not tones of constant pitch, the composer and songwriter is caught in a dilemma between servicing the information content of a verse, and following the emotion of the vowels. And in any case, a music where the voices are no longer synchronized is in constant danger of dissolving into a chaos of disembodied tones and syllables.

But perhaps this dissolving chaos is precisely the state of ecstasy the composers of renaissance polyphony had in mind. When the words are already familiar to your audience, such liberties may be permitted. Like the music of Hildegard—or indeed, the electronic *Gesang der Jünglinge* of Karlheinz Stockhausen—the listener can choose to be elevated into a state of higher consciousness, of language as pure music, or pure information.

"O salutaris hostia" by Thomas Tallis is a text rich in consonants, and one way of achieving the appropriate state of no-mindedness, a natural goal of meditation, is for the listener to focus attention on the disembodied consonants as they flicker and dart from voice to voice, as though each singer were furnished with a tiny set of jingles. The experience is particularly fascinating because consonants in normal speech do not arrange themselves in regular patterns, but seem rather to fire off at random like a low-key firework display. The effect of a reverberant acoustic is therefore not confined to sustaining and stabilizing the melody, but has the additional effect of dissociating consonants and vowels of a text to a point where they can be listened to on completely separate levels. (Studio microphones have the same effect, though more discreetly, on the voices of radio announcers.) This is yet another factor in explaining the origins of song.

We learn from the experience that vowels carry the emotion, the melody *and the predictable continuity* of a song, while at the same time, superimposed on the melody, is a *random* and *unpredictable* texture of consonants such as [sh] and [st], [p], [f], [t], [k], etc. Furthermore, reverberation is selective, sustaining and prolonging only vowel sounds, and not the consonants, which come and go in a moment. This seems very odd, until one realises that vowel tones are purer, stronger, and more coherent signals in the mid-frequency range, whereas consonants are noises having only the power of a whisper. That consonants appear just as audible as vowels is because human hearing is more sensitive to higher frequencies.

15
Clear intimacy
John Dowland: lute song "Dear if you change." 3:25 minutes. Early 17th century. Emma Kirkby, Anthony Rooley. In *The English Orpheus*. Virgin Classics 0777 7595212 4 (track 4).

Chamber music is private, intense, and philosophical. Its world is the home. Its thoughts are personal thoughts. If you compare this song with the public world of plainchant, the differences are very obvious. Plainchant is part of a system of moral instruction for an entire community. Its message is affirmative: this is what you do, because this is what we are commanded by tradition to do. Plainchant is sung in unison to express group solidarity, and in Latin to express permanence. It is celebrated in a vibrant acoustic that contributes a sense of awe and divine endorsement. Chamber music, like chamber art, began to emerge in fifteenth-century Europe when (to put it simply) people began to think for themselves. This song, the words and music by John

Dowland, a contemporary of Shakespeare, is a private meditation on the permanence of human love. Though the message is equally poignant sung either by a man or a woman, the singer in this recording is female—appropriately, perhaps, for a song composed in the era of Queen Elizabeth I. All the same, an image of female leadership is controversial. The songs of Hildegard, remember, were banned from public performance and could only be celebrated in the privacy of her enclosed female order. Even in Dowland's time, a woman would not be allowed to sing in church, in public. Added to which, Dowland's lyric is in English, the language of ordinary people, not the Latin of institutional religion. Its message is thus available to everybody, whatever attempt might be made to suppress it in public.

Religious music is about security and tradition. This song is about what will happen in the future. The keyword is "change." At the human level the change seems to refer to an emotional estrangement between a man and a woman. One has the impression that an argument has taken place; the male partner has threatened to leave her and the woman responds by saying she will always remain faithful to the love they shared and will never love another. The language is very rich and sonorous, with many internal echoes and elevated imagery. At a more abstract level, however, the lyric faces up to the new reality of an uncertain future, that terror of the unknown that arises from society turning its back on the assurances of traditional religion, numerology, and alchemy, a doubt expressed visually in Albrecht Dürer's engraving *Melencolia I* and echoed much later in Rodin's sculpture *The Thinker*.

This very personal but also apocalyptic message is delivered in the simplest of musical terms, a voice and a lute. A private chamber is a restricted space with the acoustic of a modern bathroom. The walls, floor, and ceiling are relatively flat and very close to the singer, so the voice tone is reinforced directly, but not prolonged. Because the room space is small, it does not take much effort to fill it with sound, and because the acoustic response is so quick, a singer or instrumentalist can execute rapid and intricate patterns without the sound becoming blurred. In a concert hall or in a cathedral, the emphasis is toward projection: sending the music into space, and provoking a response from the fabric of the enclosure. Chamber music is very much more centered on the individual performers, and arises from a perception of persons as existing in isolation, so it invites a more intense empathy from an audience in effect eavesdropping on a private conversation.

The voice and lute (or voice and guitar, since this music belongs to essentially the same genre as a ballad by Joni Mitchell) are a matched pair. The voice is a soft instrument that through an effort of physical and emotional self-control is able to produce steady tones. The voice also has language, to add precision to any emotion. The lute is made of hard materials, so is inherently stable. It guides the voice and adds definition to the timing, tuning, and articulation of every note; in a domestic environment the accompanying harmonies of the lute also act as assisted resonance to the singing voice, a resonance that, unlike the indiscriminate reverberation of a stone cathedral, can be *modulated in real time* by the lutenist in sympathy with the changes of key and mood of the singing voice.

Acoustically, the message of Dowland's song matches the philosophical issues of the lyric. The message of plainchant is of a small human presence exciting a powerful unseen response. The human component is the transitional element, and the answering presence, represented by the stone fabric and reverberant acoustic, the eternal component. In Dowland's lute songs the priorities are appropriately reversed, the message of the lute expressing impermanence in tones that hang in the air for only a moment, then rapidly fade, to which the voice brings an assurance of strength, continuity, and direction.

16
A song in praise of music

Franz Schubert, "An die Musik" (To music). 2:42 minutes. Early 19th century. Ian Bostridge, Julius Drake. In *Schubert: Lieder*. EMI CDC 724435 56347 2 6.

This lyric song or *lied* is an example of the interest in human nature that overwhelmingly characterizes western art and music in the romantic era. Like Beethoven, Blake, Goethe, and Byron, not to mention the painters Goya and J. M. W. Turner, Franz Schubert's art connects the classical values of the late eighteenth century with the new post-revolutionary era of industrial democracy and natural law. The new middle classes were more interested in tunes they could sing than

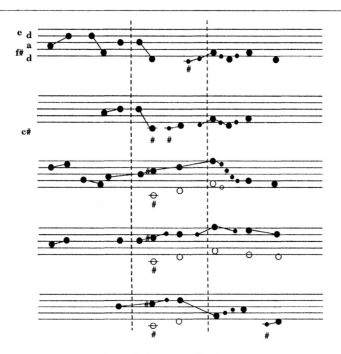

Franz Schubert: "An die Musik"

symphonies and string quartets that seemed very complicated and abstract, and reminded them all too clearly of the previous era of aristocratic rule. Schubert is a remarkable composer. His music seems natural and artless, and yet is as precisely calculated as a mathematical equation. We can see this in the structure of the verse, which is interesting to compare with the earlier "Mandad' ei comigo" by Martin Codax. Schubert's song is for a cultivated singer. There are octave transpositions and elisions, but the verse consists essentially of a beginning or anacrusis, centered on the A–D interval; a middle, in which the voice shifts to B and moves back to D; and a final cadence, which circles round the F sharp and back to D.

The range of notes is somewhat greater than Codax, but the cyclic form looks back to the same tradition, and connects with the chant forms of oral cultures of ancient times. The spirit of the song, in words as well as music, is more quietly meditative, like Dowland, a sentiment

---

universal in implication (music is good for you) but expressed in the manner of chamber music (music is good for me).

17
Song without words

Sergei Rachmaninov: "Vocalise" 4:57 minutes. Early 20th century. Brian Asawa, counter-tenor, Academy of St. Martin in the Fields, Neville Marriner. RCA Red Seal 09026-68903.

The symbolist poets of the late nineteenth century believed that music existed on a higher plane of pure feeling and was thus superior to poetry, in which pure feeling is obliged to compromise with language and its rules. The genre is associated with composers of the romantic era such as Felix Mendelssohn, but a "song without words" in the early romantic sense is normally either a transcription of a song from an opera, or an instrumental piece written to resemble a vocal melody and having no words for the simple reason that the instrument is incapable of speech. A *vocalise* by contrast is deliberately a composition without words *performed by a singer* who assumes the character of a disembodied voice or spirit.

Rachmaninov's "Vocalise" is a piece well-known in many different arrangements for a variety of solo instruments. Its publication coincided with the arrival in America of an early electrical synthesizer called the theremin, invented by the Russian Leon Termin, an instrument controlled by simply moving the hands in the air without touching the apparatus, producing an eerie voice-like wail. In this recording the vocal line is sung by a human voice, but it is an unexpectedly high male voice, of eerie intensity and purity of tone, offset by low strings beautifully orchestrated in close harmony: violas, cellos, and double basses.

Absence of lyrics is absence of words, and in the absence of words the vocalist is able to focus on purity of tone without the distractions of pronunciation or interpretation. All the meaning of the song is concentrated in the quality and movement of tone, which is free to glide continuously up and down, now louder, now softer, in a manner reminiscent of the song of Hildegard, an earlier celebration of spiritual ecstasy. Some listeners may tire of hearing a single vowel oscillating endlessly up and down; after the art deco contours of Rachmaninov, to go back to Perotin or Tallis is like rediscovering with a sense of relief the expressive qualities of modulated vowels.

18
Speech song

Arnold Schoenberg, "Mondgestrunken" (Moon-drunk) from *Pierrot Lunaire*. 1:37 minutes. Early 20th century. Maureen McNalley, reciter; Orchestra of our Time, Joel Thome. Vox CDX 5144 (cd 1, track 1).

Pierrot Lunaire is the earliest and most celebrated example of a short-lived but interesting genre of accompanied verse declamation that seems to have been inspired by the new medium of cylinder recording. In much the same way as the imagery of impressionist painters Renoir, Seurat, and others came to be influenced by the new view of reality revealed by photography, so young composers of the early years of the twentieth century took inspiration from the new, though primitive, technology of acoustic recording. Some, including Bartók, Kodály, and Vaughan Williams, were inspired in a more practical way to go out into rural communities, to record and transcribe folk music, researching into native traditions for surviving evidence of tribal and cultural identity. Others, including Schoenberg and William Walton (composer of *Façade*, music for a suite of surrealist poems by Edith Sitwell, chanted through a megaphone), were more impressed at the ability of the new medium to capture and preserve the movement of the speaking voice. Sound recording made listeners newly aware of the refined and subtle *musicality* of speeches such as the message of Florence Nightingale, a music just beyond the reach of conventional melody and harmony.

In the early days nobody, not even its inventors, quite knew what the phonograph was best suited to do. Alexander Graham Bell, whose wife was hearing impaired, was disposed to apply the new technology to speech therapy. To be perfectly honest, the phonograph was far from being a very suitable medium for reproducing music. (The famous painting of Nipper, the listening dog, and even the brand name "His Master's Voice" are, after all, statements about the suitability of the medium for voice reproduction rather than music.) From the 1890s, newsworthy political speeches, delivered by actors, were as vital a part of the record trade as items of music. They were joined soon after by the first sound effects recordings. Speech, music, and incidental noises came together in a 1900 production of a fundraising recording of "It's a Long Way to Tipperary" to celebrate the departure of British troops to the Boer War, in which are blended the music of a brass band, singing, sounds of cheering crowds, and noises of the ship leaving the quayside.

A listener's first impression of *Pierrot Lunaire* may be one of surprise that classical music could be written for a speaking voice—and a rather creepy voice too, casting spells in the darkness like one of the witches in Shakespeare's *Macbeth*. But the sound of Florence Nightingale's disembodied voice emerging from an old gramophone horn is also rather spooky, so Schoenberg may simply be responding to the strangeness of the medium as well as the spirit of the times, a new era of electricity, X-rays, Kirlian photography of energy vibrations, and the telephone—an age, that is to say, of delving into the subconscious mind that was to inspire Sigmund Freud, Ibsen's psychological dramas, and Edvard Munch's painting *The Scream* in addition to the ghostly wail of the theremin. It is also of some scientific interest that Schoenberg's vocal line, while not music in the orthodox sense, is written down in a precise notation. It was the composer's contribution to the new science of phonology, a science deeply involved in the meaning and emotional subtext of vocal expression.

19
Atomizing the voice

Pierre Boulez, *Le marteau sans maître* (The Hammer without a Master). Mid-20th century. 3 movements *ca.* 8:00 minutes. Hilary Summers, mezzo-soprano; ensemble conducted by Pierre Boulez. DG 00289 477 5327 (tracks 1–3).

Pierre Boulez is one of the truly great composers of the 20th century, and a dedicated advocate and conductor of the music of the modern era. The distinctively brittle sound of his first masterwork, settings with instrumental interludes of verses by the Belgian surrealist poet René Char, was likened admiringly by Stravinsky to the sound of ice cubes clinking in a glass. Composed in 1954–1955 and revised in 1957, *Le marteau sans maître* is a music of a kind labeled "pointillist" by music critics, in the same way as the music of Ravel and Debussy had been labeled "impressionist" a half-century before. The description is apt because it is a music of dancing lights and bright reflections, an austerely rich music gleaming of polished steel, glass and stone, like the famous Barcelona Pavilion of architect Mies van der Rohe. It is also paradoxically very French, a very tactile and sensuous musical experience of faceted tone qualities that seem to vanish as quickly as they appear.

The atomistic quality of this music is a feature of the post-1945 era, a time when the world was very conscious of the terrible power of the atomic bomb and at the same time fascinated at the mysteries of particle physics that seemed to hold the key to the origins of life, the universe, and everything. Listening to the instrumental portions of this music, one has the impression of nuclear particles colliding, being annihilated, and fusing to form chains and organic sequences.

Boulez has chosen a very special group of instruments to accompany the solo contralto voice. This is strictly a broken consort in the classical sense, but every instrument is related in an orderly sequence to the timbre of the female voice, and to the vowels and consonants of speech. It is a uniquely successful application of the principle of *serialism*, a music based on scaling principles applied to pitch, loudness, and in this example, also tone color or timbre. It is as though the composer has gone through the alphabet and selected musical sounds that correspond to every letter from the open vowel of [a] to the buzzing sound of [z]—and then put all of these sounds together in different formations, like writing words in instruments rather than letters.

The six melody instruments of the ensemble are alto voice, alto flute, viola, guitar, xylorimba (a xylophone with bass extension), and vibraphone. They correspond to the vowels, since the vowels are the melody elements that carry the song. The melody instruments form a linked chain of connection with the voice, which has tone, vibrato, continuity, and words:

alto flute (has breath, vibrato, but no words)

viola (singing tone, vibrato, but can also pluck notes)

guitar (has vibrato, only plucked notes, no continuity)

xylorimba (wooden tone, no vibrato, no continuity)

vibraphone (ringing tone, artificial vibrato)

—and back to the voice again. A seventh player is in charge of a variety of percussion instruments whose sounds are analogous to spoken consonants: *bongos* [b, d], *maracas* [ss, ts]; *tambourines* [sh, rr], *claves* [k]—along with bells, tam-tam, triangle, gong, suspended cymbals and finger cymbals, all of which combine percussive attacks with metallic reverberations at various pitches from low to high.

The meaning of the composition, at the simplest level, is as a sequence of songs to words whose meaning is buried deep in the subconscious, in the same way as the improvised lyrics of the gipsy "Fandangos." On a technical level, the music is an extraordinary collection of sounds that make completely different sense from a normal ensemble. At the highest level, it is music that says something new and profound about the way musical relationships are articulated and perceived.

20
Siren

Edgar Varèse, *Poème électronique*. Tape music, mid-20th century. 8:02 minutes. In *Varèse: Complete Works*. London (Decca) 460 209-2 (track 3).

The word *siren* usually means a device that makes a powerful wail to alert the community in an emergency. But its older meaning alludes to the enchanting songs sung by mythical female spirits as a lure to distract sailors or male adventurers from their quest and bring them to destruction. It is interesting to note that the destructive power of beauty wielded by the female over the male of the species, a myth as old as time itself and common to every culture, extends beyond physical appearance and actions to the sound of the voice and the allure of sinuous vocal melody traditionally employed by a determined woman over a man to get what she wants. The power of the siren lies in *beauty and intensity of tone*, coupled with *ambiguity of language* and a *gliding melody* that is difficult to grasp and continuously out of reach. These are also features of the sacred songs of Hildegard von Bingen and the incantations of the Tuareg medicine woman. The allure of uncertainty is as real and fascinating in song as the swaying movement of a belly dancer to the eye.

Varèse was born in Europe and settled in New York after the

1914–1918 war. He was very taken with the monumental size and scale of America, its landscape, its industry, and its energy. In 1924 he heard the siren of a passing fire engine and liked the way it traced a powerful line of melody, gliding up and down in pitch and time (and also space, if you include the movement of the fire engine through the city streets).

Ahh!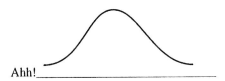

Varèse incorporated the siren as a musical instrument in his works *Hyperprism* and *Ionisation*. *Poème électronique* is a pioneering multi-track tape music composition commissioned for the Brussels World Fair of 1958. Prerecorded sounds, a dreamlike mixture of machine sounds (jet plane, road drill), mingled with musical instruments both analogue (organ, brass, timpani), and synthetic (electronic oscillators), evoking a vast and bleak landscape populated by spirits, perhaps an imaginary view of a visitor to another planet, or the time-traveller's vision of a dying earth in H. G. Wells's *The Time Machine*. Varèse's haunting imagery continues to influence the world of techno music. *Poème*'s animating spirit is a wordless female voice that seems to convey a sense of the anguish and despair of a western civilization living under the shadow of the cold war and the threat of mutually assured nuclear destruction. At times, however, the siren voice and its emotion also remind listeners that pain is also associated with the birth of new life, and thus hope for the future. After a long struggle with a difficult problem, when a person finally sees the solution and breathes out a triumphant "Ahh-hh-hh-hh!" with a rising and falling tone, that is also a siren sound, but this time an expression of very positive emotion.

Discussion topics

1. Are a violin, guitar, or piano (for example) more *musical* than a drum?
2. A monotone song has words and perhaps rhythm. What does it lack?
3. The songs of birds and some animals (e.g., the humpback whale) have

musical features: melody, rhythm, repetition, and regional identity. Are these signs of intelligence?

4.   What makes the timbre of a voice or instrument sound the same every time, even though words or music may change?

5.   Does emotion in speech or music relate to a sense of loss of control?

6.   What advantages does an audible warning signal (horn) have over a visual warning signal (flashing lights) in highway traffic?

7.   Trumpets, horns, and bagpipes were once employed to transmit signals on the field of battle. What qualities do these instruments have in common?

8.   A howling or wailing song expresses pain because the tone is unstable and also suggests uncertainty. Why is it employed to help alleviate pain in others?

9.   Many listeners believe that an improvised song (like "Fandangos") is more truthful of human experience than a song that is written. Do you agree?

10.   "One singer could be making it up; two or more singers in unison means there has to be a script." What does this say about individual initiative?

11.   A harmony of sameness (voices, strings, brass) is a harmony of *nature*, but a harmony of difference (broken consort) is a harmony of *consent*. Discuss.

12.   Is Hildegard's song a feminist counterpart to masculine plainchant?

13.   A river or a passing train can be fast and changeless at the same time. What does Perotin's "Viderunt omnes" say about the perception of time?

14.   "Vowels carry the melody, consonants carry the meaning."

15.   Chamber music is about privacy. How is this expressed?

16.   What does Schubert's music add to the significance of a poem in praise of music? Would you agree that his music makes the poem superfluous?

17.   A wordless *vocalise* expresses the late romantic view (Arthur Rimbaud, Walter Pater) that poetry and art "aspire to the condition of music." Is melody alone pure feeling? What effect would the addition of words have on Rachmaninov's melody?

18.   Punctuation marks are a form of musical notation, since they direct the rise and fall and also the timing of a reader's voice. For comparison, read aloud a familar passage or poem (e.g., Milton's sonnet *On his Blindness*), first with, and then without attention to punctuation. What is the difference?

19.   Evaluate the *sounds* of the letters of the alphabet for their suitability for musical expression, and their resemblance to actual instruments of music.

20.   Before the 1920s, public emergencies were communicated by handbells or steeple bells. Evaluate the advantages of a siren as a warning signal.

II

ECHOES AND ABSENCE

You might imagine the composer's primary function, or indeed his (her) only function, would be to compose music for people to listen to. This is not the case, or at least, is not the case in western culture. The artist's primary role is to make people think in new ways, and abstract art, painting, and poetry of the twentieth century uses the forum of art as Socratic dialogue to make works that are statements about art and invite the viewer or listener to consider those necessary implications of art that are normally hidden from conscious awareness.

During the 1950s a movement called *abstract expressionism*, led by Wols, Barnett Newman, Jackson Pollock and others in art, and Cage, Pierre Boulez, Morton Feldman and others in music, sought to wipe the slate clean and start afresh. Previously, under Nazism and Communism, artistic expression had been controlled by the government, and only art that promoted a nationalist ideology was officially recognized. The arts had come a long way from the Age of Napoleon when an artist was regarded as a national hero and social propagandist.

After 150 years, a policy of using art to entrench nationalistic sentiment, justify war and persecute those of different views, had obviously failed and was being boycotted by younger artists. The question was how to create an art that changed public attitudes without imposing any hint of dogma or censorship. Surrealism was part of the answer, a stream-of-consciousness art of intuitive image-forming that in musical terms could also embrace emptiness of content.

21
Silence

John Cage: *4'33."* Tacet for any instrument or instrument combination. Mid-20th century. Recordings include Koch International 3-723888-2, Floating Earth FCD004, and Amadinda Percussion Group, Hungaroton SLPD 12991.

Cage originally staged *4'33"* as part of a regular concert by pianist David Tudor, who sat in full formal evening attire at a grand piano and mimicked the behavior of performing a work in three short movements, but without touching the keys. In later years Cage modified the conditions of performance to eliminate even those controls over the performers' actions. The audience is asked to decide if the absence of music is also music. It is an interesting question because similar ideas arise in other contexts, for instance the moment of silence on a day of remembrance, and may also be taken into account when we listen to music of much earlier times and contexts.

In advertising, for example, the term "white space" is used of the blank areas surrounding the text copy, which are carefully managed to focus the reader's attention on the key parts of the message. In architecture and interior design, empty space has to do with the relationship of the structure to the street, to neighboring buildings, to the provision of natural light, spaces for passageways allowing the movement of visitors in and out of entrance and lobby areas, and for the definition of quiet zones. In poetry and typography, white space is what frames the words on paper, and guides the eye from line to line, or (in the case of a poet such as e e cummings) from word to word.

In a radio or studio context, silence becomes a more intense part of the listening experience, because in the absence of a visual image, the listener relies completely on hearing, and after a very short period of silence one begins to wonder if the equipment has suddenly failed. When you can see it happening, however, silence can be funny. In a sketch for television the British surrealist comedian Spike Milligan appeared as a longhaired concert pianist in a scratchy old archive black and white movie. He strode to the piano, sat down and went through the motions of playing, but since it was supposed to be a silent movie, of course there was no sound. Every so often, in place of dialogue, a fragment of music notation flashed up on the screen. In a strange kind of way the sketch made sense, because it asked the very valid question: "In a movie—even a regular movie—where do you suppose the music is coming from?"

So what is Cage saying, in this silence of 273 seconds? Some commentators say that the duration corresponds to one side of an old 78 rpm record, and mention instances of early coin in the slot jukeboxes with a silent disc among the selection on offer, which a customer could choose if he or she wanted a moment of peace and quiet. Cage himself said that the number 273 corresponds to the temperature of minus 273 degrees Celsius, which is absolute zero, and a music of 273 seconds of negative activity also represents a state of absolute zero. The music in this piece was created by the incidental noises (for instance, coughing) that tend to happen in a concert situation. There is no such thing as silence, he would say. (And in fact it is a very interesting exercise, whether you own a listed recording of this work or not, to try sitting still and listening for that period of time—or record that length of silence on tape—and note how much sound occurs, and the effect it has on a perception of silence or absence.)

In the long run, a silent item in a concert programme is a useful reminder that when music is playing, it takes over your hearing and covers up other sounds that are going on, just as when a chat show host talks, the guest has to be quiet, leading an audience to suspect that the only reason the guest has been invited is to show that the chat show host is the one in control. A silent concert item makes you ask, "Why am I here? What is really going on? Am I being told what to think? Am I being asked to endorse a particular point of view? Could I be doing something more useful or enjoyable?" And if you don't have answers to those questions, perhaps they are questions worth thinking about.

22
Absent friend
John Dowland, *Semper Dowland, semper dolens.* Christopher Wilson, Fretwork. 3:37 minutes. In *Goe Nightly cares.* Virgin Classics VC7 91117-2 (track 24).

The ultimate problem with the idea of a music of silence is that you cannot always be sure that the listener will get the point. The playwright Harold Pinter is an expert at creating meaningful silences;

another was Samuel Beckett, and both became acutely aware of the power of silence through working in radio drama. The sculptor Henry Moore discovered the sculptural value of empty spaces through his studies of Etruscan art and sensing the "lines of force" in dried bones and shells bleached and worn smooth by the action of the waves. A void is meaningful in terms of its surrounding. Even Cage's moment of emptiness was designed to be framed by music before and after. Since coping with absence and gazing into the void are universal aspects of the human condition, one is led to the interesting thought that music of other times and cultures might also have been created to convey loss or absence.

Plainchant, for example, is about filling the void, the void being the empty space of a cathedral or chapel. In similar fashion, the message of piped music in a supermarket is about filling the space between the rows of canned goods with the comforting impression of a friendly presence. People drive with the radio on to alleviate the boredom of a long journey. And so on. In many ways the presence of music, in the media and in the everyday lives of people in urban industrial cultures, can be interpreted as a cover-up for an absence of meaning or content in everyday work activity, a lack that becomes acute in times of stress and isolation.

John Dowland, the composer of "Dear, if you change," shared in the climate of uncertainty of the early seventeenth century following the separation of church and state. Dowland had a reputation as a melancholic, and *Semper Dowland, semper dolens*, a famous work for lute and viols, can be interpreted as a meditation on mortality, like Hamlet gazing on the skull of Yorick in Shakespeare's play, or, like Cage, as a meditation on the meaning of absence, of "not being." How does he communicate the idea of absence? For a renaissance composer and specialist in song, the most powerful suggestion of absence is a song without a singer, which is what we have here: an instrumental version of the composer's already well-known song. A song without *words*, in the style of Mendelssohn, does not have the same power, nor does the wordless vocalise by Rachmaninov. It is clear from the character of their music that neither more recent composer is unduly concerned with the absence of a human singer: for Mendelssohn, a piano makes a reasonable substitute for the voice, and for Rachmaninov the absence of a text is a means of drawing attention to the spiritual essence of song, which by definition exists on an altogether higher plane.

Dowland's musical meditation for viols and lute is a highly wrought music of interwoven strands, like a maze, through which the listener is guided by a leading melody in which the viol deputises for a missing voice. It is a restless music that seems to be searching for an answer, but the answer is always silence. There are three verses. At the end of verses 1 and 2, the music stops dead. Since it is chamber music, there is no reverberation, so each time the music stops is like switching off the light: a black silence descends, and one really feels as though confronting the void. It is a sensation like the old Chinese proverb about finding the locus of all movement, which is the hole at the center of the wheel: the point, that at the center of the wheel is emptiness.

Dowland is the philosophical English face of the new humanism that was spreading across Europe. The lyric of his song "Dear, if you change" sends much the same message as Shakespeare in his famous sonnet "Shall I compare thee to a summer's day?" In a time of religious uncertainty, what are the true values? The answer comes back: religion may pass, but love, art, and self-belief will endure.

23
Freedom of expression

Giovanni Gabrieli, *Canzon Duodecimi Toni a 10 No. 2* for 6 trumpets and 4 trombones. Late 16th century. 4:13 minutes. Recommended: The Wallace Collection, Simon Wright Nimbus NI5236 (track 1: UHJ surround sound encoded). Also Naxos 8.554129 (track 4).

Dowland's doubt is essentially private. The Venetian group of composers that included Giovanni Gabrieli responded to the new dynamism that was sweeping over Europe in an equally radical, but upbeat and positive way. Venice in the late sixteenth century was a European center of trade where the prosperous west met and connected with the mysterious east, and where silk and spice traders from Africa, Lebanon, and cultures as far away as India and China delivered their exotic wares. The old music, represented by plainchant, emphasized *unity*: unity of place, unison harmony, uniformity of behavior, unanimity of belief. When plainchant is performed in a great cathedral, it does not

matter which door you go in: the music is the same, you are part of the
same space, the same group. The values of unity are appropriate for
isolated communities living in walled cities and anxious to preserve
and defend their identity from marauding heathens. As a trade center
for the civilized world, Venice represented a new and more open consciousness. Where different communities meet to trade goods and ideas
in friendly and open exchange, different points of view have equal
validity.

The word *renaissance* means "a rebirth." The new polychoral
music of the Venetian school is exciting to listen to, and captures, both
literally and metaphorically, the optimistic dynamic of the age. Where
there is a culture of unity, alternative views are suppressed. Where
there is a culture of diversity, however, alternative views are embraced
and discussion becomes very animated. Guided by the same scientific
discoveries in optics and lens-grinding that allowed Galileo to identify
the moons of Jupiter, Italian painters had created a new art of perspective painting, images of people and objects in spatial relationship,
that conveyed the message that what you are seeing, and therefore
what meaning you extract from the painting, expresses only a single
point of view.

The Venetian composers invented surround-sound over four centuries ago. In this music by Gabrieli the musicians are divided into
groups located at different points among and around the audience,
some in galleries at a higher level, others at ground level. The music
consists of a series of brilliant and combative exchanges from group to
group. For the audience it is very exciting, because the exchanges are
actually coming from different directions. The separation of groups
means that a listener will gain a different perspective on the music
depending on where that person is standing, so the older church doc-
trine of hearing the same music no matter where you stand, no longer
applies.

The basilica of St. Mark's, where this music was first performed,
is a religious building, making the musical statement of a coexistence
of different points of view under one roof appear very challenging to
orthodox opinion. It is furthermore a very exuberant music in which
the leading trumpets engage in a virtual competition to find who is the

most accomplished performer. The musical script demands that they all play the same elaborately decorated solo passages, creating the possibility that in a live performance (as distinct from a recording) a winner will in fact emerge.

This music is excited, not solemn; expressing diversity rather than unity: already serious challenges to the dignity of traditional religion. The concept of instrumental music without any words represents a further threat. Dowland and Shakespeare wrote unconventional lyrics to express their humanist values, but eliminating words altogether created the possibility of a freedom of expression to transcend even language. The church authorities were understandably shocked. A music without words, they reasoned, was a music over the meaning of which they had no control. In the past, instruments had been permitted to accompany religious singing. Singing honored the scripture, and instruments honored the singers. Now this music of the Venetian school did away with a text, and even with the limitations of the human voice. A trumpet could play faster, and higher, and more elaborate figurations than any singer, and when the excitement of competition is added to the mix, serious questions of propriety begin to arise.

Progress and trade is about sharing information, and a key to sharing information is making multiple copies. Gabrieli follows Gutenberg in celebrating a new age of shared information in a music in which the same melody passes rapidly and freely from one musician to another. In an astute piece of marketing the word *canon* in modern society has been adopted as the brand name of an office copying machine. Its older meaning is the echo effect that can be heard in Gabrieli's music. The two go together.

24
The echo song

Orlando di Lasso, "Hark! hark! the echo" (O la o che buon eccho) tr. W. G. Rothery. 2:22 minutes. Mid-16th century. Glasgow Orpheus Choir, Hugh Roberton. Moidart MOICD 007 (track 9).

This charming piece for two four-part choirs, one of which is concealed, is self-explanatory: a lyric about a dim-witted courtier who encounters his own echo and tries to engage it in conversation. We all know the legend of Narcissus who fell in love with his own reflection, but the person who chances upon a rocky place or cavern where a singing or speaking voice returns as an echo is likely to be just as fascinated. We are all curious to hear what our voice sounds like to other people, because when we speak our voice is heard for the most part inside our head. For this reason, places that echo have a special attraction, since they are proof that the words we speak are actually transmitted into the space around us, and thus that the world is independent of our senses. The irony of all this (which applies equally to the story of Narcissus) is that the reflected image is fuzzy and unclear. Only after the development of voice recording in the nineteenth century did it become possible to capture a person's voice with anything like reasonable fidelity. Then many people found that they did not like the sound of their own voice. For audiences in the sixteenth century, however, the experience of an echo was still a novelty.

The composer seems to be playing a game. You can imagine the scene. A choir standing in full view of the audience sings "Hark! hark! the echo falling"—and lo and behold, there the echo is, but the choir is not singing it, so it must be real. This is novel. All of a sudden the room where guests are being entertained has become an echo chamber. The guests laugh. The choir also laughs, and back comes the echo, also laughing. The audience listens further. "Where are you?" sings the choir. "Will you sing for us?" But it won't, being an echo. "Well, then, go away!" sings the choir, which is an equally ridiculous request. At the end the truth is revealed: a second choir steps out from behind a screen, or appears at a gallery.

Hidden in the joke is a small but serious purpose. In drawing attention to the echo as a natural acoustic effect, the composer is making a point about space and time that for sixteenth-century Italy is very up to date. It reminds the listener that sound travels through the air at a constant speed: the delay in the echo is a measure of distance as well as direction, and that distance in space corresponds also to distance in time. In simulating an echo, the composer is also affirming that empty space—the air between people—is measurable, heralding a new age in which the world can be mapped, and the motion of the planets exactly quantified. In its own way this is an affirmation as significant as acknowledging the zero in arithmetic, or the reality of irrational numbers that underpins the tempered scale.

25
There and back again

Claudio Monteverdi, *Magnificat.* "Quia fecit mihi magna," 1:02 minutes; "Et misericordia," 2:14 minutes; "Deposuit potentes de sede" 2:37 minutes. Early 17th century. From *Vespers of 1610.* Recommended: Boston Baroque, Martin Pearlman. Telarc 2CD-80453 (disc 2, tracks 7, 8, 10).

Monteverdi was a celebrated composer and consummate diplomat. In his monumental *Vespers* he manages to reconcile the interests of church and state, tradition and the new, in a music of wonderful economy. In these three brief pieces from a lengthy collection, the new renaissance world of space, time, and dimension are celebrated: lateral space, in the left–right dialogue of tenor voices in "Quia fecit;" vertical space, in the ascending melody of "Et misericordia"—aptly setting a text about feeling depressed and having one's spirits lifted—and the full three dimensions of length, breadth, and height in the complex left–right, front–back echo canons of "Deposuit potentes." The players in this marvelous work represent the two opposing views of reality, a choir singing sacred texts with organ accompaniment representing the timelessness of traditional religion, onto which the composer overlays solo and instrumental music demonstrating, almost in textbook fashion, the various dimensions of perspective space.

But he doesn't stop there. We can understand the juxtaposition of spiritual and temporal worlds in Monteverdi's montage of traditional plainchant and new material, but in "Et misericordia" the sense of vertical upward movement is both real, rising from the basses on the floor to the trebles at a higher level—and also a movement in pitch space, from low to higher tones. The realm of pitch is one where we talk about movement up and down, but in reality there is no up and down to pitch: it is an imaginary dimension. In "Deposuit de sede" the composer hints at additional dimensions of what might be called "virtual space." To the audience's right are solo *cornetti*, at the front of the picture, artificially echoed by another solo cornett located some significant distance to the rear (a combination of real separation in

space and virtual separation in musical terms). To the audience's left
are solo violins who perform the same music, once again in front and
echoed to the rear. At first encounter, the opposition of cornetti to the
right and violins to the left seems to make little sense. But by juxta-
posing the two Monteverdi draws attention to the functional opposition
of louder instruments such as trumpets or cornetti, that *project* signals
out into the world for other people to hear, and smaller-voiced strings
such as violins or lutes, whose orientation is more inward, to *reflect*
internal sensations and emotions. So in music lasting a mere two
minutes, Monteverdi conjures up a multi-dimensional space in which
past, present, and future, left and right, forward and back, up and
down, exterior and interior space, and time and eternity magically
coincide.

26
Dancing in church?

Claudio Monteverdi, "Deus in adjutorium" chant and response. 2:14 minutes. Early 17th
century. From *Vespers of 1610*. Boston Baroque, Martin Pearlman. Telarc 2CD-80453
(disc 1, track 1).

Johann Heinrich Schmelzer, *Sonata per chiesa et camera* (sonata for church and
chamber). Mid-17th century. 3:37 minutes. Ensemble Gradus ad Parnassum, Konrad
Junghänel. Austrian Radio. DHM 05472 77326 2 (track 1).

Monteverdi reserved the most complex and imposing music of *Vespers*
for the introduction, which is short, but powerful. The music opens
with a traditional invocation sung by a solo tenor in authentic Gregorian chant. As the reverberation dies away, the decorum of ritual erupts
in a splendid, rousing chorus for voices and instruments. This music is
loud, almost aggressive; it marches to a steady beat as if the sacred
space of the cathedral has been invaded by a stately procession of
princes, magistrates, merchants and bankers, all robed in their finery.
This is a worldly music, expressing the power and splendor of the new
merchant classes, in telling opposition to the reserved piety of traditional ritual. The sound of the massed musicians is anchored in the key
of D, but is so complex that the listener cannot hear everything that is
going on. This ability to create musical noises that are too intricate to
hear properly, is a consequence of notation, of being able to write

music down and calculate relationships by eye. Any listener from a foreign power that heard such music is likely to have been intimidated, because the culture that can make music of such extraordinary power and complexity is by definition capable of organizing its people to perform great deeds on the field of battle.

At times during this grand processional the music shifts from a solemn march in two time to a lighter, dancelike rhythm in three time, the back beat remaining the same. This jaunty rhythm speaks as clearly of human life and emotion as the triple-time decorations of Perotin's "Viderunt omnes." Triple rhythms may have some religious significance: that is a matter for experts. For the ordinary listener, a music that breaks into three time is beginning to dance, like the joyful celebration of the song "Mandad' ei comigo."

Human beings have two legs, so a music in two or four time can be walked in a straight line; music in three time however tends to lead in a circle. This more complicated and ambiguous sense of timing fits well with baroque architecture, in which straight lines and box-like shapes are abandoned in favor of restless and dynamic contours of curves and voids. The triple rhythms of Monteverdi's "Deus in adjutorium" reappear in the stately church sonata composed a half century later by Johann Schmelzer, incidentally in the same key of D (the term *sonata* meaning music for instruments alone). Like the cornetts and violins of "Deposuit de sede," Schmelzer's trumpets and violins are heard in alternation, the more out-going trumpets sounding from the rear and limited to plain declarations of fanfare, the inward music for violins much closer in sound, more intense in emotion, and more intricately worked. What the music says, in effect, is that for communicating in the public arena, a degree of simplification of text and meaning is always necessary; only in the privacy of the mind or heart can the subtler harmonies of human relationship be adequately conveyed.

27
Space, time, and color
Giovanni Priuli, *Canzona Prima a 12.* 4:52 minutes. Early Music Consort of London, David Munrow. Virgin 7243 5 61288 2 8 (track 4).

The Venetian polychoral style spread northward, to become established in Austria. Giovanni Priuli, a contemporary of Monteverdi, found employment in the service of Prince Ferdinand of Graz, whose private chapel provided much the same acoustic qualities and opportunities for spatial deployment of musicians as St. Mark's in Venice. In this beautiful example Priuli goes further than either Gabrieli or Monteverdi. Three groups of musicians are disposed in different locations in call and answer relationships, at times joining in chorus. In the Gabrieli canzona the various players are all instruments of similar type, so the principal degrees of separation are spatial and temporal. In Monteverdi, as we have seen, additional polarities of existential time and instrumental color are included, but the relationships are oppositional. In this slightly wistful but glowing work Priuli evokes a sound world where space, time, and instrumental color are variously combined, like the three layers in a color print.

28
Corelli's joke

Archangelo Corelli, Concerto Grosso in D major, Op. 6/7, Vivace–Allegro–Adagio. 2:40 minutes. Late 17th century. Recommended: Clarion Music Society, Newell Jenkins, Benjamin Hudson. NCD 70075 (track 1).

A century after Gabrieli and Monteverdi, the innovations of musical perspective and echo forms are beginning to fade and become stereotyped, even among Italian composers. The focus of music-making has moved out of the church and into the ballrooms and mansions of the wealthy. The new music is dynamic, lively, and complex, reflecting a new European culture of exploration and trade. Most of all, the new environments for performing music are different acoustically. In place of the complex interior stone surfaces of a cathedral or baroque church, structures built to a superhuman scale, with long reverberation times, furnished with galleries and side chapels suitable for a music exploring spatial effects, the residential accommodations of princely patrons tended to be simpler rectangular boxes, with wooden floors and low-relief plaster walls and ceilings. These structures produced a slighter, more immediate reverberation that allowed for a music of faster tempo and abrupt changes of key. These music rooms were typically located above cellar or kitchen rooms in the basement, spaces that not only provided additional resonance, but left the wooden floor of the music room above free to vibrate, reinforcing the bassline as it modulated from key to key. So the entire structure of a performance environment changed from a relatively inert stoneclad space, relying on multiple reflections, to a comparatively thin-skinned box resonator that acted to amplify the music within. During this period of transition, a distinction emerges between portable instruments such as flutes, trumpets, violins, and violas, instruments that do not touch the ground and whose sound is totally airborne, and supporting bass instruments—cello, double bass, and harpsichord—that rest on the floor and are thus able to make the floor structure vibrate in tune with the music.

This music by Corelli shows that composers were able to laugh at themselves. The opening music of a *concerto grosso*, a term of convenience for music for a relatively large number of players, has two functions: first, to quiet the audience, and second, to get the musicians organized and comfortable. We need to remember that even by the end of the seventeenth century it was quite an achievement to keep a large ensemble of musicians under control, a group often of varying ability, like a college orchestra today.

So what is the joke? In a chamber orchestra of this period, which is also the time of J. S. Bach and Handel, there were normally two lead players: the conductor, usually the composer himself at the harpsichord, and the principal violinist or concertmaster, whose role was to guide the melody line. If there were any doubt in an orchestra's mind about who was in charge, confusion could result. Corelli's joke is about that possibility.

The music begins with a short, standard overture in plodding, attention-getting rhythm, to alert the audience to sit down and be quiet. Then begins the movement proper, a lively *Allegro* in canon. This is a standard formula to get the music going, and it involves the lead violin beginning a brisk melody, followed a few steps behind by a second violin playing the same melody. It is in effect a speeded-up version of echo canon given in an acoustic that no longer conveys the spatial illusion of Gabrieli's time.

Corelli's lead violin begins the *Allegro* all by himself, and is followed soon after by a second violin. But here it appears as though

the silent harpsichordist has been caught napping, creating a problem
for the rest of the orchestra of which violin to follow. After a few bars
of hesitation the conductor at the harpsichord signals the rest of the
orchestra to begin playing, but it quickly becomes clear that he has no
idea where the two violins have got to. He tries one chord, then
another, then another, going round in circles, like trying to catch a
butterfly with a net. All the rest of the orchestra can do is try to stay
with the harpsichord. The audience, sensing the joke, has started to
laugh. Then the entire ensemble gets stuck in the key of D, unable to
move, sinking lower and lower as if into quicksand. More laughter.
Finally the movement extricates itself with a flourish, but to a chord
based on G sharp, about as alien from the key of D as it is possible to
get. At this point a graceful and apologetic melody from the lead violin
restores order so that the remainder of the item can continue in more
organized fashion.

29

Celebration in stereo

Antonio Vivaldi, "Lauda Jerusalem" RV609 (Psalm 147). Mid-18th century. 8:02
minutes. Recommended: Margaret Marshall, Ann Murray, John Alldis choir, English
Chamber Orchestra, Vittorio Negri. Philips 420 648-2.

Famed for "The Four Seasons" and not much else, Vivaldi has been
given rather a hard time by scholars. It is more than a little unfair on a
composer admired by J. S. Bach who was also a vital contributor to the
development of the modern orchestra, still very much in its early stages
during his lifetime. Vivaldi was a priest and musician employed for
much of his life as teacher and music director of a school for young
girls. His music is fresh and deceptively artless. He wrote an enormous
number of concertos, works for a range of solo instruments and
orchestra, that subsequent commentators assumed had been composed
to a production line formula. In fact Vivaldi's purpose was rather more
serious. One of the major issues of the day was the future of the concerto grosso: where would music go next? With so many different
combinations of instruments becoming available and performance
skills rapidly improving, the question was what permanent form a
symphony orchestra might eventually take. It was an issue to be

decided over many years, through the next generation of Haydn and Mozart, even into the nineteenth century of Berlioz and Wagner. Vivaldi's task as he saw it was to evaluate the instruments available for their suitablility as members of a more or less fixed ensemble, the classical symphony orchestra. He did this by the efficient but labor-intensive method of composing concertos of straightforward design, often recycling themes or whole movements from earlier works, so that the balance of a particular instrument could be assessed against the string orchestra, both as a soloist and also within a blended ensemble. Many of the instruments Vivaldi composed for were unaccustomed to performing in a solo role, one reason why the music is kept simple. The instruments themselves were often in a transitional state, requiring changes in design to make their tone and control acceptable for an eighteenth-century ensemble. Flute, clarinet, oboe, bassoon, and trumpet are among those to be adapted during Vivaldi's lifetime, on the way to attaining the quality of tone they now enjoy. If Vivaldi's concertos now seem simple and repetitive to play on modern instruments with supplementary keys, consider how much more skill would have been required to perform them on instruments of earlier design.

Composed in Vivaldi's later years, the "Lauda Jerusalem" returns to the same diplomatic balancing act between religious piety and secular energy as is shown by his great predecessor Monteverdi in the opening "Deus in adjutorium" of the *Vespers*. The new work is music of considerable élan, bubbling with vitality, to be performed perhaps at a wedding celebration. The spatial interest of the Venetian school returns, but is reduced to left-right stereo mode, as if the music were specially composed to show off the latest hi-fi equipment. The unusually fast pace is only possible in an eighteenth-century concert hall: it would never work in a cathedral acoustic. The ensemble is divided into two matching units, of solo soprano, choir, and strings, with the organ arbitrating in the middle. In a traditional echo dialogue, the answering voice is traditionally more distant, but here, as in Corelli, that relationship of time and distance has been forgotten in favor of a dialogue between equals in competitive mode. Like opposing players in a tennis match, the music volleys back and forth, the delays sometimes longer, sometimes shorter, with more overlap. The

recommended performance under Vittorio Negri has an astonishing
rapturous vitality that belies the doctrinaire piety of the chosen text.
For a composer of Vivaldi's time of life it is a wonderful tribute to the
revitalizing power of adolescent high spirits.

30
Infinite space

W. A. Mozart, Minuetto from the *Notturno in D major*, K286. 8:18 minutes. Late 18th
century. London Symphony Orchestra, Peter Maag. Decca 289 466 500-2 (track 3).

The word *canon* comes from the same root as *canyon*, a cleft or gorge
cut by a river on its way to the sea, and a place where repetitive echoes
are heard. It is a shame that composers of the classical era seem to
have lost interest in simulating echo effects from nature, though harpsi-
chordists continued to play with echo repetition (loud, then soft) on
dual keyboards, while melodic imitation, as we find in Corelli, continued in popularity as a technical device. A rare exception from the late
eighteenth century is this Notturno for four orchestras by Mozart. A
notturno (night piece) is an occasional work, often to be performed out
of doors, perhaps on a summer evening when the air is still, while
guests stroll among the ornamental gardens of an aristocratic estate. As
a child Mozart traveled widely around Europe, so it is not out of the
question that he may have experienced the rolling echo of a canyon at
an early age, possibly from a boat navigating down the Rhine from
Basel through Germany, through the same massive cliffs and natural
scenery that were to provide a majestic setting for Wagner's "Ring"
cycle of operas a century later.

The reason one suspects Mozart may have heard the echoing of a
real canyon is the relative accuracy of his simulation. Lack of regular
contact with natural echo can explain the trivial, or at least artificial
echo effects in Corelli and Vivaldi, and one might have expected
Mozart to be equally out of touch with reality. The impression of the
triple echo overlapping, receding, and dying away is so alluring, however, that even though the music is pastoral in tone, a listener imagines
the composer to be making a discreetly philosophical point about the
vastness and monumentality of the forces of nature when measured
against the scale of human affairs. The four orchestras are not arranged

in a circle, in the manner of Priuli or Gabrieli, but in a straight line that seems to extend to a vanishing point out of sight and out of hearing. The four orchestras are evenly matched, with strings and two horns in each, the string harmonies sounding more than usually diffuse in the open air, and the horn cries evoking the sound of the chase.

31
Stereophony

Béla Bartók, *Music for Strings, Percussion, and Celesta.* II Allegro. 20th century. 7:25 minutes. English String Orchestra, Yehudi Menuhin. Nimbus NI 5086 (track 5).

The seating arrangements of musicians over the centuries is a fascinating and neglected area of study. Where the choir and orchestra players sit, in relation to the structure as well as to one another and to the audience, seriously affects how a music will sound. A choir in a cathedral may sit off to one side and out of sight, to make the sound of voices appear diffuse and numinous like a halo of sound. The players in a baroque orchestra of the eighteenth century were arranged round the harpsichord in the center of the room, leaving the audience free to sit where they liked, or to promenade. The idea of grouping players on a stage at one end of the concert chamber, making a concert resemble a dramatic entertainment, did not appear overnight. It was not until the zoning arrangements of a concert were properly agreed, with the players occupying one area and the audience another, that the issue arose of positioning the players so that their sound would be in balance and uniformly projected toward an audience.

Throughout the nineteenth century and into the twentieth, concert halls and orchestras increased dramatically in size and numbers. This led to the present zoning arrangement, of players seated onstage facing an audience, also in fixed seating, becoming firmly entrenched. If they wanted freedom of movement, people could go to a promenade concert in the park, or watch a marching band. Concert promotion in the Victorian era was driven by economics: larger halls, ever grander displays, and the need to fill as many seats as possible. It is not surprising that under those conditions, interest in the spatial dimension of music withered on the vine.

It was pure chance that led to the rediscovery of space as a dramatic element in musical performance. A French engineer, Clément Ader, who had a financial interest in the new telephone industry, organized a public demonstration at the Paris Exposition of 1881. Land lines were laid from the stage of the Paris Opéra to the exhibition site, where for a fee of five francs (quite a sum in those days) members of the public could listen in to an opera performance relayed from transmitters ranged across the front of stage. Following complaints that a single microphone or "transmitter" could only pick up half of the action, he tried listening with two earphones to two transmitters, one to the left, the other to the right side of the stage. To his surprise, he found that the movements of the actors and singers across the stage were clearly reproduced. Listeners could also pinpoint where the musicians were sitting in the orchestra pit; indeed one critic, who was wearing his earphones back to front, complained that the trombones were on the opposite side from where they should be. The demonstration created enormous reverberations in the industry, arousing speculation of the possibility of cable entertainment in stereo some forty years before public broadcasting by radio was to become a reality, and 75 years before the first vinyl stereo records appeared on the market.

Fast forward to the 1930s, a new era of radio and sound recording, and a time when the silent movie industry, facing competition from both, was busy reinventing itself as "the talkies." Leading manufacturers in Britain and the United States were now committed to stereo, though not for radio, and not for gramophone recording, but for the silver screen, using optical film as the recording medium.

In 1936 the conductor Paul Sacher commissioned a work for double string orchestra, piano, and percussion from Béla Bartók. As well as being a champion of contemporary music, Sacher was also interested in reviving music of the preclassical era and in 1933 had founded the Basel Schola Cantorum to perform forgotten works of the Italian baroque, including Albinoni and Vivaldi. It was Sacher's idea to have a work composed for double string orchestra, to the left and right of the conductor, which raises the interesting possibility that he had come across works like the "Lauda Jerusalem" of Vivaldi and was interested in revisiting the older polychoral style.

Bartók's *Music for Strings, Percussion and Celesta* is in four movements, alternating slow and fast. The second movement is music in stereo, full of high spirits, like a speeded-up version of Vivaldi. Ideas flash from left to right and back, sometimes turning upside down in transit. A tennis match would be too slow: the flickering exchanges are more like table tennis, and very hard to follow. So fast, in fact, that the listener begins to wonder if the composer really appreciated that echo canon is based on real acoustics, and that for spatial effects to be heard and enjoyed, the ear needs time.

Discussion topics

1.   Discuss the implications of a *collective* moment of silence or stillness in human affairs: a concert, or a public ceremony. Is this what Cage's music of silence is about?
2.   To those in the know, Dowland expresses the ideas of absence in the substitution of a melody instrument for the voice, and a sense of loss in the dead silence between verses. Compare this effect with images in art such as a still life, an installation, or a *vanitas* of musical instruments.
3.   Gabrieli's echo illusions keep changing orientation, suggesting a world of multiple perspectives. What does the energetic character of his music add to this perception?
4.   Monteverdi's spatial symmetries are poised and precise, analogous to mirror-images and male-female relationships in renaissance painting. What is the hidden meaning of such reflective imagery?
5.   The perspective effects in Monteverdi's *Magnificat* can be interpreted as a meditation on spatial relationships as a consequence of people having two eyes and two ears.
6.   Would you agree that trumpets (or cornetts) conventionally represent an outgoing, decisive, active masculine sensibility, whereas violins convey the inward, feminine, less certain, more reflective and emotional side of humanity?
7.   In contrast to Monteverdi, Priuli's canzona is organized in threes: high, middle, low; left, center, right; woodwinds, strings, brass, etc. A music based on three-fold symmetries has religious and symbolic implications, like the panels in a triptych.
8.   Corelli's joke in the concerto grosso has elements in common with the BBC comedy "Dad's Army." In both the comedy turns on conflicting ideas of who is in charge, who is giving the orders, and the confusion that arises among the ranks when more than one person appears to be in command. Discuss the military implications of good discipline in an orchestra or band.

9.   In "Lauda Jerusalem" Vivaldi's matching soloists, choirs, and string orchestras engage in a rapid dialogue that you might think has more to say about human relations than spatial perspective. Discuss the opinion that this is music for a marriage celebration.

10.   Plainchant is a music about unity of space and time, and the music of Gabrieli and Monteverdi is about a space in which multiple events and perspectives coexist. In both cases it does not matter where the listener is located: in the case of plainchant the musical effect is essentially the same, and for the listener to Gabrieli and Monteverdi perspective effects may vary, but every point of view is equally valid. In composing his *Notturno for four orchestras* where would Mozart have intended his audience to be located in relation to the orchestras? Can the size and scale of the music be interpreted as a premonition of romanticism, acknowledging the grandeur of nature?

11.   Bartók's rather turbulent dialogue of two string orchestras in the *Music for strings, percussion, and celesta* seems far removed from the artful spatial illusions and echo effects of Orlando di Lasso, Gabrieli, or Vivaldi. In some places the symmetry is speeded up, or even turned upside down. Is this a musical game of tennis, a game of combat, or something else? What kind of emotion do you think the stereo dialogue is intended to convey?

III

PRECISION INSTRUMENTS

Earlier examples of the Shinto chant and Herbert Morrison's "Hindenburg disaster" broadcast have shown that in performance there is not only a value to composure—that is, to delivering information without getting emotionally involved—but also a value to a performance that conveys signs of passion. The two values are not very compatible. The Shinto priest chants in a monotone that leaves the sacred words absolutely clear and free of any contamination of personal interpretation. The radio broadcast begins in an acceptable way, the reporter speaking with very little emotional inflection, until the airship explodes and he is overwhelmed by strong emotions of fear and anguish. Morrison's loss of composure affected his ability to speak and report clearly, so from a professional point of view it stands as an example of what happens when you let emotions take control. Ironically, for most people the broadcast is powerful and memorable precisely because the reporter becomes overwhelmed by emotion.

The professional and ethical distaste expressed by the male church hierarchy, the singers of plainchant, toward the passionate music of Hildegard, is another example of the same conflict of attitudes. Plainchant is supposed to be emotionally neutral and serve the interests of the text, whereas the sacred songs of Hildegard use a text simply as a vehicle to release powerful natural impulses. Even the pairing of voice and lute, as in Dowland's song, can be interpreted as a meeting of opposites. The voice is a naturally unstable mechanism, so for the voice to deliver a message clearly and steadily requires sustained mental and physical control; the lute on the other hand is constant and reliable in tone and pitch, but incapable of speech.

The legend of Apollo and Marsyas elevates the functional polarity of musical and vocal expression to a conflict of aesthetic, or even moral values. In the legend Apollo, the god of music and a leading authority on the physics of stretched strings (violin and lyre as well as the bowstring), is challenged to a competition by Marsyas, whose instrument is the panpipes, simple reed tubes. Artists such as Jacopo da Palma depict Apollo as a god crowned with laurel leaves, while Marsyas is depicted as a satyr, with goat horns and shaggy legs. The implication is that his rustic (and by implication, also licentious) music is no match, either in quality or nobility of purpose, to Apollo's mastery of the violin, and in the story Marsyas is dealt with severely.

At face value, this is a story about skill and powers of expression as essential values of art. The panpipes, both in fact and by implication, do not require any skill to play, and have next to no flexibility of expression. Though even violinists carry a set of pitch pipes in their violin cases for tuning purposes, the violin—for obvious reasons of age, craftsmanship, and quality of sound—is the insured item while the pipes are little more than a disposable toy. In Mozart's last great opera *The Magic Flute* the song of Papageno, representing pastoral innocence, is accompanied by the artless sound of toy panpipes.

In every music of every culture a balance is struck between certainty and uncertainty. By establishing codes and rules that everyone knows, it is possible to share information of an ostensibly factual and mutually understandable kind. Language and notation are systems of information sharing, and musical instruments provide standards of hardware design and performance that to a greater or lesser degree help to ensure consistency in interpretation within and even across national boundaries.

A set of panpipes may not be a vehicle for virtuoso display, but at least it stays in tune. A violin does not. That is the difference. The choice is between a system and instrumentation (notation, keyboards) that is standardized for greater efficiency in communication, and those allowing more freedom of expression, for a higher degree of accuracy and truth to experience.

32
Gamelan

Tabuh Kenilu Sawik for gong ensemble. 4:17 minutes. Kulintang ensemble of Labuhan Maringgai dir. Japar Raja Alam. Lampung, Sumatra. From *Gongs and Vocal Music of Sumatra*, Smithsonian Folkways SFW CD 40428 (track 8).

To western ears this music for tuned and untuned gongs and drums, a music suitable for playing in or out of doors, is a calming antidote to the stresses of city life. It is music for six performers playing different percussion instruments, in western terms a broken consort where different instruments have different roles and close teamwork is part of the message. The skin and ringing metal sounds are predominantly in the mid to low range, glowing reverberant sonorities with a dash of drum to enhance the sense of touch. This music expresses a mildly elevated excitement, but within a context of disciplined patternmaking. It is music suitable for playing at a wedding. The listener is aware of layers of rhythm under a gently undulating surface. No one player demands special attention; the parts are subordinate to the whole, like the limbs of a dancer in graceful motion.

Percussion ensembles like the gamelan, or the solo drum of Iran, are tranquil to listen to in part because they are played by hand or soft beater, and also because their tuning, however strange, is fixed in advance. Like the panpipes, these are instruments preprogrammed for pitch, so making and listening to their music does not involve the constant attention to tuning associated with (say) a performance of massed guitars or violins. Absence of tonal variation (which is also an absence of tension) is a source of relief for the listener, and allows the musician to focus on dialogue and ensemble interactions. This is a music that flows like a stream, but stays in one place.

33
A meeting of cultures

Francis Poulenc, Concerto for Two Pianos and Orchestra in D minor, I. Allegro ma non troppo. 8:04 minutes. Early 20th century. Peter Toperczer, Marian Lapsanský, Slovak Philharmonic, Zdenek Kosler. Point Classics 2672122 (track 11).

This likeable piece dating from 1932 is among the first of a number of works composed during the interwar years (1918–1939) to embrace the delicate and (to western ears) haunting sonorities of Indonesian gamelan. During the 1880s this music had been heard in Paris, greatly impressing Claude Debussy and others. Poulenc belonged to a later generation further influenced by movie travelogues that from the 1930s were beginning to arrive in Europe from countries of the far east, bringing music as well as images of exotic landscapes and peoples. This movement begins briskly in neoclassical style, an idiom combining the astringency of Stravinsky with the jovial good humor of a René Clair movie. For a moment at the very beginning one catches a glimpse of a different acoustic world, but it is only after four minutes into the movement that the mood deepens from witty and sophisticated to mysterious and otherworldly. The writing for two pianos becomes briefly ethereal, like a gamelan, a music of shimmering piano harmonies in the upper register. The two idioms of east and west appear to coexist, but not to interact, as though an unseen hand is switching channels on the radio. If one were to dance to this movement of Poulenc, one might contrast energetic and angular moves during the neoclassical segments, with lighter and more graceful moves, emphasizing the vertical, in the gamelan segments.

"In a choir, nobody wins." When gamelan is set side by side with music of a western sensibility the contrast in mood is very striking. Western music is goal-directed, dynamic, restless: a listener has the impression that it is going somewhere, that the purpose of life is progress and discovery, and that pain and suffering are a necessary part of the process. But when the gamelan music appears, those undercurrents of restlessness and constant tension suddenly dissolve. In music of such contrasts it is possible to understand the romantic allure of the legend of Shangri-La, and the power of myth of a lost paradise on earth assiduously cultivated by western explorers of the eighteenth and nineteenth centuries. Since it is nonvocal, gamelan has no text; being collective, it has no leader; and being for instruments, it has no emotional inflection, hence no passion, so this music lacks the three major distinctive features of western music. At a time in European history when the music of war, and rampant nationalism, seemed to be leading humanity to doom and destruction, Poulenc's message of gamelan stands out clearly as a beacon of hope.

34
A gamelan in New York

Edgar Varèse, *Ionisation* for 13 percussionists. 5:56 minutes. Ensemble cond. Pierre Boulez. Sony SMK 45 844 (track 1).

Varèse thought he was being very brave in composing for a percussion ensemble. Thirteen musicians play a total of 37 instruments, including a pair of sirens (which provide the melody component, and are not percussion at all). The remainder, among them Chinese blocks, Cuban guiros (scraper gourds), gongs, cymbals, anvils, celesta, and piano, could be regarded as an ad hoc collection of instruments of conflicting ethnicities with no recognizable cultural identity. It is certainly a long way from the calm and peaceful music of Eastern philosophy. Despite the composer's own protestations, so ebullient and powerful a music, especially with two sirens involved, could not fail to evoke the newsreel imagery of a fast-paced, bustling urban industrial community such as New York.

It takes a little time for the listener to recover from the initial impact of this music. The abstract artist Kandinsky compares a sinuous line to a line of melody, and one can imagine Varèse's music as the musical equivalent of a Kandinsky "Improvisation," the sirens representing the artist's trademark whiplash black line undulating across the canvas and leading the eye through a composition of patches of color and abstracted rhythmic shapes.

In the absence of cultural signposting, the listener has to listen out for alternative unifying features. A percussion orchestra is perhaps the ultimate broken consort, organized by pitch (high, middle, bass), material (metal, wood, skin), tone (pitched, clangorous, unpitched), and quality of sound (sharp, soft, dry, ringing). Transitions between categories can also be heard, for example from triangle (metal, ringing, no pitch) to anvil (metal, dry, pitch) to celesta (metal, ringing, precise pitch); or from the dry rustle of maracas to the metallic shimmer of sleighbells, and so on. By putting to one side all knowledge of the instruments and their associations, and developing a sense of what the sound is doing in purely acoustic terms, a listener begins to appreciate the artistry of the composer in combining and modulating from sound group to sound group.

35
Prepared piano

John Cage, *Sonata II* for prepared piano. Mid-20th century. 2:30 minutes. Boris Berman.
Naxos 8.559042 (track 2).

Cage began composing for percussion-only ensembles as a young man
in 1935. Until surprisingly recently, the world of classical music tended
to regard percussion instruments as little more than rhythmic noise-
makers. Varèse had begun to challenge that attitude in a number of
compositions, culminating with *Ionisation* in 1931. But Varèse was a
big man, interested in making loud and forceful statements on an
industrial scale. Cage preferred the more tranquil associations of
gamelan. The latter influence is easy to hear in his *Double Music* of
1941, composed in association with Lou Harrison.

Cage went on to invent the prepared piano, as he said, because it
was easier and cheaper to prepare a piano on site for a concert than to
have to transport a percussion band from place to place at a cost that
could not be recovered from the performance fee. The prepared piano
is a regular piano treated by the careful and deliberate insertion of
foreign objects between the strings. A piano has massive single strings
in the deep bass, which are left alone, double strings in the medium
bass, and triple strings upward from middle C. When a wedge of cork
or rubber is inserted between double or triple strings, they are unable to
vibrate as freely, and the tone quality changes. By experimenting with
positions and materials, some unusual and beautiful effects can be
created, sounding like cymbals, bells, bongos, or wooden drums. If the
inserted object is a metal screw, or a bolt and nut with a loose washer,
sharper and more clangorous tones can be created.

Though the very idea of interfering with the sound of a piano may
seem offensive to many musicians, Cage's idea is as revealing and
memorable in its own way as the "Hindenburg disaster" broadcast.
Morrison broke the golden rule of a radio reporter. Faced with the
reality of a tragic event, he lost his cool. But in losing his cool, he
struck an emotional chord with the public. People realised for the first
time that radio could affect them directly. In tampering with the piano,
Cage was also breaking the rules. The piano was a musical icon. It
embodied certain values, in particular the idea of a continuum of pitch

from low to high, and every note consistent in tone color and response. The mechanical keyboard had been specially developed to allow a composer complete freedom of movement up and down in pitch, of modulation from key to key, from loud to soft, and chord to chord. At a stroke Cage changed all that. His prepared piano forced the musical world to understand that these uniformities are also limitations on freedom that come with embracing a dynamic of progress.

In Cage's prepared piano, what you see on the music page is not always what you get in terms of sound. Conventional notation and the piano keyboard evolved together. A dot on the chart signifies a location on the keyboard. But under Cage, the perfect, even regularity of the keyboard is revealed as an illusion. Instead of marking a location on a continuous spectrum of pitch, a key becomes the trigger to a specific instrumental quality or sound, different from all the rest, but always the same for that key. Conventional melody (which is based on continuity of pitch) and harmony (which is based on compatibility of tone) are suddenly off the agenda. What is a great pianist to do? He (she) has to abandon all thoughts of conventional virtuosity and embrace the lucid detachment of a different mentality that just happens to have elements in common with the far east.

36
Expressionless music

J. S. Bach, Prelude 1 in C major for piano, BWV 846. 2:21 minutes. Early 18th century. Recommended: Vladimir Feltsmann, MusicMasters 01612-67105-2; also Jenö Jandó, Naxos 8.553796-7 (track 1).

This is a famous piece of piano music that many piano students learn to play at an early age. It is not difficult to master the notes—much less difficult than many of the other preludes and fugues in the total series. The problem is more one of deciding what the music is about. There are great pianists in recent history who have been completely thrown off balance by this one piece, among them the famous Canadian pianist Glenn Gould, who recorded it with a great deal of ostentatious un-certainty, even gingerly, as though the music were a hot potato, or a trick question. There is no trick. The notes are there. Don't ask in advance what they are supposed to mean. Just play.

This is the first prelude of Bach's "48" Preludes and Fugues, pieces composed to endorse a generalized system of tuning the notes of the scale so that playing music in any key, black or white, sharp or flat, major or minor, would sound acceptable. The issue of tuning the scale to permit free modulation from key to key is complicated and paradoxical. Vincenzo Galilei, uncle of the famous astronomer Galileo, was

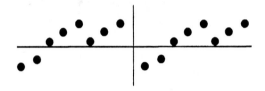

Bach: Prelude in C major: the pattern

among a group of leading scientists and intellectuals who a century before Bach had agonized over the problem of tempered tuning, which is responsible for the positions of the holes on a flute and the pitches programmed on a synthesizer. To cut a long story short, the tempered scale is a compromise, here and there a shade out of tune. (The out-of-true intonation of western music after Bach is one reason why singers sing with a vibrato and why the multiple strings of modern pianos are tuned slightly out of pitch: effects comparable to smearing petroleum jelly on a movie camera lens, to disguise wrinkles in intonation.)

Virtuoso pianists like to show off, and are sometimes embarrassed to play music that gives them nothing to express. What is Prelude No. 1 for? Could you sing to it? No. It has no melody. Could you dance to it? Also no. There is no beat. What is it, then? A pattern of notes that sits under the fingers and moves up and down the keyboard. This music is about the fact that the keyboard is a neutral mechanism for the study of tonal relationships, both by the simple movement of a configuration of notes up and down the keyboard, and by the slight alteration of finger positions to produce alternative harmonies. The music starts in the cleanest and whitest key of C, and moves by degrees away from the home key, driven by a logic of key relations that leads it into strange and exotic places, at one point reaching a Sargasso Sea of weirdness where tonal movement threatens to come to a halt, only to be rescued at the last moment to return to home base with a hint of celebration.

To appreciate the delicacy of Bach's harmonic journey the piano should ideally be tuned to the system that Bach developed himself, which is somewhere near the tuning recommended by his contemporary Andreas Werckmeister. On a suitably tuned instrument a listener is better able to detect the telltale tremors and dissonances that signal the movement of a harmonic sequence into dangerous territory. In the absence of appropriate tuning, a plain performance style is best, to clarify that this music is not about style or emotion, or even about technique. Rather it is music to draw attention to the virtues of the keyboard as a mechanism to ensure objectivity and evenness of tone and touch, to eliminate unwanted human variables such as accents or crescendos, and thereby to reveal in fascinating detail the possibilities of animated shapes traveling at will across the musical screen.

How is this music related to the gamelan music of Indonesia? It demonstrates an attitude to sound that is free of expressive intention, and focused on acoustic relationships of pattern and movement. When we hear this music played appropriately on a modern piano, it becomes easier to understand what Cage had in mind for the prepared piano.

37
Study for guitar
Heitor Villa-Lobos, *Étude No. 1 (Animé)*. 1:49 minutes. 20th century. From *Twelve Études* for solo guitar. Fabio Zanon, MusicMasters 01612-67188-2.

In many outward respects this study for guitar in E minor by the Brazilian Villa-Lobos resembles the Prelude No. 1 in C major by Bach. The music unfolds in a sequence of *arpeggio* figures (rolling chords), each one repeated a second time. This repetition device might have been originally designed as an echo effect, the first phrase performed loud, the repeat soft, played on a harpsichord with dual keyboards, but repetition in this work for guitar seems to be intended more for emphasis than dynamic contrast. For a guitar, the key of E minor is the natural point of departure equivalent to C major for a keyboard. Like the Bach prelude, the sequence of chords moves gradually away from the starting chord, but whereas in Bach the trend is more passive,

moving gently downwards, as if seeking its own level, in Villa-Lobos
the trend is directed upwards in an image of growth and increasing
power. Villa-Lobos has little interest in purely tonal relationships. This
is a deliberately ostentatious virtuoso exercise to demonstrate technical
competence at high speed and impress the opposite sex. Unlike the
austerity of Bach's keyboard—an instrument played at arm's length by
levers controlled from the fingertips—a Spanish guitar is a curvaceous
resonating body cradled in the arms and touched all over with the
fingers, the left hand moving up and down the neck of the instrument
in constantly-changing positions, while fingers and nails of the right
hand tug at the strings. A guitarist feels the vibrations directly in the
body. It is a tactile experience of conscious mastery. A wonderful work,
a real party piece, ending with a sigh of delicate harmonics.

38
White music

Erik Satie, *Gymnopédie I* for piano. Late 19th century. 3:38 minutes. Daniel Varsano.
SBK 48283 (track 1). Alternative version (5:57 minutes) by Reinbert de Leeuw, Philips
462 161-2.

"The artist should regulate his life," wrote Satie in 1913, shortly before
the outbreak of World War I. "I only eat white food: eggs, sugar, grat-
ed bones; the fat of dead animals; veal, salt, coconuts, chicken cooked
in water; moldy fruit, rice, turnips; camphorated black pudding, pasta,
cheese (white), cotton salad and certain kinds of fish (without skins)."
Behind the dry wit is a serious message: art should aspire to whiteness.
There is a similar message in Kasimir Malevich's painting "White on
white" of 1918, the year the Great War ended. Composed in the 1880s,
Satie's *Three Gymnopédies* are examples of "expressionless" music
after the model of the Prelude in C major by J. S. Bach. Bach's deliberate lack of expression is in a spirit of objectivity widely practiced by
the "music programmers" of the early keyboard era, composers such as
Domenico Scarlatti, Johann Froberger, and Louis Couperin. Satie however is also protesting against the posturing heroics and cult status of
the romantic era virtuoso performer, a trend in his day all too easily
associated with an increasingly aggressive nationalism. Perhaps encouraged by the arrival of new recording media, the player piano and

the phonograph, Satie pursued an art related, as he saw it, to the sublime indifference of classical antiquity, to timelessness, to religion, and to elevating the spirit above the physical world of action and emotion.

It is a tribute to Satie's judgement, both moral and technical, that after over a century this disarmingly simple piano piece is still so great a challenge for "virtuoso" pianists to perform. In three time, inscribed "Lent et douloureux" (slow and seemingly sad) the music asks the question, What do you do when there is nothing to interpret? And what music could be more simple? And yet recordings of this one piece are unable even to agree on an appropriate tempo. Some performers treat the work as a slow dance, which means that it has to be played fast enough to dance to, resulting in a duration of under three minutes. Others take the composer's instruction literally (which is only fair, after all) and conclude that the piece should be played slower and more thoughtfully, at a pace where dancing becomes unsteady and no longer graceful. To give the impression of a white composition, bereft of emotional coloring, an interpreter has to find a way of expressing the music's passage as floating through time without the distraction of physical movement. The perfect example of such a process is the ticking of a grandfather clock.

Another insuperable simplicity in this piece is how to interpret the shift in dynamics from soft to loud. Of the two recommended recordings, Daniel Varsano glides gracefully and imperturbably, but the change in loudness comes with a jolt. For such a quiet piece, the effect of a *forte* can be achieved by the slightest alteration of pressure and a little added sustain. Nearly twice as long, the unexpectedly intense interpretation of Reinbert de Leeuw moves at so slow a pace that the listener's attention is attracted to the inner life of the piano harmonies, very close in spirit to the prepared piano of John Cage.

"By creating a piece which sounds mechanical, Satie makes it seem as if nobody is there at all, and the music is creating itself."

39
Inner voices
Anatoli Kuular (jaw harp), "Talking *Xomuz.*" 1:53 minutes. In *Tuva, Among the Spirits.* Smithsonian Folkways SFW 40452 (track 17).

Kaigal-ool Khovalyg, "Fantasy on the *Igil*." 5:33 minutes. In *Tuva, Among the Spirits.*
Smithsonian Folkways SFW 40452 (track 4).
The voice is also a precision instrument. Language is a precision affair.
Most people pay attention to the sounds of the words they speak and
are sensitive to shades of pronunciation and their effect on meaning.
Puns, jokes, and other forms of wordplay test our sensitivity to vocal
sounds and their meanings. Just how the astonishing variety of sounds
is produced in the vocal cavity is less well appreciated, except by
scientists and specialists in speech and hearing disabilities. The focus
of such studies is naturally remedial; speech and hearing are important
for communication. But there is a much more ancient interest in the
nature of speech and its relationship to music, and it is found in surviving traditions of *mouth music* or *throat music* in Siberia, Mongolia, and
the Shetland Islands, and more widely in jaw harp music which involves inserting a twanging device inside the mouth as a substitute for
the vocal cords. The typical "dong, dong, ding-a-dong, ding, dang,
dong" of a jaw harp is a familiar sound in country music. Nobody
thinks of this rustic device as a scientific instrument. And yet it can be
fairly described as a voice analyzer, and the knowledge derived from
playing the jaw harp as a knowledge base from which an entire tradition of tone synthesis, from the history of organ building through to
electronic music and artificial speech in the late twentieth century, can
be extrapolated. Jaw harp and throat music are based on the same
principles as synthetic speech employing an artificial tone source.
Sometimes the intention is to mimic speech directly, as in the first of
these two examples, in which the musician sings a verse of a love
song, and then imitates the same words using a jaw harp. Other times,
as in the second example of throat music, the vocal apparatus is reinvented as a multiphonic musical instrument that manipulates vowel-
like resonances to produce whistling melodies over a steady drone.
      Whether such ancient recreations conform to scientific practice as
we know it is neither here nor there. They arise from oral traditions
that have been passed from generation to generation by imitation, not
in written form. All the same, in order to acquire the skill to perform
jaw or throat music, a person has to develop an analytical ear for vocal
resonances, and in order to make melodies, a musician has to be able to

arrange the sounds of speech in ways that make no sense as language. Here are two examples from everyday speech: say (or whisper) the phrase "Uh-oh," and then, slowly and continuously, the phrase "How are you?" The first phrase can be heard as two notes in succession, the second note a third or a fifth lower than the first. The whispered difference in vowel is clearly audible as a difference in resonant pitch: we even speak the phrase as a two-note melody. Whispered, the second phrase is heard to produce a wavelike resonance sliding down, then up, then down again. The effect is even more striking if, instead of being spoken or whispered, both phrases are intoned on one note. Then the vowel resonances change from bandwidths of noise to crystal-clear harmonics, a very beautiful and musical effect.

Both throat and jaw harp music are unmistakable evidence of disciplined and systematic inquiry into the abstract frequency composition of spoken language. The social implications of voice analysis are profound. The person who understands how words are formed has the godlike power to form new words associated with magic spells, shamanistic utterances, and speaking in tongues. A culture that can turn language into music has the incentive to develop more elaborate mechanisms of tone synthesis.

40
Ambrosian chant
Antiphon: Ton stauron sou proskinumen / Crucem tuam; Psalm 149: Laudate Dominum. 7:23 minutes. Lycourcos Angelopoulos, Marcel Péres. In *Chants of the Cathedral of Benevento*. 7th–11th centuries. Harmonia Mundi HMC 901476 (track 3).

There is a simple reason for developing the jaw harp as an independent mechanism for the production and study of vocal resonances: it produces a tone of steady and invariant pitch, which is difficult for a singing voice to achieve. A jaw harp thus releases the performer from the duty of maintaining a steady pitch, to focus attention on controlling the resonances within the mouth and throat. Since these resonances are harmonically related to the underlying pitch, they can only be properly evaluated if the underlying pitch is constant. In addition, because the instrument is independent of the performer, the discoveries made with its aid can be shared with and reproduced by somebody else.

Having developed an independent drone source, the next logical step in the process of musical inquiry into language and meaning, is to stabilize the wind supply. The goal of producing tones of indefinite duration, at constant pitch and amplitude, is achieved in the organ and portable instruments of the bagpipe family. The fixed drone is a feature of music of many cultures, as we know from the Spanish "Mandad' ei comigo," the Tuareg chant to ward off fever, and the Perotin "Viderunt omnes." In this austere example from the byzantine era the constant drone is sung by wordless bass voices over which the celebrants sing the text alternately in Greek and Latin. This example of drone accompaniment alludes to the musical function of the pipe organ, then a very primitive affair. It was not until the sixteenth century that the organ attained its classic form as a keyboard synthesizer capable of blending artificial waveforms of different timbres. That tone synthesis emerges as the ultimate objective of organ construction, suggests a long evolutionary process, via the drone function, from the simple and effective culture of mouth music.

41
Morning Raga

Singi-Bhairavi: morning Raga. 14:58 minutes (mono). Ravi Shankar *sitar*, Nodu C. Mullick *tamboura*, Chatur Lal *tabla*. *The Sounds of India: an Introduction to Indian Music*. Columbia CK 9296 (track 5).

The distinctive sound of this music is representative of the Indian subcontinent. The timbres are plucked strings and tuned drums. The strings consist of a melody instrument, the sitar, and an accompanying harmony or drone instrument, the tamboura. It is a singing music of great sophistication and resonance that does not rely on a reverberant acoustic, but on the combined assisted resonance of gourds and sympathetic strings maintained in continuous vibration. The glossy sound and intricate melodic inventions of the sitar, rich in high frequencies, are offset by the drier and deeper tones of the two tabla, tuned bowl drums that produce ringing overtones. It is a very tactile and ostensibly emotional music of noticeably speechlike quality, improvised to a combination of melodic and rhythmic patterns chosen from a vast repertoire and appropriate to the season, mood, and time of day.

When listening to music of another culture it is easy to feel ignorant and to think that one's own impressions are of no importance. The alternative view is that art and music develop their own rules and mythologies to account for the way a particular form of expression is organized, and to explain the importance of culturally sensitive features. In the long run, the beauty and significance of a music is in the sound of the music itself, which is available to everybody whatever their culture. If a listener who is not an expert in the musical traditions of India notices that this music has a number of features in common with Ambrosian chant, or jaw harp music, that is evidence perhaps of universal traits that reflect our common humanity. The relationship of the principal melody to the drone accompaniment is a case in point. The drone provides a steady reference line against which the movement of a melody can be precisely judged, including expressive deviations and tremors from the true note. The similarities between the ornamental tremors of Ambrosian chant and the excitable tremors of improvised sitar melody are easy to hear, even though the one is vocal and religious, the other secular and instrumental.

Both are related by implication to jaw harp and throat music, in which the vowel resonances of the mouth cavity are diverted from a speech function to a higher music function. Ambrosian chant is outwardly intended to serve the needs of a text, but the speech function is overlaid with solo melodic transitions that quite clearly refer to the higher (i.e., more abstract) layer of meaning represented by vowel melody. In this example of classical Indian music the sitar melody is inflected in a speechlike manner, but purely for the implied emotion, and not necessarily with particular words in mind.

As the improvisation continues, the artists hope to attain a state of inspiration in which the music flows of its own accord. This desirable state of elation or release, where the musician becomes a medium, can be compared to the trancelike state of the Tuareg medicine woman. The hypnotic drone accompaniment has a vital role to play in this transformation of consciousness, because it provides a focus of meditative concentration.

Compared to the spacious and reverberant enclosure of a western church, the Indian ensemble, seated on a deep-piled, sound-absorbent rug, makes sounds of a more intimate and sensuous, "close-miked" character, in keeping with a music of tactile qualities. There are similarities between the sitar performance and the bravura display of the Villa-Lobos study for guitar: both kinds of music are physically demonstrative, both tend to grow in excitement and rise in pitch level as they progress, and in that sense too the message of the music is found in the quality of the activity as well as in the purity of the sounds. In comparing the two, a listener detects a more macho, assertive manner to the Brazilian character, in contrast to the more tender, ecstatic quality of the sitar.

42
A Singing harp

George Crumb, *Ancient Voices of Children.* Jan de Gaetani, ensemble cond. Arthur Weisberg. Elektra Nonesuch 79149-2.

The human vocal cavity is a programmable resonator, and language is the program. By substituting the fixed pitch of a jaw harp for the movable pitch of the vocal cords, one is able to determine that differences in the vowel sounds of speech are related to specific zones of harmonic reinforcement (or *formants*), mouth resonances that under certain conditions are audible as partial tones.

At the end of his song cycle *Ancient Voices of Children* the American composer George Crumb has the soprano solo move to the rear of the open grand piano and sing into the instrument while the sustain pedal is depressed. The piano acts as a resonating chamber for the voice, which takes on a ghostly, cavelike quality.

This is something anybody with access to a piano can try. Open the lid so that the strings are exposed, and depress the sustaining pedal so that they are able to vibrate freely. Then sing different syllables in a steady voice at different pitches, and listen to the result. The pitch of the voice is prolonged, *and only that pitch.* What happens is that the strong frequency elements in the voice interact with the corresponding strings in the piano, and set them in motion. This is called *sympathetic vibration.* Not all the piano strings vibrate, only those that are in tune with the partial tones of the singing voice. That is the crucial point. By singing into the piano and observing which strings are vibrating it is possible to determine the frequency components of the voice at that instant.

We are used to the idea of a guitar or lute helping the singing voice to stay in tune, but it now appears that a string instrument is also able to detect and reinforce the singing voice at a desired pitch. A piano is a very massive piece of equipment, and it is rather surprising to discover that the energy of a singing voice is sufficient to stir the heavy strings into vibration. A guitar or lute is a much lighter instrument, and more responsive, but has very few strings compared to a piano. The perfect compromise would be a lightweight string instrument with many freely vibrating strings covering a frequency range extending far beyond the singing range of the voice. In other words, a harp.

In the story of Jack and the beanstalk, Jack refers to the plectrum, the beanstalk to the long neck of a theorbo or bass lute, and the beans to the notes that sprout into melodies and cause the musician's fingers to move up and down. According to the folk tale, in the realm beyond the clouds, which is the realm of music (vibrating air), Jack discovers a singing harp and a sorcerer or ogre whose catchphrase is "Fee, fie, foe, fum!" These magic syllables are four vowel sounds: [e], [i,] [o], and [u] (with a hum). These vowels have distinct resonances that jaw harp and throat music employ to make music. (Indeed, the singing harp of the story may refer to a jaw harp and not a Celtic harp at all, even though we are told it is a Celtic harp in the story.) It would appear that, like many folk tales of wizards and magic, this story may be based on a misinterpretation of early experiments in assisted resonance aimed at discovering the frequency components of speech, to most people an esoteric pursuit with magical connotations.

An aeolian harp is a simple wooden frame with strings of randomly varying tension stretched across it, suspended from a tree or at a doorway, to be set in motion by an ambient breeze. As the wind increases, the ambient music also rises and falls in pitch and intensity. The instrument can be interpreted as a primitive detector, based on real voice experiments with the harp, designed to intercept and amplify the spirit voice of the wind, another recurrent image of the music of all cultures. Alternatively, the aeolian harp may be modeled on a spider's web, designed to pick up the sound vibrations of flying insects.

43
Tibetan Buddhist chant

"Rituals of the Drukpa Kagyu Order: Mahakala Sadhana: Dun-kye." 12:29 minutes. 16th century. In *Tibetan Buddhism: Ritual Orchestra and Chants*. Monks of the Tashi Johng Community, Khampagar Monastery, rec. David Lewiston. Elektra Nonesuch 9 72071-2 (track 2).

This extraordinary music alternates a loud wailing of folk oboes and long trumpets, together with clashing cymbals—a music of biblical intensity, seemingly designed to bring the house down, like the trumpets of Jericho—with vocal chanting of a quieter and more inward quality. The ritual music of Tibet has attracted a following in the west, particularly the United States, and has featured, albeit briefly, in movies such as the remake of *Seven Years in Tibet*. This is music adapted to the mountainous landscape of the Himalayas, and to temples of a richness of resonance akin to the cathedrals of Europe. Of the louder instrumental music one can say that the combination of winds and percussion, and the deliberately strident idiom of this music occupy the same acoustic territory as the music of Varèse, and as with Varèse (for example, *Intégrales*) a listener's initial impression of overwhelming loudness gives way to a new sensation of hearing with unusual clarity and transparency: a music not noisy but colorful, vivid, and larger than life. One also has the impression of powerful animating forces at work.

This Tibetan ritual music is *composed* music, notated in a cursive script perhaps distantly related to the punctuation marks of early plainchant. Unlike jaw harp or throat music where the meaning of a text is sacrificed to the demands of melody, in this music a very clever accommodation of text and musical effect can be heard. The chant is sung by choir in deep-throated unison, and the texts are real prayers. As in Tuvan throat music, the voice sings at a low fundamental pitch making changes of vowel audible as a much higher and more ethereal line of resonance forming a melody. But in an unusual twist, the Tibetan chant manipulates the lower voice line simultaneously with the changes of vowels as they occur in the sacred text. The effect can be heard by a discerning listener as the upper and lower voice lines moving in paradoxically contrary motion, the resonance rising in pitch as the bass line descends, and vice versa. Technically it is not very difficult to do, but to the unassuming listener it sounds like magic. Try singing the gliding phrase "Ah–eye" on one note. Pay attention to the resonance rise with the change of vowel. Now sing the same phrase,

a- -i

but with a downward glide in pitch. You now hear contrary motion in two parts in one voice, a very strange and mysterious effect that could easily give the impression that the singing voices (the monks) and the resonances (the vowels) are two distinct and independent entities: one human, the other spirit.

44
Stimmung
Karlheinz Stockhausen, *Stimmung*. 70:20 minutes. Mid-20th century. Singcircle, dir. Gregory Rose. Hyperion CDA66115.

When this music for unaccompanied voices was first performed in Amsterdam in 1968 a disturbance broke out among some radicals in the audience, including a number of composers. The "hippie" era was drawing to an end, and the highly motivated and focused style of Stockhausen's music offended some who thought it too authoritarian. That is a very interesting perception, and in its way perfectly true. Though serene and gentle in tone, one can understand this inward and disciplined music making representatives of the counterculture feel exposed and a little uncomfortable.

Stimmung means "tuning," and also agreement. In German, the *stimme* is the voice, so the agreement is vocal. There are six singers with individual microphones, and the music consists of a static drone harmony of up to six notes, sustained by the singers, modulated by the voices as they chant pure vowels, syllables, and divine names. In a context of jaw harp, throat singing, and Tibetan chant—not forgetting didgeridu music of the Australian indigenous people, yet another example of tribal ritual employing amplified voice resonances—today Stockhausen's music no longer seems particularly alien or hard to understand. Its special added value, as it were, lies in the fact that the voice multiphonics are also superimposed on a multivoice harmony, in effect taking the idea of melodies of vowel resonance to another level. This composition is over an hour in length and despite its apparent stillness and lack of harmonic movement, reveals itself as extremely busy and animated in the detail of individual voices. In this respect it invites comparison with the "Viderunt omnes" of Perotin, being both timeless in the larger sense of the drone, and animated from a human time perspective. Stockhausen even incorporates the willful dissonances and ribaldries of the earlier work.

Discussion topics

1. Some instruments offer only a limited range of notes (open strings or finger holes). Others provide an entire scale. What effect does this imply for musical performance as a test of skill?

2. In Poulenc's concerto for two pianos, what do the differences in character of "European" and "Asian" idioms say about the different traditions and aspirations of European and Asian cultures?

3. Is Varèse's percussion music simply noise, or is it music?

4. Cage's prepared piano changes the piano keyboard into a special effects interface, like a modern sampler. Discuss.

5. Many professions are valued for their objectivity. What is the message of absence of expression in music, especially music for keyboard?

6. Villa-Lobos's fiery guitar study could be performed more efficiently and easily on a piano with two hands. But would it be the same music?

7. If Satie's *Gymnopédie I* is "white" music, what is "colored" music?

8. Explain why a robot voice sounds like a robot.

9. By assigning drone and melody functions to separate instruments, Indian classical music is able to achieve greater freedom of expression.

10. Discuss the effectiveness of an aeolian harp, a piano, and a spider's web as sound and vibration detectors.

11. Like Perotin in "Viderunt omnes," Tibetan chant explores the inner resonances of real words with religious significance. Is this respectful?

12. A Serbian folk tale tells of a man who played only one note on the violin. His wife told him, "People in the village say that by moving your fingers you can play more than one note." The man replied, "Woman, what do they know? They talk about searching for the right note. *I have already found it.*" What is the humor of this story?

IV

TEAMWORK

Teamwork on a large scale is a distinctive feature of classical music and its evolution. The organization of large numbers of people to work cooperatively and harmoniously to achieve a common goal is essential for the survival and prosperity of society. It is a traditional requirement of attack and defense in conflict situations, and the key to mass production and distribution of goods for commercial success on a large scale in the industrial era. The term *organization* is a musical term with links to medieval *organum* (Perotin) and the design objectives of the *organ*, which were to discover the underlying principles of harmonious interaction among many different voices or pipes. The history of western music can be viewed in part as an evolutionary process in social organization from the uniform actions of plainchant, for example, to the sophisticated teamwork of a late Haydn symphony.

Prior to 1600 research into the underlying principles of harmony was centered on the church and expressed a vision of centralized authority aimed at replicating on earth the guidance and control systems already implemented in the heavens. The universe was seen as an oscillating system with many partials (the planets) following different cycles. Musical instruments such as the organ were developed to inquire into the underlying rules of harmony, divine laws that allow the coexistence of multiple cycles within a stable and self-supporting system. Western rules of harmony are grounded in experiments designed to explain the coexistence of dynamic change and stability in the universe. These are very strong and influential laws: as late as the seventeenth century Isaac Newton interpreted the orbits of the planets by musical analogy, while during the twentieth century the orbital motions of electrons were found to conform to discrete energy states related to harmonic ratios. Even today the most esoteric theories of the origins of matter and the universe continue to discuss the existence of multiple fundamental particles in terms of vibrating strings at different harmonics or energy states. So the use of musical models to account for the existence of matter and the dynamics of the universe is at the same time very ancient, and also very modern.

With the discovery and agreement across Europe on a system of standard notation, a more complex music based on paper calculation began to develop. Under the patronage of the church, the new complexity manifested itself in multi-part vocal music such as the Tallis "O salutaris hostia," which is an example of complexity within a unified timbre (the voice), and in keyboard music where the complexity of multiple parts comes under the control of a single intelligence and pair of hands, as well as being unified in timbre. Real progress in teamwork organization had to wait until the patronage of music moved away from the church and into the free market of secular power. The rise of the symphony marks the coming of age of people organization on a large scale in a purely instrumental music free of archaic symbolism and hierarchies.

45
Rite of spring

"Yuanshi" (Primordial). 5:39 minutes. Traditional Naxi music from Southern China, Lijang province. Dayan Ancient Music Association Nimbus NI5510 (track 6).

The organizing principles specific to western music that have been embraced by Asian industrialized countries in the growth period since 1945, and are the reason why western classical music is socially acceptable in urban Asian communities that have their own distinct cultures and musical traditions, can be appreciated more readily by listening to music than through political science or economic analyses. This example of a Chinese traditional music that has survived political disfavor and religious reform in China, is haunting and beautiful in its own terms and also an idealized image of group harmony. This kind of instrumental unison chant, with percussion markers, is known as *heterophony* and is a feature of oral cultures across the world. It is instrumental music to accompany a religious chant. It incorporates a great number of different melody instruments, some high, others low in pitch, and they all follow the same basic melodic shape in a demonstration of unity of purpose among a diversity of musical functions and identities. To western ears the tone qualities are strongly characterized, even raucous. We think the same of folk instruments in the west such as the shawm (bagpipe chanter), rackett, or saxophone, reflecting a late western preference for instruments that sound smooth and blend well. This uniform melodic movement is typical of oral cultures that have no established notation. In noting the absence of western-style harmony a listener can begin to understand the advantages of a written code that enables different musicians in an ensemble to play different lines of music at the same time without having to worry about breaking the harmony of the group. Here, by keeping to the same basic melody the performers are showing agreement and unity, but are limited in the ways they can demonstrate individual qualities, which rest with the distinctiveness of each timbre and permitted ornamentations of the musical line. So in this example, a listener can appreciate the aim of *melodic unity* within a context of *timbre differentiation*, whereas for a western ensemble the opposite aim is *melodic differentiation* in a context of relative *consistency of harmony*. Only through a highly-developed system of notation that is the same for all instruments is a western-style complexity of organization and role differentiation possible. The advantages of notation include those of universal literacy, which in turn implies a standardization of forms and meanings in language throughout a country or region (or industry). These conceptual advances underpin the organization of modern industry, and are a significant reason why western music is now valued and cultivated in Japan, Malaysia, Singapore, China, Korea, and elsewhere.

46
Wassoulou

Sali Sidibe (vocalist), "Ntanan." 7:07 minutes. Traditional song of Mali, with ensemble. From *Wassoulou: Women of Mali*. Stern's Africa STCD1035 (track 7).

There is a strong Arabic influence in this engaging song, an influence also recalled in the strong vocal line and proud female presence of the fourteenth-century song "Mandad' ei comigo" by Martin Codax, which dates from a time when Spain also had strong cultural ties with northern Africa. Though studio recorded, the idiom is clearly out of doors music: a penetrating voice timbre, a strong sense of rhythm, and a wonderfully assorted collection of accompanying instruments. This is another example of a broken consort, but on this occasion clearly hierarchical, dominated by the voice, and coordinated by rhythm rather than by a common tuning. Indeed, what makes this piece so charming to classically-trained western ears is the absence of normal harmony, a delightful looseness and freedom of tonal association coupled with inspired timing and sharing of roles among the various members of the group. It is a good example of birdsong in a plains environment that, as the man said, "relies more on temporal coding." It serves as a reminder to western listeners of the tight controls on tuning and tone relationship that characterize classical music—and by an inverted logic, of the virtue of sometimes loosening up a little in matters of intonation. In this song every participant is distinctive in sound, and that sense of separate identity is reinforced by a willful indifference to uniform tuning. In this respect it is also very different from the heterophonic style of Naxi tradition.

47
Baroque orchestra

Johann Sebastian Bach, Brandenburg Concerto No. 1 in F major BWV 1046, II. Adagio. 4:22 minutes. Early 18th century. Academy of St. Martin in the Fields, Sir Neville Marriner. EMI 7243 5 69877 2 2 (track 2).

J. S. Bach, Brandenburg Concerto No. 2 in F major BWV 1047, I. (Allegro). 5:21 minutes. Artists as above. EMI 7243 5 69877 2 2 (track 5).

It may seem rather strange for non-European listeners that classical musicians in the west should be involved in an ongoing and often fractious debate about whether early music should be performed on original period instruments or modern instruments. The older view, taking the printed music at face value, aims for a beautiful sound that expresses the best the notated score may suggest; the more recent view argues that in order to achieve a more authentic sound, truer to the composer's original intention, reproduction instruments of the same period have to be used, and their techniques of performance mastered anew. Authentic performances of the latter philosophy tend to be more strongly differentiated in sonority than a modern orchestra. This has its reasons and also its attractions. In these examples of Bach orchestration, however, the smooth corporate finish of a modern orchestra is persuasive evidence in its own right of an authentic style of ensemble management, one that also allows the sophistication of the composer's musical organization to be heard without distraction.

The slow movement from No. 1 of this orchestral series composed by Bach for a princely patron, Margrave Christian Ludwig of Brandenburg, offers an excellent introduction to western orchestral practice. The orchestra is arranged in bands of instrumental color: oboes, high strings, low strings, and organ. Bach himself was an organist, and composed extensively for the instrument. His approach to orchestration combines an Italian sense of instrumental color contrast, as we hear in Monteverdi and Priuli, with an organist's perception of live instruments as animated organ stops.

In this recording the bright harmonies of oboes unfold in opposition to the more muted textures of the organ and strings. Bach's harmonic movement is unusual and daring, each layer following its own logic, giving rise at times to striking harmonic clashes that reveal a mindset that places a higher priority on action (i.e., movement and change) than on maintaining perfect harmony at all times. The music speaks of a dynamic of controlled instability, like riding a bicycle or learning to walk: a philosophy of keeping going at all costs, implying that unstable harmonies are not only a necessary consequence of harmonic movement, but also an essential means of initiating movement in the first place. Restlessness is a defining trait of baroque art and music. In this slow but powerful movement, flowing like a boat on a river, the problem is not how to keep moving as how to bring the movement to a halt. The ending to this Adagio is pure genius, a unique moment in classical music. Abruptly the corporate flow of the orchestra sound separates into bands: oboes, violins, and organ, resolving into alternate patches of instrumental color, like the famous unfinished portrait of Mozart where the eye travels beyond the face to lose itself in broad strokes of background color.

The first movement of Brandenburg No. 2 has no tempo assigned to it, but is classed as an *Allegro*, meaning fast. Here the issue of tempo is the same for Bach as for Satie in *Gymnopédie I*: how fast is fast? Could you sing to this movement? No: the melody is a toy trumpet style fanfare passed from one instrument to another, jaunty but not very singable. Could you dance to it? Again, no: there is no sense of a dance rhythm or movement either, the music just keeps on going without a stop. There is more activity here than the Satie piece, certainly, but the principle is the same: music that is really designed to simulate a clockwork toy—a machine that moves across the floor under its own power, of its own accord, only stopping when it bangs into the wall. At the time this music was composed, a pocket watch was the rich person's executive toy of choice. A portable timepiece allowed its owner *to tell the time*. This new awareness of organized time had nothing to do with human feelings of duration or fatigue; in fact it was a perception completely independent of human experience. Bach's movement has no tempo assigned to it because it is not intended to correspond to any human sensation of time, but rather to the movement of a watch.

Compared to the slow movement of Brandenburg No. 1, this is a more complicated interweaving of voices, held together by the harpsichord. The solo motif passes from trumpet to oboe, to violin, to recorder, the same image in constantly changing instrumental colors. Bach's orchestra is a model of team organization. All the instruments are treated with equal respect, there is no hierarchy of masters and servants, and everybody has an interesting line of music to play.

48
Spring

Antonio Vivaldi. Concerto No. 1 "Spring." 3:44 minutes. From *The Four Seasons*. Early 18th century. I Musici, Felix Ayo. Philips 438 344-2.

Vivaldi's *Four Seasons* is not only one of the most widely recorded works of classical music, it has also become very popular in recent years as background music for advertising campaigns on television for banks and investment brokers. Either the advertising agencies handling these accounts have a passion for the composer, or a financial interest in marketing the recording, or they consider Vivaldi has the right "image" to attract investors and borrowers. What is it about this music that makes it so attractive to banks and their customers?

This music is exactly contemporary with the Bach Brandenburg concertos. Bach is German, and the German mind enjoys complexity. The Brandenburg No. 2 *Allegro* is hard to grasp; it has many threads of different colors, and part of the music's fascination lies in following the leading melody as it passes from one instrument to another. For best results, this music needs to be listened to with close attention and reproduced on high quality equipment. Vivaldi's "Spring" is shorter, laid out in a series of tone pictures, composed for only one sonority, the strings (with harpsichord)—and more clearly structured. Music that not only lends itself to quotation in an advertising context where time is precious, but is also robust enough to sound acceptable in a performance by amateurs, or when reproduced on the poor quality speakers of a normal domestic television receiver.

Vivaldi belongs to the Italian tradition of direct expression. The sound of massed strings is diffuse and atmospheric, and the movement also embodies echo repetition, adding to a sense of space. The full orchestra plays with a strong beat, steady and reliable, but also moving ahead, above which distinctive melodic motifs leap upwards in an imagery of new growth. In between choruses, solo violins join in birdlike trills that swoop and chirp high above the rest of the orchestra in another image of awakening new life. There are alternate verses suggesting a rippling stream and a spring shower. It evokes an image of nature at her most benign and positive.

49
Music on the Thames

Georg Frideric Handel, Andante–Allegro 2:02 minutes. From the *Water Music*. Berlin Radio Symphony Orchestra, Lorin Maazel. Philips 454 029-2 (cd 2, track 10). Also Naxos 8.550109 (track 16).

This short piece comes from a sequence or *suite* of short pieces for orchestra, composed to accompany a newly-crowned King George I on a trip in the royal barge up the river Thames to Chelsea in 1717, and his return later the same evening. This is outdoor music designed to present the king to his subjects as a powerful and kindly ruler.

Since in those days it was a rare occurrence to hear music being played outdoors, the music would attract the attention of all who heard it, and they would know that it signaled a special event. Music is a structured acoustic signal that cuts through the humdrum murmur of daily life. A person in a position to put on a public show featuring a great many players performing on expensive musical instruments is clearly a person of rank and style. At the very least, the music "commands the airwaves," from the jovial and upbeat character of the music a listener would also know that the occasion was intended for people to enjoy and not be intimidated. Since the music in effect stands for "the voice of the king" its characteristics are to be interpreted as features of the royal patron himself. This is a king who is in command, in a good mood, reaching out to his subjects; a royal personage who has something to say, and is saying it with confidence, in clipped, concise, well-measured phrases.

The music was composed to be played from a second vessel in close attendance on the royal barge. The river Thames is an open space with no walls, only the surface of the water to reflect the sound. Handel's music is simply drawn, a music of bold steps (trumpet and horn fanfares), straight lines (the strings' descending scales), and insistent repeats, easy to hear at a distance, and using color contrast in place of loud and soft. It is music of a vitality that says "All systems go!"

Handel's echo dialogue (in which the mellow horns repeat the bright trumpets an octave lower) is a device the composer acquired during his studies in Italy. The echo tells his audience that the king is "a listening monarch," and that his brilliance (the high-pitched trumpets) is *reflected* and *endorsed* by the kingdom and its people (the horns, which play the same notes, but at a less elevated pitch). The king's trumpets express high spirits and penetrating leadership, to which the horns add body and weight. From the music we know that this is an intelligent and physically active king who takes a lively interest in his people and is not a remote or intimidating figurehead.

Since the royal procession is traveling past the listener standing on the riverbank, its short segments of music ensure that everyone has the time to hear a complete musical statement as the barge glides by. It is a thoughtful consideration on the composer's part, giving the impression of a royal wave, a gesture of greeting directed at every listener personally. Finally, the alternating calls of trumpets (instruments of the battlefield) and horns (instruments of the hunt) signify that the new king is a successful leader to be trusted both in war and in peace.

"A composition of bright contrasts, flat planes, and angles, like a Canaletto Venetian canal scene with gondolas."

50
The symphony comes of age

Christian Cannabich, Allegro from Symphony No. 50 in D minor, Op. 10, No. 5. 3:38 minutes. 18th century. Nicolaus Esterházy Sinfonia, Uwe Grodd. Naxos 8.553790.

"History is selective though cruel," observes Allan Badley in his introductory essay to *The World of the Eighteenth-Century Symphony* sampler cd (Naxos 8.554761) of which the present movement is a taste. The eighteenth century was a period of remarkable growth of interest and activity in ensemble music. Vivaldi and his contemporaries had done their duty and prepared the way for the modern orchestra and its major form, the instrumental *symphony*, a new term meaning "sounding together."

The subsequent neglect of this rich repertoire of pieces, many of them ideally suited for amateur and secondary school orchestras, is perhaps not so much the fault of history as the consequence of social revolution, the decline of private patronage, and the ascendancy of a nineteenth-century middle-class culture ill-disposed to acknowledge the achievements of an Age of Enlightenment era perceived as oppressive. Fortunately, much of this music has survived, and society has progressed to a point where popular taste is ready to appreciate the confident message and technical skills of the period.

This movement was made the subject of a listening test for non-musicians. The objective of the test was to discover just how much information about the period and culture could be gleaned from the evidence of the music alone. The student commentaries were appropriately enlightening.

Special Assignment

You have been sent on a mission from the future to an eighteenth-century European state. You do not understand the language and you have no access to secret documents. Your only source of information is from attending a performance of this Allegro. *Your report on the state of civilization and development in this location and period is based on the following considerations:*

1. How big is the orchestra? How many instruments are involved? What skill levels are in evidence?
2. For what size of space and kind of acoustic is the music designed?
3. What is the general mood of the music, in terms of its sense of energy, confidence, and preparedness?
4. Estimate the level of teamwork and organizational skills required to create a musical demonstration of this magnitude and effect.
5. How intelligent, stable, and resourceful is such a community? How would one prepare to negotiate with such a culture?

Answers

"Determination, teamwork, and leadership designed to make the audience feel strong. There are surprises and sudden changes, but these only reinforce a listener's impression of discipline and control. This is a hard-working community capable of being aroused and of feeling passion."

"It starts off deliberately, to the point, as if anxious to get going. Playful, smooth, and melodic at times, the piece always returns to a darker mood with a sense of purpose. These people have an obvious zest for living and a sense of control of their own destiny."

"Energetic, as the name suggests. It is fast-paced throughout; yet what varies in intensity is actually the relative loudness and softness of the fast-paced tempo. It is, I would say, 'confidently crazy.' It does not falter in its language or message, just in how certain it wants to be about the message. It flows easily, with no breaks, thus there is a sense of musical stability. It lacks in *emotional* stability, however. It acts very much like an unstable personality—up and down—and growing more intense. It is more *emotionally* complex than *musically* complex; more emotionally resourceful than musically resourceful. It does, however, convey a sense of uniformity. There is no 'call and answer' dialogue, no musical pauses, slowing in tempo or variation in instruments."

"There is [a sense of] immediate reaction to any musical suggestion, that does not leave much to contemplate. The real element of surprise is the manic-depressive personality coming to focus on one solid, sturdy thought in the end."

"The mood shifts and swings from anticipation to urgency to action, with a dash of danger and the occasional echo of music that might be folk-dance. Still, the tight choreography of the movement and its rapid but confident shifts of pace and mood (and even volume) speak well of the musicians' technical skill, precision, and powers of description."

"These people are clearly very capable in both intellectual and technical pursuits, a sure sign of a sophisticated and stable society. That said, a piece like this is also evidence that they still appreciate a good scare now and then. They strike me as a robust, excited people ready to grab the world by the tail and take it wherever they please."

"These people *will stop at nothing*."

51
Storm and stress
Joseph Haydn, Finale (Presto) from the Symphony No. 94 "Surprise." 3:53 minutes. The Hanover Band, Roy Goodman. Hyperion CDA66532.

The rise of the symphony over Haydn's long lifetime (1732–1809) and the increase in skill of rank and file musicians over this period helped to build a consciousness among the workforce that, when properly organized, they were a force to be reckoned with. The image of teamwork cultivated over several generations during the eighteenth century, coincided with a period of growing popular unrest at the culture of extravagance and indifference of a powerful aristocracy. When one realizes that from around 1780 the symphony orchestra was the most highly organized expression of teamwork ever known, of greater skill even than the army, the message of symphonic music begins to sound warnings of direct social aspirations as well as more abstract and intellectual conceptions of data organization.

Haydn was a gentle and likeable person, working for much of his professional career with an amiable and considerate patron, but he was not insensitive to the social unrest of the times, especially since, in his role as the Esterházy court composer and music director, he not only had to provide music that reflected the temper of the times, but also look after the musicians under his direction and represent their interests when they had a grievance. Such an occasion was the famous request for time off that Haydn diplomatically conveyed in his "Farewell" symphony.

Sturm und Drang ("Storm and Stress") is the label attached to the rising tide of social unease that affected the arts in general and came to a head in the revolutions that swept the European colonies in the United States before reaching a gruesome climax in the French Revolution and its bitter aftermath. Classical music has the reputation of being cold, hard, and intellectual, but a listener has only to scratch the surface, especially of a symphony, which is a very public showcase, to discover the emotions lying within. In the present case, the finale (or last movement) is a typical *presto*; the word means "very fast," with a bit of "hey presto" magic thrown in, a show of speed teamwork to excite the audience and end the four-movement symphony on a high. Mixed in with the closely-knit precision, energy, and fast pace, however, is a mixture of more troubling emotions. Listen carefully to the opening of the movement. Could you dance to it? No. Why not? It is at a speed that teeters on the brink: nervous, unstable, like a pot of water just coming to the boil. The quietness is not tranquil, but under pressure, ready to explode, so the listener is not entirely surprised when the music suddenly does erupt in turmoil. There are two moods to this fast tempo: one is nerves, the other is panic. Just because the orchestra remains completely in control at all times does not mean that the audience can ignore the pent-up energies and their implications. After all, who is in charge, the aristocracy or the orchestra? That is the unsettling question.

Most of the energy in this and similar symphonies is generated by the string orchestra, which instead of creating an airy, spacious ambience is co-opted as a powerful source of abrasive and turbulent noise through which the clearer sounds of woodwinds can distantly be heard.

The moment of surprise comes toward the end of the movement, when it appears the unsettled and stormy middle episode has passed and an uneasy calm has settled. Suddenly, like a bolt from the blue, the heightened stillness is shattered by a clap of thunder from the timpani. It is Haydn's way of signing to his audience that the crisis about to hit the upper class is not just a social revolution, but divine retribution.

52
Mozart enraged

W. A. Mozart, Finale, Symphony No. 40 K. 550. 4:46 minutes. Recommended: French National Orchestra, Josef Krips (recorded live November 2, 1965). Montaigne TCE 8821.

Mozart has been portrayed insultingly by Hollywood mandarins as a foul-mouthed delinquent with an uncontrollable talent. The movie industry, alas, has never felt totally at ease with classical music—or music of any quality—and this finale from one of Mozart's last symphonies is worlds away from the simpering caricature of Peter Schaffer's play *Amadeus*.

This music is more than ominous. It is angry. How is a composer to express anger, and why should Mozart want to do so? To answer the second question first, Mozart was closer to the action than Haydn. He knew from bitter personal experience how capricious and disdainful his patrons, bishops, or princes, could be. Mozart was a skillful craftsman, an enormously hard worker, and he knew his own value. He could see disaster looming, and over the last few years of his short life his operas and his music sent out a terrifying warning of the destructive forces that were about to be unleashed on a complacent and increasingly fragile governing class.

Today's symphony halls are large, purpose-built structures, designed to accommodate large numbers of fee-paying members of the public. The space is carefully zoned. The orchestra occupies a raised platform or stage at one end of the hall, and the audience faces the orchestra from seats in the auditorium on one or more levels. Between the two groups is a wide lateral passageway, like a moat, as if to keep the orchestra members quarantined, at a safe distance. In Mozart's day a concert was more presidential, and took place in an aristocratic ballroom with parquet floor and chandeliers. The orchestra occupied one end of the room and the distinguished guests sat on comfortable chairs facing them, *on the same level*, the front row only a few feet away. Imagine yourself among the audience at such a concert. These are difficult times. There is open talk of rebellion on the street. The guests have come to hear the orchestra. The late eighteenth-century orchestra is a highly-trained and disciplined representative group of a newly politicized professional class and it has a message to deliver. The revolution is imminent. *There is no escape.*

How is anger expressed? It is a combination of collective unity, moving with the headlong speed and power of an avalanche, and violent mood swings, of an in-your-face intimidation relieved by moments of deceptive serenity. Mozart uses the interview psychology of the good guy and the nasty guy familiar from television series like *NYPD Blue*, the technique of alternately roughing up and soothing an uncomfortable suspect hauled in for questioning. The most unsettling feature of this movement of Mozart, as also of Haydn, is the unstable bassline, in both cases a hugely energetic display of awesome power (and remember, the energy is right there in front of you and making the floor shake). If I had been among the audience at the first performance in 1791, I would have felt very uneasy indeed.

53
The artist as hero

Ludwig van Beethoven, Overture "Coriolan" Op. 62. 8:26 minutes. Early 19th century. Slovak Philharmonic Orchestra, Stephen Gunzenhauser. Naxos 8.550072 (track 3).

Beethoven composed this overture to a play by a contemporary Viennese writer on the same subject as Shakespeare's more famous drama. The story of a Roman general who successfully defends his people from enemy attack, and is then criticized and ultimately ostracised by the people for continuing to behave in a similar manner after victory, has topical overtones in the era of Napoleon, who was admired as a revolutionary leader, but also feared across Europe as a threat. In this music Beethoven sketches a character portrait of the romantic hero as leader, drawing on his feelings toward Napoleon, along with his own experiences as an artist and moral leader in post-revolutionary Europe.

The popular revolution had come and gone. Unlike the orchestra of Haydn and Mozart, Beethoven's orchestra no longer needs to conjure up an image of imminent crisis or rioting in the streets. Why? Because the professional classes, represented by the orchestra, are now in power. Beethoven's focus is rather on the effects of yielding power to the masses. The question is, what happens now? How is that awesome power directed? How is it to be controlled?

Like his contemporaries Goethe and Goya, Beethoven is having to deal with the uncontrolled energy of a new social order that is no longer tightly repressed, and sweeps all before it, like a force of nature. The romantic hero is an idealized superhero, larger than life, with immense charisma and the authority to restore and maintain order. The very first phrases in this powerful musical study can be interpreted as fateful images of the guillotine descending on the French aristocracy. They set the tone of apprehension. At the same time, there is a surgical or geometrical finality about these defining actions: they signal the end of an era, perhaps even the end of civilization: a musical right angle, horizontal, then vertical.

It should not come as a surprise to discover that composers are intelligent people, just as motivated and in tune with issues of the day as poets and painters. Beethoven's epic scale of gesture is as grandiose as Goya or Turner. He sees the new world in terms of benign but overwhelmingly powerful natural forces. There is no menace in the power of Beethoven's orchestra: it is simply an overwhelming presence that crosses your path like a Leviathan, without any attention to rank or protocol. For Beethoven there was also a personal side to the big gesture, the obsessive repetitions, the refusal to back down, the apparent indifference to others. *He was deaf.* When you are deaf it is a struggle to communicate: you shout, you gesture, you repeat yourself.

54
The good-humored Rossini
Gioachino Rossini, Overture "La Cenerentola" (Cinderella). 9.07 minutes. 19th century. Cincinnati Symphony Orchestra, Thomas Schippers. Vox CD3X 3036 (cd 2, track 1).

Another country, another overture, and a completely different take on the signs and symbols of early romanticism. Like Beethoven, Rossini

inherited the musical skills and terminology of the late classical era of
Mozart and Haydn, and survived into a more troubled and politically
unstable world coming to terms with a new sense of citizen power and
new directions in popular taste. Rossini's familiar tale of Cinderella is
nothing like the story of Coriolanus, to appreciate which a classical
education and grasp of political symbolism are required. Fairytale
reaches back to the world of oral tradition and myth; it emphasizes
magic intervention over intellectual prowess, and as one might expect
imagines a world of royal privilege and wealth to which the poor and
abused may nevertheless aspire. It is escapist fantasy rather than the
philosophical realism of Beethoven, but fantasy in the general style of
Hollywood, and with the same topical implications.

The orchestra is still a powerful beast, like Beethoven's, and Rossini manages this power with the flair of a lion tamer. One one level
this is a routine overture with a function to settle the audience in
preparation for the drama to come. But on another level this overture is
a remarkably modern exercise in musical montage, almost an improvisation, with no initial sense of direction but a masterly feeling for the
power of rhetorical gesture. Like the finales of Haydn and Mozart, it is
a music of sudden and extreme contrasts. The old echo imagery of
Italian tradition is now transformed into a dramatic chiaroscuro of
brilliant light and deep shade—though designed however not to cause
panic in the ranks, but simply to entertain. That power over loud and
soft is now the people's power, and playing with it is the composer's
prerogative.

What appears so modern to listeners today is the loose, improvisatory style of Rossini's overture. It unfolds as a series of almost
isolated gestures: a bang, a leisurely descending melody by clarinets in
thirds, a rising melody on bassoon, they meet: bang again, and the process repeats. It is a bit like watching the movement of an artist's brush
on a new canvas, and waiting for the forms to emerge. Out of nowhere,
a sighing phrase on lower strings. Again. And again.

Then, in a bizarre, funny, and gruesome parody of Beethoven's
guillotine, the music is suddenly caught up in a chopping motion that
appears to take on a life of its own, and just keeps on going, like an
obsessively robotic butcher dealing with a particularly large and bony

carcass. Equally suddenly, the violent chopping action ceases and a more serene pastoral music takes over, with distant trumpets and horns alluding to an idealized landscape tradition. The most imaginative aspect to the overture is Rossini's unprecedented freedom in handling the orchestra (and controlling the audience). Here is music without form and without logic, created as it were on the spur of the moment and of a deliberately willful and arbitrary nature. Whether modeled after the conventional unmeasured prelude of French keyboard composers d'Anglebert and Couperin, or in imitation of the improvised cadenza of the classical era, this overture is made to form spontaneously out of casual and isolated gestures. Today's audience can appreciate it as a momentary glimpse into a twentieth-century future of chance and aleatoric music envisaged by John Cage and his friends.

55
A Byronic pilgrimage

Hector Berlioz, III. Allegretto "Pilgrims' march." 7:30 minutes. 19th century. From *Harold en Italie* Op. 16: Symphony with viola solo. Gérard Caussé, Orchestre Révolutionnaire et Romantique, John Eliot Gardiner. Philips 446 676-2 (track 2).

In many ways the changes of sensibility that mark the transition from the classical era to nineteenth-century romanticism resemble the shift in emphasis from church to state that had taken place two centuries before, in the time of Monteverdi and Gabrieli. In the earlier case the dominant symbolist aesthetic of a ruling class (the church) was overwhelmed by an aesthetic of science and free enterprise; it is echoed in the Napoleonic era two centuries later in the transition from an authoritarian classical aesthetic (Newton's optics, Voltaire's "best of all possible worlds")—which, rightly or wrongly, was also identified with an oppressive élite—to a populist aesthetic. It is remarkable that in both cases, music is emblematic of *power*: the power of religion, then of science, finally of numbers. Audiences of the nineteenth century were like movie audiences today; they wanted a good story, they wanted to be entertained, they were impressed by charisma, beauty, and special effects, and they had a keen sense of national identity.

In both form and content the symphonies of Berlioz are very

different from the earlier symphonies of Cannabich, Mozart, or
Beethoven. In the sensational *Symphonie Fantastique* the young
French composer orchestrated a five-movement fantasy of love, despair, rejection, and revenge, fictionalized out of his own emotional
struggles to win the attentions of a young and beautiful opera star: a
sentimental fiction directed very astutely at a new female constituency
among the wives of an expanding business class. Wealthy heiresses
and widows of merchant bankers began to emerge at this time as a new
and significant source of influence in art and music, providing essential
patronage to composers and symphony orchestras throughout the nineteenth century and well into the twentieth. It is not surprising that one
observes the artistic priorities of romanticism changing to accommodate the objects and preferences of these women of taste.

Prior to 1800 the focus of musical innovation lay in developing
and refining teamwork skills, improving musical instrument design,
expansion of the orchestra, and philosophical debate on such abstract
issues as time and motion. In opera, as in drama, such abstract ideas
were expressed in human terms, as for instance the discussion of
leadership qualities in Beethoven's "Coriolan" overture, itself the
prelude to a play addressing the same issue.

Nineteenth-century audiences by contrast were more interested in
heroic deeds than the nature of heroism, and they were also newly
curious about past history. *Harold en Italie*, Berlioz's "symphony with
viola solo" is loosely based on the composer's reading of *Childe
Harold's Pilgrimage* by the English poet and iconic romantic hero Lord
Byron, here reinventing himself as a medieval wanderer on a personal
quest that also manages to resemble the Grand Tour of more recent
history. The message of the music is typically pictorial and literary,
concerned with beautiful images, exotic encounters, and personal
emotion. It is an occasionally enchanting sound picture of the arbitrary
actions and motivations of a nominal narrator (the viola solo), deemed
to be a person of exceptional charisma, in whose natural impulses a
listener is invited to discern the character traits of a superior being. The
unusual designation "symphony with viola solo" is deliberate. This is
not a concerto: the viola role is reduced to occasional commentary, not
·intended to dictate the course of events, but to give expression from

time to time to the sense of awe and wonder of a puny traveller in a vast and unfamiliar landscape. (The composer Felix Mendelssohn celebrated his own travels to remote and awesome parts of Scotland in the overture "Fingal's Cave" and the "Scottish" symphony.) Berlioz's orchestration is masterly, by the way; the rarely-heard and darker timbre of the viola is aptly identified with the dark, enigmatic inward emotions of the romantic hero. The composer conjures up magical visions that are translated into sound by the orchestra acting as a high resolution image projector. The orchestra has now changed in public perception from a team of expert operatives to a machine for the reproduction of exquisite visions.

56
Stream of consciousness

Claude Debussy, "Gigues." 7:48 minutes. From *Images* for orchestra. Early 20th century. BRT Philharmonic Orchestra, Alexander Rahbari. Naxos 8.550505 (track 1).

Maurice Ravel: "Malagueña" 2:12 minutes. From *Rapsodie espagnole* for orchestra. Early 20th century. Czecho-Slovak Radio Symphony Orchestra, Kenneth Jean. Naxos 8.550424 (track 2).

A new, weightless aesthetic emerges in the music of Debussy and Ravel at the end of the nineteenth century. This music is consistent with a culture of vaporous sensuousness associated with French perfume, fine wine, elegant fashion, cigars and brandy. It takes a position at the opposite extreme from the traditionally solid German cuisine of Beethoven, Wagner, and Brahms. The name *impressionism* is used to describe this music. Impressionism is an elusive, time-dependent art in which an essential image is captured in an initial moment of awareness. The paradox is that with closer scrutiny the initial impression of organic unity disappears in a swirl of brush strokes. The artist Turner was among the first to render atmospheric effects with this sort of immediacy, a feature of impressionism that has something to say about the way the eye senses images before the brain has time to interpret them. In the light, airy music of Debussy and Ravel images constantly form and dissolve; the musical focus is high in pitch, and the instrumental mixtures are selected for their sheer color and transparency rather than for weight or texture. Music, unlike painting, unfolds in time, so the composer of impressionist music retains control over the flow of a listener's thoughts. Here the melodies and harmonies float free of classical chord bases and progressions.

France was the birthplace at this time of some of the first movies, by the Pathé Frères, and Meliès, the pioneer of surrealist trick movie photography. Young French composers and their literary counterparts were greatly impressed by the flickering images on screen, which seemed to evolve and change at the speed of thought, and their work captures that dreamlike quality while at the same time continuing to develop the narrative aesthetic of Berlioz and others of the romantic era. In this example by Debussy, a version of the familiar sea shanty "The Keel Row" wends its way through the musical texture like a folk memory. The anecdotally brief "Malagueña" of Ravel, composed in the first decade of the twentieth century, catches a moment of Spanish glamor and warmth, a tribute to the traditions and also the grace of Spanish dance, expressing a physicality missing from the sheer intoxication of Debussy's imagery.

57
Blissful end

Gustav Mahler, IV. "Adagietto for strings" From Symphony No. 5. 12:03 minutes. Early 20th century. Polish National Radio Symphony Orchestra, Antoni Wit. Naxos 8.550528 (track 4).

This lingering song without words for string orchestra and harp seems to look back over a nineteenth century of romantic achievement with a mixture of nostalgia and regret. The heroic mindset of high romanticism had turned brooding and uncertain. Lacking a sense of purpose or direction, it looked inward, searching after human motivations beyond the reach of normal (or at least, polite) consciousness, to the drives and taboos of an emotionally self-repressed middle class that were about to be analyzed and mythologized by Sigmund Freud and Carl Jung, and later celebrated in the eroticized surrealism of Salvador Dalí. Mahler's darkly serene slow movement harks back to the German song tradition, mingled with the Wagnerian fantasy of an endless melody representing a state of permanent arousal. Unlike the perfumed light and shade of

Debussy and Ravel, Mahler's harmonic language is recognizably conventional, its rise and fall of emotional tension recalling the ancient tradition of Apollo and his lyre, as well as finding an echo in the sitar improvisation of Indian classical music. But in drawing so heavily on the past, Mahler is also distancing himself from the present, and, one suspects, turning his back on an imminent future of four-minute phonograph recordings for which both his music and his temperament were ill-adapted.

Perhaps the most startling analogy of all can be made with the "Semper Dowland, semper dolens" by John Dowland, composed three centuries earlier. Not only does Mahler employ essentially the same instrumentation as the lute and viols in the Dowland, his music also captures a moment of soliliquy, of private thoughts, now seemingly projected onscreen in close-up for public view. Mahler's emotional uncertainty is also akin to Dowland's; both expressing apprehension about the future, both conveying feelings of simultaneous epiphany and loss, and both works driven by a restless compulsion to seek some kind of resolution.

58
Summer morning by a lake

Arnold Schoenberg, "Farben" (Chord-colors). 3:06 minutes. III. Movement of *Five Pieces for Orchestra*, Op. 16. Early 20th century. Recommended: London Symphony Orchestra, Robert Craft. Koch International 3-7263-2H1 (track 3).

Schoenberg's "impressionism," unlike that of Debussy or Ravel, is grounded in the ambiguities of real life rather than the momentary flashes of dreams. This three-minute impression of sunlight reflected on the surface of the Traunsee is not a transient illusion, but a glimpse of something beyond the physical presence of water, mountains, and light. A something, nevertheless, that retains its mystery even after the brain engages. That perhaps is the distinction between a French style of intangible sensation, and a German impressionism, that is more deliberate and philosophically inclined. Schoenberg himself disliked titles, because to him the act of contemplation was the subject matter, not the object of contemplation. Urged on by his publisher, he settled on the title "Chord-colors" which he thought sufficiently abstract, and which refers to the fluctuation of the underlying chord in harmony and instrumental coloring. The play of light on water is a recurrent motif of impressionist art, as we see in Monet and J. M. Whistler, through to the oval abstractions of Mondrian that reduce the sparkle of reflected sunlight to a pattern of plus and minus signs. (Perhaps the piece can also be understood as a tribute to Mahler, a composer revered by Schoenberg, who also liked to escape to a cottage by a lake to gather inspiration for his symphonies and symphonic song cycles.)

Schoenberg's notion of a transcendent vision, achieved through contemplation of nature, is reminiscent of Perotin and Hildegard: the "eternal chord" of "Viderunt omnes" functioning in much the same way as Schoenberg's endless chord, its changes of vowel corresponding to the changes of instrumental color in Schoenberg's study. At the same time, the composer's aesthetic of transcendence displays clear emotional affinities with the courageous serenity of Hildegard's "O vis aeternitatis"; a contemplative power reminiscent of Mahler but reduced here to an almost perfect stillness.

Most music is focused on activity for the simple reason that it occupies time, and activity is how most people tend to deal with time. Under Weber, Wagner, Brahms, Bruckner, and Mahler the romantic symphony settled and spread until it became an immersion experience, guided tour, or literary journey through which a captive audience was obliged to navigate with the aid of a virtual map or programme. Static pieces like "Farben" represent a rare culmination of this trend in western music, though the experience is normal among cultures of the east. Timeless compositions such as this not only allow a listener to rest mentally, which is desirable in itself, but also make the point that the emotion or impression aroused by a piece of music—in other words, what is identified as the *object* of contemplation—is also *an exact description of the process* by which a listener arrives at that perception.

Music, in other words, is a way of demonstrating that reality consists in mental activity, but with the interesting footnote that even though the object of attention may not be certain to exist in itself, the mental activity associated with its perception can all the same be exactly defined. This somewhat Freudian view of the nature of reality has interesting implications for the use of music for therapeutic purposes, as an aid to contemplation, or merely as an aid to privacy.

59
Through a microscope
Anton Webern, *Five Pieces*, Op. 10 for orchestra. 4:27 minutes. Early 20th century. Ulster Orchestra, Takuo Yuasa. Naxos 8.554841 (tracks 13–17).

With the arrival of sound recording around 1890, a new minimalist aesthetic of brevity and jewel-like precision was created, employing as few instruments as possible and expressed in an absolute economy of statement and gesture. At the same time as the new technology was encouraging miniaturization in musical affairs, a new science of microphotography was beginning to arouse public attention with images of diatoms and microorganisms revealing an unsuspected reality below the threshold of ordinary vision. Seen through the eye of the camera, it was a world of tiny geometric structures, mineral crystals, and living cells, at the same time real and also abstract, beautiful and totally natural, structured and yet randomly organized across a surface with no depth, no perspective dimension. It was a view of reality that inspired the artist Wassily Kandinsky to create a series of watercolor and oil improvisations in which the world on a human scale is similarly transformed into abstract shapes and splashes of movement as if viewed through a celestial microscope.

The new miniaturist aesthetic suited Webern, a pupil of Schoenberg and a composer of very intense and focused sensibility. Like Debussy, his images form and vanish in a moment, but unlike the French composer, with Webern one always feels a sense of completion, of having experienced something to the full: as Schoenberg commented, "a novel in a sigh."

60
American grandeur
Charles Ives, "Washington's Birthday." 11:31 minutes. From *Holidays Symphony*. Early 20th century. New York Philharmonic, Leonard Bernstein. Sony SMK 60203 (track 2).

There is an Emersonian breadth and dignity in Ives's music, a consciousness of vast spaces that is very American, not only in the movies of D. W. Griffiths and John Ford, but also the art of Robert Motherwell and Willem de Kooning. There is also a natural bigness in American perception that is different from the grandiose or the monumental in European art: a space that extends in every direction and through which the mind is left free to wander.

Charles Ives is a musical phenomenon, a painter in orchestral sound whose conception of music has much in common with the romantic pastoralism of Berlioz, the narrative grandeur of Wagner, and the impressionism of Debussy, but whose ideas of harmony and texture are closer to Schoenberg, his exact contemporary, though they never met. Composed in isolation in the early twentieth century and virtually ignored until the 1950s, his music has troubled the world of conventional music for almost a century because it is very demanding to perform and very hard for the listener to fathom. Ives requires a different kind of listening: one simply has to let go, like the movies, and allow the extraordinary images and textures in the music to take over. Ives's inspiration comes from the sights and sounds of the late nineteenth-century midwest, where he grew up. He was fascinated by the experience of a complex total sound field: the fact that human ears could take in more information at one time than the human brain could ever deal with. His music recreates that natural saturation experience with the result that a listener is not directed where to go and what to hear, as in conventional European music, but instead is encouraged to wander at will and focus on whatever catches the imagination. Here and there a popular tune will emerge through the musical texture, like the "Keel Row" melody in Debussy's *Gigues*, in the role of a guiding thread.

A century on, the fabulous beauty and originality of Ives's music is still only beginning to register with audiences. His music's grandeur and sense of freedom and personal responsibility, struck a chord with younger generations of American composers, including John Cage and Morton Feldman. Though his music remains difficult and elusive to many listeners, his approach to music as an art of acoustical montage has been a major influence on movie composers, though the imaginative and technical complexity of his music is still unequaled.

The *Holidays* symphony of which "Washington's Birthday" is one movement is Ives's American take on the European convention of a music to celebrate "The Seasons," as by Vivaldi, Domenico Scarlatti, or Haydn. Though based around festival dates in the American calendar, and the activities associated with them (for instance, square dancing to a jaw harp accompaniment), the presence of nature is never far away. The bucolic ending, to an expertly harmonized music-hall tune over a distant church bell, is unlike anything in European music, and quite breathtaking.

61
New chamber music
Igor Stravinsky, Second Pas-de-Trois. 3:02 minutes. Mid-20th century. From *Agon*. Orchestra of St. Luke's, Robert Craft. MusicMasters 01612-7113-2 (tracks 36–38).

In this music of the 1950s the symphony orchestra is reinvented as a lean, keen, dancing machine. As a young composer Stravinsky was greatly influenced by Debussy (the opening measures for strings of his fairytale opera *The Nightingale*, for example, are almost identical with the opening woodwinds of "Nuages" (Clouds) from Debussy's *Trois Nocturnes*). Stravinsky was also an early convert to the miniaturist aesthetic of the phonograph era, which inspired Webern, and also the charming neoclassical pastiches of Fritz Kreisler as well. Composed just before the Great War of 1914–1918, the Russian composer's *Three Japanese Lyrics* and *Three Pieces for String Quartet* are masterpieces of precision and economy.

In later years, living in Los Angeles among a community of European exiles that also included Arnold Schoenberg, Stravinsky evolved a new, terse aesthetic. The ballet suite *Agon* is like a diary or notebook of his ideas and inventions as his new idiom took shape. There are elements of classical form and practice interwoven with melodic and rhythmic features of his own earlier "cubist" period. The title and conception of a suite of dances draw on French classical models from the time of Rameau. This excerpt begins with a two-part canon for trumpets, a clear allusion to baroque practice. Stravinsky's orchestra, though large and variegated, is used very economically, each dance movement and segment defined by a particular combination of instruments treated as a chamber ensemble in a manner clearly based on a close study of Webern's orchestration, and perhaps even *Le marteau sans maître* of Pierre Boulez.

Immediately after the canon for two trumpets, the instrumentation becomes very like Boulez, though perhaps more tense and physical. In the "Bransle Gay," flutes seesaw awkwardly against the strict rhythm of castanets: two very different time-layers superimposed. The overall mood of this three-part segment is highly active and demonstrative: an energy, humor, and gestural inventiveness that combine classical sensibilities and skills with the dry wit and professionalism of the Hollywood animated movie.

62
Atmospheres

György Ligeti, *Atmosphères* for orchestra. 6:52 minutes. Mid-20th century. New York Philharmonic, Leonard Bernstein. Sony SMK 61845 (track 1).

This work will be familiar to many listeners as the "Overture" to Stanley Kubrick's movie *2001: A Space Odyssey*: background music to a movie text printed in simple white on black, a gesture referring back to the silent movie era and a very effective way of subduing the audience and building expectation toward the title sunburst to the strains of Richard Strauss. Some of the same music by Ligeti later returns in a montage that accompanies the capsule traveling through a wormhole or time warp into another dimension.

When we hear music we are literally "in the dark" because what the music means is not necessarily revealed or explained in what we see. This is cluster music, seemingly boundless in space and time, with no discernible edges or borders. The orchestral sound is dense and powerful, capable of filling a listener's consciousness, and of masking all other sounds of reality. In the years leading up to the cluster compositions of Ligeti and Giacinto Scelsi, infamous and well-publicized experiments in sensory deprivation were conducted by government agencies; volunteer subjects were bathed in light, or saturated in "white noise," or suspended in warm saline baths so that they lost all sense of visual, aural, or tactile discrimination. The effects of these experiments were disorientating, hallucinatory, and, for some, psychologically distressing. Scientific interest in sensory illusion and the limits of perception provided composers with a pretext for using the orchestra in a completely new way, in acoustic experiments designed to provoke out-of-body or out-of-mind experiences. The use of clusters of notes played on the Hammond organ to simulate dizziness or the effects of narcotics was already a routine sound effect employed in radio drama and the movies; now came the idea of transferring the experience to the concert hall and symphony orchestra.

For an audience seated in a movie theater the lights are low and the listener has nowhere else to go, essential ingredients for creating fear and mystery. In a concert setting, on the other hand, the platform lights are on and everyone can see the orchestra playing, adding to a sense of dislocation between what one is seeing and the meaning of what is actually playing. Despite giving the impression of a static and endless cloud of sound, it does not take long for a listener to sense that Ligeti's music is actually changing shape, like a vast cloud of plankton glowing under ultraviolet light at the bottom of the sea. Gradually the listener becomes aware of a sense of location and movement up and down in pitch, of a presence approaching and receding in dynamic space (moving between loud and soft), and changing texture, color, and brightness (alterations of timbre). After about 3 minutes the body of sound contracts to a high-pitched focus of laser-sharp intensity (piccolos), only to revert suddenly to grumbling double basses (no drums), thereafter mutating to a buzzing sound in the midrange like a swarm of bees. So there is a real sense of progression from suspense to movement, but a progression that avoids any clearly outlined shape or form. Like impressionist art, it is a music that teases the audience by never revealing itself completely, and for that reason describes a world of sensation the meaning of which remains tantalisingly out of reach.

63
Images of Japan

Olivier Messiaen, III. "Yamanaka–Cadenza" 4:22 minutes; and IV. "Gagaku" 3:44 minutes. Mid-20th century. From *Sept Haï-Kaï* (Seven haiku). The Cleveland Orchestra, Pierre Boulez. DG 453 478-2 (tracks 13, 14).

Composer Olivier Messiaen visited Japan in 1962 and composed this suite of "Seven Japanese Sketches" in the same year. The sounds and sensibilities of far eastern culture had fascinated French musicians since the 1881 Paris Exposition, where Debussy encountered the sound of Indonesian gamelan. Messiaen studied the scales and rhythms of Indian classical music as a young composer, and devised a personal code of practice that had already generated works of vivid colors and striking harmonies in the sensuous tradition of Debussy and Ravel.

A *haiku* is a short poem of a fixed number of syllables, a title choice suggesting the brevity and concentration of Webern. By the composer's own admission, however, these are segments cut from much longer formal processes, so their timescale is abbreviated rather than short, offering an insight into the difference between western and eastern ways of thinking about time.

Of interest to western trained ears are the density of Messiaen's harmonies, the static nature of his musical imagery, and the reduction in scale of the orchestra, emphasizing instruments of high pitch and strident tone, especially "Gagaku," whose title alludes to the sounds and formality of Japanese Imperial court music. But, like Stravinsky in *Agon*, there is also an echo of baroque music, here the pastoral imagery of Vivaldi. And like the Italian composer, Messiaen was fond of incorporating impressions of birdsong. The "Yamanaka-Cadenza" is a musical description of the composer roaming out in the forest, sketch-book in hand, in search of birdsongs to transcribe as material. The music alternates choruses of woodwinds, representing the natural randomness (to human ears) of a dawn or evening chorus, with inter-ludes for solo piano depicting the composer at home, transcribing and harmonizing the songs he has collected in the field, all precisely identified in the published score.

"Gagaku" is tighter, more astringent music of great resonance and sheen, of a more robust exoticism than Debussy, suggesting the potent and penetrating incense of burning sandalwood. The movement is made up of layers that cycle and recycle at different periodicities, creating constantly new mixtures. The sound of clustered violins, a particularly happy invention, is inspired by the Japanese ceremonial mouth organ or *shô*. Messiaen's account of his travels in exotic lands, in an art skewed to a western perception of unfamiliar cultures, can be related back to the Grand Tour of early romanticism, the age of Goethe and Byron, reflecting much the same fascination with the exotic as the nominal hero of Berlioz's *Harold en Italie*.

64
American polyphony

"A Celebration of some 100 × 150 Notes." 3:09 minutes. From *Three Occasions for Orchestra*. Late 20th century. London Sinfonietta, Oliver Knussen. Virgin VC 7 91503-2 (track 1). Also SWF Symphony Orchestra, Michael Gielen (live recording). Arte Nova 74321 27773 2 (track 4).

The extraordinary musical career of Elliott Carter spans virtually the entire history of American music in the twentieth century, from personal encounters with Charles Ives as a student, via graduate studies in neoclassicism with Nadia Boulanger in Paris, through to his discovery of a personal rhythmic language in the mid-1940s and growing reputation from the sixties as a composer of difficult, dense, and large-scale works to set alongside some of the major European composers of the period. From his eighth decade Carter's music has become looser and less intense, expressing that freedom, even elation, often encountered in artists who survive to a great age: one is reminded of Monet and his waterlilies, or Matisse's cut paper works on jazz themes.

Despite its furious pace, there are similarities linking "Celebration" with the Messiaen of "Gagaku." Both composers design their music on paper, with their ear to guide them, and both works represent layered processes having the potential to recycle indefinitely, but edited to an arbitrary duration. This is the same clockwork image of musical time and motion that has its roots in the "Brandenburg" concertos of J. S. Bach. The differences separating Messiaen and Carter are more aesthetic and temperamental than procedural. Like his American musical forebears Ives and Varèse, Carter's imagery is vast in scale and impact, creating a first impression of pandemonium that with repeated hearings reveals unexpected and beautiful lyric qualities. Listen out for the strings, which have a generally calming function, compared to the brass and horns, which are strident and excitable. Composed as a celebration, this is music not only for a special occasion, but a tribute to the extraordinary skill of the modern orchestra in every department.

Carter's European heritage is just as real if less easy to discern. It derives from his studies of classical counterpoint in Paris from which comes his later expertise in managing a music of multiple timescales. His music has the sense of discipline and latent order we can hear in Varèse; the same sense of modulated instrumental colors, as in Webern; and from the Italians, a sense of perspective and movement in depth that the live SWF recording demonstrates with particular clarity. Somewhere in the distance, beyond the turmoil, a listener can still make out the antiphonal energy of Gabrieli, the primary colors of Priuli, the instrumental role-playing of Schmelzer.

Discussion topics

1. Describe the team spirit expressed in Naxi ensemble music.
2. What does the out-of-tuneness of Wassoulou signify?
3. In what ways does Bach's orchestra resemble a live pipe organ?
4. What qualities of Vivaldi's *Four Seasons* make the music suitable to advertise an investment bank on television?
5. What does the finale of Mozart's Symphony No. 40 say about teamwork in the orchestra, and what effect are the violent mood swings of the music calculated to have on the eighteenth-century audience?
6. What does Beethoven's use of repetition for emphasis in the "Coriolan" overture have to say about leadership in the age of Napoleon?
7. In the landscape of romantic art, nature is awesomely big and the human occupant reduced to insignificance. Show how this is depicted by Berlioz.
8. What makes the exquisite art of Debussy and Ravel distinctively French?
9. Is there a touch of orientalism in Schoenberg's contemplative landscape?
10. The delicate precision of Webern resembles a surgical operation. Does that make his music less beautiful, or capable of expressing human emotion?
11. In what ways does Ives' music resemble the impressionism of Debussy?
12. What is the physical and gestural message of Stravinsky's *Agon*?
13. Consider the possible emotional associations of Ligeti's *Atmosphères* for audiences still able to remember the effects of industrial pollution, mustard gas, and radiation.
14. Compare the "natural chaos" of the aviary (the orchestra) in Messiaen's "Yamanaka-Cadenza" with recorded sounds of birds in their natural habitat.
15. As an image of modern city life, how does Elliott Carter's *Celebration* for symphony orchestra compare with the urban landscape of Varèse's *Ionisation* of 1934 for percussion ensemble?

V

LEADERSHIP

Any music that involves a solo instrument and orchestra accompaniment represents a leadership situation. It is not only necessary in a practical sense for the group to follow a leader, it follows from the situation that the music is a *demonstration* of leadership, and thus a *description of leadership qualities*. The same human qualities can be observed in music for solo performer, but only in relation to a group can the image of leadership be clearly communicated. In the romantic era of Beethoven and Berlioz, the image of the hero was popular: thus "Coriolan" is a portrait of heroism, and *Harold en Italie* is a musical narrative based around the idea of the poet as hero and wanderer. Neither work however is a demonstration of leadership in the sense that a concerto demonstrates it. This section is about the concerto as a classical musical form, and the skills and styles of leadership that can be perceived in the role of concerto soloist through the centuries.

The term *concerto grosso* refers to music for the loose group of musicians that made up the baroque orchestra. In the time of Vivaldi, Bach, Handel, and Corelli the orchestra consisted of a keyboard instrument, usually a harpsichord, and associated instruments standing around the open casework where they were able to see the conductor at the keyboard, signal to each other, and keep a close ear on the underlying harmonies. (Though its musical idiom is outwardly very different, the organization of big band jazz in the twentieth century, for example, Duke Ellington's orchestra, has close affinities with the baroque era, from the role of the soloist to that of the conductor.)

The classical solo concerto arose out of the same period of experimentation that preceded the formation of the eighteenth-century symphony orchestra, experiments that by their very nature involved trialing different instruments by having them perform solo with string orchestra accompaniment. As the natural leaders in a baroque ensemble, there were regular opportunities for the concertmaster (violin or flute) as chief melodist, or the conductor as keyboardist, to perform in a solo role, and their musical functions included improvising graces and decorations of the written text to help keep the players functioning as a unit.

Given their roles it is not surprising, therefore, that violin and keyboard artists came to be perceived as musicians of special status and accomplishment, and these instruments continue to dominate the concerto repertoire to the present day. The concertmaster and the keyboardist represent two distinct styles of leadership. The leadership provided by the melodist is *demonstrative*: the soloist is there to coordinate the melody line, which in baroque music represents the action leading to a desired goal, and the spirit in which the action is undertaken. A melody soloist is an executive director, a person who carries out orders (interprets the notes) and inspires and guides the people under his (her) immediate direction.

A keyboardist, on the other hand, is the composer in disguise. In baroque terms, the keyboardist is the conductor as well as the composer: the leader who is in charge of the overall operation. He (she) has a plan: the role is strategic. The chief of operations issues orders to be carried out, controls the timing of events, and like a modern conductor has a duty to look after the support services and morale of the entire team, not just the frontline troops. In simple terms, the concertmaster directs only one line of the script, the lead melody, providing inspiration and leadership in executing actions that have been planned in advance by others (and in the process adding to his (her) reputation as a charismatic figure. By contrast, the baroque keyboardist and conductor has sight and control of the entire operation, and has both hands engaged in coordinating the bassline and support harmonies as well as reinforcing the pace and tuning of the melody line.

Leadership 315

65
A singing tone

Alessandro Marcello, II. Adagio from Concerto in D for oboe. 4:15 minutes. Late 17th century. Jósef Kiss, Ferenc Erkel Chamber Orchestra. Naxos 8.550556.

Unlike the harpsichordist in a baroque orchestra, whose instrument is clearly audible only to the musicians standing nearby, and is not intended to dominate the orchestra acoustically, the lead soloist or concertmaster is the voice of the orchestra, both to the team and to the audience. A good quality of voice is therefore desirable. The violin already had an outgoing voice and personality; it was thanks to the violin that the baroque orchestra came into being, and it was in order to blend in with the string orchestra that existing wind instruments were adapted and refined. The oboe is a special case, a Cinderella-like transformation of a rough and rustic outdoor instrument, the double-reed shawm (it survives as the melody instrument of a set of bagpipes) into a noble voice of great richness, concentration, and depth of timbre. In a modern symphony orchestra the oboe gives the note to which all other instruments are tuned, a tribute to the high penetration and stability of its tone.

This slow movement by Alessandro Marcello (his brother Benedetto Marcello was an equally gifted composer) displays the virtues of the oboe as a solo and leader. The tone is high and full, and one can hear that this melody inhabits a region of elevated emotion beyond the reach of a normal singing voice. It "sings" with longer phrases and greater breath control, and its tone is more consistent and engaging. It also has the ability to move from note to note, and to end a phrase, with a smoothness and grace that even the violin was unable to match at the time, since the baroque violin had only a short bow, and limited powers of phrasing.

A slow movement is normally like an aria in opera, an opportunity for a leading soloist to adopt a meditative role and display the depth of character and qualities of tone for which the voice is valued. In this example, the part played by the orchestra is reduced to a minimum, in order not to distract attention from the soloist. The melody unfolds in a stylized fashion, in repeated phrases that become more elaborate with each repetition and allow the soloist some freedom to enhance and decorate the emotional message. Note also that at the end of each opening phrase the supporting harmony changes, moving from chord to chord in a formal sequence that has the effect of exposing the melody shape, and its attendant emotion, to a spectrum of chord combinations, some of which may be more dissonant than others (the same as we hear in the Bach Prelude in C major). It is clear that the role of the strings in this relationship is to provide an assisted resonance that follows and changes key to adapt to the willful shifts in mood (or mode) of the oboe solo.

66
A melody for lute

Antonio Vivaldi, II. Slow movement from the Chamber concerto in D for lute, violins and harpsichord RV93. 4:54 minutes. Early 18th century. Eliot Fisk. MusicMasters 01612-67097-2.

Though in the right place and under the right conditions a lute can be heard surprisingly clearly, it is not a familiar solo instrument in the concert hall. For one thing, its tone is light and refined, and for another, it is not a natural melody instrument, its normal role (as in the Dowland song *Dear, if you change*) being accompanist to the voice or viol. In this familiar, delicate movement, however, the roles are reversed: the plucked lute taking the melody, the violins providing harmonic support—once again, in the role of assisted resonance. Vivaldi composed a great many concertos for plucked solo instruments: among them the lute, mandolin, and guitar. The unsuitability of these instruments as soloists in a modern concert hall setting with a large audience is so obvious that one has to consider alternative, more technical reasons for composing concertos for them. Acoustically, these plucked-string concertos can be seen as studies of the relationship of *attack* to *resonance*: the two components of the playing action of a harpsichord. Composer interest in acoustical issues is natural in a period of instrumental research and development leading to the invention, by another Italian, Cristofori, of the *fortepiano*, a touch-sensitive keyboard. In assigning the attack component to the solo lute (or mandolin, etc.), and the resonance component to strings, Vivaldi introduces a new freedom of touch sensitivity to the melody role that is not achievable on a conventional clavichord or harpsichord, instruments designed for complete evenness of touch. Speculation on the relationship of attack and resonance is consistent with a perception of the baroque orchestra as a composite synthesizer (or virtual grand organ) rather than as a broken consort.

67
A harpsichord as solo

J. S. Bach, Allegro from Concerto in D minor BWV 1052. 18th century. 8:20 minutes. Gustav Leonhardt, Collegium Aureum. From *40 Years Deutsche Harmonia Mundi.* DHM 05472 77820 2 (track 4).

J. S. Bach, II. Adagio from the Concerto in F minor for harpsichord, BWV 1056. 18th century. 2:18 minutes. Anthony Newman, Brandenburg Collegium Orchestra. Newport Classic NCD 60023.

As soon as a listener moves from the close-up world of Vivaldi and his lute to the bolder and more spacious sound of Bach and the harpsichord, the differences between the two solo instruments in musical and practical terms become immediately obvious. The harpsichord is more robust and even in tone: compared to the lute, it is a machine for plucked sounds. It has a deeper tone, due to its larger casework and soundboard; it also has considerably greater range in pitch, from bass to treble, together with the ease and freedom of movement that a keyboard interface and touch control make possible. These mechanical virtues are arguably neither musical nor artistic, bearing in mind the story of Apollo and Marsyas: they are values, in a scientific and engineering sense, of consistency and reliability of operation, and avoidance of human uncertainties of expression.

The other advantage of a keyboard, quite obviously, is the option of two-handed performance of multiple notes at a time, as chords or interweaving patterns of melody. From the opening statement it is clear that this Allegro is primarily about the relationship of harpsichord in a leading role to strings in a supporting role. It is not about melodic expression or purity of tone, but disciplined coordination. In the refrain element, a unison chorus of high-stepping, jagged and dynamic character, the solo takes full advantage of the mechanical virtues of the harpsichord to demonstrate agility and speed in holding position and

changing direction. The movement has the same relentless drive as
Beethoven in the "Coriolan" overture, and is clearly intended for disciplined musicians of a relatively high level of accomplishment. They
have to stay together, on note and in time, throughout a strenuous
journey, without respite, without relaxing, and without relief, through
very rocky terrain. One can imagine this music being composed to
accompany a forced march by army recruits, or a fast and bumpy ride
in a coach without any springs.

The slower Adagio, by comparison, is lyrical and melodic in
character: especially interesting since the normally multi-voice harpsichord is reduced to a single-line melody role. In comparison to the lute
movement by Vivaldi (from whom Bach was accustomed to borrow
ideas from time to time), a listener appreciates the greater strength and
consistency of tone of the harpsichord, and, in a reversal of roles, its
lingering resonance against a background accompaniment of *pizzicato*
(plucked) violins.

68

Imitation Bach

Joaquín Rodrigo, II. Adagio from the *Concierto de Aranjuez* for guitar and orchestra.
10:27 minutes. 20th century. Norbert Kraft, Northern Chamber Orchestra, Nicholas
Ward. Naxos 8.550729.

Villa-Lobos's Study No. 1 for solo guitar was an illustration of the
differences that emerge when a twentieth-century composer of Spanish
culture and temperament pays homage to the classical era of Bach.
This charming movement for guitar and orchestra is another example.
Temperamentally Rodrigo is closer to the Italians Marcello and
Vivaldi. This is singing music for a plucked instrument slightly more
powerful in tone than Vivaldi's lute, supported by an alternate solo
voice, the cor anglais, of the same instrumental family as Marcello's
solo oboe. It also has clear melodic affinities with the slow movement
of Bach's harpsichord concerto in F. The composer's leading sonorities
of cor anglais and guitar are warm and glowing rather than brilliant,
the gestural language discreetly ostentatious, with more than a touch of
traditional improvised ornamentation.

The return to neoclassical models by composers and artists of all cultures, not only Spanish, in the twentieth century, was driven partly by a political desire for a music to represent order and calm in times of war, and partly an aesthetic reaction against extremes of expressionism in favor of a return to a common musical language. This concerto was composed in the aftermath of the infamous attack and destruction in 1937 of the historic Spanish town of Guernica, and perhaps serves as an elegy to that event.

69
Eloquent simplicity

W. A. Mozart, Adagio from the Clarinet concerto in A, K. 622. Late 18th century. 8:47 minutes. Recommended: Jack Brymer, Royal Philharmonic Orchestra, Sir Thomas Beecham. Seraphim 7243 5 68533 2 4 (track 5).

Composed in 1791, the year of his death, and the same year as his Symphony No. 40, Mozart's concerto for the darker-toned clarinet in A can be appreciated as an equally emotional response to a Europe in turmoil as the concerto of Rodrigo in the twentieth century. It is music of an eloquence to bring tears to the eyes, and yet its restrained emotion is created with the simplest of means and draws the utmost from an unusual and effective combination of timbres.

The clarinet is noted for its agility in negotiating intricate melodies, and has a pleasantly matt tone compared to the glossier oboe. In slow melodies, however, the clarinet has a remarkable ability to begin a note imperceptibly, without audible attack, giving the melody line in this movement an ethereal and poignant quality. Mozart was fond of stretching his solo voices and instruments to the limits, moving from the highest notes in a controlled leap to land gently on the lowest. This contributes to a listener's sense of elevation or vertigo that, as we know from Monteverdi and Marcello, has strong spiritual associations. The highest notes of the clarinet glow cool, like the moon, while the lowest notes have a characteristically shadowy, introspective quality.

Mozart's sense of timing is exact: this is "white music" in the sense intended by Satie in *Gymnopédie I*, but more sublime, given the human presence driving the clarinet and the orchestra. Note the deliberate contrast of stepwise and diagonal melodic movement, in particular the choruses in which the harmonic tendency glides first upwards, then downwards, with the same eloquent simplicity as the voice line of "O vis aeternitatis" of Hildegard von Bingen. Mozart's moment of epiphany is more subdued in tone, the clarinet having the advantages of a greater range than the voice, and absence of words. If the Symphony No. 40 is about anger and the threat of war, this music (in a wonderful recording from 1960) is all about redemption. Right at the last moment, the full orchestra is revealed in a final chord that seems to draw open the curtain and let in the full light of day.

70
The artist as magician

Luigi Boccherini, I. Allegro moderato from the Concerto No. 9 in B flat arr. Grütz-macher. 8:00 minutes. Late 18th century. Recommended: Steven Isserlis, Ostrobothnian Chamber Orchestra, Juda Kangas. Virgin VC7 59015 2.

The same sense of elevation, of the ability to soar (and then come down to earth) that can be heard to such eloquent effect in Mozart's clarinet concerto, is also a feature of this cello concerto by Boccherini. A sense of floating upwards is Monteverdi's spiritual message in "Et misericordia" from the *Vespers*. In the late eighteenth century, how-ever, a more secular reason for a taste for extremely high solos can be found in public fascination with the early balloon flights undertaken by the Montgolfier brothers in 1784, shortly before Europe was overtaken by revolutionary panic. Certainly the cello, a latecomer to the stable of concerto soloists, has exceptional voice and range, from low C in the bass to soprano high C four octaves above—and greater power as well, since it is a much larger instrument than the violin, with a bigger resonating chamber.

In its previous existence as a baroque bassline support instrument, a cello would sit to the keyboardist's right and the double bass to his left, aligned with the harpsichord bass register. Both cello and double bass also rested on the floor, transferring vibrations to the wooden structure of the concert chamber in much the same way as a sub-bass speaker sitting on the floor in a modern surround-sound audio system. Because the cello rested securely on its spike and the left shoulder, the player's left hand was free to move up the fingerboard like a spider, enabling him (her) to carry a melody with ease into the pitch range of the violin. It is this extended range and freedom of movement that are highlighted in the Allegro–moderato.

Boccherini himself was a cellist, and it shows. The solo here is presented as a star and magician, the orchestra of strings and two horns taking a back seat. The movement opens with a standard overture to settle the audience, after which the cello takes the stage with a dazzling exhibition of broad arpeggios, wide leaps, rapid trills, and even two-note chords. During all of this the orchestra is reduced to a deferential pair of violins, who act as markers so the audience can appreciate the full extent of the cello's range and power. It is not hard to imagine the audience's enchantment at the skill and brilliance on display. At one point the cello floats upward to so high a note it seems to disappear into the clouds: a moment of suspense from which the melody finally reemerges and rapidly descends to ground level.

The image of leadership portrayed in this Enlightenment era cameo is a combination of rhetorical skill, superb technical accomplishment, and magic. There is hard science here, but science combined with great audience psychology. The movement reaches a climax with the solo *cadenza*, a point in the written music where the orchestra falls silent, the conductor folding his hands, while the soloist improvises at will. Nowadays a cadenza is generally played from a script, but in the eighteenth century the performer really did make it up, and to audiences of the time this sudden unscripted leap into the unknown was a dramatic affair. Time no longer ran in a predictable way, the music simply happened in brilliant fits and starts, like a firework display. No doubt there were a few "Bravo!" cries from the audience, and perhaps a few ladies in the front row could be counted on to show their approval by fainting away, just like excitable teenage fans at a pop concert of the present day. When the soloist felt he had done enough of a personal riff, in order to signal the orchestra to resume he would play a recognized formula ending in a trill, at which the conductor would raise his baton to the orchestra and bring the movement to a rousing conclusion. This concerto by Boccherini is a brilliant affair, and without any doubt expresses an aristocratic conception of leadership. In this music the soloist does virtually all of the work, but by implication is the only one with the skill and the wit to bring it off.

71
Extreme trumpet

Michael Haydn, I. Adagio from Concerto in D major for trumpet, strings, two horns and basso continuo. 7:17 minutes. Late 18th century. Recommended: Don Smithers, Concerto Amsterdam, Jaap Schröder. ProArte CDD 279 (track 10).

European orchestras after the time of J. S. Bach recognized two divisions of trumpet and horn players: those specializing in the high *clarino* register, at the top of the range, and those specializing in the lower part of the range. A clarino trumpet is heard as one of the four solo instruments sharing the lead melody in the first movement of Bach's "Brandenburg" Concerto No. 2. Since trumpets and horns of the baroque era had no valves to modify the pitch, they were limited to a single range of overtones at a time, like a bugle. In the lower range, composers and players were reduced to fanfare-like melodies with gaps, but players in the high clarino register were able to reach more or less every note in the scale, and even some half-steps. The Concerto in D by Michael Haydn, the younger brother of Joseph Haydn, is a rarely-performed item for the clarino specialist. Performances today are rare largely because the lip skills associated with the eighteenth-century clarino trumpet repertoire faded with the arrival of the valve trumpet, such as the trumpet in F of Joseph Haydn's more familiar concerto.

For those who imagine the highest note in Dizzy Gillespie's range is as high as any trumpet can ever go, this movement reaches higher by a third. Why anybody would want to play as high as this is musically unclear, but the physical exhilaration is real enough, a moment of connection with Gabrieli and Monteverdi, whose cornetti (curved woodwinds with fingerholes and a trumpet mouthpiece) fulfilled much the same role two centuries earlier. Almost certainly the younger Haydn composed this work with a particular soloist in mind. The art of playing high trumpet is not down to lung pressure but to mental attitude, according to Don Smithers, who features in this recording. Nowadays clarino parts tend to be played on a half-size piccolo trumpet, a more reliable alternative but lacking the freakish intensity of the authentic instrument. The nearest approach to such a trumpet sound in present-day music would probably be an extreme solo by the lead electric guitar of a heavy metal band.

72
Line and color

W. A. Mozart, II. Adagio from Piano Concerto No. 23 in A, K. 488. 6:25 minutes. Late eighteenth century. Jenö Jandó, Concentus Hungaricus, Mátyás Antal. Naxos 8.550204 (track 2).

Composed for the brittle sound of the fortepiano, this slow movement tells its own story of the relationship of keyboard and orchestra. It is a very beautiful story, in fact, with hints of the legend of Pygmalion and Galatea, Pygmalion being the sculptor and Galatea his statue of the ideal woman with whom he falls in love. The gods took pity on the artist and brought the statue to life. In this movement there are two distinct personalities: the piano, representing the artist and composer in the role of planner and visionary, and the orchestra, representing grace and frankly voluptuous beauty.

The movement is set in a pensive F sharp minor, a strange and remote tonality suggesting emotional distance or simply abstraction from everyday reality. It opens with the piano solo playing a methodical but hesitant passage containing unusually wide intervals, and apparently uncertain about where to go next. One has the impression of a navigator charting his ship's position in unknown seas, and plotting a way ahead. It is a lean, minimalist music of dividers and set squares, and long straight lines connecting widely separated positions on the map. Since the piano is playing solo, the impression is also one of isolation, as for chamber music, with the same hint of melancholy of Dowland and his lute. In effect, the piano is talking to himself (herself) and those of us in the audience are listening in. There is no identifiable note of grief or loneliness in the music itself, more a kind of sympathy toward someone whose work is solitary by nature. There is something of the same quietude in Satie's *Gymnopédie I*.

It is perhaps a strange kind of leadership that works alone and apart from society, but it is real enough. One thinks of the poet, the astronomer, the mathematician, the architect, and the philosopher, as well as the scientist: one thinks for example of Mozart's contemporary Captain Cook exploring in the southern Pacific. Mozart's portrayal of single-mindedness and individual excellence is more seriously intended than the showmanship of Boccherini, and exactly complementary to Beethoven's later portrait of obsessive leadership in the "Coriolan" overture. The composer's message seems to be that the acquisition of knowledge is due to self-motivated individuals and not to the collective will of society, even though the task of the individual may often be a lonely one.

Just as the piano reaches the end of that thoughtful opening statement something miraculous happens. The orchestra enters, in full bloom, without question or hesitation, filling the room with gorgeous harmony. Although the underlying tempo does not react, the orchestra's music flows in much larger time units, introducing a serene confidence and sense of direction to the uncertainty and hesitation initiated by the piano.

What makes the entrance and transformation so miraculous lies partly in the contrast of intellectual piano and sensuous orchestra, and particularly in the confidence with which the orchestra sweeps onto the scene and takes over. There is no dialogue. The orchestra does not wait for the piano to finish, or ask permission to invade the piano's space. The door simply opens and feelings of light, love, and serenity flood the workroom, *as if invited*. In the legend, when the marble statue of Galatea came to life, she stepped off the pedestal and greeted Pygmalion as a person she had always known. In this movement by Mozart the orchestra conveys exactly the same impression: of two people not *falling* in love, but of already *being* in love. The difference is crucial.

There are two such encounters in the slow movement. After the first, the music changes to the key of A major, in an image of pastoral contentment. But the tranquility doesn't last: the dream fades, and soon the composer is back at work in the key of F sharp minor, still worrying over how to find an answer. (A listener can clearly hear that the melody is unable to reach a comfortable resolution or sense of closure.) A second time the orchestra surges in to offer companionship and amiable relief. This time a second miracle happens: the piano and orchestra *begin to dance*. The piano draws confidence from the orchestra, but continues to calculate aloud: here a high note, there a low note.

The movement ends with a kiss. On both cheeks.

73
Art of persuasion

L. van Beethoven, III. Rondo from the Violin Concerto in D Op. 61. Schlomo Mintz, Philharmonia Orchestra, Giuseppe Sinopoli. DG 463 064 2GH.

The Revolution has come and gone. Throughout western Europe the people have taken control. The people still value music, but they want music to express their aspirations, and tunes they can sing. The composer is forced to reach a compromise with the values of a civilian government. In this concerto movement the relationship of artist and society is redefined. In the wake of the French Revolution both Beethoven and his former teacher Joseph Haydn responded to popular sentiment by composing music based on folksongs and traditional airs. National pride and a sense of local history were popular feelings stimulated by social change. In addition, the conventional leadership role of the soloist in a concerto underwent a subtle transformation. The early romantic era recognized artists as moral leaders with a duty to enhance and dignify national and cultural identity. That leadership however was not the same as political power and influence, which rested with the people. Artists were obliged to negotiate very carefully in order to satisfy public demand for images that celebrated national identity without appearing to claim moral or intellectual superiority for themselves.

The issue of leadership, expressed in imagery of artistic authority in confrontation with the power of the masses, is searchingly argued by Beethoven in the slow movement of his Piano Concerto No. 4, the object of a separate study. In the Rondo from the Concerto for violin, however, the composer adopts a more ingratiating manner. The *rondo* or round is an ancient song and dance form in which participants form a ring and take turns to invent alternate verses to a familiar chorus that everyone sings. In other words, a form of music that says "Let's all be friends together." In this relationship of solo violin and orchestra it is very obvious that even though the violin has the lead, the orchestra has the numbers, and therefore the power. The movement is in the form of a dialogue between the violin and the orchestra, starting with the violin's opening theme, which has the rhythm of a folk-dance and is pitched at a level for an audience to sing along. In fact, one can

imagine this same tune being sung in a bar by a group of revelers.
After allowing time for the audience to begin nodding and joining in
the singing, as it were, the violin brings the music to a pause, and then
starts the same melody again, but this time two octaves higher, in the
musical stratosphere, way higher than anyone in the audience could
sing. It is Beethoven's way of saying "I am higher than you"; and also,
"I can take any old song and raise it to the level of art, and at that level
you can only listen."

Immediately after that surprise demonstration, the orchestra rushes
in, joining in the melody in a robust reprise. It is not a very elegant
chorus—it sounds rather like a parody of the orchestra entry in the
Mozart concerto, in fact—but is quite obviously intended as a chorus
of approval, since the whole orchestra reproduces the violin melody at
its original tempo. The irony, for a listener, is that while the orchestra's
endorsement is politically significant, and its obvious enthusiasm a
welcome sign of acceptance of the violinist (the artist) by the orchestra
(society), one cannot help noticing that when it comes to singing and
dancing, the orchestra is rather clumsy and left-footed. So for listeners
in the know, a picture emerges of the artist as a gifted individual of
skill and refinement, but little power, whereas society has the power of
numbers, and in this case considerable energy and goodwill, but is self-
consciously lacking in refinement. The orchestra sounds incongruous,
in fact, like a troop of dancing elephants.

74
Artistic temperament
Robert Schumann, II. Slow movement (Langsam) of the Cello concerto in A minor, Op.
129. 4:14 minutes. Mid-19th century. Maria Kliegel, National Symphony Orchestra of
Ireland, Andrew Constantine. Naxos 8.550938 (track 2).

Boccherini's cellist was an expert technician and a dazzling performer
in the eighteenth-century mold of the artist as leader. Some seventy
years later, Schumann's solo cellist presents a very different figure,
exciting admiration not by actions, but ostensibly by the person he
(she) is. On the evidence of this movement, Schumann's romantic artist
is a creature of taste and sensibility rather than physical skill, a style
icon rather than a person of intelligence. Schumann was a gifted

songwriter in the romantic style, and in this movement has composed a song without words for his temperamental solo cello. Alas, this song without words turns out to have little to say. It is an image of leadership reduced to a pretty voice and an affected pose. The cello melody is languid and voicelike, of limited energy and movement but beautiful tone that says, Listen to me, I am an artiste. It is not much of a melody either, mostly simple enough to be mastered by a moderately skilled teenager. (An extended and rather more satisfying melody in the same mood can be heard in the Adagietto from Mahler's Symphony No. 5.)

But how do we arrive at this impression of artistic temperament? In two ways: first, from the balance of melodic precision and uncertainty, which are both functional (notation) and emotional (intonation) in implication. The sense of wavering between self-control and losing control is every bit as meaningful for this music as for the wail of the Tuareg medicine woman, or the emotionalism of Hildegard compared to the careful precision of plainchant. It can be heard just as clearly in the alternating fanfares and diagonals of Handel's *Water Music*, or the wailing sirens and precise trumpets of Varèse, and just as clearly in the relationship of stepwise melodies and poignantly measured up and down scales of Mozart's clarinet concerto. The nature and scope of that emotional balance has also to be measured against the range of the melody itself, which is carefully limited for plainchant (heightened speech) but pushes the boundaries of acceptability in the case of Hildegard, and of loudness in the case of the siren. In Mozart's concerto for clarinet the melody reaches extremes of pitch far greater than the voice, but the accompanying emotional range is absolutely controlled, sending a message of great emotion held firmly in check. Schumann's cello persona, unlike Boccherini's, stays timidly within a limited voice range, conveying no sense of emotional extremity. This is *less* than the cello can do, and much less than one expects of a leadership figure; furthermore, within that limited emotional range the solo contrives unconvincingly to suggest a personality stressed to the end of its tether, through a technique of gliding or sighing from note to note, a popular romantic expressive device called *portamento*.

Like the Beethoven Op. 61 Rondo, this movement by Schumann is a rondo of sorts, except that the cello appears to have no idea where to go, responding in an agitated and dismissive manner to any suggestion, however tentative, voiced by the orchestra. The image of the romantic leader as a prima donna with a pretty face is rather strange, and hardly fair, even to Wagner, in his own time a notorious aesthete.

75
Another matter of balance

Camille Saint-Saëns, IV. Maestoso–Allegro from the "Organ" Symphony in C minor Op. 78. 7:49 minutes. 19th century. Philippe Lefebvre, Orchestre National de France, Seiji Ozawa. Seraphim 7243 5 73430 2 2 (track 4).

This alliance of grand organ and symphony orchestra brings together two emblems of power: church (organ) and state (orchestra). The combination was perceived by nineteenth-century audiences as an expression of cultural might as potent and symbolic as the blazing "Deus in adjutorium" of Monteverdi's *Vespers*. Town halls throughout Europe were fitted with pipe organs, and it seemed only fair to have them perform with an orchestra from time to time. It is a rare combination all the same. The reason is that the two entities create significant problems of balance. The grand organ and the symphony orchestra are the Sumo wrestlers of classical music, so any work combining them is likely to turn into a contest of strength.

Of equal interest to the contest of size and noise-making ability is the implicit contest of sacred and secular. This is not only a matter of symbolism, but also of acoustic design. The pipe organ embodies a thousand and more years of development toward particular goals of harmony and integration that in the final resort are essentially *static*. It is also designed to function in a highly reverberant structure such as a cathedral. The symphony orchestra, by contrast, is a workforce of multiple players, rather than a single mechanism of multiple keyboards. The orchestra was intended to express the dynamics of a new humanism; music for orchestra embodies the idea of *progress*. The orchestra also functions best in an acoustically lively plain structure of a much shorter reverberation time. So music combining the two is implicitly a battle between a conservative philosophy of a mechanized universe in which everything is certain (i.e. there is a scriptural reference, a key and a stop for every possibility), in opposition to a radical philosophy based on agreement and cooperation that allows for individual freedom of action—that is, moral and technical improvement—as well as uncertainty along the way (the cadenza, etc.). The resurgence of the organ in the nineteenth century is also an interesting development psychologically for a romantic era beginning to tire of the image of the artist as hero.

76
Divine madness

Alexander Scriabin, *Prometheus—the Poem of Fire* for piano and orchestra. 22:43 minutes. Early 20th century. Alexander Toradze, Kirov Orchestra, St. Petersburg, Valery Gergiev. Philips 289 446 715-2 (track 16).

Intoxication of any kind: religious, medicinal, or purely recreational, has its risks. Whether designed as an escape from the tedium of everyday life, or seeking to transcend the limits of everyday consciousness, music has always been associated with rites of passage, from the ritual sacrifices of ancient civilizations, via the wailing women at a funeral or sickbed, to today's rave culture of party drugs and sensory overload. Luckily, compared to the risks of overindulgence in wine and sex, an excessive consumption of classical music does not normally produce dangerous or lasting side effects. How music contributes to altered states of mind exactly is of interest both from an aesthetic and historical viewpoint, as an aspect of the human condition, and for its therapeutic potential to relieve stress without chemical intervention leading to hazardous consequences.

The romantic era reacted against eighteenth-century science and embraced the idea of a world controlled by powerful natural impulses of waves, wind, lightning—and also human drives and emotions. Throughout the nineteenth century, art, literature, music, and medicine alike were directed toward understanding the unseen forces directing human actions: social pressures, psychological terrors, and drink, as well as narcotics, and in opera, disease (most often tuberculosis, but a version of the disease having no effect on a singer's heroic powers of expression). Technical innovation also played its part: photography transformed society's perception of visual reality, and the introduction of sound recording for the first time allowed for the capture and preservation of the essence of a speaking personality. By the early twentieth century, X-rays were beginning to reveal the inner physical body just as psychology aspired to reveal the inner mind. Symbolist poetry and impressionist art belong to that shift of focus in the late nineteenth century, from external forces and appearances to the mysterious subliminal drives of human nature, the roots of suffering, and the inner limits of experience, that come to a head in Scriabin's music.

We sense the first stirrings of artistic narcissism in the fashionable moodiness of Schumann's cello concerto slow movement, a music that amounts to a statement about the virtue of being rather than doing. Fifty years on, in the era of Madame Blavatsky, the Russian Scriabin emerges as cult leader of a new aesthetic of transcendentalism involving all of the senses at once: light, color, perfume, and sound. His title *Prometheus*, a reminder of the mythical human being who challenged the gods and was bound to a rock in perpetuity while crows plucked at his entrails—is as good an allusion as any to the perils of a bad trip, one might think, but with the afterthought that though the mind may dream, the body remains resolutely physical and subject to painful aftereffects.

Prometheus is not a concerto in the formal sense, rather an extended fantasy-cadenza, or simulated improvisation, to be understood as an expression of artistic delirium (which, to be fair, is not essentially different from the ecstatic spirit of a classical Indian sitar improvisation). In simple terms, the solo pianist is the hallucinating or visionary artist whose fantasies are reflected and enhanced by the orchestra—more extreme, perhaps, but expressing basically the same relationship as the baroque keyboardist to his attendant musicians.

This is a pungent, sensuous, and richly textured music with all the virtues and the pitfalls of aesthetic intoxication. In later years the American minimalists Steve Reich, Philip Glass, and others, would pursue a similar objective of transcendence, but through the incessant and mindless repetition of small musical figures over long periods of time—a typically American procedure appropriate for industrialized western cultures of work involving routines of endless repetition of simple actions, but an idiom assimilated, curiously enough, from studies of tribal rituals of equatorial Africa.

77
American baroque

George Gershwin, *Rhapsody in Blue* for piano, clarinet, and jazz band (original version).
13:44 minutes. 20th century. Recommended: George Gershwin (1925 piano roll),
Columbia Jazz Band, Michael Tilson Thomas. CBS MK 42516 (track 1).

Gershwin's racy but matter-of-fact urban fantasy is an apt new-world
antidote to the feverish old-world vision of Scriabin, but it inhabits the
same emotional territory of free improvisation picked up, colored in,
and run with by a team of standby musicians. It was Gershwin's first
"classical" composition. He was a gifted songwriter and fluent pianist
with a mission to be taken seriously by the New York musical establishment.

Though he had a gift for improvisation, Gershwin initially had
little grasp of classical form, so by default rather than by design his
music tends to wander where his fancy leads him—like Schumann, but
without the headache, or Scriabin, without the liquor. The audience is
introduced to a busy but civilized urban landscape, in which the piano
solo appears totally at ease. The composer's motivation appears more
technically than spiritually or emotionally driven, displaying confidence and energy in fingerwork that would not seem out of place in a
Bach keyboard concerto.

The baroque connection extends to the role of bandleader Paul
Whiteman, who originally commissioned the *Rhapsody*. A clarinetist,
Whiteman plays a role corresponding to the concertmaster of baroque
times, discreetly introducing and signing off each section of the work,
most dramatically at the very beginning, where the clarinet imitates a
siren riding from a low F trill up to a high soprano B flat, Gershwin's
witty rejoinder to the siren of Varèse's *Hyperprism*, which had made a
sensational New York debut the previous year. *Rhapsody in Blue* was
subsequently arranged for symphony orchestra by Ferde Grofé. This
rather reserved conventional version is the one most often performed in
concert and familar to most audiences.

Gershwin died much too young in 1937. In the recommended
recording of his original score for the Paul Whiteman orchestra,
Gershwin's evocation of twenties jazz is noticeably edgier and spicier,
and the pace is a lot more frenetic, guided by a slightly spooky solo

performance recorded in 1925 by the composer himself on a reproducing piano roll.

78
End of the cadenza

Olivier Messiaen, Turangalîla 2 from *Turangalîla Symphony*. 3:45 minutes. Mid-20th century. Recommended: Jean-Yves Thibaudet *piano*, Takashi Harada *ondes martenot*, Royal Concertgebouw Orchestra, Riccardo Chailly. Decca 436 626-2 (track 7).

Composed to celebrate the end of the 1939–1945 world war, Messiaen's *Turangalîla Symphony* is a massive ten-movement work lasting well over an hour. Like Mozart's Symphony No. 40, it is a meditation on war, this time a war commented on by two solo instruments, which gives it the appearance of a concerto in the loose sense of Scriabin's *Prometheus*, or Gershwin's altogether more urbane *Rhapsody in Blue*. However, although there are two solo characters in Messiaen's vision of conflict, neither is in charge of the fighting. One, the piano, is a self-portrait of the composer as a *victim* of war. Here, in the seventh movement, "Turangalîla 2," the artist is heard defending the values of nature and freedom through cadenza-like interruptions based on his beloved birdsong. The other solo instrument is the *ondes martenot*, an early amplified electronic melody synthesizer of penetrating tone and ghostly wail, more usually employed as a musical effect in sci-fi movies. This instrument plays a dual role, representing both a spirit of fear and doom associated with war, and in more sensual guise the spirit of joy and love. The personalities of the two solo instruments are all the same consistent with their traditional musical functions. The keyboard is rational, precise, the voice of reason, the same as in Bach, while the sweeping melodic glide of the ondes martenot, like the voice-line of Hildegard's canticle "O vis aeternitatis," is the expression of ecstasy and commitment to a vision (ironically the driving force of warfare as well as human affection). In this regard Messiaen's symbolism is also no different from Mozart's in the Piano Concerto in A.

Messiaen was as much a visionary as Scriabin, and he shared the Russian composer's fascination with the relationship of harmony and color. Unlike the decadent Scriabin, Messiaen's vision is essentially religious and pastoral, after his ideal St. Francis of Assisi. Compared to

Varèse in *Ionisation*, Messiaen's treatment of percussion as gunfire seems childlike, even though his layering of rhythms and tone qualities is planned and calculated in a sophisticated way.

Discussion topics

1. Explain how the valued qualities of Marcello's oboe melody may also be interpreted as admirable qualities in a person's character.
2. Examine the contrasting roles, of tactile lute and disembodied violins, in Vivaldi's lute concerto movement, the violins acting as assisted resonance.
3. Consider Bach's harpsichord as a prototype "mechanical guitar" that is better in some respects than a guitar, but less musical in other ways.
4. Discuss how Rodrigo's guitar concerto manages to reconcile the classical spirit of J. S. Bach with the warmth of Spanish tradition.
5. The emotion of Mozart's clarinet movement is based on self-restraint, expressed in a music of straight lines and simple chords. Is this similar to the mysterious emotion of the "Mona Lisa" of Leonardo da Vinci?
6. Show how the skill expressed in Boccherini's cello concerto resembles the skill of a high wire artist or tightrope walker.
7. A child who is excited may squeal, and an adult scream or yell. Does this explain why extremely high melodies are exciting to hear?
8. Show how the piano and orchestra in Mozart's concerto can be seen as a marriage of opposites, like Jack Sprat and his wife in the nursery rhyme.
9. In the Rondo of Beethoven's violin concerto the soloist seems to be encouraging the audience, and the orchestra, to join in the song. What style of leadership does this action represent?
10. Could the emotions expressed by Schumann's cello be expressing fear of the unknown, or impatience? How do they compare with the temperaments of a Boccherini or a Mozart solo?
11. In a musical contest between the organ and the orchestra, which is David and which Goliath?
12. Who was the mythical Prometheus, and in what ways is Scriabin's concerto inspired by his story?
13. What are the practical and dramatic implications of a performance of Gershwin's *Rhapsody in Blue* with the composer as soloist on piano roll?
14. The eerie gliding tones of the ondes martenot in Messiaen's "Turangalîla 2" evoke both the horror of war, and the joy of peace. What do these two extremes of emotion share in common?

VI

TIME AND MOTION

Attitudes to music vary widely in different parts of the world. In ancient traditions and among non-industrial cultures, music is a valued element of ritual and social life, bringing precision and dignity to ritual, helping to preserve valued traditions and memories, and coordinating and patterning social life through song and dance. The story of western music is more complicated. From ancient history to 1600 the study of music was deeply involved in the most important areas of human knowledge. Not "art" in the modern sense of the merely decorative and entertaining, but *real knowledge* in the sense we understand by philosophy, psychology, science, communications, and people management.

We are brought up to think that musical knowledge is knowledge about music, and that real knowledge is something else. But making music by definition involves an understanding of acoustics, the behavior of sound, of materials, and how they vibrate—for instance how the parts of a violin work together to produce a beautiful tone—and of consonance and dissonance, the structures and processes of human hearing, and the expression of emotion in coded form, as well as meaningful communication and abstract data processing of a pretty advanced kind. Music is not just about entertainment. The instruments of music as well as music itself can be interpreted as declarations of a particular world view as well as affirmations of universal principles of physics. The pipe organ is a monument to early astronomy, geometry, and proportion. It took 1500 years to evolve to its renaissance form.

Standard music notation took over four centuries to evolve. Designed as an international code of information exchange, the development of music notation involved the same conceptual advances as the scientific graph, of which it is a significant precursor. Standard notation also created the possibility of organizing people of different skills into an orchestra. An orchestra in action today is a model of production-line management, and also a model of society.

In 1900 the sociologist Max Weber described the modern symphony orchestra as the ideal model or paradigm of western industrial society. He was probably thinking of the music of Beethoven, Wagner, Bruckner and perhaps Mahler, and he was not talking about aesthetics but about the orchestra as a model of social organization, and social organization as a manifestation of economic power. Today large sectors of former European and American industry have come under Asian management. Companies who are heavily invested in western music, like Yamaha and Sony, realize that to compete successfully in the world, industry has to operate as efficiently as a symphony orchestra and plan its operations as precisely as a Beethoven symphony. Asian cultures see western music in a completely objective manner. They have their own sophisticated musical traditions. We wonder why they are so interested in what we in Europe and the old west regard as mere aesthetics and entertainment, and then we wonder why having done so they are doing so well at making cars and computers.

Time and space are key dimensions of human existence. Our history depends on a sense of the past and the past experiences and deeds of ourselves and other people. Our lives in the present rely on a shared perception of time that enables meetings to happen, shops to open, and goods to be delivered. Who we are and where we are going are matters of personal relationship to history, to the course of our own life, where we are today, and where we want to be tomorrow. These are universal considerations. Music is part of the universal human process of coming to terms with them.

At a superficial level, movement is physical activity, including work and recreation, that makes life enjoyable and productive. At a fundamental level, however, movement of any kind (or even the sense of movement alone, as when we listen to music) addresses the two issues of how to fill time and space. The word "occupation" means what we do for a living: to occupy our time. But we also occupy space, the place where we live, this desk, this seat. For most people, too, the quality of life a person leads is defined by their *occupation*.

If human beings were all the same, our music would be all the same as well. As physical systems, of course, we are all much the same. Most differences are cultural. They reflect the habits and customs we adopt, our particular software for coping with the world. These cultural differences are realized in the patterns and priorities of the music we make. In understanding those differences in processing information we can make it easier to understand one another.

79
A Japanese universe

"Edo Lullaby." Traditional Japanese melody arr. Minoru Miki. 3:34 minutes. 18th century. In *Japan: Traditional Vocal and Instrumental Music.* Ensemble Nipponia, Minoru Miki. Elektra Nonesuch 9 72072-2 (track 4).

This music is an arrangement for instruments of a traditional Japanese melody. Edo is the old name for Tokyo. The music can be imagined as the image of a Japanese garden through which a fresh breeze passes. The breeze is represented by a Japanese flute (shakuhachi). Other instruments are: small bells, a banjo (shamisen), lute (biwa), and two long zithers (koto). These other instruments represent the effects of the breeze on the garden and its inhabitants. There are *hard, soft, sudden, shimmering,* and *bending* sounds. A Japanese garden is a microcosm of the world. It contains earth, air, fire (warmth), and water (the ornamental pond), together with creatures and life forms that live in the air, on the ground, under the ground, and in the water. The listener sits on a wooden bench contemplating the garden. When the breeze blows, the garden comes to life.

The midpoint of the piece is an image of a sudden shower of rain played by the kotos in rapid tremolandi. Elsewhere the sharp plucked and strummed sounds appear random, but their actions begin to make sense if perceived as effects of the flute in its guise as a breeze. Though the plucked sounds are intense and sharp, the overall effect is calm. This music is a mixture of tactile sensations, hot and cold, bright and dark, hard and liquid, resilient and compliant. Such music invites us to reconsider what a lullaby means. In the west a lullaby is a soothing song to lull a child to sleep. You may wonder how is it possible to go to sleep with so many sharp and abrupt sounds going on. Surely they would keep a person awake? Perhaps the intention is more philosophical, a music for meditation rather than for going to sleep. One could understand this music as the equivalent to the sounds heard when relaxing under a tree on a summer afternoon with cicadas chirping in the background; or when dozing on the beach in the sun to the accompaniment of seagulls and the roar of the waves. And yet my Japanese students assured me the flute melody was indeed a cradle song their parents or grandparents used to sing.

Absolute silence is disturbing, as John Cage realized. We need some noise as reassurance of the world continuing to exist. A silence unbroken by the sound of cicadas or birds would be of a dead world. A truly tranquil experience is one that we feel is *open to disturbance*, and yet we are never sure when to expect it. Schoenberg's musical image of a summer morning lake scene is exactly like this: from time to time the listener hears the effect of a leaping fish breaking the placid surface of the water.

The message underlying this music is not a storyline in the usual sense, although it does tell a simple story of a playful breeze in a garden setting, leading up to a brief shower of rain, and then the sun coming out. Nature, it says, is not a loose collection of inert parts that just happen to occupy the same general location. That weather happens is true, but also not very interesting. The real meaning is simple but profound. If there is no movement, there is no noise. If there is no noise, there is nothing to be aware of. Through the incidental noises made by natural processes, such as the buzzing of insects, the flight of birds, frogs croaking, a leaf dropping, water trickling, etc., a listener becomes conscious not only that there are things happening out there, but what they are made of, whether they are living or nonliving, and where they are located. In this case there is an invisible moving force in the garden, which is the breeze, represented by the flute. By implication, everything that is disturbed in the garden is responding to the action of the breeze. Leaves flutter, reeds bend, frogs croak and splash, and the surface of the pond is disturbed. The musical picture of action and response is a Japanese way of saying that nature is interconnected, a system tuned to a certain tension like a musical instrument, so that when it is energized by an external force, it vibrates: not in unison, but in a connected fashion: a harmony of being. But there is more to it than a natural process. The flute also stands for the inquiring mind of the observer, considering each element in the universal equation, what it is, and how it fits in with all the rest.

"It describes miniscule little things that are not usually noticed or enjoyed, quiet actions that cannot speak or make a noise: falling leaves. Absolutely magical."

80
Afternoon in the sun

Claude Debussy, *Prélude à l'Après-midi d'un Faune*. 10:28 minutes. Jan van Reeth, BRT Philharmonic Orchestra, Brussels, Alexander Rahbari. Naxos 8.550262 (track 1).

The Japanese poster art of Hiroshige and others dramatically influenced young French nineteenth-century artists, Claude Debussy among them, who went on to become the Impressionists. Given the central importance of the shakuhachi in Japanese music, it is hard to ignore the possibility that in this composition, the work that first brought him to public attention, a work for orchestra in which the flute plays a leading role, Debussy is deliberately alluding to the newly fashionable orientalist aesthetic.

It is interesting to compare this piece with the *Edo Lullaby*. The comparison works on a number of levels: both works are pastoral in setting and mood, both assign a leading role to the flute, and each can be interpreted as a dialogue between the flute as a motivating force or idea, and the other instruments as elements in the natural landscape responding to that motivating force.

A faun, by the way, is not a young deer but a teenage Pan with a set of panpipes and an active libido. If we take his title at face value, Debussy's mini tone poem can be read as a celebration of the erotic impulse and the role of music to disarm and seduce. The work is in the form of a *ritornello*, like Beethoven's Rondo from the Violin Concerto, the opening melody provoking a series of alternate responses but always returning as a refrain (which, depending on the listener's mood, may suggest a succession either of romantic conquests, or of failed attempts at attracting the opposite sex).

Unlike *Edo Lullaby*, the opening flute melody, interestingly, is not a true melody at all, more of a movement down and up the scale, of a kind that in fact could only be carried off successfully by a modern keyed flute, and not by panpipes. Its gliding motion: down–up, pause; down–up, is both a covert representation of the wavering action of unstable emotion, as in wailing or ecstasy, and also a scanning action in disguise, as though looking for a target. Although we hear the flute stimulating a reaction, like the breeze in *Edo Lullaby*, the answering shimmer from harp and tremolo strings is a trembling effect a sophisticated French audience would be just as likely to interpret as feminine shivers of anticipation, as (say) the rustling of leaves in the wind (even though the two images are metaphorically connected).

From a western perspective Debussy's unusual whole-tone scale evokes a different emotional world from the tired rhetoric of classical tonality: an idealized back-to-nature landscape of innocent play that has more to do with wishful reverie than a respect for traditional Japanese observation of nature. The composer's musical argument, to be inferred from the succession of different continuations of the ritornello theme, is that a whole-tone melody of this simplicity lends itself to an indefinite number of possible continuations and harmonic implications —a thesis distantly related, indeed, to the panchromaticism of Bach's *Well-tempered Clavier*. Of course, it also embodies the fashionable late romantic idea of sexual freedom, popularized by Balzac and other prominent literary figures.

<h1 style="text-align:center">81</h1>
<h2 style="text-align:center">Real time</h2>

Louis Couperin, Prélude à l'imitation de M. Froberger. 6:27 minutes. From the Suite in A minor. Laurence Cummings *harpsichord*. Naxos 8.550922 (track 7).

What is time? This is a question that greatly exercised the minds of philosophers and composers of the baroque era. In the medieval era of plainchant, music notation recognized *succession* (things happening one after another) but not rhythm or measured *duration* (things moving to a beat): plainchant is timeless in implication. We encounter music modeled after clock time in the Brandenburg concertos of J. S. Bach, whose music conveys a deep interest in mechanical processes. The objection to clock time is that it has nothing to do with human perceptions. A work song, like the blues (which originated in the cotton fields), a sea shanty, or just a love song, like "Mandad' ei comigo," is at least coordinated to the rhythm of performing a task, like kneading bread, tilling the soil, or hauling ropes on board ship—and in the final resort, to the action of singing and the emotional connotations of the words, which are also temporal in implication. In such instances the music's sense of timing is naturally consistent with direct experience. On the other hand, the human experience of time varies from person to person, so is neither consistent nor reliable.

Once you live in a society where time is regulated by the clock, and not simply by the position of the sun in the sky, the nature of time becomes an intellectual issue of scientific interest, and for seafarers mapping their travels in remote oceans, precision timing becomes a matter of considerable importance.

In classical music we can identify different styles representing different ways of describing temporal processes. The first is clock time, a measure deliberately unrelated to human movement. A second is dance, because dances are established patterns of movement with definite associations of relative pace and physical action. A third is *virtual* dance, meaning a music patterned after a dance form but impossible to dance to. In virtual dance, the same patterns as real dance are employed, but in an abstract sense, and may be distorted or modified for effect.

The baroque suite for harpsichord is a sequence of dance forms, presented as studies in time and motion. The revealing feature of these suites is that they are composed for the harpsichord in the first place, since the harpsichord is a mechanical keyboard by which it is difficult, if not impossible, to convey a sense of rhythm or physical movement. There is a charming scene in Ingmar Bergman's movie *Smiles of a Summer Night* in which a gathering of well-to-do early nineteenth-century holidaymakers dance to the sound of a musical box. It seems a little incongruous for a musical box to be employed in this way, since its tinkling sound does not carry a strong beat. By comparison the harpsichord is more robust in tone, but it still lacks a strong beat. To circumvent the harpsichord's lack of dynamic emphasis performers employed decorative trills and inflections to emphasize an underlying beat structure. Couperin became a leader in developing a systematic language of ornamentation (or "graces") for this purpose. The act of taking familiar dance idioms ordinarily performed by real people to an accompaniment of strings and wind instruments, and transferring them to keyboard instruments of limited expression, such as the pipe organ or harpsichord, suggests an inquiry into the nature of movement.

A harpsichord suite usually begins with a prelude, a word implying preparation before action. A prelude, however, is not a dance. It resembles the moment of improvisation when a performer checks the tuning and warms up an instrument before the beginning of a concert, while members of the audience are still taking their seats. The players in a symphony orchestra go through the same ritual before the conductor appears onstage at the beginning of a concert.

The fact that it has no rhythm or form does not mean that the warming up process has no sense of time, however. Indeed, one could argue that a listener's sense of time is even more acute in the absence of conventional patterns. Uncertainty concentrates attention on the present moment. The same heightening of awareness occurs during a cadenza, for example, when the orchestra stops and the soloist is free to improvise. This splendidly impulsive example of a baroque prelude, composed by the French composer Louis Couperin as a tribute to his German contemporary Johann Froberger—illustrates what happens when intelligent minds turn their attention from concepts of *order* (i.e., dance forms) to constructive *disorder* (the warming-up process). As well as being intellectually challenging, the baroque "unmeasured prelude" is a real test of a composer's notational skills. Since standard music notation is predicated on a uniform timescale or beat, a music without timescale is by definition impossible to notate exactly.

Apparent randomness is a recurrent, if provocative, feature of classical music throughout history. The philosophical issues raised by this wonderfully wayward improvisation are essentially the same as we encounter in the orchestral montages of Charles Ives, the chance compositions of John Cage, and electronic music.

82
Virtual dance

J. S. Bach, III. Gavotte en rondeau. 2:01 minutes. From Partita No. 3 in E for solo violin, BWV 1006. Yehudi Menuhin. EMI CHS7 6035-2.

Bach's solo partitas and suites for violin and cello are chamber music in the purest sense, but with a subtle twist. In classical times a dancing-master would go from house to house to teach the younger members of the wealthy to dance, and he would carry a cigar-shaped or pocket-sized violin in his cloak on which to play the music. The instrument had a full-sized fingerboard, so could be played like a normal instrument, but only a tiny resonating body, producing a volume of sound perfectly adequate for domestic use, but of a quality resembling the sound of a bumblebee, or the sound of abandoned headphones. So in one sense Bach's dance suites for solo violin resemble the real thing, dance music as actually performed by a traveling dancing-master on his pocket violin.

But in truth, this music is not at all suitable for teaching young people to dance. The composer has transformed a rather vigorous leaping dance, the gavotte, into a showcase for the violinist, who is required to play with a high degree of technical expertise, including double-stopping (playing two notes at once). Dancing-masters in practice were obliged to keep the beat and call the moves, and played more like toe-tapping folk fiddlers in country bluegrass music—a direct descendant, in actual fact, of this tradition of fiddle music for dance, still popular in rural parts of Europe and the United States.

Compared to the simple tunes and strong rhythms of traditional fiddle music and orthodox dance music, Bach's gavotte is revealed as an elegant and largely solitary paraphrase for the performer to exercise his (her) technical skills, a technical elaboration of dance form in which the challenge is to maintain the flow, in the process often sacrificing the melody line and regular beat on which young novice dancers are bound to rely. The simple test of such a music is to play it for children of primary school age and see if they are able to dance to it. After only a few seconds the sense of beat vanishes completely and the poor children do not know what to do.

83
Order and chaos

G. F. Handel, I. Ouverture: Largo–Adagio–Allegro from *Music for the Royal Fireworks*
HWV 351 Original 1749 version. 7:42 minutes. The English Concert, Trevor Pinnock.
DG Archiv 453 451-2 (track 1).

In an earlier encounter with Handel we heard a movement from the
Water Music, composed soon after the accession of King George I.
This later composition is a compilation from various earlier pieces in
celebration of the signing of the treaty of Aix-la-Chappelle in the reign
of the king's son, George II. Once again the performance takes place
out of doors: this time not on the waters of the river Thames, but on
land, in London's Green Park. The title *Music for the Royal Fireworks*
is exact: it is music to accompany an actual fireworks display. The
overture is a stately processional suggesting the arrival of the King and
his retinue, scored for a barrage of wind and percussion instruments to
convey an impression of civil and military might. It is music not dis-
similar in character to Monteverdi's "Deus in adjutorium," though
without the voices.

An open park covered in grass and full of spectators is not a very
reverberant space, and Handel did not have the benefit of modern
amplification. The king is supposed to have asked on this occasion for
"no fiddles," perhaps regarding the sound of violins as too effeminate
or too rustic for such an occasion. But Handel would probably have
decided that violins were not a good idea anyway, since out of doors
they sound relatively weak in tone and in any case are not designed to
perform under less than ideal weather conditions. (He later relented
and arranged the same music for a conventional orchestra including
strings, but only for performing indoors.)

Despite being one of the composer's most widely loved and fre-
quently performed works, this orchestral suite is normally performed
and recorded without any hint of accompanying fireworks. There is no
practical reason why it should not be performed in association with a
fireworks display: every year in the United States on the Fourth of July
Tchaikovsky's "1812" Overture is performed in the open air to the
accompaniment of synchronized cannon fire and fireworks, much to
the delight of American children. The only reason one can imagine for

not incorporating the prerecorded sound of a fireworks display in a concert performance of Handel's *Music for the Royal Fireworks* is that those responsible have never regarded the incidental noises as a significant element, either of Handel's instrumentation, or of his musical conception.

Let us think about this. A composer of Handel's quality and experience does not just supply background music on demand for a fireworks display. He thinks of ways in which the fireworks and the music can be reconciled, musically, dramatically, and philosophically. Fireworks after all are a peacetime recreation of the chaos and excitement of war. The sounds are explosive and unpredictable. There is a smell of cordite in the air. Spectators are excited and a little frightened, their cries adding to the general noise level. This particular celebration was composed to mark the successful end of a lengthy period of sporadic fighting throughout Europe, so on this occasion the symbolism of fireworks is especially meaningful.

A fireworks and music performance today is a carefully choreographed event. Computer controlled detonations are timed exactly to coincide with the downbeat of the music. In Handel's day such refinements of timing did not exist. The firing is random, as in a real battlefield. What is a composer to do? What does any fire officer want to do at a public fireworks display? Reassure the public that they must not panic, that the event is under control. And this is exactly what Handel's music does, especially during the Overture. The music provides not only a firm, secure pulsation but also the strong melody and harmonies aimed at reassuring a volatile audience that the king can be relied upon to prevail in the field of battle and protect his subjects from danger. Take away the sound of fireworks and all that is left is a rather loud march past in the exaggerated rhythm of French style. But juxtapose this heavy rhythm with sporadic explosions high in the air, and its function as a reassurance becomes only too clear. This music is no trivial entertainment but a dramatic dialogue in acoustic terms between the forces of chaos and the forces of order. Random explosions, noise, and death—but also excitement—are associated with the sounds of the battlefield; regularity, order, and harmony—but also a hint of tedium —are associated with royalty and control.

To juxtapose sounds representing chaos and order is one thing, but Handel goes even further. Among the original instrumentation are military side-drums and timpani (tuned kettle-drums). The former are noise instruments, but associated with military discipline and therefore make *reassuring noises*; the latter are processional instruments for music-making, but they are *tuned to specific notes* and so help support the musical bassline: they represent a further step in the process of reconciling the instrumental music and the noise of fireworks. So in the long run the chaos of random fireworks is carefully contained and integrated by stages with the music:

fireworks	–	side drums	–	timpani	–	winds
random noises		rhythm		pitch		harmony

Naturally, the meaning of the fireworks would be entirely lost if they were programmed to detonate at precise intervals. Because then they would no longer be random.

84
Time paradox

W. A. Mozart, I. Allegro, and II. Romanze (Andante). From Serenade No. 13 in G K.525 "Eine kleine Nachtmusik." I. 4:26 minutes; II. 6:19 minutes. Philharmonia Orchestra, Sir Colin Davis. Seraphim 7243 5 68533 2 (cd 1, tracks 1, 2).

That clock time and human time are perceived differently is not a hard fact to grasp. A machine ticks away at an even pace because that is the most efficient way for it to dispose of a constant energy supply. Human time is driven by a complex of motivations sourced in both the mind and the body, so a person is conscious of time in relation to the clock and also in relation to personal pressures and work patterns. The same habits and preferences enable a person to distinguish between order and chaos, though most of us live comfortably in conditions somewhere between the two.

Tempo is the musical term for pace, how fast or how slow a piece of music is moving. Few would have any difficulty telling the difference between fast and slow. Fast is when you are running for a bus; slow is when you are taking your time and looking in shop windows. Everybody knows that. But is it true? A classical symphony typically consists of four movements: first movement, slow movement, scherzo, and finale. The word *movement* means more than just a single piece of a symphony: it carries the implication of a group of instruments playing together to convey a definite feeling of moving or being moved, which is actually quite exciting when you consider that the players on the platform are not moving very much at all, making the effect of movement largely an illusion. The four movements of a symphony are differentiated in tempo. The first movement is usually neutral, somewhere between moderate and fast. The second is slow. The third is a dance form in three time, in the style of a minuet (formal, upper class) or a scherzo (a joke, more lively). The finale is typically an exercise in how fast the orchestra can play while still remaining perfectly synchronized. So each *movement* by definition is a study in motion as well as a study in togetherness.

Composers have a variety of terms for the *tempo* of a *movement*, meaning a *sense* of time within a *semblance* of motion (the two are not quite the same). Tempo terminology is varied and a study all to itself. It ranges from the names of dances, which already imply conventions and patterns of body movement, through vaguely descriptive Italian terms corresponding to "lightly," "leisurely," "moderately," "animatedly," etc., to totally abstract metronome numbers like "quarter-note at 80," meaning eighty beats per minute. Of all the available terms, the dance name and the metronome indication are the most precise: the dance because as a pattern of movement it has an optimum pace that is geared to tradition and the pace of human execution, and the metronome because it is related to clock time. Of these two, only the dance corresponds to a human sensation of movement.

Invented in seventeenth-century France as an aid to ballet dancers, the metronome introduced objectivity into the study of motion. By swinging a pendulum and shortening the length of the string until the weight swung at the same pace as the dancers, one could work out the number of steps or beats per minute for each dance. That labeling of tempo in terms of beats per minute is still engraved on traditional metronomes today. The slower the beat, it says, the slower the movement: the same as in the movies, where fast motion is the movie speeded up, and slow motion is movement slowed down.

As early as the renaissance era composers recognized that a basic beat could be maintained while the tempo of the song or dance changed—say, from two steps in the beat to three. (This can be heard in the Monteverdi "Deus in adjutorium".) After the arrival of the metronome, baroque and classical composers became more interested in the idea of measuring time, and noticed that a fast metronomic beat could paradoxically apply to a slower movement as well. It seemed that human perceptions of fast and slow were no longer simply a matter of counting the number of beats in a minute. Rather, the sensation of pace or tempo relied on other factors.

In numerous works from the classical period it is possible to observe a consistency of beat frequency from movement to movement, employing the same metronomic value for fast and for slow. The first two movements of Mozart's *Eine kleine Nachtmusik*, for example, are respectively an Allegro (fast) and an Andante (leisurely pace). The names are given, so one is in no doubt of the composer's intention. And indeed, when one listens to the two movements one after the other on a recording, the first sounds fast and energetic, and the second serene and graceful. And yet, if a listener flicks back and forth between the two movements, the underlying beat of both movements is virtually the same: a deliberate illusion. To understand how the illusion is produced, one analyzes the musical content. It turns out that a listener's sense of pace is conditioned not so much by the beat as by the degree of change within the musical texture. Sudden changes in loudness, irregularities in rhythm, a jumpy melody, and frequent and unpredictable alterations in musical texture and density all contribute to a sense of dynamic uncertainty. More simply, they add up to a great deal of mental work for the listener. And that excess workload imposed on the audience contributes to the impression of greater speed. There is too much to keep up with. The second movement, by contrast, is music of steady flow, smooth contour, constant dynamic, and even texture, so there is less work for the listener to do, and the music appears slower and more graceful.

The same techniques of varying the texture, density, and contour of music while maintaining the same beat frequency are also heard in the F minor slow movement of Mozart's Piano Concerto No. 23 in A. The piano solo music sounds empty, withdrawn, and the orchestra ample and in full flood, but the underlying beat is the same for both. Another very clever example is the Introduction and Allegro of the first movement of Beethoven's Symphony No. 4 in B flat, which opens to a music expressing absence of movement and proceeds by slow degrees of alternating "full" and "empty" passages to a noisy climax out of which a fast-tempo Allegro suddenly appears, all over a constant underlying pulsation. It is a very impressive achievement.

Pierre Boulez once remarked "tempo is only a quality of speed in the passage of time," a curious observation that further suggests that a perception of movement—in music, at any rate—may also be influenced by cultural factors. Sound recording and electronic music are certainly responsible for, or have renewed an appreciation of, a difference between *playback* time, which is mechanical (fast motion, slow motion), and *action* time, which relates to the moving content of an edited segment. That action movies contain so many pointless chase sequences may signify in the same way that it is not the content of the action that creates excitement, but rather the increased density of information the viewer is expected to digest.

85
One beat per second

Arthur Honegger, "Évocation des forçats" (Life of the convicts) from the film score *Les Misérables* (1934). 1:55 minutes. Slovak Radio Symphony Orchestra (Bratislava), Adriano. Marco Polo 8.223181 (track 3).

Erich Wolfgang Korngold, "Robin Hood and His Merry Men." From *The Adventures of Robin Hood* (1938). 4:28 minutes. London Symphony Orchestra, John Williams. National Public Radio, "Music in Film" compilation. Sony SMK 60991 (track 1).

Miklós Rózsa, "Parade of the Charioteers." From *Ben-Hur* (1959). 3:13 minutes. Hollywood Bowl Symphony Orchestra, Miklós Rózsa. NPR/Sony SMK 60991 (track 11).

John Williams, "Main Theme" from *Star Wars* (1977). 5:51 minutes. Skywalker Symphony Orchestra, John Williams. NPR/Sony SMK 60991 (track 17).

Metronome 60 is a measure of one beat per second. Film composers like it because music at this tempo is easy to manage in a context of movie scenes that run for an exact number of minutes and seconds. From a musical perspective, composing to a uniform pulsation of one per second, 60 beats per minute, makes no sense at all. Firstly, it does not correspond to the tempo of any normal human action. The normal heartbeat is 72–76 beats per minute. In times of stress, as for a driver overtaking on the freeway, or the pilot of an aircraft coming into land, the pulse rate can rise momentarily to 140 beats per minute or thereabouts. Secondly, a uniform beat at 60 per minute is neither fast nor slow, and certainly not both at once. How is it possible to create music geared to the ticking of a stopwatch that can also satisfy the film-maker's reasonable demand for pace and atmosphere? The answer to that question can be heard in the examples cited here, and in many others. With an eye on the digital second counter of a cd player, it is possible to listen to the music and count the seconds at the same time.

Swiss composer Arthur Honegger began his film music career in the silent movie era. In those days exact coordination of vision and live music was neither essential nor even possible: live music was designed to provide atmosphere rather than accompanying the action like ballet. After the arrival of optical sound on film in 1930, a new art of precision editing arose, since the music was now firmly attached to the visual action, and could be perfectly coordinated with it. Henceforth the timing of events within individual scenes would be a critical issue. Wolfgang Korngold, a young German opera composer who emigrated to Hollywood during the silent era bearing recommendations from Gustav Mahler and Richard Strauss, devoted his considerable skills to the impossible task of creating a movie music in complete synchronization with the screen action. It was a doomed enterprise, both musically and dramatically, creating comic effects more suited to the exaggerated world of animated movies than for "realistic" serious drama or heroic romance.

The early example by Arthur Honegger is music composed for a small orchestra amd intended to convey the monotonous routine of prison life, a neutral emotion closely related to clock time. By comparison, Korngold's *Robin Hood* title music is a three-part character sketch for full orchestra, a music by turns heroic, tranquil, and epic, as though describing the leading male, the female love interest, and the landscape in quick succession. In this 1938 example the transitions in energy and characterization are of particular interest, since the beat remains constant throughout, and one can clearly hear that the factors determining the perception of tempo are rhythm, line, and instrumentation, exactly the same as Mozart's *Eine kleine Nachtmusik*. At the beginning an uneven rhythm, a jagged melody line, and bright brass timbres generate energy, after which a smoother melody played by strings in even note values creates a slower, more feminine and lyrical sense of tempo.

The same techniques of musical scene-setting are readily identified elsewhere, from Bernard Herrmann's iconic stabbing music for strings in the shower scene from Alfred Hitchcock's *Psycho*, at two beats per second, to the title music of *Ben-Hur* and *Star Wars*, both scored to a one-second beat. For these movie composers, as for the Bach of the Brandenburg concertos, the relentless pulsation of mechanical time is a valued part of the action and its emotional subtext. At one level, clock time is an assertion of control by the movie over the audience, a rhetorical position encapsulated in the motto of the classic television series *The Twilight Zone*: "we control the horizontal, we control the vertical." On a deeper level, a devotion to clock time tells the listener that life is short, time is fleeting, enjoy it while you can. Or, more realistically, "pay no attention."

86
A German dance

W. A. Mozart, No. 3 from *Three German Dances* K.605. 2:54 minutes. Late 18th century. Recommended: Philharmonia Orchestra, Sir Colin Davis. Seraphim 7243 5 68533 2 4 (cd 1, track 7).

In the final year of his life Mozart composed a number of occasional dances for small orchestra with additional folk instruments such as the tambourine, flageolet, and hurdy-gurdy. This particular dance has an element of humor that most (presumably German) commentators prefer to ignore, calling the piece "a musical sleigh-ride" because it happens to incorporate post-horns and jingle bells. That would be fine, except for two things. One, it is called a German Dance. That is its title. Meaning, it is a *dance*. A *German* dance, that is, a description of a typically German type of dance, or style of dancing. Second, it is hard to conceive of a sleigh-ride in three time, in which the jingle bells only appear in the mid-section or "middle 8." Horses do not canter in three time: if they did, the sleigh would go round in a circle and get nowhere. Nor do they switch off their sleigh bells from time to time as it suits them. As a dance, the music works perfectly well. In this recording, it is also very funny.

In the late eighteenth century, as the aristocratic regime came increasingly under fire from the newsreading public, an irreverent art of political caricature burst on the scene, associated in Britain with Hogarth, Rowlandson, Gillray and others. Considered as a genuine dance, this piece can be read as a caricature of the German upper class at play. Mozart himself was Austrian by birth, and the merchant Austrians considered themselves vastly more cultured than their agrarian neighbors to the north, a contrast perfectly expressed in the folk tale of the town mouse and the country mouse.

Listen to how the dance begins. Ask yourself if this is the music of an elegant and refined group of dancers. It is loud, coarse, and heavy: good for dancing, but not music suggesting a delicate sensibility or for the light of foot. The opening theme (for post horn) resembles a military bugle call, suggesting that the male revelers are already a little the worse for wear and have to be woken up; either that, or they share a mindset that only responds to military orders. (Or perhaps both.) It is masculine, heel-clicking "oom-pah-pah" music, interrupted by an interlude somewhat lighter in style, with accompanying sleigh-bells shaken in rhythm. This is the ladies' cue to dance, dressed "with rings on their fingers, and bells on their toes." Now it is clear that the dancers in this comic portrayal of country revels are all in costume: the men dressed for the hunt, the ladies as plump rococo shepherdesses like candidates for a saucy painting by Watteau or Fragonard. The short dance draws to a close with ladies and gentlemen dancing together, but when it is time to end, the bells continue to shake, indicating that the ladies, like little Bo-Peeps, have lost their way home. Again the music calls time, and again the ladies miss their cue. Finally the post horn emits an ear-splitting high C that continues to ring while the action on the dance floor peters out in confusion.

To perform Mozart's *German Dances* in a way pretending that they are not dances at all is about as silly as performing Handel's

Music for the Royal Fireworks without the sound of fireworks. Musicians today often seem to miss the joke. Of course, it could be a musical impression of a sleigh cresting a rise and disappearing round a corner. But that would not be anything like as funny, and Mozart was at a stage in his short life where he needed a good laugh.

87
Haydn's suspension bridge

Joseph Haydn, III. Minuet and Trio, from Symphony No. 101 "The Clock." Late 18th century. La Petite Bande, Sigiswald Kuijken. DHM 05472 772451 2.

In classical music a bridge is a short cut or connecting passage that brings a wandering theme back on track. In this example of virtual dance by Haydn, the audience is led away from the standard pattern of a minuet and trio, a formal dance of deliberate symmetry, into an extended passage of rhythmic suspension that for a while seems as though it could go on forever. If listened to as a real dance, the effect is witty and surprising. After a normally symmetrical opening of four measures by four, the alternate party (the female partner in a regular dance) appears to get caught off her step in a rhythmic loop that would seem to be leading her farther and farther away, to the other side of the hall, through the door, and down the corridor. It all sounds very plausible, but the effect is amusing and would be appreciated by an audience in the know (who, needless to say, would not be dancing but just enjoying the show).

This movement is from a late Haydn symphony, but a music displaying no hint of political stress or impending catastrophe. What is fascinating is the composer's daring extension of dance-related rhythmic conventions into a new architectural domain of poise and counterpoise. The baroque roots of minuet and trio form consist of repeated short phrases conforming to the moves of the dance: left then right, forward then back. The music guides the dancers and reminds them of where and how to lead and respond. It is a solid, conventional structure in repeating segments like the columns of an arcade, or the arches of a viaduct. Into this conventional pattern of simple repeating structural units, Haydn introduces an interesting and radical notion of rhythmic leverage that allows an answering arch to extend over a much greater distance than one would expect, a design feat worthy of Brunel. It is in fact true that engineering concepts of weight, balance, and leverage are imitated in the balancing act that is dance, an art where body weight is

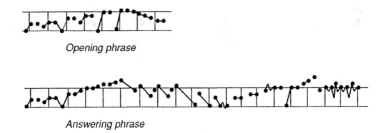

Opening phrase

Answering phrase

poised alternately on one foot and the other, and movement from place to place is interpreted in the spirit of stop motion photography, and the step pattern—in Haydn's day already notated on paper—revealed as a sequence of graceful and matching arches. In the opening phrase of the minuet there is a clear pattern of five upward leaps, firmly anchored in the bass, equally spaced, rising to an octave in height, from which the countermovement angles gently downward like a seesaw. The same structure, in the answering phrase, is converted into a gantry from the high point of which the remainder of the melody is freely suspended. One is reminded of a mobile sculpture by Alexander Calder, a finely balanced system of pivots and weights that all the same is able to swivel freely.

A virtual minuet and trio is still available to be danced, but to do so without losing control would require special choreography. This music could make a very interesting pas de deux, a duo for male and female. The use of an unstable rhythm to generate dynamic momentum is a classic device that can clearly be heard in the Bach Brandenburg Concerto No. 2, and in the Mozart Symphony No. 40 finale, but here is a rare example of an actual step pattern manipulated to alter a conventional symmetry of balance and movement on a human scale to create a dynamic equilibrium on a larger scale. Haydn passed on this ability to work with large-scale forces to Beethoven, whose whole mindset was geared to larger than life gestures.

88
Stage directions

Franz Schubert, Ballet Suite No. 2 from *Rosamunde*. 6:57 minutes. 19th century. Orchestra of the Age of Enlightenment, Sir Charles Mackerras. Virgin VER5 61305-2.

Ballet is real dance, but with a script. It tells a story and is danced by specialists. "Tells a story" is only the surface meaning, for popular consumption. In practical terms a classical ballet is more like a symphonic suite for dancers. What is really going on is music translated into movement and gesture, sometimes intricate, often demonstrative, involving a solo or numbers of soloists, or full ensemble. In the baroque era, the growth of music for instruments alone led to a new style of extended singing, beyond the prowess of a normal voice. In a similar way, instrumental music also provoked a new art of extended movement aimed in a similar way at stretching the physical capabilities of a normal person. As of gymnastics and competitive ice skating, part of the attraction and motivation of modern ballet lies in pushing the body to the limit. The fact that ballet is executed in costume and to music (unlike gymnastics, but similar to ice skating) does not *mean* that its only purpose, or even the main purpose of ballet, is to decorate a fairytale. In terms of telling a story, ballet is more abstract than opera, since there is no text and no singing, the narrative being conveyed purely through music, costume, and movement. It is also more abstract than mime, since a mime artist is expected to move in a natural manner and without reference to music.

Formal dance, such as a minuet and trio, has its own layer of symbolic meaning encoded in the cyclic pattern and character of its movements, all of which are within the scope of a person of good health and coordination. Classical dance forms celebrate states of being or aspects of the human condition: love, anger, despair, melancholy, hope. As demonstrations of the affections they are not intended to lead anywhere, and end as they begin. Like the Japanese *Edo Lullaby*, these formal dances can be interpreted, on the one hand, as affirmations of nature, and on the other, as display rituals amounting to corporate expressions of human and social relationship, dignified in graceful moves that also acknowledge the balance of male and female principles, sun and moon, time and motion, in the universal scheme.

Formal dance follows a memorized pattern of steps and moves that repeats over and over. The name of a formal dance: minuet, sarabande, gavotte, etc., is the name of the pattern, and any music that fits the pattern can be called by the name, whether or not it is intended for dancing. A ballet, by contrast, has a script; the name identifies the script, and that name is identified with a particular author and composer. Having a narrative storyline and course of action means that the principal characters are no longer symbolic or abstract male and female qualities, but are transformed into identifiable personalities or character types whose special status is demonstrated in movements of exceptional physicality. And whereas a classical cyclical dance form can be interpreted as an expression of order and stability in the universe and in human affairs, a storyline is essentially linear in implication, a message of dynamic change and progression, involving actions that in effect challenge the existing order and introduce a new scheme of relationships. On a philosophical level a storyline is predicated on the idea that *things could be different*, and that individual actions can change the world. At a practical level, it is a lot harder for a dancer to remember a storyline that leads to a completely changed situation, than to remember an abstract pattern of limited duration that ends just the way it began. So a dancer's memory is stretched in ballet as well as the physical body.

Music to accompany dance has a duty to assist both the memory process and the dancer's interpretation of the moves. Like classical poetry, music has its own code of stressed and unstressed beats, of characteristic rhythmic groups (known in poetry, interestingly, as *feet*), and phrasing, in lines and verses. In virtual dance, such as the Haydn minuet, these conventions of stress and phrasing can be employed in an abstract fashion, so that their meaning becomes ambiguous or self-contradictory; but in ballet, which involves real dancers, the cues have to be exact—so much so, that many choreographers prefer to create their ballets from preexisting rather than new music, to ensure a perfect match.

Schubert's second ballet suite, a dance interlude from the opera *Rosamunde*, is familiar music and an excellent example of structured composition designed to assist dancers. A ballet differs from classical dance in that in a formal dance such as a waltz the dancers are on the dance floor from beginning to end, so are always in motion and within earshot of the orchestra. Ballet, on the other hand, consists of a sequence of dances for different groups or soloists, so many of the participants have to spend time offstage, where it is not so easy to hear the music, with the result that the music is relied upon not just to co-ordinate step patterns, but also to cue exits and entrances.

To a casual listener Schubert's score seems deceptively simple, like folk music. It flows effortlessly and is easy to follow. There is a lot of repetition, helpful both to the listener and to the dancer, and in keeping with the conventional symmetries of traditional ballet: now male, now female, now left, now right. And for a dancer waiting in the wings, Schubert's music is also very easy to count. If a phrase is stated twice in succession, the second time is slightly changed in instrument or key, as in the introduction, where the first line of the four-line verse is scored for violins in G major, the second answering line in A minor, the third line for clarinets in D major, and the fourth for flutes, return-ing to G. The entire sequence is constructed in dance modules, each given a distinct masculine or feminine character and appropriate instru-mentation. At the end of the movement the pace quickens from two to three time, a normally problematic change, beautifully managed within a constant beat, so that the dancers do not have to change their rate of counting in order to stay in time.

89
Movement in all directions

Nikolai Rimsky-Korsakov, "Flight of the Bumble-Bee." 1:24 minutes. From *Tsar Saltan* Op. 57. Early 20th century. London Symphony Orchestra, André Previn. RCA Victor VD 60487.

Because gravity pulls people down, ballet and dance consist largely of movement on the level surface of a platform or dance floor, describing patterns essentially in two dimensions. This is not to say there is no vertical interest, since defying gravity through leaping and lifting is an important element of both traditions, only that the ability to fly and maneuver above ground is ordinarily limited nowadays to trapeze artists, or actors suspended by a wire in pantomime.

By 1900, when this little piece was composed, the idea of aerial flight was fast becoming a reality. What makes this composition even more interesting is the care with which the composer has translated a random continuous movement in three dimensions into music. As it moves through the air, the wing motion of a bumblebee or flying insect creates a traceable sound of variable pitch and loudness, and a flying insect trapped in a room tends to fly back and forth in search of a way out. Though a bumblebee is a more amiable subject for a public concert item, the flight pattern described here is more likely to be that of a house fly or bluebottle, insects that tend to fly with erratic changes of pitch and direction. Bumblebees and wasps, by contrast, tend to buzz at a constant pitch. If the composer had really wanted to describe a bumblebee in flight, it would have turned out a lot more monotone.

Describing continuous movement in three dimensions is a feat that even a Monteverdi would have found hard to match. The example "Deposuit de sede" from the *Vespers of 1610* expresses an architect's conception of space in a series of musical exchanges located at a set of cardinal points: left, right, up, down, front, and back. To draw a line of music that moves freely through space requires a different set of musical skills. This is an *illusion* of movement in space, remember, not movement between real locations in an actual building. The composer relies on careful observation of real movement, expressed in changes of timbre (tone color), loudness level (dynamic)—and, to a certain extent, on the actual trajectory of the melody in concert from instrument to instrument on the concert platform, the closer buzzing violins being located at the front and to the left of stage, the more distant sounding flute further back, nearer an imaginary vanishing point.

90
Hero . . .

Richard Strauss, Introduction from *Also sprach Zarathustra* (Thus spake Zarathustra) Op. 30. 1:49 minutes. Late 19th century. Slovak Philharmonic, Zdenek Kosler. Naxos 8.550182 (track 1).

Among the distinguishing features of western music in the romantic era of the nineteenth century, are an interest in literary and political themes, in the artist as hero, and the hero as an emblematic figure of emergent nationalism. These themes and stereotypes reflect the rise of a popular culture unwilling to relate to the abstractions of classicism, and they continue to thrive in the Hollywood mythology of the action superhero. At their most typical, the operas of Wagner can be interpreted as a music theater of wishful thinking in which formal demonstrations of group cooperation and leadership associated with classical symphony and the concerto are fictionalized into epic dramas of national unity out of an imaginary preclassical past.

The hero of romantic opera is often a paradoxical figure of historical cliché whose great deeds and choices are predestined rather than expressions of free will. The abiding problem with sanctifying past dramatic actions that appear heroic at the time is that they may also be accused of contributing to the crises in which contemporary society finds itself. If heroic figures from the past are called upon to rescue society in the present, they are likely to be the same heroic figures whose great deeds contributed to the problem in the first place, so what is really called for is a vaccine against heroism, or a heroism diluted out of existence, as in homeopathy.

For whatever reason, a generation or so after Wagner, the romantic image of the mythic hero had become tainted to a point where an increasingly world-weary public could interpret the irritating noise and futile gestures of Rimsky-Korsakov's bumblebee as a caricature image of a Wagnerian hero cut down to the size of a trapped insect, his heroic mission to save the world reduced to a furious buzzing in a vain effort to save himself.

Heroism in its several guises, and the fate of the heroic impulse itself as a source of artistic or moral inspiration, is a recurrent dramatic and musical theme of Wagner's younger compatriot Richard Strauss, an orchestrator of great virtuosity many of whose hero figures are recognizably flawed: Macbeth, Don Juan, the composer himself in the tone poem *Ein Heldenleben* (A hero's life), and extending to the female of the species in musical portraits of Elektra and Salome. In "Coriolan" Beethoven offers a realistic and also sympathetic portrayal of the hero as a singleminded but socially inhibited visionary. In his own time the German Strauss (unrelated to the Viennese dynasty of waltz composers) lived to regret the disastrous social consequences of heroic nationalism run rampant, though his own choices of model heroes are tinged with irony.

A lingering distaste for the supremacist philosophy of Friedrich Nietzsche's *Also sprach Zarathustra* cannot detract, however, from the brilliance of the music's opening gesture, adopted as the title music to the movie *2001: A Space Odyssey*, Stanley Kubrick's cinematic testament to evolutionary hubris. In the movie the music accompanies a vision of the sun rising—which is also Nietzsche's—an effect exactly reproduced in acoustic terms by a music that opens with a rumbling C at the lower threshold of hearing, followed by trumpets in a stepwise movement leading upwards, and then the whole orchestra bursting into sound.

The visual analogy is exact because the lowest sounds, while very powerful, are so large in wavelength, around 12 meters from crest to crest, that human hearing cannot precisely locate the source. A listener is aware of a vague presence, and that is all. The entrance of the trumpets at middle C rising to upper harmonics G and C, introduces wavelengths of approximately 120 cm, 90 cm, and 60 cm respectively: these lesser measures are scaled to human hearing and interact with irregularities in the room structure to make the interior structure clearly audible and create a sense of volume and direction. When the doors swing open, as it were, to let in the orchestral light, the full breadth and range of human hearing is activated, up to the highest audible resonances of brass harmonics, violin partials, cymbals, and triangle. So the listener is led through a transition from a sense of all-encompassing gloom and obscurity to awareness of a pinpoint of sound in the exact middle of the pitch range; this point location moves upward in pitch and implicitly in space, and then all is dazzlingly revealed in a simultaneous lateral and vertical expansion, a virtual "big bang" in musical and acoustical terms.

A similar gesture can be heard in the opening measures of Brahms's Symphony No. 1, another imposing work, also in the optimistic key of C major. Both introductions demonstrate the strengths and also the weaknesses of the grand opening gesture: a powerful and memorable impact, but fatally self-extinguishing: everything thereafter can only be an anticlimax.

91
. . . and anti-hero

Richard Strauss, *Till Eulenspiegels lustige Streiche* (Till Eulenspiegel's merry pranks) Op. 28. 16:26 minutes. Slovak Philharmonic Orchestra, Zdenek Kosler. Naxos 8.550250 (track 3).

Strauss's sublime evocation of the vastness of space is at an opposite extreme from Rimsky-Korsakov's miniaturized, wayward, and slightly comical bumblebee in flight, but Strauss also has sympathy for the anarchic anti-hero of folklore, now entrenched in popular culture in the cartoon figures of Bugs Bunny and Daffy Duck. The introduction to *Till Eulenspiegel* is mock-heroic in style, rises to a climax that is the imaginary hero's entrance cue; he fails to show, so the music repeats a second, then a third time, at which point a cheeky clarinet figure makes an appearance. (You can almost hear him say "What's up, doc?") Till Eulenspiegel is a confidence artist, a delinquent and amoral version of Berlioz's doomed lover of the *Symphonie fantastique*, and he comes to no good, but he enjoys life while it lasts, which is welcome relief from the moral agonizing of most regular opera.

92
Belly dance

Söyleyin yildizlar sevgilim nerde (Desert night dance). Turkish belly dance. 3:36 minutes. Ensemble Hüseyin Türkmenlar. From *Best of Bellydance*. ARC Music EUCD 1358 (track 10).

Belly dance is "a woman singing, not with her voice, but with her body." The listener has to imagine the dance as a dialogue with the different solo instruments: in this example a kind of oboe, a violin, and a dulcimer (a table harp played with lightweight sticks). Hand drums provide rhythm, and a group of unison violins, the chorus line.

Sometimes a simple dance is more profound in implication than the grandest of grand opera. The Salome of Strauss's opera danced for King Herod to such effect that he promised her whatever she wished. She asked for the head of John the Baptist, and Herod with some reluctance gave in. The traditional femme fatale image of the middle-eastern seductress is part of the apparatus of ancient and exotic myth appropriated by western artists to provide an antithetical figure to the hero of romantic fiction. The conventional operatic image of the female nemesis (Delilah, Salome, Elektra, Lulu) using her sexuality to undermine the powers of the masculine hero is a simplistic fiction that says more perhaps about attitudes towards women among middle-class western male society than about attitudes in traditional nonwestern cultures. (Richard Strauss himself insisted that Salome's dance be performed in a chaste and nonsalacious manner: a request usually overruled in actual performance.)

The idea that belly dance is little more than sexual in interest is beginning to disappear as the art becomes more widely practiced in the west. Audiences are beginning to realise that the dance has always stood for a more sophisticated understanding of the male–female relationship as a meeting of two realities: the macrocosm or outgoing world of the male explorer, and the microcosm or inwardly oriented world of the nurturing female. (The same association of outward and inward realities is encountered in Monteverdi's instrumentation in the Magnificat, where matching cornetts (also male) to the right are voices in dialogue with an exterior world, in symmetry with violins to the left (also female) representing voices of the inner world of the emotions.)

That belly dance exists in male-dominated societies is, after all, a testament to male attraction toward women. The dance itself creates a situation where by consent and in fact the female is in full control; furthermore, the accompanying music has as much to do with the enthusiastic responses of the male spectators as with dictating the movements of the female dancer.

The female belly is the cradle of new life, and a belly dance is a form of display to honor the female of the species as the bringer of life. The subtext of this dance is not at all salacious, but a message of mental and physical health and muscular control as desirable attributes in the ideal woman. You have to be fit. The dancer conveys her message without words. Her message is in the skill with which she attracts and holds the attention of her male audience. The accompanying music expresses pace, a measure of gestural control, along with hypnotic excitement, representing the audience's adrenaline rush. From time to time a violin breaks out in a wild improvisation that seems to join in the dance.

93
Panic

Arnold Schoenberg, I. "Vorgefühle" (Premonitions), 2:04 minutes; IV. "Peripetie" (Crisis), 2:09 minutes. In *Five Pieces for Orchestra*, Op. 16. London Symphony Orchestra, Robert Craft. Koch 3-7263-2H1 (tracks 1, 4).

It is one of those ironies of life that classical music fans who say they hate modern music, along with young people who would never dream of attending a symphony orchestra concert, both go happily to the movies and listen to, and *enjoy*, and *understand*, exactly the same kind of dissonant music as long as there is visual action to go with it. Schoenberg's *Five Orchestral Pieces* (which include the "Summer Morning by a Lake" previously noted) were composed in 1909, in the silent movie era. Their titles indicate, if it were not already obvious, that these two pieces are studies in extreme emotion. You could not dance to them, you would not sing to them, but you would certainly react. To find ways of isolating and expressing emotional states without recourse either to words (opera), familiar images (painting, sculpture), or actions (dance) was the challenging objective of many young artists. Schoenberg himself was associated with the "Blue Rider" art movement in Vienna, and sympathetic to the expressionist and abstract tendencies of Edvard Munch and Wassily Kandinsky.

It was the new world of the silent movie, however, that offered a platform for musical expressionism. As drama, it dealt with human lives in extreme situations; in the absence of speech, the drama had to be conveyed in movement, gesture, and facial expression. The silent movie introduced a more intensely focused dramatic experience, along with a return to an older formalism of stereotyped gesture, against the Wagnerian trend of realistic opera. There are no long speeches in a silent movie: like the music of Webern, meaning has to be conveyed in a look, or a sigh. In turn that demand introduces a new concentration of timescale into the narrative, since the visual sense is very quick. These contextual issues of brevity, intensity, and immediacy, are distinctive features of Schoenberg's *Five Pieces*, and evidence of the composer's remarkable intuition of where the new expressionism was heading.

It is strange but true that both silent movie, which is vision without speech, and radio drama, which is speech without vision, provided the same incentive to create music of an expressionist kind to represent inner thoughts and extreme states. In both the movies and radio drama background music is internalized, not intended to be listened to with the same attention as a concert performance, which is "out there," but all the same capable of acting directly on the listener's subconscious. Recognizable figures and images distract the attention of the observer, so abstraction in art, and atonality (absence of harmony) in music are *actual requirements* if this music is not to be consciously noticed.

Though his own music never became widely popular, Schoenberg's expressionism from the silent movie era has left an indelible mark on composers of Hollywood epics celebrating fear, panic, horror, and other emotional extremes.

94
Sound effects

Erik Satie, "Petite fille Américaine" (American girl). 3:42 minutes. From *Parade: Ballet Réaliste.* Early 20th century. Orchestre Symphonique et Lyrique de Nancy, Jérôme Kaltenbach. Naxos 8.554279 (track 2).

Carl Stalling, "Feed the Kitty." 1:30 minutes. Music for the Warner Bros. animated movie (1952). Session orchestra, Milt Franklyn. In *The Carl Stalling Project: Music from Warner Bros. Cartoons 1936–1958.* Warner Bros. 9 26027-2 (track 13).

Silent movies and radio changed classical music in other ways. *Parade*, subtitled "realist ballet," was devised by a young Jean Cocteau to entertain Paris during the 1914–1918 war. Cocteau took inspiration from the loose structure, flat presentation, and sudden jump cuts of the movies to create a work of live theater having the earnest humorlessness and improvisatory feel of a newsreel about life in New York, at the time regarded in battle-scarred Europe as a haven of prosperity and progress. Picasso designed the sets and costumes, which included characters dressed as skyscrapers. Satie's music is only a step removed from the improvised accompaniments of movie houses of the period. Like his friend Debussy, Satie was an avid moviegoer, fascinated by the fragmentary music improvised by ad hoc groups of musicians to follow the visual action of silent movies, a music sounding like the aural equivalent of cubist painting. Performed by trios or quartets seated in front of the screen, the seemingly random montages of familiar tunes were punctuated by sound effects such as doorbells, car horns, or firearms. Instant psychological realism was the key. As long as the music matched the actions and emotions onscreen, it did not matter how crudely it was put together. In 1952 veteran composer Carl Stalling created an affectionate parody of an improvised silent movie score for the cartoon "Feed the Kitty," based on the melodic clichés of classic music hall.

Satie's score for *Parade*, like Cocteau's script, has a fey charm; the Europeans did not quite know what to make of the movie medium at this stage, but were fascinated by its energetic, blank, matter-of-fact depiction of the perfectly ordinary. An avowed antiromantic, Satie celebrates the antiheroic qualities of the modern newsreel with music of a deliberate nonchalance, into which he introduces at appropriate moments the rapidly clicking texture of an office typewriter and bell, a starting pistol, and a ship's horn. All for fun, but from then onward sound effects gained the right to be considered as material for music.

95
Enchantment

Alban Berg, 1. "Seele, wie bist du schöner" (Soul, how more beautiful you are). 2.53 minutes. From *Five Orchestral Songs*, Op. 4, to texts by Peter Altenberg. Early 20th century. Vlatka Orsanic, Südwestfunk Symphony Orchestra, Michael Gielen. Arte Nova 74321 27768 2 (track 10).

Self-annihilation is the ultimate romantic fantasy. Wagner called it *Liebestod*, "death in love"; for Wagner as for Hildegard before him it signified a momentary state of supreme happiness associated with a life of ultimate sacrifice or religious devotion—a state more often associated today with experiences of sexual climax, fast cars, intoxication, and any number of dangerous games that risk life and limb for the sake of an adrenaline rush.

To experience bliss can take a lifetime or happen in an instant. To *express* bliss in music, poetry, or art is a more complicated affair requiring exceptional powers of self-analysis together with the technical skills to translate extreme perceptions into artistic processes that can be freely shared. The arts of the late nineteenth and early twentieth centuries provide an extensive database of individual dream images and private fantasies that defy conventional reason: images from the impressionists, expressionists, vorticists, dadaists, futurists, suprematists, abstractionists, and surrealists, through to the post-1945 nuclear bomb generation of Jack Kerouac, Jackson Pollock, and John Cage. To go beyond the limits of the possible is a natural human impulse, even though it may end in self-destruction. To convey a sense of exceeding the bounds of reality is a function of art. Records and documents relaying messages from the limits of experience, or the subconscious, could even be said to fulfill a religious role of helping society as a whole to come to terms with the supernatural and the irrational in human history.

Painting and sculpture are permanent representations of the real and the sublime. Poetry, drama, and music however, unfold in time, so are more than just images of the ultimate experience, being also descriptions of the process by which the desired state is attained—as we know from the movies where the director decides when and how much the viewer is entitled to see and know.

In the slow movement of Mozart's Piano Concerto No. 23 in A, the moment of epiphany comes with the entrance of the orchestra; in Strauss's depiction of sunrise the moment of climax is the same, the entrance of the full orchestra, though in making the comparison the latter appears rather vulgar and grandiose. Both Wagner and Mahler dreamed of an ecstasy prolonged indefinitely in an endless melody, an experience encapsulated in the yearning Adagietto of Mahler's Symphony No. 5. The generation of Schoenberg, Berg, and Webern opted for brevity, influenced among others by the instantaneous images of contemporary photography, the transience of cylinder recording, and the enigmatic concentration of Japanese haiku. Berg's *Five Orchestral Songs* are as ephemeral as Webern, but composed for large orchestral forces and exotic intrumental effects, suggesting the dazzling visual effects of the art of Gustav Klimt.

In music, brevity is a specific against memory, and thus against expectation. Here, by the time the audience has realised what is going on the experience has vanished. At the time of composing these songs Berg was in his late twenties. He had just married. In this brief sigh he captures a glimpse of paradise.

96
Progress

Maurice Ravel, *Bolero*. 20th century. 16:29 minutes. London Philharmonic Orchestra, Enrique Batiz. Concerto Digital Classics XQ 0010 (track 15).

At the opposite extreme from the sudden moment of epiphany is a sense of utter helplessness in the face of inevitable doom. This celebrated composition by Ravel has been described as the longest upbeat in history and ranks with Perotin's "Viderunt omnes" as a study in musical gigantism. Whether Ravel was overcome by a premonition, or whether, as the story goes, he was merely exacting revenge on an orchestra that did not take his music seriously, we do not know. That he regarded *Bolero* as an exercise in "antimusic" and its huge popular success as an unfathomable irony, is certainly true. The music builds from a distant, seemingly languid flute melody, almost a middle-eastern version of the flute theme of Debussy's *L'Après-midi d'un faune*, that in the course of some twenty repetitions is gradually revealed as a vision of an approaching army heading inexorably toward the listener. The music has the same relentless momentum as "Mars," hymn to the god of war in Gustav Holst's orchestral suite *The Planets*. (Interestingly for music so evocative of an army on the advance, *Bolero* is based on a dance in three-time, while the Holst movement marches ahead to an unequal rhythm of five beats to the measure.)

Performing a single movement more than a quarter hour in length, without breaks or variation in tempo, and building continuously in density and amplitude to a shattering climax, is a tough call for any orchestra on the concert platform, and even more problematic in a recording studio (not an issue in 1928 when this work was composed). Such a music is virtually impossible to stop and retake in the event of a mistake, since the music before and after any edit point has to be matched perfectly in tempo, amplitude—and also tuning, because the pitch of instruments can wander with room temperature over the course of a session. That it is easy to follow as well as a technical challenge is perhaps why *Bolero* is feared and admired by players and audiences alike. As well as challenging the conductor to maintain strict continuity of overall dynamics and timing, individual parts demand exceptional breath control and phrasing of the melody from a succession of solo players, as well as absolute accuracy and evenness of tone in the rigid accompanying staccato rhythm, a discreet parody perhaps of the *dit-dit-dit-dah* motif of Beethoven's Fifth Symphony, and an experience of purgatory for all orchestral musicians, including the side drum.

Dynamics is another ambiguous term from the musical lexicon. A listener's perception of increasing loudness, as in the case of an approaching sound, depends on three factors: total frequency range, timbre, and amplitude. Sounds at a distance lack bass and extreme high frequencies, so to convey an approach involves gradually extending the frequency range, introducing more bass for increased presence, and more high frequency information for greater definition. Amplitude has to do with the energy of the total sound, and is determined by the physical effort put into playing, and to a certain extent by the number of players involved. In itself amplitude does not equate to loudness, however, because a perception of loudness is frequency-dependent: the energy has to be concentrated in the upper midrange where human hearing is most acute. Instruments of richer timbre such as the trumpet, violin, and oboe, whose energy is more widely distributed throughout this optimum range, for this reason sound more penetrating in tone, and thus appear louder, than timbres such as the flute and clarinet, whose energy tends to be focused on fewer partials.

Needless to say, *Bolero* is also a fascinating listener's introduction and guide to the instruments of the orchestra. The sequence of lead instruments, which includes one or two rarities, accumulates roughly as follows:

1. Flute, side drum, pizzicato (plucked) cellos;
2. B flat clarinet, harp;
3. Bassoon;
4. E flat soprano clarinet;
5. English horn (cor anglais);
6. Flute and muted trumpet;
7. Tenor saxophone;
8. Soprano saxophone;
9. Oboe d'amore and piccolo;
10. Oboes in harmony;
11. Alto trombone;

12. Flutes, oboes, bassoon;
13. Unison violins and piccolo, flute;
14. High strings in harmony, woodwinds, timpani;
15. Violins and violas in octaves;
16. Harmonized strings and woodwinds;
17. The same, with added muted trumpets;
18. Added winds, horns, trombone;
19. A change of key, added trumpets (unmuted);
20. Added bass drum and tam-tam.

Remarkably, the entrance of the strings, normally the body of a symphony orchestra, is delayed until nearly the halfway point in the piece. Up to that time Ravel has engineered a virtual crescendo by a careful choice and blending of instrumental timbres; only after the entrance of the violins do instrument doublings, harmonies, and dynamic levels in general (soft, medium, loud, very loud) begin to play a greater role. Like a mouse hypnotized by a rattlesnake, the audience is held in suspense wondering when the end will come, and how the music could possibly get any louder. In addition to doubling parts at the unison, Ravel also superimposes instruments to give the effect of new sonorities, for example the combination of oboe d'amore and piccolo, sounding like a wheezy pipe organ. It is only in the very last moments that trumpets, trombones, and horns jointly appear at full blast, before the orchestral caravan grinds to a juddering halt.

97
Abstract speech

Gertrude Stein reading "If I Told Him: A Completed Portrait of Picasso." 3:34 minutes. 20th century. In *The Caedmon Poetry Collection: A Century of Poets Reading Their Work.* Caedmon CD 2895(3) (cd 2, track 12).

Just as a person signing a document is making a personal mark and is less concerned with the formation of individual letters, and just as in the same way Japanese calligraphy is an art of signing that goes beyond the word or text to draw attention to the emotion associated with the gesture of letter-forming, so too poets are interested in the sounds and shapes of spoken language as much as the literal meanings that attach to them. An attention to the music of speech is as old as poetry and continues to play an important subliminal role in the modern art of product branding and advertising. Dowland's verses for his song *Dear, if you change* deliver a message of faith as words on paper, but that message is overlaid by a music of vocal sounds that have their own resonance and appeal for a listening audience:

> *Dear, if you change   I' le never chuse again;*
> *Sweet, if you shrink   I' le never think of love. . .*

Public interest in the sounds and textures of poetic speech was rekindled in the nineteenth century through a combination of factors, including the revival of oral traditions and verse forms, the invention of the first voice recorder, the phonautograph, by the Belgian Léon Scott in 1852, the rise in popularity of letter codes and word games, and not least by the symbolist poets, who sought inspiration in dreams and incantations, and found occult meanings in word association.

A number of English writers, Lewis Carroll and Edward Lear among them, made fun of the new fashion for wordplay in nonsense verse: Carroll in parodies of Coleridge and Wordsworth, Lear in limericks of inventive silliness. At the same time, poets such as Algernon Charles Swinburne and Gerard Manley Hopkins—the former an avowed decadent, the latter a religious ecstatic—embraced a new aesthetic of musical speech in sound-images of visionary presence and conviction, but hovering tantalisingly at the edge of reason. It was out of this climate of textual analysis and experiment that the American poet Gertrude Stein emerged. After studying biology and the history of poetic diction at Harvard, she settled in Paris in the early twentieth century and became patron and mentor of an important group of young artists including Picasso and Braque. As a poet and writer Stein took a particular interest in the way movie photography broke down organic movement into a succession of momentary states, a process she believed to replicate the stream of consciousness in human beings. Her verse and prose writing, which even today is still not widely appreciated, resembles the flickering continuity of film, a continuous succession or superimposition of verbal afterimages repeatedly modified in the manner of cubism and futurism in painting.

Today, a listener is struck by the similarity of Stein's musical speech, its insistent rhythms and jazz-like refrains and repetitions, to contemporary rap or hip-hop, an art form supposed to have emerged spontaneously from the urban street culture of the nineties. Stein strongly objected to her writings being described as repetitious, insisting they were images of organic growth and change, as much for her processes of thought as for the images contained in successive frames of a movie. That perception of altered consciousness arising from repetitive utterance connects her art in turn with mantric traditions of prayer, and also with the minimalist school of American music, for whom the model is the tape loop, and hip-hop, which is speech music based on the sample.

98
Ultimate peace
Giacinto Scelsi, I. from *Konx–Om–Pax* (Peace) for orchestra. 7:26 minutes. Mid-20th century. Orchestre de la Radio-télévision de Cracovie, Jürg Wyttenbach. Accord 200402 (track 9).

Scelsi's title, the word "peace" in Greek, Sanskrit, and Latin, alludes to the inscription over the portal through which the initiate passes to enter the mystic fellowship of occult magicians. This eerily contemplative music has been described as an image of watching the sun rise: "something very powerful, slowly and patiently approaching." The synaesthesia is strange and effective: a listener visualizes a matt shape seemingly shining by reflected light of increasing brilliance, and also the afterimages that remain on the retina after one has looked at something dazzling. Scelsi's layered orchestration creates an enveloping ambience that draws the listener in and builds a sense of anticipation. Using a technique more usually adopted by movie composers to suggest mystery or suspense, the composer deliberately creates a foggy and shadowy imagery where the listener has to work to discern shapes and movements. Long sustained trombone and horn sounds resemble foghorns or the blare of distant passing freight trains. Once again a symphony orchestra is employed as a source of colored noise, to fill the acoustic space and create a narcotic experience for the audience. Though described as an amateur composer, Scelsi shows a remarkable sensitivity for fringe effects, for example high partial tones that at one point seem to be rotating over the heads of the audience. To some the music may resemble a mysterious hologram, changing perspective as the viewer passes by; others may detect signs of life in the subtle changes of instrumental balance. And while it may seem a little odd to mention Beethoven in such a context, Scelsi's musical vision evokes much the same early romantic perception of an intimidating superior presence indifferent to the affairs of mere mortals. Compared to the sunrise of Strauss's *Also sprach Zarathustra*, or Ligeti's *Atmosphères*, which it resembles more closely, this musical presence seems rather more aloof.

"There are three elements: one, a fear that pushes; two, a perverse tranquility; three, a sense of being left completely in the dark."

99
Flashback

Morton Feldman, *Madame Press Died Last Week at 90.* Duration 4:10 minutes. 20th century. Orchestra of St. Luke's, John Adams. Elektra Nonesuch 7559-79249-2 (track 8).

Madame Press was Feldman's piano teacher. He composed the work after she died in 1970, so it is a piece in her memory. Repetition is a feature (count them), but it is not quite the mechanical repetition a listener associates with the minimalism, say, of Philip Glass or Steve Reich: it has more in common with the modulated repetitions of Gertrude Stein, which the poet claimed should be interpreted as an organic growth process. Nevertheless, the layers of meaning Feldman's music reveals have a great deal to do with how a listener interprets repetition and its connotations. This is not at all menacing like Ravel's *Bolero*. Something dramatic happens in the middle: a moment of silence, after which the music resumes with a little more urgency than before. Some listeners are upset at the apparently relentless repetition, and wonder if the music will ever end (even though the work is relatively short). Others discover an interest in the fact that every repetition is a little bit different, and though the differences do not seem to add up, they still seem to carry a message.

"As the music plays on, it seems to be learning itself," said one. Once the listener grasps the point of the repetitions, the meaning of the music becomes crystal clear, even though it may not make the music any more likeable. Part of the message of this piece is that you don't have to like what you hear in order to understand what the composer is saying. Repetition and time, memory, and growth come together in many guises: the cuckoo-clock, the rhythmic clack of the carousel as transparencies of a life are reviewed through a slide projector; the laborious repetitions of the young pianist practicing to master a musical phrase, along with the idea that perfection in life and in music is attained through persistent repetition and attention to detail. These are images of the learning process in real life, but beyond that they also comment on the nature of life and the relationship of the individual to time and eternity. In Feldman's austere, patient, self-effacing ritual it is possible to perceive an idealized simplicity of lifestyle and Puritan work ethic that are distinctively American. The rhythms of work and routine are ways of coping with time, but also of transcending it.

In comparison to the clockwork of Bach's Prelude No. 1 in C major, Feldman's music conveys a greater sense of human involvement and progress, but the progress is not always smooth: unlike Bach's mechanical sequence of arpeggiated chords, it is not possible to guess what the next chord will be. Like Satie's music, there is always a human presence, a certain wit: a hint too of American opposition to the bravura rhetoric of European tradition. As a young man John Cage attended Schoenberg's composition class at UCLA, and was asked if he had learned any of the traditional skills in harmony and counter-point. Cage said no, they did not interest him. In that case, Schoenberg warned, Cage would have to be prepared for a life of banging his head against a brick wall. So be it, said the young American, and an echo of Cage's defiance also emerges in Feldman's tribute to his own teacher, a Russian émigré with connections to Scriabin.

Two-thirds into the piece, a distant bell is heard, like the church bell in Charles Ives's "Washington's Birthday."("The bell is recess," said one.) For a brief moment the repetitions lapse into silence, and the music seems to drift. Then it resumes, with a trumpet taking the place of the earlier flute. It is a moment of reflection, as if her life has come to an end, the music resuming showing that her knowledge has been passed on to another generation. But in a strange twist, the pause at the sixty-first repetition turns out to be a premonition of the composer's

own death in 1987, at the age of 61, at the time of composition a full
seventeen years in the future.

100
Kaleidoscope

Igor Stravinsky, IV. Interlude and V. movement from *Movements for Piano and
Orchestra*. 2:22 minutes. Mid-20th century. Christopher Oldfather, The Philharmonia,
Robert Craft. MusicMasters 01612-67195-2 (track 13).

Igor Stravinsky, "Tableau II: Petrushka's Room." 4:03 minutes. Early 20th century. From
Petrushka. Columbia Symphony Orchestra, Igor Stravinsky. CBS MK 42433 (track 5).

Carl Stalling, music for the 1956 Road Runner cartoon *There They Go Go Go*. 5:27
minutes. Mid-20th century. Studio orchestra, Milt Franklyn. In *The Carl Stalling Project*,
Warner Bros. 9 26027-2, (track 6).

Composed at the age of 77, for sheer high spirits the finale of Stravinsky's piano concerto *Movements* is hard to beat. After moving to Los
Angeles, the composer made the difficult and life-changing transition
from neoclassicism to an idiom joining the spare molecular aesthetic of
Webern—a music of positive and negative charges in which instruments attract and repel like atomic particles—with the manic exuber-
ance of animated movie. The admiration was mutual. During the thir-
ties, Stravinsky's gestural piano music for the 1911 ballet *Petrushka*
became model and template for composers of music for Terrytoons and
Merrie Melodies cartoons, the wonderfully expressive Tableau II (incorporating the mother of all cat and mouse chases) perfectly adapted
to the faster-than-life action and sudden stops and starts of the world of
cartoon animation. Carl Stalling, a master of the genre, pays tribute to
Petrushka in a frantic and brilliantly crafted score to the 1956 Road
Runner animation *There They Go Go Go*.

As its title suggests, *Movements* is a study in the movement of a
musical line from instrument to instrument, with the piano acting as
agent provocateur and coordinator, much in the manner of the keyboard conductor of a baroque concerto grosso. There are echoes too of
the witty theatricality of Rossini's overture to *La Cenerentola*; indeed,
one can also pick out the same delight in a geometry of wide intervals,
and the deliberate offset of neutral piano tone against a rich range of
orchestral textures and colors, that can be heard in the slow movement

of Mozart's Concerto No. 23. Although in a technical sense there is very little density of information in Stravinsky's serial music, in practice there is such an abundance of musical fiber to be digested, so many symmetries and refractions of themes, rhythms, and timbres to be considered, that like a modern Brandenburg concerto *Movements* is still very difficult to assimilate, though wonderfully exciting just to listen to.

With this music we reach an altogether higher level of information management. In the past music has been designed to lead the listener through a memorization process, hence the dance forms, the repetitions, and the often leisurely pace of change. With few exceptions, from Perotin and Hildegard to Debussy and Schoenberg, western music has tended to unfold in "real time" at the speed of the listener. With the arrival of sound recording, however, "real time" is no longer necessarily commensurate with performance time. Being able to listen to a recording over and over again changes the experience (of the meaning of the music) from an ideal concert performance, to a data assimilation process that can only be resolved in the timeless world of the mind. It is music for the computer age of instant information, and also of total recall.

101
Artificial intelligence

Pierre Boulez, *Répons* for 6 keyboardists, orchestra, and computer generated sounds: Introduction and Section 1, 9:24 minutes; Coda, 4:34 minutes. Late 20th century. Ensemble InterContemporain, Pierre Boulez. DG 289 457 605-2 (tracks 1, 2; 10).

Plus ça change. . . . (The more it changes, the more it stays the same.) At the dawn of history human beings took refuge in caves and rocky enclosures. For people living in caves as much as for birds living in the forest canopy, security and protection are associated with reverberant spaces that reflect sound, aid vocal communication, and disclose the presence and location of any source of potential harm. Every living creature that occupies space has a natural interest in defending it from outside interference. A shelter protecting against intruders and from wind and rain is naturally desirable, and a reverberant enclosure can be monitored by hearing as well as by sight.

Since reverberation is a mystery and its effects benign, those who benefit from its protection are inclined to treat it with respect as a hidden but benevolent presence to be negotiated with through a dialogue of stylized vocal and musical utterance that, for the greater human tribe as for songbirds, barking dogs, and small children, combines a declaration of individual existence *and the right to be heard* with a petition that the individual existence may be acknowledged as worthy of continued protection. Cave dwellers of prehistory discovered the more reverberant locations within their dwelling space and honored them as sacred places, decorating their walls with images of the animal spirits against which they sought protection. The same propitiatory message underlies the chanting of the Tuva herdsman across the river to the cliff face beyond. The human occupier of the space emits a vocal signal to match the acoustic of the natural environment in order to provoke a response confirming the presence of a benevolent spirit.

A cathedral or temple enclosure is constructed in the joint image of cave and forest, and the musical rituals that take place within such environments have much the same underlying purpose. It is a remarkable tribute to the persistence of human behavior that in a world outwardly far removed from the stone age, music is still respected as a medium by which humanity establishes contact with the divine. Even more surprising, the same ritual forms continue to be employed. During the 1970s Boulez masterminded the establishment in Paris of IRCAM, a center for acoustical and musical research, its centerpiece one of the most powerful digital computer systems designed specifically for musical applications, among them a synthesis program with the interesting name "Chant" with which the sound of a singing voice can be transformed into the sound of a bell, and vice versa.

Boulez has led the way in composing a number of major works involving dialogue interactions of solo players and the 4C computer. In effect, they are rituals in which a solo instrument sends out a signal that is captured by the computer, transformed, and returned through loudspeakers. The difference lies in the transformation process, which unlike the reverberation of a cave or cathedral acoustic, involves an artificial intelligence modifying the harmonic content of the original voice or timbre, and returning it in new note formations. To a casual listener it seems as though the gods are not only responding, but are actually talking back.

The title *Répons* (responses) is also a term in traditional church music, alluding to the dialogue forms of Catholic ritual and exchanges between the voice leader and the choir or congregation in response. This new work attaches to a distinctively French scholarly tradition, of Pierre Janequin, medieval composer of birdsong, and Perotin of the cathedral of Nôtre Dame, whose "Viderunt omnes" combines religious piety and scientific interest in the inner resonances of the human voice. Boulez himself is a former pupil of Olivier Messiaen, another Paris-based composer and mystic in the French pastoral tradition whose music for organ reinvents the instrument as a modern tone synthesizer and in doing so makes the powerful argument that tone synthesis is what the instrument was really designed to do in the first place.

For all its technical complexity the underlying message of *Répons* is relatively easy to grasp. There are three elements in this modern ritual, laid out in concentric circles resembling a painted target by Jasper Johns, or perhaps to suggest the ripple effect of sound travelling from a center to an outer periphery. In the center, the orchestra, representing a turbulent source of energy; around it, in a ring, the audience as a congregation, literally "facing the music" but also containing it. Behind the audience, positioned at equidistant points on the periphery, six solo keyboardists: two pianos, harp, vibraphone, xylophone (also glockenspiel), and cymbalom (a form of dulcimer, an instrument of Turkish belly dance). These soloists are the mediators whose musical signals are intercepted by the computer in real time and returned as the "responses" of the title. It is interesting to note that the superior status of the solo instruments in this musical ritual appears to consist in their being keyboards. Apollo and his violin are forced once again to yield to the panpipes of Marsyas. On the surface, the digital keyboard represents a higher, more objective state of musical knowledge than the subjectively emotional and unstable violin. In practical terms, however, keyboard instruments are more suitable candidates for computer recognition, since they are preprogrammed to a limited scale of pitches, have a separate mechanism for every pitch, and offer consistent onset and dynamic characteristics. (The reality, then, is that keyboards are chosen not because they are morally superior, but because they are totally predictable.) Their tone qualities deliver the same virtues we respect in an expressionless performance of Bach's Prelude in C major.

In the Introduction of *Répons*, the orchestra evokes the congestion and turbulence of contemporary life. It is exciting, stressful music, and the stress is accentuated by the instruments being crowded in a circle in the middle of the auditorium, an image of a world of too many people. The music pushes outward, rising to an initial climax at which the first set of responses suddenly appear, from speakers located behind the heads of the audience. It is a magic moment. There is a cool intellectualism in the clipped speech of the six soloists, and a touch of science fiction in the magnified brushed-metal chimes of computer-generated melodic figures that seem to wriggle and cavort like microorganisms in a drop of pond water.

Ideally, a system that allows performers to interact in real time with a computer, should also allow for an ongoing dialogue in which the keyboards respond to what the computer has to say. But that does not happen in church, so we should not be surprised if the conversation in this case is also a little one-sided. At the end of *Répons*, however, is a coda that seems to take on a life of its own. The orchestra falls silent, leaving only the keyboardists in telecommunication with the unseen intelligence, like a small roomful of telephone helpline operators dealing with emergency calls in the dead of night. Finally even they fall silent, leaving the computer alone with its thoughts.

Discussion topics

1. Explain the following: "The voice is made of soft stuff, instruments are made of hard stuff."

2. Discuss the following statement: "Religious singing builds on an agreement that the text is all-important, not the messengers of that text. Secular music is no longer using singing as a means of getting an identical message across; rather, it explores ways of changing the delivery of the message, or even the message itself.

3. How does reverberation in a cathedral environment influence the manner and style of singing and playing?

4. Ornithologists observe that birds living in the forest sing more tunefully,

and birds in the open plains sing with more attention to rhythm. Explain why this is also true of music in the human community.

5. Modern music notation and punctuation marks are related. How is this?

6. When two or more voices are singing exactly the same melody, what does it signify?

7. What freedoms of expression are available to the solo musician, and why are they highly regarded?

8. "Noise is something we cannot help: it is the price we pay for the gift of hearing. Music is a blessing that comes with that gift. Silence is something we crave when this gift overwhelms us." If noise is a curse, and silence is a blessing, where does music fit in?

9. How does plainchant or unison ritual music express the idea of unity?

10. Why is the inside of a cathedral bigger than the outside, and what effect does that have on the music performed there?

11. What interest is there to music without expression, like the Bach Prelude No. 1 in C major, or the *Gymnopédie I* by Erik Satie?

12. What are the design advantages of a keyboard operated instrument, and are they in the best interests of art or science?

13. Describe the leadership roles of the concertmaster (lead violin) and conductor (keyboard) of a baroque orchestra of Bach or Corelli.

14. In what two ways does Monteverdi express the idea of the spirit being lifted from a depression in the "Et Misericordia" of the Magnificat (from the *Vespers* of 1610).

15. What change in the performance environment enabled instrumental music to become faster-moving and more complex?

16. What is chamber music, and what are its intimate qualities?

17. In a song for voice and guitar, what are the complementary roles of each?

18. Notation enables complex music to be exactly specified, but only as exactly as the system of notation allows. What are the limitations of notated music compared to the music of oral traditions?

19. If an orchestra is regarded as a team, what core message does its music send to the wider community?

20. What contribution does standard notation make to the functioning of a symphony orchestra as a team?

21. What are the team implications that distinguish music for a choir (i.e., a group of the same family of instruments) from music for a broken consort (a group in which the instruments are unrelated)?

22. How did orchestral music in the late eighteenth century express the "storm and stress" undercurrents of imminent social revolution?

23. Compare the image of the solo artist as entertainer in Boccherini's cello

concerto, with the image of the artist as prima donna in Schumann's cello concerto. What does this tell you of the changing criteria of leadership from the eighteenth to the nineteenth century?

24. The artist Wassily Kandinsky observed that painting is superior to music, in that music requires time to communicate its message, whereas the message of a painting is instantaneous. Is that right? And is there an advantage to music *controlling* the unfolding of a message, whereas the interpretation of a painting is left to the spectator?

25. A composer and computer scientist, Lejaren A. Hiller, remarked "music is a compromise between chaos and order." How is this statement exemplified in the *Music for the Royal Fireworks* by Handel? What does such a definition signify in a context of programming a computer to compose a melody?

26. "Movement in weightlessness reminds us of how clumsy and ungraceful human beings are." In the movie *2001: A Space Odyssey* director Stanley Kubrick chose to accompany images of spacecraft maneuvering in space with the Viennese *Beautiful Blue Danube* waltz by Johann Strauss II. In what ways is his choice appropriate?

27. Discuss the remark "In real life, music is the foreground and incidental noise the background. In the movies, incidental noises are the foreground and music is the background."

28. Does music tell the truth?

29. Consider the observations "Music is a language without words. It is what is left when words are removed," and, "Music helps you to stay sane. Staying sane is not meaningless."

30. Picasso (in *The Blue Guitar*) and Ben Shahn (in *The Blind Accordian Player*) portray street musicians who are blind. Are there reasons other than sentimentality for associating music in a painting with an image of blindness?

INTRODUCING
BOOK SIX

The big adventure is discovering music for yourself. There is a world of classical and traditional music waiting out there. Not a cult, not a religion, not a form of mass indoctrination to which you are being asked to subscribe: just an alternative way of listening. Compared to only a generation ago, traditional music of all kinds and cultures has never been easier or cheaper to obtain, and is now readily available in reproductions of a quality and transparency previously unobtainable outside a recording studio.

Acoustic music, where all you hear is the person playing and no amplification, is different from an ordinary band concert where voices and instruments have to go through amplifiers in order for the audience to hear anything at all. There is a natural and agreeable balance to the sound of classical music, a quality of dialogue from instrument to instrument, and a sense of balance with the acoustic space, which, if you are lucky, will have been designed with the requirements of acoustic music in mind.

The ultimate experience has to be a live performance. For those who have never been before, attending an orchestra concert can be quite amazing, simply because of the numbers of musicians involved, their discipline, and the special quality of three-dimensional live sound that makes the complexities of classical music instantly understandable and intriguing.

Away from the city and the concert hall, there are still many opportunities to enjoy listening to classical music, or simply to have it in the background. For those on a long car journey, or overnight flight, classical music is an agreeable and completely private option. My art and design students found that listening to classical music, while they worked, sharpened their perceptions and led their art in new directions.

BOOK SIX

Impressions of Beethoven

The impressions of Beethoven recorded here are the spontaneous reflections of mainly young students hearing a short but complete movement of classical music that they had not heard before or previously thought about. They listened to the piece three or four times over a half-hour period and wrote down their impressions, guided by a very few items of basic information. The majority, young artists and designers, were more used to expressing themselves in lines, shapes, or textures, than in words. Some, indeed, were writing disabled to a greater or lesser degree. To many, the world of classical music initially appeared a remote, elitist, and even hostile reminder of social attitudes and pressures that had led them to take up art. These students were not hostile to music, but were more at ease listening to singer-poets of the present day with whose message they identified emotionally. Live music was understood as a form of relaxation from work, and recorded music, which they listened to on headphones from portable players, as a means of screening out the outside world and its distractions in order to focus on the artwork in hand. The short one-term course in music appreciation from which these reports are taken had two aims: first, to equip students with the basic critical skills to listen with confidence to *any* music, and second, to persuade them to study and express their responses to music in simple, clear language.

Listening is about finding words to fit impressions. All of us have impressions. They are not a problem. The real issue of putting impressions into words, for many people, is whether those impressions have any value. Many young artists are faced with a dilemma. On one hand they ask how anyone else can possibly know what another person is thinking, especially in a medium where no words are exchanged. On the other hand, for those who have invested a great deal in the principle of freedom of self-expression, the very idea of forming an opinion on another artist's work may seem to concede that others also have freedom of access to their work, and the right to question their most private thoughts and motives. The awful paradox arises from realizing that their own art also has a public dimension, that the career of an artist depends to a certain degree on self-promotion, and that even the music with which they identify amounts to a very public "private world."

Classical music, in being both familiar and in a sense alien to many listeners, offers situations and images that in one sense are remote from personal experience, and therefore non-threatening. That makes it apt for experiments in criticism. Critical training still requires the observer to draw on a personal vocabulary of experiences, however, so is no less revealing. Classical music is easier to deal with, but in doing so the writer is also entering on a surprising journey of self-discovery that can also be a breakthrough.

> This class taught me a lot about critiquing. Critiquing music is very difficult much like critiquing art is. Critiquing art is just about the hardest thing for me to do and by taking this class I was forced to critique music pieces that I truly did not know much about. All I could do was just listen to my instincts and gather how the particular piece affected my emotions. Through critiquing these pieces I realize that there is not much of a difference between critiquing art work and music pieces. They both consist of talking about pattern, movement, rhythm etc. Now I know that when I am critiquing art all I have to do is listen to my instincts and my emotions.
>
> Before taking this class I had no feelings about classical music. I never had the time to listen to it because it just is not the type of music that I prefer to listen to while doing everyday things. This class forced me to open my eyes and try something new. I was able to listen to these various beautiful pieces and get some feedback on

the artist. It really helped me to relate to what I was listening to and try to figure out why the pieces were done the way they were. Having to listen to the tapes at home was a wonderful idea. I would listen to them as I drew and painted. The music changed my work completely. It showed me a whole new side of my work.

Beethoven (1770–1827): Piano Concerto No. 4, *Andante con moto* is a slow movement in which the *con moto* seems to be ironically intended. It can be read as a dialogue between the piano (representing the individual artist) and the orchestra (representing the mass of society). If you think of it as a dialogue between two individuals you get it wrong. The group does not think or behave like an individual. It behaves like a crowd at a political rally. The group has a sense of unity and a desire for power (i.e., a desire to win and to get things done). It reduces the complexities of the real world to a simple formula or litany, in this case "Unity is strength!" But beyond the rallying cry, the crowd typically has no idea or agreement on how the people's goals are to be achieved.

This is music reflecting the time after the Revolutions of France and elsewhere that deposed the aristocracy and left composers and artists with a sense of responsibility for offering moral leadership to a new middle-class power base. The new democracy is composed not of peasants, but a majority of professional people with skills but only a limited grasp of the finer things of life, which they view with suspicion as élitist extravagance. Beethoven's message in this piece is that leadership, even a leadership of artists, has its uses.

A concerto is about leadership. Leadership is not a property of a group, but of an individual. A good leader has experience, intelligence, planning ability, a strategy, and a certain eloquence and persuasiveness in debate. In the guise of the pianist, Beethoven adopts the mannerist tone of the deposed and despised aristocracy. They are the ruling class he has learned to deal with. The piano is the one, the strings are the many. The language of the piano part (originally improvised) is measured, even flowery. His may be a solitary voice to enter into dialogue with the masses (the orchestra), but he clearly has something to say. He

listens to what they have to say—a sort of brusque, rhythmic refrain in
the spirit of "The people! United! Will never be defeated!"—and responds in phrases that seem each time to draw a moral from the
crowd's inconclusive slogan. Compared to the crowd, representing the
power of numbers, his is a small voice, but it makes up in ability to
lead, to carry a musical line, for what his instrument lacks in fullness
of tone. The piano is the voice of reason.

In this movement the full orchestra is reduced to strings alone, and
they play in unison with a deliberately abrasive tone expressing energy
and a sense of impatience. The uneven rhythm of the strings expresses
repressed energy, like a motor trying to fire, and also frustration at their
inability to formulate a complete statement, having no real idea of how
to decide on, let alone attain, a goal. The crowd is not so much angry
as eager, hot, and excited at the power of numbers. The unity of their
unison refrain signifies "no dissent" and also "collective might."
Beethoven knew and admired the music of Handel, and had studied
with Haydn, whose lifetime overlapped with Handel and J. S. Bach.
The abrasive zigzag of his string writing in this movement may be
taken as a small and perhaps ironic allusion to the short bow movements and dotted rhythms of the aristocratic baroque style of Handel's
music for strings: for example, the Op. 6 No. 5 Concerto Grosso,
betraying a hint of his attitude to the music of an earlier era.

The piano's music is measured in even beats, polished, elegant,
logical, and emphasizing harmony and resolution (chords). On principle, there is no harmony in the orchestra, since harmony implies a
reconciliation of differences. The fact that the orchestra is initially
silent while the piano speaks shows that its attitude is one of respect,
but the orchestra cannot respond to what the piano says, other than
repeat the same refrain over and over in the same irregular rhythm,
showing that the collective mind has no freedom to think or act despite
having power. Nor does it have leadership, since a leader is by definition an individual who stands out in a crowd. So the drama of the
dialogue has to do with the piano winning over the orchestra. Will the
crowd listen to reason? The piano makes several attempts at dialogue
but the orchestra either does not understand or will not listen, and starts
interrupting the piano. The piano changes its approach and appeals to

the emotions of the orchestra by means of an elaborate and passionate cadenza climaxing in a tearful tirade of trills. This expression of un-classical fervor appears to have the desired effect. The orchestra becomes subdued in tone and in the final few measures makes its first tentative steps toward harmony, abandoning its earlier aggressive rhythm in favour of a quietly affirmative chord of E minor, repeated three times, as if saying "Yes. Yes. Yes." The piano, quietly triumphant, celebrates the truce with an overarching phrase that puts it literally "on top."

This was the last concerto in which Beethoven appeared as soloist. He was becoming increasingly deaf. In making a point about leader-ship in post-revolutionary society, he might also have been reflecting on the composer's right to be heard in a society deaf to the values of classical art and music, as well as intimating a personal sense of alien-ation arising from the fact that his own ability to hear himself was also slipping away.

This piece triggered a great variety of responses. Some young listeners imagined the piano to be on trial, pleading for his (or her) life before a court that refused to listen. Some interpreted the piano as a young woman pleading with an abusive father. When an interpretation is colored by personal experience or stereotype situations, it is im-portant for the writer to be able to show that the imaginary scenario is thoroughly consistent with the music, which actually ends, in this case, in a resolution of the opening conflict—or at least, coming to a truce (it is, after all, a low-key ending). A listener jumping to conclusions about the relationship between the piano and strings may be revealing an inner truth, but one that runs the risk of overlooking the composer's intended message. The lesson in such a case is not that an interpre-tation is incorrect, only that it has not been worked through in terms consistent with what the music is saying.

❧

TEST

"The music to be played is the second movement *Andante con moto* of
the Piano Concerto No. 4 by Beethoven. It lasts 4:33 minutes. It will be
played in two versions, one an early string orchestra with solo fortepiano, the other a modern piano and symphony orchestra.
This music is a dramatic dialogue between the string orchestra,
representing society, and the keyboard, representing the artist or composer. What are the personalities of the two sides, and how does the
story develop? What do you think the music says about the relationship
of the artist and society in the time immediately after the French
Revolution?"

ANSWERS

1
Anglo-Egyptian male
A conversation of emotions. The cellos create an initial impression of
strength; the piano answering back with an almost transparent sound
which builds up and takes the spotlight. It also overcomes a barrier and
becomes free, playing quite rapidly, and then falling back to grace. The
music ends quite frankly. The piano did suggest qualities that are feminine, the cello, more deep, like a man. Respect between the two comes
at the close.

2
male
Each party seems to be competing for control. Maybe they don't
understand each other. The orchestra sounds like a heavy, slow, un-
changing force, while the piano seems to be fluttering about, making
rapid changes. The mood is of sadness. The piece ends as if it were
going to sleep. The piano in the second version is a little too harsh, and
could be considered as powerful as the orchestra. The fortepiano
sounds a lot more subtle, and delicate, which is the perfect contrast:

more feminine than the modern day piano.

3
African-American male

The orchestra is asking a question loud and noticeably while the soloist answers back nice and calm as if it already knew what the orchestra was going to ask. All the instruments in unison provide the orchestra with its own personality and style. The orchestra seems to be bold, steady, and loud, while the piano is calm, relaxed, and enjoying the time. The piano seems to set the mood. Since it is slow, it sets the whole dialogue slower than the orchestra wants. The music seems to end with a question. A relaxed and open-ended question that could have many answers.

4
female

It is his melody, whether the orchestra likes it or not. The emotion of the pianist is slow and dreamy, and feels as if, in his world, days prolong themselves eternally. In the cadenza the soloist seems more aware of the "rest of the world": however, even that short outburst is stopped by solemn chords. The music ends on a note of higher pitch and sadness, as if saying "will this world ever change?"

5
male

It seems as though the cello is a living force which is intent on silencing the perfection of the piano. But "still the piano gently weeps," refusing to give in to the deep scolding of the cello. The unrest between the Royal Establishment and the manipulated artist is portrayed through this argument, the more powerful "angry father" attempting to keep the piano silent. There is a drawn out moment towards the middle of the piece which allows the piano to become slightly agitated. The ending is unexpected, the cello backing off, and they finally play together. It seems like a strange statement for Beethoven to make, to accept (possibly with reluctance) the support of society.

6
male, wheelchair bound
The Romantic Artist is telling the world to relax somewhat and look around to appreciate what it has. The orchestra grudgingly admits it isn't as bad as it first stated. The orchestra was very fast and aggressive while the soloist tried to soothe it by a musical "cooing" or calming effect. One has the feeling that the peace won't last long and that the upper-class soloist still has no clue why the orchestra is upset and thinks that the problem has been solved. The orchestra knows otherwise and is just waiting for the moment to strike.

7
male
It sounds like they are speaking. The soloist or piano is a pretty sound. They take turns speaking and the orchestra seems to be dominating the piano. The Artist is small compared to the World. The Artist wins in the end though. More instruments may not always mean more power. It is the content of the music which holds the power. The contrast could tell a listener that it was a hard time, or that it was hard for Beethoven to fit in. It was him against the world and he won.

8
male
The piano's soothing sound differs from the deep *da, da, da-da* of the strings: threatening, a sense of danger or overcoming. Finally the world accepts the artist and both kind of fade out. The strings add everything to this piece of music. Without the strings there would be no threat to the pianist; no balance between good and evil. The effect of the ending is to show that the pianist (artist) is just as powerful as the orchestra (world).

9
female

A dialogue as if to say to the orchestra "Can I please try something new or ask a question?" The orchestra replies in an aggressive manner No No No. The playing of the piano seems improvised, especially after hearing the second version: it sounded quite different yet very much the same. The mood I got from the piece was a young person with new ideas trying to express herself in a very close minded and competitive world. I see someone sitting in the corner of a room, in a scene of a movie about the eighteenth century, playing a sad tune on the piano, longing for something. The contrast is between the soft timid piano playing and the harsh aggressiveness of the orchestra's response. It tells us that Beethoven lived in a time when his ideas were not being taken seriously by the public, and he is feeling very sad about all this. The music ends almost unresolved, but with the piano playing last as if to say that he will keep on playing no matter what.

10
female

The string section is deep and powerful, while the piano is slower and more mournful. The two almost seem to be arguing. The piano solo moves into an agitated state towards the end, as it trills very quickly. The piano soloist perhaps represents the working class in turmoil, while the strings represent a strong and overbearing aristocracy. The end of the piece may be interpreted as sad or maybe it shows that nobody wins and nothing is resolved. In the second version the cello is not as dominant; in the first version the tinny sound of the fortepiano seems to add to the emotion of the solo. It almost seems to be quivering in fear of its opposition.

11
female

The orchestra seems to be trying to get the piano to go faster. The piano doesn't listen. The movement says the world is against the artist, but in the end the artist prevails. Beethoven lived in a world when the artist could easily face rejection, and therefore had to constantly be strong. I prefer the second version. The piano is softer, but stands its ground.

12
male

The piano expresses elegance and sophistication, while the orchestra adds an element of seriousness. The two don't go well together, but this is intentional: the piano representing something that doesn't quite fit in, like a black sheep in the middle of a white flock. Since the orchestra is not using its full range of tone, the piano is the bright rich color standing out against the orchestra's dark background. The elegance of the piano contrasting with the mood of the orchestra relays the fact of not wanting to follow, but to do things for the right reason, wherever that might lead.

13
African male

Separate entities, human and spiritual, are noticeable. The dialogue is quite animated. Even though the orchestra is not heard continuously throughout the entire piece, its presence is constantly felt. It seems to dictate what the piano might say next, and even when it is through playing a certain part, the piano hesitates as if it's not sure the orchestra is really finished. The depth of the orchestra gives the piece its axis and the speed and elements revolve around that. The contrast in size makes the dialogue very celestial and at the same time extremely human.

14
male

We could say that the orchestra represents an angry father punishing his son. He responds in a low delicate manner; the child would be represented by the piano solo. The difference in power and volume gives it an atmosphere of intensity, having two sides: the delicate (the piano) and the strong and angry (the orchestra). Anger is not just yelling out without making any sense, it is taking its time and in a way it sounds as if each one was thinking, well, what is he going to say, so he takes his time. One speaks, the other listens. The ending is surprising, as if all the pressure of that buildup is released in anger. Not like the anger of the orchestra, but as if the artist is responding to the world in his own way.

15
male

It seems to say that artists don't have as loud a voice but they can still make the world see things differently at the end. It takes some convincing to have the world accept your art, when the world determines what is acceptable. It ends very quietly, as if to say that differences can be worked out. If we can learn to see art neutrally, and not judge by our own biases of right or wrong, we can all get along. I prefer the modern piano because it seems louder and richer, and more emotional.

16
African-American male

The violins and bass sounded like a harsh person ridiculing the soft-spoken piano. It cowers and plays slow as if it is scared. After the build in the song the piano starts to trill. This represents a change. Maybe that the one represented by the piano has died or left. From that point the music is played so soft that you know something bad has happened and I feel that the music is remembering or thinking about a time when the one represented by the piano was around. I take the song as being a depressed person that is feeling overwhelmed and unable to go on, and is finally gone. The other person, the one being so harsh, the orchestra, did not expect it to actually turn out the way the depressed person said it would. This is something Beethoven must have felt and he brings it across very clear. I thought it was a very impressive piece.

17
male

The dialogue sounds *very* vocal, as if a chorus (the strings) were echoing a vocal soloist (the fortepiano), like a male chorus. The piano sounds more like a melancholy woman lamenting; its notes being higher and sharper also hint at feminine qualities, while the deeper, "thicker" sounds of the cellos hint more at masculinity. The piano is making the sounds of a more "refined" society, one of powdered wigs and ballroom dancing. Its notes are clear and distinct. The strings, however, represent a "working-class" sound. The piece as a whole sounds very East European and the solos like an East European national anthem. Very proud music. The strings are talking of work and muscle and hardship while the piano is talking about the posh life of servants and luxuries. Near the end the piano becomes feverish, but everything is finally settled and the two end the dialogue in unison.

18
Spanish-American female

Romantic, mysterious. Some sort of question and answer: the answer that everything is strong and doesn't end in tragedy. The piano is making a Romantic, but yet somewhat adventurous, or better maybe, *challenging* confrontation with the orchestra. The music from the piano is very sweet, somewhat sad. It is full of feelings, like someone trying to run away, and the orchestra is trying to make it stay. There is a very tense relationship between the artist and the world, maybe inspired from real life, a parting from a loved one or some other tragic event. The ending is represented as a very slow, painful death.

19
female

A lot of bass and a deep, hollow sound suggest some sort of power over the piano soloist. Not that the piano can't take control, because as you get to the end of the piece, the pace slows and the orchestra and piano are brought to a more comfortable, compatible level, like a compromise or peace between them.

20
female

If the piano represents the voice of the Romantic artist, maybe it is a female artist. I feel that there is a very strong female to male conversation taking place because the piano plays higher notes. It seems like a question has been asked by the orchestra; with the piano's sorrowful and heartfelt response it is clear that this conversation may turn into an argument. Towards the end the piano becomes increasingly defiant, arguing with repeated high notes played very loudly. One might expect it to end with a huge clash of instruments to signify a parting of ways, but instead the music becomes slow once again, the outcome a sorrowful reconciliation, or the piano giving way, like a submissive female who has stood her ground for a minute, only to realize that she has to obey.

21
female

Maybe there isn't a conflict at all. Maybe the orchestra's tone is one of excitement and agreement.

22
male

The piano has a soft voice as if trying to please or perhaps persuade the orchestra. The orchestra comes in with a strong, brash voice as if angry at the piano. It's as if all the strings are united in a struggle against the piano part. In the end, the piece just drifts away, as if the conflict between the strings and the piano can never be solved.

23
female

A lovely, heartfelt piece of music. The orchestra seems to be at odds with the soloist here. For every painfully sweet note played by the soloist, the orchestra retaliates with a dark and melancholy argument. The piano talks patiently, but the orchestra seems not to want to listen, even cutting off the piano at times. The music ends with a soft reply by the piano, almost like he's giving up, but he still got the last word.

24
male

It seems to be a conversation: the piano calm, almost like a mother, and the orchestra much more harsh, like an upset teenage child. But in the end the mother wins, like she always does. The music ends with the piano getting excited and then calming down. It shows that the calm rational one has said enough and maybe even won the argument—but it also shows how the calm person got upset for a minute and maybe lost control, but then regains it again. At the end the orchestra also calms down and joins the piano; that could show that they have resolved their differences.

25
male

The world is telling him to conform to their ideas, while the artist in quiet dignity is saying that he will not, to the point of bursting into tears. In the second version the piano sounds more sympathetically, and the strings more ominous.

26
female

At times the piano, thoughtful and melodically slow, seems to be pushed to the edge, as though running and running and then at one point teetering on the brink of a cliff. When they play together, the orchestra coming after the piano creates a tension that is almost tangible. On one side the calm of the artist who is thoughtful and creative, whereas the rest of the world is pushing the artist to do what they want it to do: conform. The artist stands his ground. The movement ends on a very unusual note. It leaves you hanging in suspense or anticipation, as though saying goodbye but not really meaning it.

27
male

A definite struggle: the piano seems to be pleading, the orchestra seems to fight every word. Maybe the orchestra is telling a young intrepid youth that the world is a cold harsh place and that you can't have everything. The cellos are played only in the lows probably to set the mood of a large cold population that cares nothing for the piano. Like an overseer. The piano plays mainly higher notes to symbolize youth and innocence. The ending, very slow and ominous, appears to signify loss of hope because the piano chimes in as if it was giving in to the orchestra. But the last few notes are higher, and that may show the piano still holding on to its individuality. The modern piano is too big and bold. It sounds theatrical and fake, empty and lifeless, whereas the fortepiano shows the piano full of life.

28
male

A depressing piece, expressing anguish and loneliness. It sounds as if Beethoven just lost the love in his life. The dialogue is as if the world is demanding something from Beethoven and he is replying in great sorrow, as if he just wants to be left alone.

29
female

The orchestra (strings) are very authoritative, very strong. The piano (soloist) is timid and appears to be quite fragile. It seems as if the soloist is trying to stand on his or her own two feet and prove a point. The orchestra won't hear of it. The orchestra appears to weaken, and the soloist, playing with more tone, becomes "stronger," almost out of control. The artist (piano) is saying stop for a minute and listen to me; the world replying you do not have a right to an opinion, do as I say. I think this is a very dramatic, moving piece.

30
male

A dialogue of good and evil. I would have expected it to end a little more abruptly, but with it fading away one does not know for sure what happened.

31
male

Strings are the strong arm of the middle class. The orchestra knows right off what they want to say.

32
male

The strings eventually understand that to fix the problem they must also listen.

33
male

A piece that puts me in a sad and unhappy mode. I feel the piano is acting the role of a lowly broken-hearted artist that is being driven away from the rest of the world (the orchestra). Yet the artist tries to talk his way back into the world. The solos by the piano are very elegant in the sense that you can feel the artist moving away from the world; then when the piano solos get shorter in alternation with the orchestra, it is as if the artist is asking to come back, and from the way the piano ends on a high note you sense that he is denied readmittance into the rest of the world.

34
male

A carefree artist in a fast-paced, unforgiving world. The piano's quiet and graceful sound is smothered by the powerful orchestra: "Dum de dum—de dum DUM DUM." The piano dies away almost unnoticed. At this time in history there was love and war, and no shades in between.

35
Thai female

The strings represent war, the piano the sadness of war.

36
male

The orchestral sound is that of power, domination, maybe even anger. The piano answers in sadness, a melancholy reflection opposed to the orchestra's decisive notes. As the piece continues, the pianist begins to respond without hesitating and discovers that it is exciting to be rid of its emotional burden.

37
male

Like a mother, the peacemaker, trying to calm her child, the piano tries to calm the orchestra, who is continually interrupting. Later the piano becomes upset and raises her voice; at this, the orchestra finally listens and lowers its tone. During the 1800s there were wars being fought all over the world, also there was a great separation of the classes which I think can be heard in this movement.

38
female

Beethoven being deaf, the first performance of this concerto, which he conducted from the keyboard, would have been even more dramatic.

39

Spanish-American male

As if there is an argument brewing. The music from the piano is a very soft, calm emotion while the orchestra is harsh and agitated. I expected a full-blown confrontation, but the piano avoided the challenge through intimidating the orchestra into backing down. The two go together: the orchestra is the tough shell of the turtle, the sensitive piano the turtle itself. The music portrays both the protectiveness of the shell and the vulnerable, delicate body within.

40

male

The piano represents the machine of government, the strings the voices of imperfect people.

41

male

Like most of Beethoven's music it has a majestic, somewhat somber feel to it. The piano, representing the artist, plays very melodic sweet music (although a little tragic), as the orchestra, representing society, plays very harsh heavy music. The pianist is also trying to say a number of different things, while the orchestra can only say the same thing over and over again. An image of the classical artist competing with the factory worker.

42

female

The piano is soft and eloquent while the orchestra is loud and angry. The artist is full of passion and pain. The world is overbearing and unsympathetic to the artist. The orchestra is made up of strings. A very different texture of sounds. I don't believe it is slow, it was intoxicating in speed. I could keep with the rhythm as if it were the speed of a conversation, maintaining a steady flow of ideas. I could recognize the emotion. The dialogue was wonderful: subtle, but not to the point of not being able to understand what was going on. I expected the orchestra would smother out the piano. Instead, the piano won over by the strength of its inner emotion.

43
African-American male

The solo piano is responding to the rest of the orchestra. Compared to the orchestra the piano is minute, but it makes its point as an individual.

44
male

The artist is outnumbered and his voice cannot possibly be heard over so many. One can hear the struggle and the sadness especially when, in the end, the artist seems regretfully to join the world, or the pianist the orchestra.

45
male

The soloist piano represents the artist, a being of exquisite taste and refinement, one who is peacefully perceptive, eloquent, and romantic. The orchestra describes the harsh, brutal, uncaring world of the early 1800s, a world that is unwavering in its purpose. Each depends on the other, for contrast if not for their existence. Even though the two forces are so vastly different, peace can be made by acquiring some traits of your opponent.

46
Spanish-American male

The style of music the piano is making is tiptoe, sympathetic. The orchestra is rough, harsh, and yet eager. The relationship says they both can't live without one another. The music ends by the soloist continuing on and not stopping until the orchestra dies out. A strong story with a *pietà* ending.

47
African-American female
It is an argument between two lovers: the music ends with the piano in the forefront and the strings in the background, though you would expect to hear the strings with the piano on the same level together.

48
African-American female
The soloist part sounds like you are in a nice, quiet place listening to the introduction of a song. The orchestra sounds like a heavy voice in a dark room. At the beginning of the piece it seems like a nice sunny day, but as the heavy sound comes in, it becomes dark with cloud and thunder all of a sudden.

49
Spanish-American male
The piano is begging for peace and the orchestra is showing no mercy. The orchestra is demanding equality, liberty, and justice for all.

50
female
A wonderful contrasting dialogue. The soloist is shy at first. The music slow and soft, as though quietly saying look at me. The piano is different, like the artist. The orchestral sounds are very large bodied and deep. Finally, the orchestra stops and listens, because the soloist becomes louder, braver, and stronger. The world listens and seems to accept a little, and quiets down and lets the artist add color to the world.

51
Spanish-American male
The artist is refusing to submit to the voice of society, to prove his individuality and the beauty of his music. Arthur Miller said, "Society always forgives the criminal but never the artist."

52
female
The orchestra is trying to make the piano see reality, but the piano has a heartfelt but naïve view of the world in general. The slow tempo gives the piece extra attentiveness.

53
female
The piano seems to be pleading for life with an eloquence the world does not share. The orchestra is very dramatic because of its low pitch and abruptness. This demonstrates how the world at large may move faster and with more force than the single romantic artist represented by the piano. The strings also show the unity of the outside world.

54
Anglo-Indian male
It seems to me that the piano player and the orchestra are having some kind of conversation, and as you listen to them going back and forth, that the soloist is talking calmer and the orchestra is talking much stronger. In the end the piano seemed to have gotten his point across and the orchestra had no more to say.

55
African-American female
The orchestra represents the world because the sounds of the instruments are loud and want to be heard. Just like people in the world

today, they speak their mind and everyone wants to be recognized.

56
female

A slow relay of emotions which flow from piano to orchestra. At first the piano seems to speak its ideas softly and later finds the means to express itself more forcefully and elaborately. The strings then reply with a discerning tone, their sounds seeming less agitated. In the end, there is a mutual agreement, though the piano has the last words.

57
female

It opens with a very dark statement by the orchestra, to which the soloist replies with a melody very delicate and gentle to the touch. The piano is trying to stay sweet and young while the rest of the orchestra seems to be trying to make it change its mind. You would expect to hear by the end of the piece that the orchestra would take control and smother the single piano but instead the orchestra gives in to the influence of the solo player and supports him.

58
Chinese-American female

The dialogue reminds me of a conversation between a woman and a man. The soloist is the woman, with a clear, crisp sound, powerful at times, expressing quiet firmness. The man (orchestra) has a low tone, and the way the string instruments are stroked resembles the manly, macho struts of a man. The strings sound upset and the soloist calm and gentle, then the soloist picks up the pace and exposes the most powerful, strong emotions that just could not be calmed any more, feelings well hidden at the beginning of the piece. The movement describes the complaints and emotions the artist has against a chaotic world that is massive and insensitive. The music begins slowly, but the emotions are not slowly delivered. We understand instantly as an audience that this is a contrast between light and dark, good and evil. As we know, Beethoven was deaf; perhaps the music he created was his expression of what the world ought to sound like. The second recording is in front of an audience. It feels more like we are a part of the performance, or that we are present in the room where the conversation takes place. The fortepiano sounds a little static, yet crisp and sensitive.

59
Spanish-American male

This movement is expressing a feeling of sorrow or sadness. It is saying the world is not an easy place to live in: the soft sounds of the piano beautifully expressing sadness and melancholy. The orchestra expresses greater power, size, and strength. A very sad piece I should say. The feeling is not resolved until you hear the very end, and it ends in a completely different experience, making the listener reflect on the conflict in their own life.

60
African-American female

The orchestra is very harsh, hard, and bold. It seems unconcerned about the sensitive, caring, soft, and low piano. It's like the piano is crying out to the world about his feelings. The orchestra sound is dark and dull, giving the listener a sense that the world is cold and mean, and the artist needs love, happiness, and joy. The piano has a point to express and the orchestra has a point to state. People didn't want to hear him out or listen to his music. Seems like a difficult time.

61
male

The piano represents something small and peaceful and the orchestra represents something large and stern. The piano speaks in a soft reserved style while the orchestra's style is very harsh and coarse. The orchestra—basically the string section—adds to the situation by suggesting in a very short, abrupt manner that it has a point to put across. This piece carries on at a steady pace but it takes a while for the ideas on each side to sink in.

62
male

Piano is slow, medium forte, elegant, peaceful and relaxed. Orchestra is a little more upbeat, loud at the beginning, cellos and violins very tense. The world is coming down on the Artist and the Artist is trying to get away from the world, but realizes he can't. Sounds like the Artist is standing up for his right in life, but no one is listening, which causes hardship on him and he tries to get away from all the drama.

63
Kenyan male

The power of the orchestra in contrast to the softness of the piano makes the artist seem overpowered by the world, as if he were just a small child trying to be heard. Eventually the world listens to him, and later even plays at a lower tone, as if to be at the same level with the artist. The music ends with the piano overpowering the orchestra. This is very interesting since the music starts so powerfully yet ends quietly and peacefully with the piano, a really big change. The piano players in both versions are very good and seem to be the ones holding the piece together.

64
female

The artist seems to be shunned or reprimanded by the orchestra, a looming, sinister personification.

65
Korean male

This is a combination of strong power (of cello and violin), and beautiful power (of the piano). The cello represents man, by its thick and short sound, and the piano represents woman, by its soft and slow tone.

66
Korean female

The piano as voice of the Romantic artist is seeking beauty. The orchestra is saying to the piano, wake up from your dream and face reality. To me it seems that the piano is a rebel, trying to do things differently and more beautifully than the rest of the world. The words *Andante con moto* refer to the pace of the music, and to the emotion that the piano and the orchestra give to each other. They are not heard as fighting against each other, rather that they are contrasting each other, slowly, one by one.

67
female

A beautiful display of talent on the piano. The strings have a strong and deep, very serious tone, a tone that the piano plays right into. The piano is a great contrast, but also a great complement. It adds a feminine lighthearted feeling. This could be a husband and wife arguing, or a father and daughter, because of the feminine and masculine role-playing portrayed by each instrument. Finally at the end it sounds as if they are coming together; quietly and slowly they stop battling each other and come to some kind of term. More attention is paid to the piano because of the beauty, difficulty, and calmness of its music. The fortepiano has an old, courtly elegance to its sound.

68
Spanish-American male

The soloist and orchestra seem to counterbalance each other. In my opinion the piano represents someone who is blinded by love and in a state of disillusion, while the orchestra represents an understanding of the harsh realities of love. The orchestra is the voice of sensibility, and it is trying to make the piano understand that love is not all about happiness, but also involves pain. The orchestra gets right to the point and does not hold anything back. It represents the idea that the truth can hurt. The orchestra puts out shades of red, while the piano sounds out shades of blue symbolizing a feeling that is soft, smooth, and very refreshing. What the contrast tells a listener about the historical period in which Beethoven lived, is that love has always been, and will always be the same in any period of history. At the end of the piece the piano is beginning to grasp the reality, and the truth begins to cast a shadow over what was once happiness.

69
female
The orchestra is faster and stronger, marching on while the quiet, slow piano is basically wanting to relax and not move on. The piano is the sad partner that is not ready to let go and still feels like the relationship will work, while the orchestra is the partner that thinks the relationship is over.

70
female
In both versions the piano delivers a light, contemplative and almost feminine mood, while the orchestra delivers a heavy, dramatic, deep and masculine mood. In the more modern version the orchestra strongly dominates and the piano seems to accent only certain notes. A definite clear ending. The piano holds its last note which the orchestra would presumably follow, but instead it ends alone and suddenly.

71
male
This is much like an interrogation where the orchestra is grilling the soloist and therefore the soloist has to answer. I think the Rest of the

World is asking the Romantic Artist why he chooses to be different. The mood is very sad. The orchestra just keeps repeating itself. I was expecting more dialogue, but I was not surprised how it ended with the piano. Even though the orchestra was loud and quite violent sounding, the piano answered quietly and calmly stood his ground. I know that if I heard this piece live it would send shivers down my spine.

72
female

While the piano is a romantic civilized voice, the orchestra is dogmatic and programmed to bring into line all those who stray. The range of instrumental color adds a lot to the listener's sense of meaning to the piece. The world is opaque: dark and cold, with little light coming through, and the piano is light and soft. The dialogue is steady with constant questions from the piano and rebuttals from the orchestra.

73
male

The piece begins with downward strokes from the orchestra. The silence opens a doorway for the lone voice. The piano replies, timid, shy, and beautiful. A call and answer begins. The subtly defiant piano holds its pace and its mood, unbroken. It is a show of the struggle of the artist under the oppression of a strict code. Whether it be against the laws of music, or laws of society, or laws of man, beauty will always prevail. The struggle against oppression has continued for many years and because of it the message of this piece will forever be timeless.

74
male

The sound of the piano is very elegant and smooth whereas the orchestra is very forceful and hard. It is as though the piano is trying to express himself but cannot overcome the power of the establishment.

The slow tempo draws attention to how the artist of the day must have been feeling. There was not as much freedom then as there is today. The artist is describing his emotions towards those that are against the freedom of expression he seeks. The piece ends very soft. It feels as if it is going to end loud and hard. It does not. The artist is the last one to speak. This offers hope that one day artists may be able to express themselves freely in society.

75
male

It sounded like a small ship lost at sea in a large storm. You can tell through the piece that the artist put up a struggle but couldn't escape the power of the "whole." In the second version the piano and orchestra kept the same meaning but changed their styles. The piano is now a beacon for those at sea: a guiding light. The artist is in no hurry to join with the rest of the world. In the second version there is a greater sense of mystery. The two sides become one, and they do it less noticeably, so at the end you are suddenly aware that the two sides have come together. This creates a feeling of inner peace.

76
male

The piano is begging the orchestra to spare its life. The orchestra doesn't listen to the piano though, and cuts him off. The piano becomes full of fear and is sped up in tempo as it grasps at something, life perhaps, and fails. The piece ends with the piano slowly dying and fading out. Only in the death of the piano does the orchestra show mercy. The piano was only doing what it knew how. Perhaps the piano doesn't die though. But it isn't in any condition to go anywhere.

77
female

Almost a confrontation: the orchestra seems to represent a man and the soloist seems to represent a woman, as if she is speaking about love and life. The man as the orchestra toward the end of the piece seems to break down, as if understanding what the woman is saying to him —and of course the woman has the "last note," saying "goodbye." The term *slow* refers to the pace of the piano; I feel that it is explaining and emphasizing the emotion behind the character portrayed by the piano. The music ends with a fading note after a small serious combination of the two. I as a listener expected it to end as it did, fading softly.

78
female
The strings begin the piece with a unified statement, very structured and almost military. The piano answers with a romantic, almost spontaneous melody of its own. The dialogue goes back and forth, with the piano gaining strength and power until the strings cut it off rudely with their motif. Suddenly the piano changes from an unstructured melody to a clear one; it gains strength and wins a final argument with the strings who, after a token resistance, slink off leaving the piano in triumph.

79
male
The strings are like the school bully: "Give me your lunch money."

80
male
The dialogue in the piece is almost like a father being stern with his daughter. The orchestra has a very stern, almost menacing tone to it, whereas the piano is very sweet and gentle. In the very beginning there is a sharp contrast between the two. As it progresses, however, the piano grows in intensity and the strings become more quiet, to the same level as the piano. The piano's intensity of emotion then changes again, to a more dominating and resonant tone. Its beauty also

increases, almost as if the daughter had grown into a woman, and the father had nothing left to be stern for. And in the end the strings return for a few quiet moments, mingling with the piano as if they were saying "goodbye." Even though the strings decidedly dominate the beginning of the piece, it is the piano that takes control. This is clear to me by the fact that throughout the strings are very repetitive, but that the piano is allowed to roam and go its own way.

81
male

The tone of the strings is deep and strong. The strings eventually help the piano to gain a sense of strength as well. The piano starts out peaceful and tranquil, and then develops its own sense of strength, built up by the help of the strings pushing it along. Being that it is a conversation shows that they are engaging in it together, such as they are playing music together. So, the dialogue from the piano stays peaceful and slow, then escalates to a chaotic fast pace in order to set the strings in line, and then finally comes back down to its softer, peaceful state. The strings stay strong throughout the piece. The piano thus takes control with the change of emotion and then ends with another change of emotion back to its original state, as if to say "See, there's no reason to argue."

82
male

It is similar to a fighter who is relaxed, going in to fight someone who is all excited and powerful. The outcome of the fight is always going to be in favor of the relaxed fighter because he or she is able to think and conserve energy rather than the anxious fighter who is more likely to rush things and make a mistake. I think something of that caliber is happening between the piano and the orchestra. The piano's coordination seems to reign supreme and he has more flow than the orchestra.

83
male, dyslexic

The orstra respniting sciety verry powerful abrupt notes. They sound angry and ciptil of the pinno. Not quite seing what the panio stands for or what it is trying to express.

The panio (Artist) has a verry dignfied systcated tonation to it. Strong but systcated. At one place they clash and almost argue with notes and keep doing it.

They baddle back and forth intell the panio (Artist) wins and demonstrates his skill in wrighting complex music, and creating somewhat of a scudling mood. The orstra almost acceps the panio and Backs off.

This all can be put in to perspective of a governent over trown by the people then the people questning Artis for being aletist and testing to see were your morals lie.

The Renfinement of the panios Dignified educated style is important to cast It as the roll of the Artist.

The Strength and power of the orstra defently sounds like scioty's Angry voice questning and Ridiculing the artis But in the end finding out that he just creats things that are budiful to lisin to.

[The orchestra representing society [plays] very powerful abrupt notes. They sound angry and skeptical of the piano, not quite seeing what the piano stands for or what it is trying to express. The piano (artist) has a very dignified, sophisticated tonation to it: strong but sophisticated. At one point they clash and almost argue with notes, and keep doing it. They battle back and forth until the piano (artist) wins and demonstrates his skill in writing complex music, and creating somewhat of a scolding mood. The orchestra almost accepts the piano and backs off.

This can all be put in the perspective of a government overthrown by the people, and then the people questioning artists for being elitist, and testing to see where their morals lie. The refinement of the piano's dignified, educated style is important, to cast it in the role of the artist. The strength and power of the orchestra definitely sounds like society's angry voice questioning and ridiculing the artist, but in the end finding out that he just creates things that are beautiful to listen to.]

84

male, dyslexic

The whole orchestra shows all of society rich, rich, poor, and the working. Then the orchestra goes to strings showing that time have changed and that the working class is in charge, and they want none of the old way, none of the rich Bull crap. So they see the artist, the piano, as a memory of the old way. So they are not happy to the artist, but the artist just wants to please. So starts the artist must prove his self to society. Artist say wait and look and see what I mean. No we will not, we now have what we want. So he try to win over society he needs to refine his work make it so they will like, and understand, but at first they say no go away, so the artist change then he trys again slowly they see the emotion in the work and see him trying and they both unite and live in harmony. The tone of the orchestra are quick, they will hear none of it. The tone of the artist is trying and precieful. Slowly the artist please the orchestra and coach them into liking it. They end in Harmony and the artist is pleased and the people are happy and please with the artist.

[The orchestra as a whole represents all of society: rich, poor, and the working class. Here the orchestra consists only of the strings, showing that times have changed: the working class is in charge, and they are not interested in the finer things of life. They see the artist, represented by the piano, as a reminder of the old regime, even though the artist just wants to fit in. Because they are not too well disposed toward the artist, his first task is to prove himself to society. The artist says, "Listen, be patient, and hear what I am saying."—"No, we are not interested, we have power and that's all we are concerned about." So the artist realizes that if he is going to succeed and win over society he needs to refine his message and make it so they will like it and understand. But again they reject it, and again the artist changes his manner, until gradually society understands the emotion in his message and respects his persistence and they come together in harmony. The tone of the orchestra is quick and abrupt, and dismissive at first. The tone of the artist is persistent and reasonable. In time the artist convinces the orchestra and coaxes them into agreeing with him. The dialogue ends in harmony and the artist expresses his satisfaction at the outcome.]

85
female

Piano Concerto No. 4 slow movement by Beethoven is composed of a piano soloist and a string orchestra each taking turns speaking to each other. Ths piano is clear and intelligent; the orchestra, however, is rather coarse and rough and a bit pushy. The piano represents an individual, an artist, a logical thinker that speaks out in a crowd. The orchestra represents the crowd, unfamiliar with the idea of individuality, hence they play a simple melody in unison. Its tone is bold, energetic, filled with enthusiasm, but there is no real direction. The orchestra makes it known that it has enthusiasm, but for nothing in particular. The piano replies patiently to the orchestra by playing elegantly and logically as it demonstrates the power of an individual. It gets more and more assertive to compel the orchestra that is at first reluctant to [face] this strange new concept. It is when the piano lays it on thick with emotion that the orchestra is moved to venture into the strange, new world of harmony. It follows the piano's lead, catching on gradually. At last, the piano rises triumphantly over the harmonizing orchestra with a clear melody, announcing its success.

86
male

The orchestra is persistent in its style of a loud and powerful melody, but the piano responds with a subtle reminder that it does not have to play in a loud fashion to receive attention from listeners. The piano reminds the orchestra that there is beauty in being subtle, and power in being an individual.

87
female

It is obvious that the message of the piece and the emotion involved are the point of the piece, since the music is not overly difficult technically. The orchestra is the people, Beethoven's new audience. At this time in Europe, society was in an upheaval as various revolutions did away with the aristocracy and the "common people" took power. And since there were no more wealthy patrons, the composer had to produce music that the masses would embrace, or starve.

88
female
At the beginning of the song the strings play together, to show unity and strength. Then you hear the piano. It plays solo. The chords play slow and quiet. It represents harmony. The piano has a long solo. It plays fast and scattered, but then goes back to harmony. Near the ending of the song both orchestra and piano play taking turns. They play softly and slow. They harmonize creating a beautiful ending.

89
Japanese male
The strong orchestra sound is getting gentle, as if the piano has caused an injury.

90
male
Through persistence society can be changed.

91
African-American male
It is like a dad and mom arguing. All the mom does at first is say "yes," and "I know," and she lets him get mad and then tells him to calm down, and after that is when she starts to take over.

92
female
The orchestra is annoyed; the piano listens patiently, then starts to play more difficult, more impressive melodies.

93
female
I didn't see it as two different characters at all, but rather two different sides of the same character.

94
male
The solo piano has the liberty to do what it wants, but the orchestra *is* forced to follow the same line.

95
female
They meet and blend in harmony in the final notes. When two opposing elements meet in the middle, that is learning rather than debating.

96
African-American male
The piano compromises by taking time to incorporate some of the strings's harshness and disorder to create an effective tune that both sides can agree on.

97
Chinese male
A family argument. The orchestra collectively gangs up on the piano, one of their own, for doing wrong. The accused is shaking with fear at the end.

98
African-American female

This is a dialogue between a person (the piano) who is on her death bed, and a close friend or relative who is upset. "It is okay," says the piano, "let me go." And the other voice is angry and won't accept what she says, and won't let her go. The music of the soft voice finally dies and the angry voice accepts the truth of what has happened.

99
male

In the beginning the strings have longer segments, in the middle the piano dominates, and at the end both are virtually equal.

100
male

The orchestra is arguing over what they should do now.

101
female

The artist plays a long segment rich in changing tones, while the orchestra listens. It seems to me they are both searching for a certain level of understanding.

Notes

The two performances of Beethoven's Piano Concerto No. 4 second movement were by Anthony Newman (fortepiano) with the Philomusica Antiqua of New York, conducted by Stephen Simon (on NCD 60081); and a transcription of a historic concert recording by Clara Haskil (piano) with the Orchestre Nationale conducted by André Cluytens (on Disques Montaigne CD ANT 90).

Index

About the Author

Born in Auckland, Robin Maconie studied piano with Christina Geel and majored in English literature and contemporary music at Victoria University under Don McKenzie, Frederick Page, and Roger Savage. As a graduate bursar he studied under Olivier Messiaen at the Paris Conservatoire in 1963–1964, and in Cologne with Karlheinz Stockhausen, Herbert Eimert, Bernd-Alois Zimmermann, Aloys Kontarsky, and others. He has held teaching appointments at the universities of Auckland, Sussex, Surrey, Oxford, and the City University, London, and for five years was Professor of Media and Performing Arts at the Savannah College of Art and Design.

During the 1970s as music correspondent for *The Daily Telegraph, The Times Educational Supplement* and *The Times Literary Supplement* he gained a reputation for clarity and directness in defence of new music. He was editorial assistant to John Mansfield Thomson in the founding years of *Early Music*. His reputation as a writer and musicologist is founded on his writings on Karlheinz Stockhausen, most recently *Other Planets*, published by The Scarecrow Press in 2005 to wide critical acclaim.

His other titles, *The Concept of Music* (1990), *The Science of Music* (1997), *The Second Sense* (2002), and now *The Way of Music* pursue a lifelong ambition to restore intelligent conversation to classical music through a transfusion of ideas from the familiar worlds of design, architecture, computing, fashion, the movies, and favorite TV shows. Robin Maconie returned to New Zealand in 2002 and lives and works in Dannevirke.